A CHRISTMAS KISS WITH HER EX-ARMY DOC

TINA BECKETT

SECOND CHANCE WITH THE SURGEON

ROBIN GIANNA

MILLS & BOON

First Published in Great Britain 2019
by Mills & Boon, an imprint of HarperCollins*Publishers*
1 London Bridge Street, London, SE1 9GF

A Christmas Kiss with Her Ex-Army Doc © 2019 by Tina Beckett

Second Chance with the Surgeon © 2019 by Robin Gianakopoulos

ISBN: 978-0-263-26994-9

MIX
Paper from
responsible sources
FSC **C007454**

Printed and bound in Spain
by CPI, Barcelona

A CHRISTMAS KISS WITH HER EX-ARMY DOC

TINA BECKETT

MILLS & BOON

PROLOGUE

THE FUNERAL MADE her squirm, her grief and tears for
her husband having already been spent long ago. The
second the news had reached her that Jacob's chopper
had been shot down in a remote part of Afghanistan,
Hollee Cantrell had instinctively known he hadn't survived. But protocol demanded he be listed as MIA until
the helicopter and his body were found.

A year later, both had been.

It was official. She was a widow. The ache in her
heart bloomed to life all over again.

She stood on the plush lawn of the cemetery beside
her parents as guns fired one blistering shot after another until all she wanted to do was press her hands to
her ears and muffle the sound.

Instead she stood frozen in place.

The military salute ended and almost against her will
her eyes shifted to a spot to her right.

He was watching her. Again.

When he mouthed, *Are you okay?* her eyes filled
with hot tears.

All she could think about was herself, and here was

Jacob's best friend—looking as handsome as sin in his dress blues—asking her if she was okay. He'd separated himself from their little band of friends before she and Jacob had started dating, deciding that playing the field was a lot more fun than hanging out with them. So she was surprised to actually see him here. And even more surprised that he cared about how she felt. If only he'd known all those years ago that, given the choice, she would have chosen...

No, it would have changed nothing.

She forced herself to give an imperceptible nod, even though she wasn't okay. Not at all. What she felt was numb.

Her dad put an arm around her shoulder and dropped a kiss on her head, which made her tears come even faster.

Using her fists, she rubbed them away and prayed neither Clancy, his sister nor his mother came over to speak to her after it was all over.

She felt the worst sort of traitor. She'd married Jacob and only a couple of years later had she realized she'd made a mistake. But there'd been no going back, even as the ring on her finger had become a noose she had been desperate to escape. She'd planned on having a long talk about their future once he came off deployment. Only he'd never come home.

And now she was done with love. Done with relationships. Forever.

As soon as she could, she was slipping away. Far away from Virginia. Far away from Jacob's memory.

And most of all far away from the man who hadn't wanted her. A man she'd never quite forgotten, no matter how hard she'd tried.

CHAPTER ONE

Five years later...

CLANCY DE OLIVEIRA SETTLED behind his new desk, putting the picture of his significant other on the corner of it with a smile. Gordy might not be human, but he was the only kind of permanent companion Clancy needed or wanted nowadays. The part basset hound had followed him to his car after the funeral, and they'd been together ever since—except for his nine-month stint in Syria. The last one of his career.

It was almost like Jacob had sent the dog to apologize for what he'd done. At least that's what Clancy would like to think. The truth was they'd barely spoken since Jacob had confessed that he was in love with Hollee all those years ago.

Clancy tried to find her after the funeral, but she'd been long gone. Besides, would he really have told her the truth about what her husband had done while overseas? Probably not. Better to just let the truth be buried with his old friend. The last he'd heard, Hollee had moved away from Arlington, probably needing a fresh start.

Clancy was now a civilian taking his place in a vast network of hospitals and private practices in the area. His plastic surgery skills would morph from treating combat injuries to treating children with facial injuries and defects. The devastation of war had changed him in ways that no one could imagine. In addition to the scars he wore inside, he'd suffered a physical injury, a shard of shrapnel that had sliced a path through his eyebrow and across his cheek, barely missing his left eye. The thin scar had faded somewhat—leaving just a line and a narrow bald patch in his brow. The exterior package had been cleaned up. The interior, however…

He shook himself free of his thoughts and opened his laptop, logging into the hospital's computer network and clicking the different tabs to see what was there. The administrator had told him to take the first week to acquaint himself with the way the hospital did things. There was a staff meeting in fifteen minutes, where he'd meet some of the folks he'd be working with, which included trauma and general reconstruction specialists, and there was a volunteer opportunity he was interested in. He was anxious to get started. Sitting still had never been one of his strong suits.

Which was why he'd decided not to take a vacation after leaving the military. The offer from Arlington Regional Medical Center couldn't have come at a better time.

Prying himself from his chair, he took the elevator to the third floor, where the administrator had said the meeting would be held. Some of the muted but elegant decor made him frown. He took a deep breath and let it hiss back out. It would take time to transition from the sparse military installations he was used to. Arlington Regional believed in focusing as much on atmosphere as it did on quality of care, saying it was all part of the healing process.

And it probably was. He'd just never practiced in a place like this. But at least here he would never have to worry about things like whether their stock of gauze pads would be depleted before the next supply run.

He turned a corner, following the blue stripe on the floor that would take him to the business areas of the hospital. There. People were ducking inside a door to the left, and a couple of others were standing outside the room, talking. Just as he got ready to enter it, one of the people waiting glanced up at him.

Bright green eyes—all-too-familiar eyes—met his, and her soft gasp came as complete recognition dawned. Hell. It couldn't be. She no longer lived here.

But that had been years ago. And she'd been a vet tech back then. So what was she doing here at the hospital? *His* hospital? Dressed in scrubs?

"Hollee?"

The word came out before he could stop it, and the person she'd been chatting with must have decided to get while the getting was good because the woman murmured a goodbye and shot through the door.

Hollee stood there without answering for a minute and memories from the past washed over him. Specifically, the moment when his nineteen-year-old eyes had met hers and he'd thought he'd captured something swirling in those green depths. Intrigued, he'd moved in to take a closer look. Before he'd known what was happening, his lips had brushed over hers.

The light touch had deepened into an actual kiss that had had his hands cupping her face. When they'd finally parted, they'd both stood there staring at each other, and she'd whispered his name. The wonder in her tone had almost transformed a friendship into something else. Almost. Until he'd remembered that she was the apple of her daddy's eye, and Clancy was a motorcycle-riding rebel.

A few days later his best friend had told him he'd asked her to their prom and that she'd said no, but he was hoping she'd change her mind. Clancy had instinctively known that Jacob was right for her in all the ways that Clancy was wrong. So he'd set out to prove that to her. And had succeeded far too well, since she had indeed accompanied Jacob to the prom.

Only what he'd found out about his friend later had made him rethink that decision.

He shook off the thought.

"Clancy, what are you doing…?" Her eyes widened slightly when they passed over his chest, and it took him a minute to realize she wasn't looking at him, rather at his lanyard. Maybe she'd been hoping he was just here to visit someone.

No such luck, sweetheart.

And since she was sporting a matching lanyard and had a stethoscope draped around her neck, she was here on business as well.

His gut tightened. So much for this job being a god-send. "Did you change professions?"

"I did, actually."

His gaze strayed to her left hand. Jacob's ring was gone and no one else's graced it. Dammit. It was none of his business whether or not she was involved with anyone.

More people were entering the room, a few of them sending quizzical glances their way as they passed. "Well, I guess I'd better head in," she said. "I was wait-ing on someone, but they're evidently running late."

Waiting on someone. A boyfriend? Friend?

His gut gave a painful spasm. She'd already been married once. And Jacob wasn't around to care.

But Clancy was.

Again, none of your business.

"All right. I'll see you in there."

He let her go, purposely waiting a minute or two be-fore moving into the room. That way he wouldn't feel obligated to sit by her. Not that she'd want him to. If anything, she'd made it pretty obvious that seeing him hadn't been a pleasant surprise.

Why would it be? He had done a good job of play-ing the field. He'd convinced her and everyone else—including himself—that he was not the settling-down type.

He grabbed the first seat he could find, forcing him-self not to try to locate her in the group. But of course he did, because what his mind dictated wasn't always followed by his body. She was two rows ahead of him, talking to the person next to her. The same woman she'd stood outside with.

She was a nurse.

Hollee loved animals, so he was surprised by her career change. And dismayed. It was going to be hard to avoid her, and after not seeing her for five years... Well, the memory of their past and that kiss had hit him a lot harder than it should have.

She hadn't changed much, that red hair combined with the tiny freckles that dotted her nose were all still there, and still just as beautiful.

Fortunately, before he could dwell on that thought any further, the hospital administrator went up to the podium and called for everyone's attention.

"Thanks for coming. I'll try to be brief." A few chuckles went up, which Clancy took to mean that brevity wasn't normally the man's forte.

"First of all I'd like you to welcome the hospital's newest addition. Clancy de Oliveira will be joining our reconstructive surgery team. Dr. de Oliveira, could you stand so people can see you?"

He did as he was asked, nodding to those who turned to look. He gave a small smile at the one head that hadn't turned toward him before taking his seat again.

The administrator went on to talk about the terrible tragedy that had befallen several small towns in Appalachia. The poverty-stricken area had suffered flooding from the record rainfall, and just as the waters had begun receding, and they'd been trying to dig out from beneath the mud, a tornado had ripped through, leaving a wide swath of destruction. Dozens were dead, and a big part of the population was in misery. People in the area had opened their homes to those who were without. But there was a lot still to be done.

Arlington Regional would be sending in a team to help with medical care and to get the biggest of the clinics back up and running again. They needed both doctors and nurses to volunteer.

Hollee sat up a little taller.

Was she thinking of going? Damn. He'd already expressed an interest to the administrator. It would be hard to back out now.

"The catch is the team will be gone the first two weeks of December. Close to the Christmas holidays, I know. But that's even more reason to go and help. We'd like to have about ten to twenty people from Arlington Regional participate. A soup kitchen and field clinic are being set up as we speak."

Someone raised his hand. "I'm interested. Where do we sign up?"

"Great, I'm just getting to that. I'm sure there are a lot of questions, and I've prepared a handout with some of the details. I know there's not much prep time, but Arlington Regional is all about quick response, so look at your schedules and decide if you have room in it to participate. If your department needs help with coverage, come see me and we'll take a look at what we can arrange. Lodging will be provided and meals will be served on site."

Clancy could remember mess meals. Despite the desire to be home, Christmas was still celebrated with gusto complete with a holiday meal with all the trimmings. When the meal was over, though, it was back to work. It was after one such meal that they'd come under attack from a missile, and he'd been injured. Several others hadn't been quite so lucky, with five people dying.

He'd been haunted by those deaths long after his wounds had healed.

He shook off the memory and concentrated on the administrator, his thoughts racing. He knew he would be an ideal candidate to participate, since he had nothing on his schedule yet and could keep those surgery dates open. And he was used to less-than-ideal working conditions.

And if Hollee was going…

Since when did his personal issues supersede doing the right thing? They hadn't back when they'd all been friends, and they didn't now.

The information sheets were passed out row by row. Clancy took his and gave the stack to the person beside him with a smiling nod. Then they were dismissed. Glancing over the paper, he worked through the logistics then sensed a person standing nearby. He looked up to make sure he wasn't blocking someone in. Instead, his jaw tightened when he saw Hollee.

"Sorry if I seemed short earlier. Welcome to the hospital," she said. "I didn't know you were back."

He nodded, knowing she was talking about his deployment. "I could say the same of you." He stopped short of admitting to visiting her mom years ago. Besides, Shirley had probably already told her daughter about it.

"I've been back for a while." She hesitated and then touched her left brow. "What happened?"

He wasn't sure what she was talking about for a second then realized with a jolt. She'd noticed his scar. "Wrong place. Wrong time." He didn't actually want to tell her, and he wasn't sure why. If she wanted to think he'd gotten into a bar fight or something, that was fine with him.

He changed the subject, nodding at the page in her hand. "Are you thinking of going to help?"

"I am, why?"

"Just curious." Her voice was reawakening synapses in his brain in a way that he didn't like. Synapses that suddenly couldn't grasp the concept of "in the past."

"With the devastation in that area, I'm sure there are some pregnancies that have been affected. I want to help, if I can."

"Pregnancies?"

"I'm a labor and delivery nurse."

That surprised him. "Do you regret trading being a vet tech for being a nurse?"

"There are always things to regret. But it seemed like the right thing to do."

Her answer could have been taken right out of his own playbook. Hadn't he done what he'd thought was right, only to discover later that he'd set Hollee up for a world of heartache? Luckily, he'd never had to deliver on the ultimatum he'd given Jacob in the months that preceded his friend's death. "Will my going on the trip make things awkward?"

"It'll be no different than working at the hospital together, right?"

Except if Clancy had known she was here, he would have given more thought to accepting the position. Would it have stopped him? He couldn't honestly say for sure. And she didn't know what he'd done back then. Just that he'd turned a cold shoulder to her a few days after that kiss. "True. Only I'll be working on a different floor."

He was still surprised that she was a labor and delivery nurse, although he wasn't sure why. Having children wasn't a prerequisite for working there or anywhere else. But it was a relief to know her face—as beautiful as it was—wouldn't greet him every single day. Because the question that had beaten in his skull for years was: *Had he done the right thing?*

Jacob's confession that he'd asked someone to the prom hadn't been what had shocked him into silence back then. Neither had the fact that his friend had thought he was in love with that person. It had been the who behind the speech. Because it had been Hollee. Their Hollee. *His* Hollee. Only she hadn't been his. One shared kiss did not a relationship make.

Returning to the present, he stood firm, meeting her eyes. "It doesn't matter where either of us works, so don't worry about it. If you're worried about what… happened, don't. It was a long time ago. Before you and Jacob ever got together, and it was obviously a mistake."

At the swift look of pain that flashed through her eyes he went back and tried to soften his words. "Let's just let bygones be bygones." And like his retirement from the military, it was best if he just kept moving forward.

"Thanks for that, Clance."

The shortened version of his name made him clench his jaw. Mainly because hearing it on her lips brought back memories that were better off forgotten.

And if he couldn't forget?

No, he'd grown harder and wiser during his time in the military. And part of that included discipline. The discipline to compartmentalize areas of his life so that they never touched. If he had been able to do it then, he could do it now.

So he forced a smile that was less than sincere and said, "Nothing to thank me for. I've moved on. And obviously you have too."

Up went her chin in that familiar stubborn tilt. Only he wasn't sure why she'd feel the need in this case. He was giving her an out. And himself as well. There was nothing to discuss. Now. Or ever.

"Yes, I have." She moved a hand as if to brush a strand of hair behind her shoulder. Except her hair was pinned up with a clip, exposing the long line of her neck. Nervous gesture? It didn't matter if it was. "Well, anyway, the hospital is very fortunate to have you here. I'm sure I'll see you later."

He was sure she would. Only Clancy was pretty sure he'd rather just avoid her whenever possible. But if they were both going to help in the flood-damaged area, there would be no avoiding anyone. They would be working closer than they'd ever imagined possible.

And he'd imagined all kinds of "closeness"... Once

upon a time. His jaw tightened. Why was all this coming up again? Was it the shock of seeing her after all these years?

That had to be it.

As she walked away he was pretty sure it was more than that. And that he was doomed. Doomed to dig up things best left in the past. Doomed to sleepless nights of hearing her whisper his name. But there was one thing he wasn't doomed to do, and that was to dwell on the mistakes of the past.

No matter how difficult that might prove to be.

Hollee punched her pillow for what seemed like the thousandth time and tried to get her racing mind to take a break. God. Why did he have to land at Arlington Regional of all hospitals?

And why did they both have to volunteer for this trip?

She could stay in Arlington, except the thought of pregnant moms not having access to health care wouldn't let her take the coward's way out. If she'd stayed the course with being a vet tech, she wouldn't be in this predicament. She'd loved her old job with a passion, except for one thing. Putting animals to sleep. She'd thought she could get past it with time, but while she had been relieved when an animal's suffering was finally over, it had been the decisions made for financial reasons that had killed her.

She'd gone home in tears one too many times, although she'd known it wasn't the pet owner's fault in many cases. So she'd chosen to retrain, focusing on the human side of health care instead. There were still problems and things she didn't like doing, but at least people could understand what was happening to them and, for the most part, they could have a say in the decision-making.

Adopting one-eyed Tommie was the last act she'd performed as a vet tech. Glaucoma had stolen the dog's right eye, but it hadn't stolen her life. Her elderly owners had turned her over to Hollee, knowing she was the dog's best chance for survival, since glaucoma in one eye could attack the other at a later date, and they weren't equipped to care for a blind dog.

Tommie was getting older herself now, but Hollee loved her fiercely. Two weeks away from her was a long time, but Hollee's mom was going to stay at her house and keep her company while she was gone. And it wasn't like she'd be in another country. Just a different part of Virginia.

Maybe sensing her turmoil, Tommie chose that moment to hop on the bed and nudge her hand before curling up beside her. She smiled. "You know you're not going to get away with that when Mom is here."

She draped her arm over the dog's side and sighed. "But I won't tell her if you don't."

With that, Hollee finally felt a blessed heaviness invade her limbs, and her mind began to shut down. When Clancy's rugged face strayed a little too close, she nestled into her pillow, suddenly too tired to fight it off.

How could one person go from hot to so very cold and indifferent? She'd seen it not only in Clancy, but in Jacob too. A couple years after their marriage, he'd seemed to cool, and all the insecurities she'd felt after Clancy's rejection had returned with a vengeance.

She'd have to work on that problem after she'd gotten some rest.

Maybe then she'd have the strength to throw all the demons of her past away once and for all.

CHAPTER TWO

HOLLEE RACED DOWN the corridor toward the room at the end of the hallway, skidding to a stop when she saw Clancy heading toward the same door. "Clance? What—?"

"It's Ava." His head swiveled toward her, but he didn't stop walking. "She called when I was in the middle of surgery and said she was on her way. Dammit! I can't believe she drove herself in."

Clancy's sister! She'd actually meant to check on her pregnant friend this week, but with how crazy things had been, she hadn't gotten a chance. Of course if she had, maybe she would have known that Clancy was headed to her hospital. As it was, she'd only heard that a woman with pre-term labor was being prepped for an emergency C-section, so she'd come to see if she could help. But she'd never dreamed it would be Ava.

Worried he was about to burst into the room and create a scene, she caught up with him and put a hand on his arm. "Stay here. Let me see what's going on."

His eyes narrowed. "She's my sister."

Which was why she didn't want him charging in

there. He was worried. She got it. But that kind of raw, exposed emotion helped no one.

No one knew that better than Hollee.

"Yes, and that's exactly why I should go in first. You don't need to upset her." Or everyone else. Though she left that part unsaid.

At his brusque nod, she slid into the room, and encountered a chaotic scene. Ava was thrashing around on the bed as two nurses and the attending doctor did their best to quiet her.

"You need to hold still!"

"My baby! It's too early!" The fear in that voice was almost Hollee's undoing. But she held it in and went to the nurse who was trying to physically hold Ava down.

"She's a friend. Let me try."

"Okay, but put on a mask, she tested positive for influenza b."

Oh, God. Not good. She took the mask the nurse thrust in her hands and pulled on gloves, then she smoothed Ava's bangs out of the way, not liking the heat that rose in waves from her forehead. The fever explained some of her agitation. "Ava, it's Hollee. Can you look at me?"

"Hollee?" Her demeanor changed almost instantly, and she sagged against the bed. "What's happening?"

She, Clancy, Jacob and Ava had all been so close back in the day. She and Ava were still friends, but Hollee avoided talking about Clancy. And when Ava had made passing comments about where he'd been currently stationed, Hollee had just smiled and nodded, then changed the subject. Her friend hadn't mentioned him leaving the military. Of course, her friend had had other things on her mind.

"The baby's coming." Fresh pain speared through Hollee. What she wouldn't have given to hear those words during her marriage. "You need to let them take you. They're going to do everything they can for both of you."

Tears streaming down her face, Ava nodded. "She's supposed to be my Christmas Eve baby. Please don't let anything happen to her."

A promise no one could make.

Hollee stepped back to let the other nurse take over again as an anesthesiologist swept in. "What do we have?"

"Preterm labor secondary to flu. We need to get her into the OR. Do you want to do the epidural here or there?"

"There."

One of the worst things that could happen to the maternity ward was for the flu to find its way inside these protected hallways.

As if reading her thoughts, Dr. Latrobe grimaced. "We'll need to follow protocols for disinfecting the ward. I've already called it in."

Hollee needed to let Clancy know what was happening. "Does the baby look okay?"

Latrobe glanced up. "She's five weeks early, but the baby's registering some early signs of distress. The sooner we deliver her the better."

She took that as her clue to get out of their way. She went back to Ava. "I'll check in on you as soon as I know which room you're in. Dr. Latrobe is one of Arlington's finest, so you're in great hands."

"No! Don't leave!"

Fearing Ava was going to start getting agitated again, she said, "Clancy's outside, and he's worried sick. I need to let him know what's going on."

"Poor Clancy." Ava's face flushed with fever. "He had a thing for..." Her face contorted as a contraction hit.

Hollee turned to leave while she could. Peeling off her gloves and mask, she pumped a couple of squirts of hand sanitizer before touching the door. She encountered resistance in pushing it open and found Clancy with one hand on the wooden surface as if he'd gotten tired of waiting.

"You can't go in there. She has the flu. They're taking precautions to keep it from spreading."

"Damn. I asked her to get her flu shot. I thought she did, but maybe not."

Ava had always been the free-spirited, independent one in their group. Even so, she'd been devastated when the baby's father had decided he couldn't do the whole parental responsibility thing. As if to prove that fact, he'd found someone else almost immediately after they'd broken up. "You know about the dad."

He gave her a searching look before nodding. "Yeah, he made her promises he never intended to keep. He should be ashamed."

Had Clancy aimed that jab at himself? They'd shared a kiss that had been pretty hot and heavy, but a week later he'd become someone she hadn't recognized. All he'd said was that the kiss had been a mistake, show-ing up with another girl soon afterward. And another one a few weeks after that. It had been a slap in the face and had proved that bad boys did not make good mar-riage material. Even Jacob had commented on the way Clancy had been acting.

While she'd still been stinging from Clancy's rejec-tion, Jacob had asked her out, and she'd accepted. At first it had been a way to get back at him. But slowly, over the course of six months, she'd realized she and Jacob actually had a lot in common and when he'd pro-posed, she said yes. She'd loved him, but that spark of passion she'd felt for Clancy had never been there.

At first she'd thought it was because she'd over-romanticized that kiss and the connection she thought they'd shared. That feeling had gotten worse when Jacob seemed to distance himself emotionally. Initially, she'd chalked it up to her imagination. But a year before he died, that apathy had become marked, and her request to start a family as a last-ditch attempt to put things right had been met with a chilly response. She'd been crushed, and a seed of inadequacy had sprouted. First Clancy and then Jacob. Was there something about her that drove away people she cared about?

All but Ava. They'd remained close, but she'd never felt comfortable sharing her problems with Clancy or Jacob with her. Clancy was her brother. And Jacob... well, he'd been one of Ava's friends too.

In the end, Clancy hadn't even come to their wed-ding, something that had hurt both her and Jacob.

The funeral had actually been the first time she'd

seen him since getting married. That had been five years ago. It might as well have been a lifetime.

Ava was whisked out of the room and down the hallway, reminding Hollee what was really important right now—and it certainly wasn't her melancholy thoughts. Or things she could no longer change.

Clancy's face was a tense mask, and she gripped his arm, the warmth of his skin making her realize how cold her own hands had become. Ava had a big team of staff with her, and Clancy had no one right now, and she ached for him. "Come on. Let's grab a cup of coffee. And then we'll sit and wait for news."

"I want to be in there."

"You can't, Clance. You know that. Ava needs to concentrate and so does her team. And the last thing you need is to carry the virus into one of your surgeries."

"Hell, how did I not know she was sick?"

She smiled. "Are you serious? Ava is one of the strongest people I know. She's also the most stubborn. 'Show no weakness'—remember?"

That had always been the de Oliveira siblings' motto.

The flexing of muscles made her realize her fingers were still clutching his upper arm. She released him in a hurry.

"I can't believe she didn't come in sooner." He dragged a hand through his hair.

"I've been checking on her periodically but, honestly, she probably didn't even realize she had the flu. We get sick, and we wait it out. It's the way humans are geared. She had a pretty high fever, which is probably what triggered labor."

He leaned a shoulder again the wall. "She wants this baby. Despite everything."

"Of course she does." Hollee would have too, had the situation been reversed. But it wasn't. She swallowed away the sudden lump in her throat and inclined her head to point down the hallway. "The sooner we hit the cafeteria, the sooner we can come back and wait for news."

"Are you on break?

"I actually worked the night shift. I just got off about fifteen minutes ago, but I heard the noise and decided to see if I could help."

He nodded. "I'm glad you were here. I might have gotten myself tossed out of the hospital before I'd been in town a week."

"That would be unfortunate. Especially with the Appalachia trip coming up."

And why had she even brought up the relief mission? The last thing she needed to be thinking about right now were those two weeks. Not when she hadn't quite figured out how she felt about being there with him.

They made their way to the first floor, and as the elevator doors opened she was met with the hospital's Christmas trimmings that had gone up in the last couple of days. Three festive trees were clustered to the side of the huge glass entry doors, the sparkle of silvery tinsel catching the light. On the other side stood a life-sized animated Santa, his bag of toys thrown over one shoulder, his head swiveling from side to side as if looking for his sleigh.

Above them, glittery snowflakes hung from fishing line, the climate-control system making them dance.

She'd always loved this time of year. "The hospital does a great job decorating."

"Hmm…"

The sound was so noncommittal that it made her laugh. "You don't like it?"

"It's just different from the places I've worked."

Of course it was. "The military doesn't decorate for the holidays?"

"They do, it's just not normally so…" He paused, as if searching for the right word. "So extravagant."

Hollee looked with different eyes and could see how he might think that. "I'm sure where we're going, then, you'll feel right at home." Then, wondering if that sounded pompous, she added, "It's not the decorations that make Christmas special. It's the spirit behind it. Arlington Regional has a lot of children who walk through those doors. And sometimes they need a little bit of hope—a little bit of magic."

"I never thought of it that way. I guess I'm used to dealing with cynical adults whose deep pockets only give up funds for other things."

"Things that save lives." She smiled. "But you're right. I think it all depends on its target audience."

If things went as planned she would be here to help out on at least one of the hospital's "Staff Santa" afternoons in the next couple of weeks, when they handed out gifts in the pediatric ward. It was always fun to see who they got to play the part of Santa. After that, she'd be away in Appalachia, in a town called Bender, for the rest of the festivities, playing a completely different kind of Santa. Two groups so very different but that both needed a shot of hope and happiness.

They arrived in the cafeteria, which was also decorated for the season, boasting small centerpieces on each of the laminate tables. She headed straight for the coffee machine, where she dumped a couple of sealed creamers titled "Mint Fantasy" and three packets of sugar into a cup.

He smiled. "I see you like a little coffee with your flavored syrup."

"It's the only way to enjoy it." She scrunched her nose. "I'll never understand how people can drink theirs black."

"Since that's how I like mine…"

"Okay, so maybe I was being a little judgmental. But for me, coffee is a dessert. Best savored in tiny delicious sips that make you tingle all over. Sweet, luscious and silky smooth." She closed her eyes for a second, her tongue already anticipating the flavor.

Clancy didn't answer, and when she glanced up, she found his eyes on her in a way that made her swallow. Oh, God. She'd made her coffee sound almost like…sex.

Strangely, they'd only shared a single kiss but, like her dessert coffee, she could still taste him. That light touch between them had been romantic and sweet and had hinted at things that had made her skin heat.

Their kiss had happened at Christmas too, and she could still remember exactly what had led up to it. Ava had pointed above her at something on the ceiling of her and Clancy's childhood home with a wink, and when Hollee had glanced up, she'd seen a sprig of mistletoe.

And she had been standing right underneath it. And Clancy... She could still see his mischievous grin. That time he'd kissed her on the cheek. He'd saved the real kiss for later that evening, when he'd driven her home. Only that time he'd been the one holding the sprig. And when their lips had met...

She closed her eyes, suddenly angry with herself for even thinking of that night.

It might have meant something to her, but it hadn't to him. He'd made that very clear.

It was as if someone had flipped a switch and turned Clancy into a totally different person. He'd still been intense, his loose bad-boy vibe deadly to the senses. Obviously a lot of other women had found him just as attractive. He still was.

When his attitude toward her had shifted, she'd nursed that hurt until it had festered, convincing her that Jacob was the better choice. After all, she felt like she knew him, whereas Clancy had become a stranger. When Jacob had wanted to save sex for their wedding day, she'd been fine with it. But when they'd finally slept together, it had been a huge letdown, and she wasn't sure why. But she'd loved Jacob and had convinced herself it didn't matter.

But maybe it had. Maybe if she and Clancy had had let-down sex, she wouldn't be sitting here now wondering if he would have been as delicious as her coffee.

She turned away, feeling like she was betraying Jacob's memory somehow. Maybe she'd been guilty of comparing them all along, and Jacob had figured it out. Maybe that's why he'd changed.

Forget it. She concentrated on pouring and stirring her coffee and snapping on the lid. She should have just gone home, instead of offering to keep Clancy company. Tearing open old wounds was not something she was interested in doing. Especially if it would cause forgotten memories to come creeping back, dragging a matching bag of emotions with it.

"Ready to head to the waiting room?" she asked.

"Yes." Then he frowned, touching her hand. "Thank you for checking on Ava. And being her friend."

"She's always been there when I've needed her. How could I do any less?"

"Well, I'm glad you were there anyway."

"I'm sorry about the father. It was a rough time for her."

He shrugged. "Mom didn't even tell me what happened until I came home. I knew she was expecting, but not that he'd run off with someone else while I was still in Afghanistan. Maybe that was a good thing."

"Will you go back overseas?"

"No. I was ready for a change."

Something shifted in his demeanor, making her say, "It couldn't have been easy." Her glance went back to his face and the separation in his eyebrow. If anything, the scar made him look even more gorgeous, which was ridiculous. A scar was simply epithelial tissue that filled in a wound. It didn't change who he was.

Or did it? He seemed less carefree than he had ten years ago. Harder in ways she couldn't quite put her finger on. He was twenty-nine, just two years older than she was. There were no strands of gray in that thick, dark head of hair, but he almost seemed ancient, his frown line carving a deep groove that nothing would erase. She hated to think what he'd seen over there.

As they walked back toward the elevators, Neil Vickers, the hospital administrator, stopped them. "I don't know if either of you have been in the staff lounge, but I put a sign-up sheet in there. I want to get an idea of how many we have for the Bender trip." He looked from one to the other. "That is if you two are still interested in going."

Hollee didn't hesitate. "I am. I'll make sure I put my name on the list."

"Great. FEMA has just finished setting up a disaster relief camp. So they should be ready for us by the time our group arrives."

Clancy hadn't said anything, and she wondered if he'd changed his mind about going. Neil must have thought along the same lines because he glanced over at him. "How are you settling in?"

"So far, so good. I'll take a look at the sign-up sheet."

Hmm, that was rather noncommittal. What happened to all that talk about them both being adults and able to handle situations like this?

If he decided not to go, that would be a relief, right?

"That's all I can ask," Neil said.

"My sister is in surgery right now for preterm labor, and my decision has to hinge on the outcome."

The administrator frowned. "I didn't know. I'm sorry."

"Not a problem. Hopefully everything will turn out all right, and I can join the team."

Hollee had almost forgotten about that. Of course he wanted to see what happened with Ava and the baby. She felt like a fool for thinking his hesitation had anything to do with her.

She steered the conversation away from the subject, hoping to reassure Clancy that everything would turn out okay. "Do you think it would be all right if I bring some Christmas lights to decorate the tents or wherever we end up staying?"

"I didn't see anything against that in the paperwork. It might even help morale. We've already planned on bringing some small gifts for the kids. They're going to send me a rough count of the numbers once they get organized."

"That's great."

"Don't forget to sign up," he said again, before waving and heading the way they'd just come. Why not? Even Neil had to eat.

"Let's head right to Maternity," she said. "I can sign up afterward."

"Are you sure?"

"Yes, I'm anxious to see if there's any word."

Making their way there, they stopped at the nurses' station, and the person behind the desk gave them a smile, not even asking what they wanted. "She's doing well. The baby's out and being assessed. She's tiny, but perfect. I don't think she's going to need as much support as many born that early."

Clancy planted a hand on the desk as if to support himself. "Can we see her?"

"Not yet. They're still closing her up." The nurse hesitated. "And she does have the flu, so we're taking extra precautions."

"We've all had the flu shot, obviously, but we'll be careful."

Wow, Clancy had said "we" as if expecting her to go with him to see Ava. And of course she wanted to. Even if seeing the relief in his eyes had just about done her in. How hard would it be to see Clancy's niece, knowing that his family was growing, while she was alone?

In five years of marriage, Jacob had continually put off having children, at first saying they had plenty of time. The last time, he'd said he wasn't sure if he wanted children at all…with her.

Those words had hurt in a way that went beyond description. But he'd said he didn't want a divorce, he wanted to work things out, even though she'd seen no evidence of that before his last deployment.

In the end, nothing had been settled between them. Had Jacob somehow known about her youthful crush on Clancy? No. Of course not. That had been over before they'd gotten married. And Hollee never would have cheated on him. Not even with Clancy. Her infatuation had been just the foolish stuff of youth.

She was over it now. And she'd donned her anti-Clancy armor as soon as she'd seen him again. She was well protected and ready for anything.

At least, she hoped she was. Especially if he ended up going on the relief trip. The last thing she needed to do was dig up that old crush and start mooning over the man again. Especially if he still played the field, like he had when they'd been younger. If that was the case, and he tempted her to share more than a simple kiss, she would be setting herself up for a whole lot of hurt. And this time there would be no one there to catch her when she fell.

CHAPTER THREE

CLANCY PUT HIS gloved hand through the opening of the incubator and touched Jennifer Jay de Oliveira's tiny hand, marveling at the sweet face. The Jay stood for Jacob, a nod to their friend. That rankled. When he got the chance he was going to advise Ava to choose something else. But he didn't want to do that in front of Hollee.

He didn't want to hurt her if he didn't have to. If that meant taking his old friend's secret to the grave and letting her continue to think Clancy had been a jerk back then, so be it. If he hadn't been such a kid at the time, he might have sat back and thought for a while before letting his friend's veiled hints and his own insecurities convince him that he was not what Hollee—who was valedictorian of her class—needed. What she deserved. But at the time he'd thought Jacob was right.

Clancy had coasted along for most of high school, wandering aimlessly, drifting from one pretty girl to another. His friends had been the one constant in his life. Until he'd kissed Hollee and found it mattered more than he had expected it to. And then even that friendship had been destroyed. Thanks to his own stupidity.

His life had changed when he'd joined the military and had seen the need for medical personnel. It was like he'd found his purpose in life.

"She's so beautiful." The low voice of the person he'd just been ruminating about slid past his ear, making his insides tighten.

"Yes, she is." He'd invited her here. He wasn't sure why, except that Ava and Hollee were close friends, their friendship bound so tightly together that they'd weathered all the ups and downs of childhood. Not so with his and Hollee's friendship. He'd made a choice he'd never dreamed he'd regret.

But he did regret it, even though Hollee had been happy with Jacob, and since she'd never learned the truth, she continued to believe her marriage had been perfect.

Clancy had done his damnedest to stay busy, dating lots of women. He hadn't wanted Jacob or Hollee to guess the battle going on inside him, so he'd played up the freewheeling commitment-phobe aspect of his personality.

Maybe there'd been more to the act than he realized, since he was still single and had no desire to change that fact.

"At least Ava is okay, even though she can't see Jennifer yet."

They'd come to see the baby first to avoid any possibility that they'd pass something from mom to newborn. As it was, Ava wouldn't be able to see her baby for four or five days, until the period of contagion was over. It was for the baby's safety mostly, but Ava had been through an ordeal on top of being sick. She needed rest, and her body needed time to heal. She could still provide nourishment for the infant, since the flu virus didn't pass into breast milk. She couldn't feed her directly, but she could pump and have it sent to the NICU.

He turned and glanced at Hollee, noticing that she had a faraway look in her eye. She and Jacob had never had kids. Was she regretting that? He hadn't talked to his friend enough after his engagement to know if there was a reason, other than a choice he and Hollee had made. Maybe they couldn't have kids. Or maybe he hadn't wanted to be tied down by them.

That would explain a lot, actually, knowing what he did about Jacob.

"Better to wait and be sure than to endanger the baby out of impatience."

He'd have done well to heed that advice himself.

"Yes, I agree."

"Do you want to touch her?" he asked.

"Oh…um, I'm good. You take all the time you need."

A shakiness to her voice made him pause. "You don't like cuddling babies?"

"I do. My mom is watching mine."

Shock made him turn around, his hands sliding out of the incubator's access ports. "Excuse me?" She had a child? He'd assumed…

"Well, maybe I should amend that. My 'baby' has four legs and is covered with fur."

He went slack with a relief that took him by surprise. "A dog?"

"A German shepherd named Tommie."

"I actually have a dog too. Only he's a basset hound mix."

She laughed. "I love bassets."

"He's quite a character. Mom comes over to let him out during the day. She's coming up to see Ava and the baby in a little while."

"I'd love to meet your dog sometime."

A sliver of surprise went through him. She'd barely said twenty words since they'd come into the NICU area, and the change from then until now was dramatic. Her eyes were bright green and a smile revealed a peek-a-boo dimple at the corner of her mouth that he'd almost forgotten existed. It fascinated him as much now as it had when they had been teenagers. It was what had drawn his gaze repeatedly to her mouth after that kiss on the cheek, and the very thing that had instigated the very real kiss at her house later that night.

Dragging his gaze away, he focused on her eyes instead. "We'll have to get them together for a walk, although I have to warn you that Gordy doesn't always match his soulful brown eyes. Sometimes he can be a grump."

"That's okay. Tommie has enough cheer for five dogs."

What the hell was he doing? They were not two single parents planning play dates. Seeing her outside the hospital was not a good idea. But since they might be spending two weeks together in the near future, this might be a good opportunity to ease their way into things. It wasn't like they were going on an actual date. Just walking their dogs together.

"I guess we'll see. It looks like Ava and the baby will be okay, and if that's the case I'll probably go down to the Appalachian area with everyone else. What are you doing with your dog while you're gone?"

"The same as what you're doing while you're at work. My mom will come over and take care of her. She'll probably stay at the house with her, actually. She has a soft spot for Tommie. It almost makes me jealous at times."

He stiffened. That had been exactly what had gotten him into trouble with Hollee. He'd had a soft spot for her that had morphed into something else entirely. And, hell, if he hadn't been a jealous bastard the day of her wedding, even though he'd been a continent away. He'd drunk himself into oblivion just to keep from calling Jacob and saying he'd changed his mind. That the union no longer had his blessing.

Knowing what he did now, maybe it would have been better if he had. But hindsight was twenty-twenty, and there was nothing he could do about any of it now.

"My mom likes Gordy as well. He kept her company after I was deployed. She said it eased her loneliness while I was gone." Gordy had to be pushing seven now, although Clancy didn't know his exact age. And he was glad he could spend the dog's remaining years with him. Staying away had been the easier choice, but he truly believed that coming home was now the right one.

Hollee turned away, wrapping her arms around her waist. "Are you ready to see Ava?"

Damn. Had his mention of his mom's loneliness reminded her of her own loss?

"You don't have to come if you don't want to."

She turned back. "I do. She's my friend, although I should have been checking on her more. It's time I made amends for that."

Maybe it was time he made amends too for the way he'd behaved. He might have been trying to do the right thing but had ended up hurting her, according to what Ava had said all those years ago. His sister had not been happy with him. But that was okay. He hadn't been happy with himself.

He moved closer and tipped her chin up. "About what I said all those years ago—"

"Don't. Please." Her whispered words shook.

"I just wanted to say I'm sorry."

Shimmering green eyes looked into his, and she opened her mouth as if to say something before shaking her head. "You have nothing to be sorry for. We were both kids."

Yes, they had been. He paused, then decided to ask a pivotal question. "Are we good?"

"Of course." Her chin went up, and she pulled away. "Shall we go?"

Once outside his sister's room, which was no longer in the maternity ward for the safety of the other new mothers, they donned surgical caps and gloves once again. Ava was sitting up in bed, a pillow pressed over her stomach, probably to ease the pain of the incision.

She looked pale and drawn, but she smiled when she saw them. "Did you get to see her?"

"We did. She's beautiful."

"I didn't get to hold her. Or even get a good look at her."

Hollee smiled. "Well it's a good thing I snapped a couple of pictures then, isn't it?"

"You did?"

Ava said what he'd just thought. He hadn't noticed her taking pictures.

"Of course." She took her phone out of one of her pockets and punched a few buttons and then held it for Ava to see.

"Holy Moly! I did that?"

"You did indeed, honey." Hollee started to touch her, before thinking better of it.

Ava looked up at him. "Being an uncle suits you. You should see your face."

"What do you mean?"

"Come look."

He wasn't sure he wanted to, but to say no was bound to make both of them wonder why. So he went around to the other side of Holly and glanced at the images as she scrolled through them.

Hell. He looked like he was in love. Well, that's because he was. That tiny creature was his niece. It was normal to have a goofy grin on his face.

"Too bad you caught my bad side."

Their heads both came up at the same time. Ava spoke first. "Don't say that. You look fine, doesn't he, Hollee?"

He'd meant it as a joke, but evidently it fell flat. And he certainly didn't want Hollee to feel trapped into making some banal comment about his scar. Again. So he held up his hands to show capitulation. "Okay, I'm sorry. I won't say it again."

It did seem kind of incongruous that a plastic surgeon wouldn't have his own scars fixed or resurfaced. It would be easy enough to make them fade further into the background. But the reconstructions Clancy did were things that resulted from injuries or congenital conditions and he wanted his patients to love themselves, even if their after-surgery results weren't that of an airbrushed model. Not that he was the greatest example of loving himself either. Jacob had given him a pointed reminder of that a few days after he'd kissed Hollee.

I'm not like you, Mr. Bigshot. I'm a one-woman kind of guy, and between you and me, I'm crazy about Hollee, so don't go getting any ideas about adding her to your collection.

He'd never looked at himself that way, but evidently it was how Jacob—and maybe lots of other people—had seen him. It had been enough to make him pull back and put a stop to things with Hollee before he'd got in any deeper and ended up hurting her.

According to Ava, though, he'd ended up hurting her anyway. But, as he'd seen for himself, she'd recovered, and Jacob had gotten his wish.

Ava bent her head to the side, cracking her cervical joints. "They tell me that Jen-Jen is doing well."

Despite her illness, her personality refused to be

squashed. She'd always been a firebrand, but Clancy had been fiercely protective of her when they had been kids, even though she would have clobbered him if she'd known.

"Jen-Jen? Is that really what you're going to call her?"

"How about Jenny J.? Or J.J.? No?" There was a happiness in her grin that he hadn't seen in a while, despite the evidence of exhaustion in her face. Now wasn't the time to approach her about her new daughter's middle name. But he would have to make a point to tell her. And soon.

"I personally like Jen-Jen."

"Hmm…" Her smile faded. "It's still so sad when I think of Jacob as being gone forever."

Hollee tucked her phone away, her head down, not looking at either of them.

"Yes, it is." He shifted and decided to change the subject. "Any idea when the baby can come home?"

"She needs to gain some weight obviously, but her lungs are strong. I heard her cry before they rushed her away." She shut her eyes and then looked at him. "I have to tell you it was the most beautiful sound I've heard in my life."

"I can imagine. When we saw her, she seemed… content." In fact, he'd been a little worried about how quiet she was, but Ava's words made him feel better.

"She really is beautiful." Hollee smiled, but this time it seemed a little forced.

It had to be hard hearing people talk about her late husband. Which was another reason he wanted to talk to Ava about the name, although he wasn't sure why it mattered. It mattered to him, though. Jacob had betrayed Hollee in the worst possible way. A one-woman man? It seemed that had been a lie. The last thing he wanted was for his niece to bear the man's name.

He took hold of one of his sister's toes through the blanket and gave it a wiggle. "We'd better let you get some rest, but I'll come see you tomorrow." He was careful not to include Hollee in that. She could set up her own visitation schedule.

"And since I worked the night shift, I'd probably better go home and try to get some rest," she said.

"Will you come back tomorrow too?"

"If you want me to."

Ava nodded. "Of course I do. And about what I said earlier, when I was in the delivery room…" Her glance shot to him before moving back to Hollee. "I was just scared and wasn't thinking straight."

"Whatever it was, it couldn't have been too important, because I can't even remember you saying anything."

"Good." She lay back against her pillows, eyes closed.

"Do you need anything?" Hollee asked. "Water? Something to eat?"

"I'm just incredibly sleepy right now."

"We'll get out of your hair, then." This time Hollee did touch her arm. Probably because she'd put her phone away and was about to shed her gloves. "Get some shut-eye now, because you'll soon be taking care of that precious little girl."

They left the room, and he couldn't help but ask, "What did she say that she was so upset about?"

"She wasn't quite coherent because of the fever. And since she doesn't want me to remember, it's probably just as well, don't you think?"

"I guess so. Well, I'll see you when I see you."

"Yep. I'm off to dreamland."

By herself. At least he assumed she would be. The thought stopped him. Maybe that's why she seemed so uncomfortable whenever any reference to Jacob was made. She hadn't remarried or she'd have a ring on. Or maybe not, since jewelry could harbor germs, or hold them against the skin, in the case of a ring.

He watched her walk away, realizing he had more questions than when he'd started working at the hospital. And despite the fact that it shouldn't bother him, he was finding that it did. Very much. He wasn't sure how to unravel that. Or if he should even try. The only thing he could do was avoid her as much as he could—until they boarded their bus and drove off into the sunset together. Along with about twenty other people and a whole lot of medical gear.

Ugh! Hollee could not believe it. She and Clancy had joked about giving their dogs a play date and a week later she spotted him at the dog park at exactly the same time as her! Fortunately, he was some distance away and hadn't seen her yet. He was talking to some woman who was standing way too close, her Afghan hound looking tall and elegant, much like her owner, who was almost as tall as Clancy. And the way the woman looked at him, laughing at something he said…

A sick feeling rolled around the pit of Hollee's stomach as memories of the past flooded back. She guessed some things never changed. The nurses would probably also be fawning all over him soon enough.

Jacob had once joked that she'd dodged a bullet by being able to see through Clancy. Unfortunately, that hadn't been the case. But there'd been no way she would have admitted that to her husband.

Could she bear watching him make the rounds at the hospital in a way that had nothing to do with patients?

She should just turn back around and head toward her car, but when she tried to tug Tommie in that direction, her dog planted her feet, head whipping around as if to say, *What is this, human? A trick?*

"No trick, sweet girl. Just a big old dose of self-preservation."

Okay, if she couldn't retreat, she could simply head toward an obscure corner of the park and wait there until he left. Surely she could keep Tommie occupied until then. She had a ball thrower and a tote bag that held an old soft quilt that her grandmother had made. She could just sit on the grass, ignoring Clancy and enjoying the day with no one being any the wiser. Except Clancy took out his phone and put it up to his ear, giving the woman with him an apologetic shrug, and the woman handed him something before heading on her way.

The sick feeling turned into something big and ugly.

She would bet there was a phone number on that slip of paper.

Suddenly Gordy—wasn't that his name?—jerked to the right. Clancy, who wasn't expecting that or else was distracted by his call or the woman or both, careened sideways, landing right on his lean behind.

And it was lean. Just as lean as it had been ten years ago. Because, shamefully, she'd just looked.

Gordy broke free just as the woman and her fancy dog came back over and offered a hand to Clancy. Surprisingly, he didn't accept it, just hefted himself back up, but it was too late to catch Gordy, who was moving across the grass, his pudgy little legs moving like pistons. Behind him trailed his leash.

"Damn." The dog was headed in her direction!

About that time Clancy's gaze met hers and he cocked his head, bending over to retrieve his phone and the paper. He then started moving…fast, giving his new friend a quick wave as he left her behind. Within ten strides he'd caught up with his dog, snagging his leash and putting a stop to his flight, such as it was.

She realized, despite what she'd just witnessed, she was grinning like a loon. Because of Gordy, she told herself. Not because the incident had foiled the woman's attempt to hold Clancy's attention.

He made his way toward them, not saying anything as he let his dog sniff Tommie. Thankfully her dog was as friendly as his seemed to be. "Looks like they hit it off," he said. "I didn't realize you came to this park."

To his credit, he didn't look behind him to see what had happened to the woman he'd been talking to. It looked like she'd given up, since she was now walking in the opposite direction.

"I do." She was pretty sure that wasn't something to be celebrated. "Is this the park closest to you?"

Unfortunately that came out sounding like an accusation, when she hadn't really meant it to.

If he heard it, though, he didn't acknowledge it. Instead, one corner of his mouth tilted up. "Yes, actually it is. I've been here a couple of times."

That made her smile fade. Had he already met up with the same woman on other occasions?

She decided to hit neutral and change the direction of her thoughts. "How are Ava and the baby doing? Has she decided what to call her?"

Hollee was off today, and when she'd checked in on them yesterday, the pair had been doing well, with Ava finally being allowed to see her baby.

"Nope. So far J.J. and Jen-Jen are her favorites." Clancy suddenly frowned and looked closely at something. "Is your dog's eye okay? She's squinting."

Glancing down to check, she shook her head. "She's actually missing that eye. Glaucoma," she added.

"I thought glaucoma was treatable. She had the eye removed?"

"It manifests differently in dogs. She'd had it for a while before her former owners had it checked. It was too late to save her vision and was causing considerable pain. She's adjusted quite well." She reached down to ruffle Tommie's fur. "We're hoping to retain the sight in her other eye as long as possible."

She hesitated, the tote on her shoulder starting to get

heavy. "I brought a blanket—do you want to sit with us for a while?"

There was a noticeable pause on his part, then he lifted one shoulder, whether in irritation or a shrug, she wasn't sure. "We don't want to impose."

The words made her heart ache. Maybe he wanted to go back and find that woman.

Okay, she needed to answer this carefully. "I noticed you were talking to someone. I'll understand if you have other plans."

"Nope. No plans at all. Anyway, I think our dogs are enjoying each other's company."

A huge rush of relief washed through her, although it was ridiculous. He might not want to go find Ms. Afghan Hound right this minute, but he could always call her later. Or someone else would come along. She could pretty much depend on that.

That was okay, though, because Hollee wasn't interested in him like that. Not anymore, so there was no reason to sit here dwelling on it.

Why not just enjoy his company and not worry about the other stuff?

"I think so too. We can go over to one of the quieter areas, so they can stay out of everyone's way, if that's okay."

"Yes. Thanks. Gordy and I didn't think to bring anything to sit on."

More likely, he didn't feel the need to sit down, but since her legs had been feeling a little shaky ever since she'd spotted him, she'd better do something about it quickly.

That scar on his face drew her attention time and time again. He had to know she was staring at it. But it wasn't out of pity. She was fascinated by the changes that had taken place in him since the time she'd known him. Ten years had layered his face with a cynicism that hadn't been there before, the scars just adding to that feeling. It also added to that air of danger he'd carried with him back then. She'd used to fantasize about riding on that motorcycle of his, and she'd finally gotten her chance when he'd given her a lift home the night of the kiss. She'd been pressed tight to his back, her arms wrapped around his waist, and… *God*… He'd been lethal to her senses back then, and it seemed he still was. So much so that she'd done her best to avoid him in the days since little Jennifer's birth.

The man was gorgeous. And seeing him interacting with his sister's baby—the sheer devotion on his face—had opened a compartment in her brain that she'd thought was forever nailed shut. Why had he kissed her if he'd had no intention of asking her out on a date? Had he found her somehow inferior to the other girls he'd gone out with?

Her eyelids clamped closed for a second. That was a question to which there was no answer. And ultimately she'd chosen a different path. But one that hadn't necessarily turned out much better. But seeing him interact with that woman a few minutes ago had been a good wake-up call about why she needed to be careful.

She forced her attention to her surroundings. "How about over to our right? It's pretty empty."

"Looks good." He lifted the tote off her shoulder,

fingers lightly brushing the side of her neck as he did so. A shiver erupted from that tiny contact, setting off her inner seismograph. It started frantically scribbling a warning that she'd better heed.

You need to sit down. Now.

She headed off in that direction, urging Tommie to follow. She did, but not without a shrill wail of protest. Hollee rolled her eyes.

"Not you too," she muttered. "One of us has to keep our heads, girl. This is a man who doesn't stick around for long. Don't count on his dog being any different."

A minute later they arrived at their destination, Clancy having to go more slowly in deference to Gordy's shorter strides. "Could you hold him for a minute?"

She took the dog's leash as he removed the quilt from the tote and tossed it open, allowing it to flutter toward the ground. Why did the man make everything look effortless? He took the ball and its thrower and set them on one corner. "That blanket looks handmade."

"The quilt? It is. My grandmother made it. She used it for picnics and so did my mom. Now it's mine." She didn't think it would last another generation, though, as it had been mended more than once. But she couldn't bring herself to leave it in a cabinet unused. It just seemed wrong. And since she was an only child, and there were no prospects on the horizon, it didn't look like there would be a next generation. A pang went through her.

"Nice."

He took Gordy's leash again and motioned for her to sit first. She did, smiling when Tommie immediately tried to plop in her lap. She'd never quite grasped the fact that she was a big dog. Bigger than laps were made to accommodate. But that hadn't stopped her yet.

Clancy toed off his tennis shoes and sat his jeans-clad form on the other side of the quilt. Gordy didn't try to crawl in his lap, she noted. He, evidently the better behaved of the two, sat beside his owner, his tail wagging back and forth.

Sucking down a chilly burst of air, but glad the weather had warmed up enough to allow this kind of outing in December, she allowed her muscles to finally relax now that her legs had stopped their quivering. "By January this will be impossible, so we'd better enjoy it while we can."

He set Gordy's leash on the quilt beside him. "Oh, I plan to enjoy every second I get."

Giving him a sharp look and finding his attention focused in the distance, she decided he wasn't talking about her but about the weather.

She started to remove Tommie's leash, since the park allowed it, then stopped. "If I let her go, will it bother him?"

"No. If she won't run off, I'll take his leash off too. He has a tendency to play follow the leader."

"Tommie pretty much sticks to me like glue."

Once freed, the dogs came to the center and sniffed each other again before moving into the nearby grass. Gordy rolled, while Tommie sat and kept watch. It looked like she wasn't going to have to keep Tommie entertained after all. The animals looked perfectly content to romp nearby.

"How are you settling in at the hospital?"

He leaned back on his elbows. "It's a big change from what I'm used to, but I'm enjoying it. Obviously, I get more pediatric cases here than I did in the military."

"Those have to be hard."

He shifted to look at her. "They're different. A lot of them are due to accidents or burns, which definitely make you stop and think."

"Think? About what?"

"About what would have happened if things had turned out differently. About the long-term effects of a split-second decision."

Long-term effects? Oh, those were very real. One kiss had turned her world upside down and then dumped her onto her backside. It had been a heartbreaking lesson to learn: Don't let your impulsive side take control. Ever. Something she'd been very conscious of. It's one reason she hadn't dated since Jacob had died. She didn't want to take a chance on love, only to find out she'd made a mistake. Again.

Ugh. This was ridiculous. She hadn't thought of this stuff in years.

Maybe that wasn't exactly true, but it's what she needed to do: stop thinking about it. Those decisions were over and done with, and like Clancy had talked about with those injuries, they were irrevocable.

She fingered the stitching on the quilt. "I guess the same thing is true in labor and delivery. I've seen my share of surprise pregnancies. The parents' attitudes make the difference between it being a blessing or a burden. Like you said, split-second decisions carry consequences that follow you. For a long time."

Clancy stared at her, and it dawned on her that this time her tying something to the past hadn't just been in her head. She'd done it out loud, and he'd caught her. Only she hadn't done it on purpose. It just came out.

"Yes, they do."

Forcing herself to concentrate on the dogs, who were now lounging in the grass sunning themselves—Tommie's belly on full display, while Gordy's head was up, his eyes closed. "Well, they're sure enjoying themselves."

"They are."

She smiled. "So am I. I guess we got our play date after all." She quickly nodded toward the dogs. "Or theirs, I should say."

Despite her earlier thoughts, it really was nice just to sit beside him and soak in the sun. The only impulsive decision here had been to stay when she'd wanted to run. And it wasn't proving to be as disastrous as she'd feared.

"I appreciate you letting us crash your party."

She laughed. "I don't think Tommie is complaining too much."

"Neither is Gordy." He thought for a minute. "If you wanted, Tommie could stay at my place so your mom wouldn't have to move in with her. I'm sure my mom wouldn't mind feeding them both and letting them out."

"So you've decided to go?"

"It looks like Ava and the baby will be fine so yes."

She thought for a minute, trying to process what he'd

just said and the fact that he'd suggested the dogs stay together. Her mom loved Tommie and she was pretty sure she'd be devastated to have to change her plans. "My mom's looking forward to spending time with Tommie. Maybe Gordy could come stay at my place."

He looked at her, frown in place. "Are you sure? He can be a little stubborn, as you saw earlier."

"Really? Well, my mom's put up with my stubbornness for twenty-seven years. I think she can handle Gordy."

"Gordy would probably like the company, actually. My mom still works, so she can't spend the whole day with him. But he can certainly survive. Ask your mom first, though, and see what she says."

"I will, but I already know it won't be a problem. So just plan on it. Besides, your mom will probably be busy with her new grandbaby. You can drop him off on your way to the hospital the day we leave."

"I can give you a ride, so we don't end up having to leave both of our vehicles at the hospital, if you want."

Okay, so she hadn't bargained on riding over with him, but what was she going to say? No, I won't ride with you?

"Or I could give you a ride."

She only realized her chin was now sticking out defiantly when he tapped it. "You're right. Your mom can definitely handle Gordy."

"Very funny." But she did tuck her chin back in its normal position.

They spent the next half hour talking about things

at the hospital and the trip, Clancy asking her if she'd ever practiced medicine in a disaster area.

"No, never. But as far as medicine goes, I imagine it'll be more about the big picture than the minutiae we worry about at the hospital, but that's not always a bad thing. Sometimes you just have to work with what you have, something we don't always learn in medical school."

"True. We don't always learn that in life either."

"No, we don't." Something Hollee would be smart to remember. If she could remember not to focus on the minutiae or try to "fix" things between her and Clancy, maybe they could learn how to relate to each other on a professional level and leave their personal feelings in the past.

Was that even possible? Especially with the season of mistletoe fast approaching? Would she need to perpetually be on the lookout for those traitorous sprigs? It was the time of hope. And kisses. Lord knew, she'd fantasized over that kiss long after it had happened. And now with him sitting beside her, his shoulder periodically brushing hers, it was hard not to go back and remember what it had been like to obsess over every little thing about him. The earthy scent that clung to his clothes. The smooth, warm leather of his jacket against her cheek as he'd given her a ride home on his bike. The heady anticipation of his lips as they'd ever so slowly descended…

God. She could feel that kiss all over again. A spike of panic went through her, going deep and lodging there.

Please, don't start wanting him again, Hollee.

How was she going to survive two weeks with him in Bender? Or seeing him for hours on end day in and day out?

She had no idea. But she'd better figure out a coping strategy, and quickly. Or those long-term effects of a split-second decision that Clancy had talked about earlier could end up happening again. And if it did, she'd be in danger of it haunting her for the rest of her life.

CHAPTER FOUR

Strains of Christmas music came down the corridors as Hollee headed toward the pediatric ward, telling her that Santa Claus was coming to town.

He actually *was* coming to town. Arlington Regional's part of town, anyway. It was always one of her favorite times at the hospital. They had a separate room set up with a huge Christmas tree and enough space to hold a hundred people. It was their way of giving back to the community. Patients current and past could come by for the next four Saturdays leading up to Christmas and get their picture taken with jolly Old St. Nick himself—played by whichever staff member happened to be available on any given weekend. Presents were piled high around the tree, courtesy of a grant given by a local business, one who'd been doing this for the last ten years.

Ten years. Her eyes closed. The year she'd gotten married.

Over and done with, Hollee. Stop dwelling on it.

She hadn't been. She'd actually been getting on with her life. Until Clancy had walked back into it. Only he hadn't known she was working at the hospital. She'd seen the shock on his face when he saw her in that corridor. He'd definitely not planned to ever lay eyes on her again.

And who could blame him? She'd never tried to contact him after Jacob died. Or speak to him after the funeral. She only had the small bits of information that Ava had mentioned over the years.

She turned the corner and those thoughts died, a smile taking over. The music was louder in here. And the room was full of children and laughter. Some of the kids wore wristbands signifying they were patients, and some didn't.

And there was Santa, sitting on what looked like a throne. A red velvet chair with ornate gold scrollwork that someone had dug up at a local thrift store and reupholstered. It had been in use for as long as most people could remember. But Santa Claus's identity changed each week.

There had to be pillows under that red suit, because this Santa didn't have anything that "shook like a bowlful of jelly." Despite the long white beard that covered the area under his nose, the man's face had no extra flesh. It was firm and carved, and there was a deep, deep furrow between his...

She peered closer, her mouth going suddenly dry.

It couldn't be. There was no way he would have agreed to be Santa.

Then again, the requests usually came from the hospital administrator, a hard man to turn down. Not because he was harsh and insisted, but because he had a quiet way of somehow convincing people to do what he wanted. Mainly because it was normally for the good of the hospital. Or morale. Or their patients. Even though this was a private hospital, Neil was really good at making this about health care rather than the almighty dollar. He'd even been known to go to bat against insurance companies when they refused to cover life-saving procedures. And since the board had kept him on, they must agree with the way he ran things.

But Clancy? As Santa?

The one thing she couldn't imagine him saying was "Ho, ho, ho!"

But there was a sexiness about him that came through, despite the oversized clothes. It was there in those dark eyes. In the slight way his mouth kicked up to the side when he smiled. Or maybe she was the only one who noticed those things. She doubted it, though. Women had always paid attention whenever he was around.

It wasn't just his body, though. It was the way he carried himself—the way he moved and talked. Even when he'd reclined on her quilt at the dog park, he'd been completely at ease with himself—a kind of self-confidence that bordered on arrogance, but stayed just this side of it. It was what had caught her attention and carried her beyond mere friendship when she, Jacob and Ava had been teenagers.

She hadn't cared about the consequences back then. Until Ava had pointed out that mistletoe and sent the events that followed spinning out of control. There'd been no coming back from that. Not as friends.

His eyes swept the room and caught her staring. That

bushy white brow cocked at her in challenge and, sure enough, the left side of his mouth curved. Damn. The man would be sexy even when he was eighty.

She couldn't contain a small laugh and a shake of her head that she hoped conveyed her disbelief at seeing him in that chair. She pointed at him and mouthed, *You?*

One of his shoulders gave a half shrug. Then Neil got up on the stage, kicking up a bit of fake snow as he did so.

They'd done a great job on the decorations, and not just the snow. It was the whole atmosphere. There was a winter scene that boasted twinkle lights and huge shimmering Christmas ornaments. Some of those ornaments had been tossed haphazardly around the tree, as if they'd fallen and rolled into their spots. A tall snowman—a crazy patterned scarf knotted around his neck—stood off to the right, one bony stick arm raised in welcome. Someone had stuffed a set of lights inside him that changed color in time with the music. Which was now sounding off the names of Santa's reindeer.

It hadn't snowed in Arlington this year, but Hollee hoped, for the sake of the children, that whoever oversaw the weather sent a dusting of the white stuff their way before Christmas.

The administrator thanked everyone for coming. "We need a couple of staff members to be elves and pass out the presents. I see Hollee and Kristen out there. Would you two mind coming up?"

Oh, God. Why on earth had she stopped in here?

With the trip, she'd miss out on at least two of the Saturdays at the hospital, and who knew if her schedule after she got back would leave time to pop in? Besides, she'd been called on to be an elf before. It was no big deal. Or at least it shouldn't be.

But she'd not played elf to this particular Santa before. And wasn't sure she wanted to now.

Especially since Santa's lips were curved up in a smile that was full of mischief. And those lips were…

What? What exactly were they? A thread of irritation ran through her. She kept circling back around to the same issue.

That stupid kiss should have only been a tiny blip on the radar.

But it was a blip that seemed to keep coming back to haunt her. And now she was one of his elves.

The only thing she could do was to play along. This was for these kids. Not for her.

She headed for the stage, meeting Kristen halfway. She forced a smile. "Can you believe we got sucked into this?"

The brunette, probably five years younger than she was, laughed. "And yet we keep coming back for more."

"Yes, we do."

Kristen bumped shoulders with her. "You have to admit it's fun to get to see the kids' faces up close and personal. And this week's Santa is pretty dreamy."

Her stomach plummeted. Of course Kristen had noticed. How could anyone in their right mind not see past the costume to the man himself? It was a good reminder of all the reasons Clancy was out of her league. He always had been. She'd just been too young to recognize it ten years ago.

Neil was talking about the logistics as they got onto the stage. She was glad she'd worn her Christmas ornaments scrubs in honor of today's festivities. Afterward there would be refreshments. She was off duty for the rest of the afternoon, which was why she could even be here today in the first place.

And she was glad. Glad that she'd get to watch Clancy's reaction as kids came up and told him what they wanted for Christmas and then received a gift in return. Photos would be taken that would later be mailed home to the families, so they'd have a keepsake of the day. It was great for the hospital's image, but she was relieved that that's not what drove the event.

Neil's daughter had been a patient here at the hospital many years ago. The Christmas event had been the bright spot of her stay. The administrator had vowed he'd keep the tradition alive so that no child felt left out. He'd wanted to show there was a little bit of magic to be had during this season, even in a hospital.

Soon the parade of children started, and while Kristen was on the far side, handing gifts to each child after they finished their chat with Santa, Hollee had been stationed at Santa's right, making sure that each person got their turn. She ushered the next child, a boy of about five, to Santa and lifted him onto Clancy's lap. "Ho, ho, ho, what is it you want from Santa?" The words were aimed at the child, but they sent a shiver over her. Because what she wanted from this particular Santa wasn't a toy. Or a present of any type.

Her Christmases after she'd married had been fun and happy at first, but by their fourth anniversary the luster had faded. And then, once Jacob had died, she'd spent almost every Christmas at her folks' house. Their enthusiasm for the season had rubbed off on her, and Hollee had found herself welcoming Santa back into her life once again.

And this particular Santa?

The young boy who was currently with Clancy rattled off about twenty toys he wanted, making the man in the suit smile. "That's quite a list you have memorized. You're lucky Santa has a good memory too. I'll see what I can do."

Hollee directed them both to look at the camera. "Smile."

Smile. Something she was doing more and more of. Not because she had to but because she wanted to. She was getting into the spirit of the event, just like she always did. Despite her initial reservations about being up here with Clancy.

Two hours later, the last child had given Santa his wish list, and Hollee was getting ready to slip away when Neil interrupted. "Let's get a picture of Santa with his helpers for the newsletter."

What? She'd forgotten about that part of it.

She swallowed. Kristen was already on Clancy's left, and he motioned her up. Trudging back up the steps, she stood like a statue, giving the most fake smile she'd ever drummed up.

The photographer looked through his lens. "Person on the right, can you get in a little closer? And maybe look a little bit happier about being with Santa Claus?"

Happier. This had nothing to do with happiness. She managed to sidle over about an inch, only to have the photographer make another gesture, bigger this time. Suddenly a hand was on her hip, dragging her close to Santa's side. Eyes wide, she looked down at Clancy just as he glanced up at her, his grin dark and wicked, making her mouth go dry as she instinctively leaned into him. The world seemed to fade away.

It was then that a couple of blinding flashes reminded her that someone was taking photographs. She hurriedly turned her face back toward the photographer and forced herself to smile again. Except he was already gathering his equipment.

What? That was it? Her face had to have been the craziest of crazies. She looked at Kristen to see her laughing at something Clancy was saying, and her smile suddenly deserted her.

It was like being at the dog park all over again. Was there a woman on this earth who was immune to his charm?

Evidently not, judging by the way Hollee herself had stared at the man just moments earlier, her gaze dropping to his lips.

And then her mind shifted to the music that was currently playing, and she rolled her eyes. Seriously? Well, some kid's mom might have been caught kissing Santa, but she was not about to join that particular club. Especially not now.

So before she could somehow incriminate herself even further, she decided to hang up her Santa's helper costume and leave Clancy in Kristen's more than capable hands. She cringed at the image that thought evoked.

Because if he started actively flirting with her, Hollee was afraid she might scratch the other woman's eyes out. Despite the fact that it should mean nothing to her. And it looked like she had her answer after all.

This Santa had no place in her life. Not now. And probably not ever.

CHAPTER FIVE

WHAT THE HELL had possessed him to pull Hollee toward him like that the other day? The thought had rolled round and round his thoughts until he was dizzy.

He'd been trying to help the photographer, he reasoned.

Sure he had. What he'd really tried to do was get his hands on her, like he'd been itching to do all afternoon. Watching her help those kids, her warm smile as each one of them passed by, had worn away at him. Chipping away like a lumberjack preparing to fell a tree.

And sure enough, the second his fingers had cupped the curve of her hip, he could hear the distant shout of *Timber!* as he'd come crashing to the ground.

He wanted her. Wanted to toss her onto the nearest bed and do what he hadn't gotten to do ten years ago. He wondered if maybe he should sleep with her to get it out of his system, but that was not going to happen. The last thing he needed was to make a messy history even messier. No one, except he and Hollee, knew what had happened that night, although he sometimes wondered if Ava had somehow guessed, since she was the one who'd pointed out the mistletoe.

He'd been hard-pressed to hide his emotions after telling her the kiss had been a mistake. But, at the time, he'd felt Jacob had been right. So he'd made the break as definite as possible.

He'd have to be just as adept now, although there was no need. Not anymore. She wasn't interested in him. The way she'd sped out of the room after that photo told him all he needed to know.

He glanced at his watch. He was a few minutes early to his first appointment but decided to see if his patient was in her room. If he immersed himself in work, he could wipe everything else from his mind.

The phone on his hip buzzed, and without stopping what he was doing, he shifted it so he could see the screen. Hollee?

What the hell? It was almost as if she'd known he was thinking about her.

Pulling the phone free, he put it to his ear. "Hey, what's up?"

"I need you down here."

"What?" His brain stalled for a second, almost missing her next words.

"We have a problem in Maternity. Can you come?"

His thoughts sidestepped back to reality, although he couldn't imagine why they would need him. But she wouldn't have called if it wasn't urgent. "I'll be there in three."

Hanging up, he changed his route and headed for the elevator.

He reached the third floor and exited, glancing in both directions before seeing Hollee waving at him from the end of the hallway. She looked pretty upset. "What is it?"

"We have a situation. A newborn with a cleft palate. The mom came in with full-blown eclampsia and gave birth. She won't believe us when we say it can be fixed. If we can't get her blood pressure down, we're in danger of losing her."

Now that he listened, he did hear a disturbance down the hall. "Is her obstetrician here?"

"He's in there. But he thought if you came, you could explain the repair procedure to her and it might calm her down."

"And the baby?"

"She's in the nursery. Every time she caught sight of her, she just started up again. The husband is in there, but he's not much help. He almost passed out during the delivery."

"Okay. Can you bring the baby but stay just outside the door? Let me talk to her, and then we'll go from there."

She touched his arm. "Thank you. You'll understand when you see her."

Clancy knocked on the door she'd indicated and then pushed it open. Dr. Brouchet waved him over. "Marilyn, I've asked our plastic surgeon to talk to you about Sara, okay?"

The wailing he'd heard outside the door decreased in volume, becoming pained whimpers instead. The young woman was curled in on herself but shifted her eyes to look up at him. Her face was wet with tears.

"Hi, Marilyn, I'm Dr. de Oliveira. Congratulations on your new little one." No answer, but the crying had stopped, so she was listening. "I hear that she might need a little surgery. I haven't seen her yet, but I assure you I can help her."

"It's my fault." The soft voice was filled with a terrible conviction that tugged at his gut.

"Why do you say that?" He didn't want to jump to offer platitudes before he knew the situation.

"I…I…"

Her husband, who'd been standing silently beside her, touched her shoulder. "Tell him. It's okay." His voice was shaky—hesitant—like he knew something awful was coming.

"I—I was on drugs…heroin…when I got pregnant. Only I was too high to realize I wasn't having a period." She glanced at her husband. "We both were. And— Oh, *God*! It suddenly hit me, and I took a test. Afterward, we both went to rehab and got clean, but it was too… too late. My baby is *paying* for what I did. For what *we* did." Tears spilled over onto the pillow, but the hysteria wasn't there, like it had been.

Unfortunately, she was right. Addiction of any type during the first trimester could interfere with fetal development. But the fact that they'd both quit—had gotten help—showed how much they cared about this baby.

"She wasn't born addicted, because you both did the right thing. That's huge," he said. "And from what I've been told, she just has a cleft palate. Something very, very repairable."

Marilyn blinked up at him. "You promise?"

"I've asked the nurse to bring her, so I can look at her with you in the room. Is that okay? I'll give you my honest assessment."

Her hands started twisting together in a way that said she was about to get agitated again, so Clancy cut her off. "I can help her. Your baby isn't suffering, and I admire you, both of you…" He glanced up at the man. "…for getting help. You have to promise to keep up with whatever counseling sessions you've set up."

"We will." Her husband reached down and took one of his wife's hands and squeezed it. He knelt by the bed and looked into her eyes. "Let him show us. She's our responsibility now. Our little girl. We need to do right by her."

Marilyn nodded then looked up again, a sudden frown appearing. "What happened to your face?" As if realizing what she'd said, she quickly apologized, but Clancy waved it away.

"I was injured by a piece of shrapnel in Afghanistan." He smiled. "And, no, that isn't my work. I promise she won't look like me when I'm done."

She laughed. "It doesn't look that bad."

"Hey, I have to look at this mug every day in the mirror. I know exactly what it looks like."

Glancing at the monitors behind her, he saw that her blood pressure was coming down. It was still above normal, but not in the danger zone like it'd been when he arrived.

"Can I ask the nurse to bring her in?"

Marilyn nodded, while her obstetrician came forward. "I'm going to check on another patient. You'll be in good hands with Dr. de Oliveira. I'll be back in about a half hour to look in on you."

"Okay."

He gave her a smile and headed past Clancy. "Call me if you need me."

"We'll be fine," he said. "Can you tell Hollee to come in?"

Dr. Brouchet shot him a quick look before nodding.

Since Clancy had only been at the hospital for a few weeks, the OB/GYN was probably wondering how he already knew one of the nurses well enough to call her by her first name. But it was too late to try to cover the slip.

A minute later, Hollee came in with the baby swaddled in a blanket that was pulled up on the side of her face. Smart move. That way, the family's second introduction could be done a little more gently.

He was struck by the soft glow of her eyes as she cradled the baby, murmuring softly to her as if it was the most natural thing in the world. Her hair slid over the side of her face, and she tucked it behind her ear before her glance came up and caught him staring. She bit her lip, color flooding her cheeks.

He swallowed the lump in his throat. She would have made a great mother. Her babies would have been gorgeous and, oh, so...

Cut it out. You're not here for her. Or for yourself.

He dragged his gaze away and forced himself to do

what he'd come here to do, moving closer and studying the baby's face. The cleft was unilateral. He met Hollee's eyes, keeping a tight rein on his thoughts this time. "Do you know if it includes the palate?"

"Yes, but it's not a large space."

"Good. Let's bring her over to the bed."

Marilyn's husband was again on his feet, a wariness in his demeanor that needed to be addressed. It was really important for him to show support and love for his child, or he would risk Marilyn blaming herself for that as well. He caught the man's attention. "Your baby is beautiful." He said it with meaning, hoping that the man would catch his drift. He evidently did, because he gave a slight nod.

"Okay, Marilyn. I'm going to tell you how I normally repair babies with clefts like... Sara, wasn't that her name?"

"Yes." The response came as a whisper that was barely discernible.

"I like it. It fits her, don't you think so, Hollee?"

"Yes. I do." Her smile was warm and genuine. "I've always loved that name."

Would she have named her own baby Sara?

And here he was back where he'd started: on shaky ground.

He got down to business, detailing how he would go about closing the cleft and repairing the lip. He used general terms so that the mom wouldn't be more frightened than she already was. "Do you think you can hold Sara so I can show you?"

Marilyn's throat moved, and she glanced at her husband and then at Hollee and the bundle she held. "I think so."

Clancy nodded. "Go ahead and help her hold her baby, but stay close in case she needs a little extra support."

Doing as he asked, she carefully placed the baby in her mother's arms, keeping the blanket pulled high on the side closest to Marilyn. Then, much to his surprise, the baby's mom eased the cover down, looking into her newborn's still face.

"She's just…sleeping, isn't she?"

The heartbreaking question threatened to breach the wall of detachment he'd built after years of working in combat areas. "Yes. She's sound asleep. See? Her lip doesn't hurt her, but it will need to be fixed so that it's easier for her to nurse and eat."

"You're sure you can?"

"This is an easy fix." Unlike his mixed feelings about working with Hollee. "We'll put her under anesthesia so she can't feel anything, and in an hour or two she'll be as good as new. She won't remember a thing. She might have a tiny scar here…" He pointed from the open area of Sara's lip to her nose. "…but it will be barely noticeable. Not like mine."

Hollee gave him a sharp look that he ignored.

"Can I nurse her?"

"Let me talk to her pediatrician and see what his thoughts are, but I don't think that will be a problem."

Her face showed immense relief. "Can you do surgery today?"

"No. Not today. We want to give her a little time

to adjust to her world. You'll be able to take her home once you're released, and then we'll probably do surgery when she's six to eight weeks old."

"That long?"

"We want to make sure she's strong and healthy. It's not dangerous to leave it for a bit."

Sara's mom kissed her baby's forehead, as her blood pressure continued to drop.

"Do you have any questions?"

"No." Marilyn looked at Hollee. "I'm so sorry for grabbing your arm like I did. I was scared."

"Don't worry about it. Giving birth is scary under normal circumstances and everything happened so quickly that you didn't have a lot of time to process what was going on."

Clancy frowned. Had she been hurt? She hadn't mentioned there being an altercation, just that Marilyn was upset. Her concern had been wholly for her patient and the baby. Not for herself.

He'd known Hollee when she was just beginning to know who she was. Now he was seeing her standing here as a competent, self-confident nurse who was good at what she did. If Jacob hadn't reinforced what Clancy had already believed about himself, would she be where she was now? Would she have fallen in love with him instead?

It was a question no one could answer. Maybe they would even be divorced by now. He doubted he was the easiest person to live with. He didn't show his emotions easily. Even now. *Especially* now, after everything he'd seen in the world.

He pushed all those thoughts aside. "Do either of you have any more questions?" He probably needed to get back to his first patient, as he was now running a few minutes late. But this had been important.

"I want you to do the surgery."

He smiled. "I wasn't planning on letting anyone else do it, so that's a good thing."

There was something about this young family that touched him. Sara's parents had a lot of growing to do, but he saw a lot of hope in the situation.

Marilyn reached over and gripped her husband's hand, tugging him closer. And, thank God, there wasn't an ounce of revulsion or fear in the man's face.

"Hollee, can you let me know when Sara is getting ready to be discharged? I have a little something for her from Santa's visit." If anyone deserved a fresh start, it was this couple.

"I will." The smile she sent him contained gratitude, relief and a touch of something else. Attraction?

Maybe he wasn't crazy after all.

As she walked him toward the door, Hollee peered up at him. "When did you want to meet with Mom about Gordy?"

"I guess it needs to be soon, since we're less than a week out."

"Okay, I'll let you know."

"That would be great." He nodded at the couple and said goodbye to them, and to Hollee, who mouthed, *Thank you, Clance.*

"Anytime," he said aloud. And for the first time since they'd met again he actually meant it.

CHAPTER SIX

HOLLEE'S MOM HAD just left. Thankfully the meeting had been more comfortable than he'd thought it would be. Just polite chitchat that had centered around the dogs, who were now tussling on the floor.

Clancy should leave too. But he'd had a long day, and it felt good to just sit and do nothing. And since nowadays that "nothing" tended to happen when he was alone, it felt good to have company.

"Hey, do you want to stay for dinner? Tommie and Gordy seem to be getting along really well, and this will give us a chance to see if there's any squabbling when we feed them."

He thought for a minute. Was that a smart idea? Maybe not. But if she was okay with sharing a meal with him, then what would it hurt?

"Actually, that sounds good. But I don't want to put you to any trouble."

"Trouble? Nope. Cooking's my mom's specialty, not mine. I was thinking of ordering takeout, if you're up for that. Chinese?"

This idea was sounding better and better.

"My favorite. On paper plates so there are no dishes?"

"A man after my own heart."

Except he wasn't. And taking the sentence apart and reading it literally, he wasn't after her heart. At least he shouldn't be. Not anymore.

But what was keeping them from going back to a time when they had been friends?

She went into the kitchen and came back with a take-out menu. "Would you mind ordering? I like just about everything from there, so you choose. I'm going to run and change my clothes."

At least she hadn't said she was going to slip into something more comfortable, because he was already feeling way too comfortable. He'd never really done "domestic" stuff with a woman. It was more like go out to eat and then go back to his apartment and then leave for work the next day. His companion for the night was always gone when he got back. It was how he liked it. Uncomplicated.

And for the last year or two it had been less than that, because he hadn't dated at all, and he wasn't sure why. He just didn't have the emotional energy anymore.

He perused the menu, scolding Gordy once when he took something away from Tommie. "You have to learn to share, buddy."

Really? Because not everything could be shared. Toys, yes. People, no.

Choosing something that sounded good, he was on the phone placing their order when Hollee came back in a pair of gray yoga pants and a dark T-shirt. He swallowed, forgetting what he was saying for a minute.

She'd slipped into something a little more comfortable after all.

Who in their right mind had ever criticized a woman for wearing those? The stretch in that fabric was just enough so it flowed over her hips and cupped that firm behind in a way that made his mouth water.

Friends, remember?

He did remember. But a little piece of him was waving a flag in protest.

He jerked his mind back to the person on the other end of the line, who was asking if there was anything else he wanted.

Ha! He wasn't touching that. But he'd already let his pause go too long without adding something.

"Could you throw a couple of fortune cookies in with that order? Thanks."

He paid with his credit card and noticed Hollee was signaling him from across the room. "Could you hold on for a minute please?" He glanced at her. "Is there something else you want?"

"No, but I invited you. I was going to pay for it when they got here."

"It's the least I can do for borrowing your mom for the next two weeks."

"Borrowing...? Oh, the dogs."

He finished up the order and then hung up. "They should be here in about twenty-five minutes."

"Perfect. I could use some wine. How about you?"

"That sounds good. I'll come help."

He followed her into the kitchen, doing his best not to watch the jiggle of her behind as she went, but, damn, it was hard. His friendship card was quickly getting lost in the shuffle.

The last ten or so years had been exceedingly good to her. She looked better now than she had back when he'd first noticed she was all grown up, something he could not say for himself. He knew the repeated trips into war zones had hardened him in all the wrong ways. Not to mention his scarred face.

Somewhere along the way he'd forgotten what life was all about. Maybe Jacob's death had reminded him that nothing in life was certain. Or maybe it was meeting Hollee again after all these years.

Meeting that young family with the new baby had given him a jolt. That couple had journeyed through a war zone of a completely different kind, but one that was just as devastating as any he'd seen during combat. Drugs senselessly claimed lives just as guns and artillery did.

Marilyn and her husband had given him a glimmer of hope, as strange as that sounded. If they could come through what they had and learn to enjoy life again, then maybe he could too.

Maybe he could even find someone in the future and settle down and have a family.

When his eyes strayed to Hollee, he gave his head an inner shake. The time for that had come and gone, when he'd decided he wasn't the kind of person she needed. Although knowing what he did about his former friend, he wondered again if that had been the right decision.

Hollee opened a cupboard and stretched up high, grabbing a pair of glasses, her T-shirt pulling taut over one of her breasts as she did. And his mind was right back in the fray, giving the finger to his rationalizations.

Staying for dinner might just be a mistake after all.

She got a bottle of wine out of the fridge and handed him a corkscrew. "Why don't we feed the dogs before we eat dinner? Otherwise Tommie will make a nuisance of herself."

"So will Gordy."

By the time she'd put food down for each of them, he had the wine ready to go. And, surprisingly, the dogs were pretty compatible as far as eating habits went. They were both done in record time, leaving nothing for the other to devour.

"If you'll carry the glasses into the living room, I'll let them out for a while. Tommie's not a lover of winter, so she won't want to stay out long."

She called the dogs and opened the sliding glass door. Out they went.

"You don't have a tree up."

From what he remembered about Hollee's family, they were all about Christmas. He could remember his family being invited to their house for an annual holiday party. It had always been warm and welcoming... and decorated to the hilt. Hollee, however, had nothing up at all. Not a single strand of lights. It didn't seem in keeping with what he remembered of her.

"No. We'll be leaving for Bender pretty soon, and I've spent Christmas with my folks ever since... Well, for quite a while. I've been thinking, though, maybe I should start decorating again. Maybe next year."

Before he could respond, she disappeared into the

back of the house before coming back carrying a huge pillow. "For Gordy. That's the one thing Tommie doesn't really like sharing. Her bed."

And Hollee? Did she like sharing hers?

Dammit, Clancy. Just stop it.

She dropped the new pillow beside the one that was already next to the fireplace. "Do you want me to turn it on?"

Blinking, he tried to decipher—

"The fireplace."

Of course. He should have guessed. But with his mind drifting down paths it shouldn't, everything was coming back with some kind of double meaning. "I'll leave that up to you."

"On, then." She took a remote and pressed something and flames leaped to life behind the glass. "Tommie loves lounging next to it."

"Since I don't have a fireplace, Gordy will have no idea what it is."

"So what about you? Did you decorate this year?"

He hadn't given it much thought. His places of residence had been so transitory that he hadn't invested in a tree or ornaments. "No. I didn't either, actually. Maybe I will if I ever move out of the apartment into a house."

If. So he wasn't thinking of making his stay more permanent? Was he waiting to see how he handled civilian life before making a commitment to it? Well, that ship had pretty much sailed. He'd already gotten his honorable discharge. Getting back in would be an undertaking.

She sat on the sofa, and he handed her one of the

glasses, then took his spot back on a nearby chair. Although her sofa was pretty long, he wasn't sure he was up to the challenge of being that close to her. The casual Hollee was sexier than the business Hollee, as evidenced by his reaction to her at the dog park. And his reaction right now.

Taking a sip, he sighed. "Thanks for asking me to stay. I was too tired to even think about dinner."

"Hard day?"

"You could say that. I had several emergency surgeries in a row, which is unusual."

"And I dragged you here for a meeting with Mom."

He grinned. "You didn't 'drag' me. It was a good distraction. And I needed some down time."

"I'm glad you're staying then."

Was she?

Before he could unravel how he felt about that, a scratching sound at the patio door made him look up. Sure enough, it was Gordy.

Saved by the dog.

When she started to get up, he motioned her to stay where she was. "I'll get them."

He let the dogs in, and Tommie took one look at the fireplace and plopped down. Gordy followed, hesitating as if unsure what to do, so he called the dog over to the second pillow. For once, he did as he was asked.

Then the doorbell rang. "And that'll be our dinner," she said.

Once they had everything on the kitchen counter and had dished out the food, they made their way into the dining room. When Hollee held up the bottle of wine with her brows raised, he shook his head, although he was tempted to join her for another glass. "I'm driving home. Better not. I'll just have some water."

Over dinner they discussed various cases and he caught her up on how Ava and the baby were doing, starting to relax as the conversation remained on neutral topics.

Then she took a sip of her wine, and her lips lingered on the rim of the glass for a second longer than normal. And just like that, neutral shifted back into drive.

"Well, I'm glad it turned out the way it did." She swirled the contents of her glass, and he held his breath. But all she did was stand and pick up her plate. "Done?"

"Yes, I'll help you clean up."

They had just dumped their paper plates in the trash, and she was getting ready to toss away the bag the meal had come in, when she glanced inside it. "We almost forgot!"

She held up one of the fortune cookies, hopping up on the counter top and handing him the other one.

He took it, even though he had a hard time thinking about anything other than how Hollee at that height was absolutely perfect. For a lot of things. She took another slow drink of her wine and then set the glass beside her hip.

Hell, he should leave.

She tore into the cookie's packaging, glancing at him as she did. "Aren't you going to open yours?"

"Yes." He leaned a hip against the counter and took his cookie from the wrapper, breaking it in half. Retrieving the tiny slip of paper, he popped part of the cookie into his mouth as he read his fortune.

His eyes widened, and something went down the wrong way. He coughed, trying his damnedest to disguise it as clearing his throat.

"Are you okay?"

"I just tried to inhale when I should have swallowed."

She laughed. "Not a good plan."

Here's hoping he could distract her. And himself. "So what does yours say?"

"Same old stuff. Your path to success will soon be revealed."

"I think you're already on the path to success." Maybe if he talked enough, she'd forget about his. "You're doing a great job at the hospital." He shoved his fortune into his pocket.

"Wait, what did yours say?"

So much for making her forget about it. "Same old stuff, just like yours."

"Read it, then. It's the best part of the meal."

It might have been, had they been young and optimistic and on their first date. But they weren't. And a lot of water had passed under the bridge since those days.

With a great deal of reluctance he reached into his pocket and pulled out the paper, even though every word was now burned in his skull. He pretended to look at it and debated whether or not he should just make something up. Except then she might ask to look at it, and right now his head was drawing a blank on other viable options.

"The past belongs to the past, time to make a new beginning."

She blinked, then licked her lips. "I guess you're already doing that."

"I am?"

"You just got out of the military. And now you're working at the hospital. Or were you thinking of something different?"

He was. Which was why he'd almost choked on that cookie. "Those fortunes are always a crapshoot. They could mean a thousand things."

Her bare feet which had been swinging back and forth were now planted on the flat surface of a drawer, one heel on the metal handle. Oh, Lord, he was in trouble. In very big trouble.

"Like what?"

"Oh, I don't know. Like the trip to Bender or any number of new beginnings."

She used a foot to nudge his leg, letting it rest there for a second. "Speaking of Bender, have you heard anything about our sleeping arrangements?"

The room suddenly got warm. "As in…?"

"Where we'll sleep, silly. I don't think there will be many hotels open for business. Will we be in tents, or what?" Her foot bumped his leg again.

Was she flirting with him?

"I don't know. I haven't heard anything."

"Hmm… I haven't either. What if there are communal showers? Are you taking swim trunks?" She gave a grin that was full of devilish intent, her foot landing back on the drawer front. "Talk about new beginnings. And new fodder for the hospital's rumor mill."

"I'm pretty sure they'll have separate showers." His voice came out half-strangled. He could think of all kinds of new beginnings that might stem from that kind of scenario. And the last thing he needed to picture was Hollee lathering herself in a hot steamy shower, bikini or not.

"I'm sure they— What's wrong?"

"Nothing."

And then she looked at him. *Really* looked at him. "Oh."

That one word changed the atmosphere in the room in an instant, her eyes going from the cool green of today's Hollee to something he recognized from ten years ago.

They stared at each other, and he swallowed, finding the act more difficult than it should be. A lot more difficult.

The fortune that was still curled in his palm seemed to burn his skin, making him remember exactly what he'd thought those words had meant. That what was in the past—*their* past—didn't matter. But it did.

Despite that, something inside him declared war on the rational part of his brain.

Her foot touched his leg, but this time it didn't bump and leave. It stayed. Slid a few inches and then stopped as if waiting for his response.

All of a sudden he wanted one thing. Hollee. On that counter. Naked.

He turned and bracketed her in, planting a hand on either side of her.

"What are you doing, Hollee?"

The look she gave him sent a spear right through him. How many times had he regretted his decision to stop at a kiss ten years ago?

Maybe she'd read his mind, because she replied, "We're two consenting adults. It doesn't have to be anything more, does it? I don't want it to be anything more."

And that settled it. Because neither did he.

His hands slid up her arms, and as if anticipating what he wanted, her legs parted, allowing him to come close. And hell if he hadn't been exactly right about the height of that counter top.

Cupping the back of her head, he slowly reeled her in, needing to draw this first contact out and make it last.

Her lips touched his, warm and moist and just as sweet as he remembered. Only as soon as they came together, it was as if an explosion went off between them. Her arms wrapped around his neck and held him tight against her as their mouths suddenly clashed, tongues and teeth battling to take control of the situation.

And, sure enough, the feet that had been pressed to the vertical surface of the cabinets were now flattened against the backs of his thighs. Taking that as his cue, he gripped her hips and yanked her forward until there was full contact between them.

Her low, throaty moan sent a shudder through him, and his eyes closed, wanting to hold onto that sound and remember it forever. He hadn't heard anything that needy, that sexy in a long, long time.

Her hands moved to the back of his shirt and tugged it out of his waistband, the sensation of it being balled up in her fists making him hungry for her. He couldn't believe this was happening, didn't want it to stop.

Leaning back so that she could drag the shirt over his head, he found he already missed her mouth. As soon as she'd tossed it to the other counter, he took up where he had left off. Only she was now fumbling with his belt.

This wasn't the shy girl he remembered from the past. Then again, he wasn't the same cocky boy she'd once known. They were both adults now.

And as the adult he was, he was not going to stand there while she stripped him naked. Not without putting them on an equal footing.

He reluctantly broke the kiss and took hold of the T-shirt he'd admired a little while earlier and pushed it slowly up her torso and over her breasts. And confirmed that, yes, she did have a bra on, something very thin and lacy and delicious looking.

Soon the shirt was off, and his palms cupped her, the soft flesh filling his hands to perfection.

She reached behind her and unsnapped the bra, throwing it in the same direction as his shirt, before pressing herself back into his hands. His body ached, needing to touch her everywhere, even as his thumbs strummed over her. And when he covered one of those nipples with his mouth, she squirmed against him, her hands going to the back of his head and holding him in place.

There was so much he wanted to do, but it didn't look like she was going to give him that chance. There was a quickness to her breathing that seemed to border on desperation. So he let himself be swept along on the same wave she was riding, pulling back just long enough to grip the elastic of her yoga pants and slide them down, her hips lifting to help him. When her panties started to come with them, he decided to hell with it and helped them along.

He let both garments fall to the floor and then moved in close again, the thought of so little separating him from the place he wanted to be driving him to reach into his pocket and take out his wallet, securing protection.

"I want you naked," she whispered.

He was right about the change in her. This was a woman who wasn't afraid to ask. And he gloried in it. No games. No tricks. Just a man and a woman doing what came naturally.

A little tug inside his skull whispered a word of caution, but he wasn't going to listen to it.

Instead, he kicked off his shoes and removed the rest of his clothes. And then he was there. Against her... having to hold himself back from taking her, condom or no condom.

But he wouldn't.

She handed him the packet, and he sheathed himself as her lips trailed tiny paths over his jaw, his chin, his throat, leaving molten lava in her wake. She whispered against the corner of his mouth. "Do it, Clance. Please."

There was no doubt about what she wanted. It wasn't more heated kisses, or a little more foreplay. She wanted the main event. And at her words so did he.

Aligning himself with the moist heat, he pushed into

her in a rush, burying himself inside her. Her eyes fluttered closed, her fingers digging into his hair and pulling him to her.

Mouth? Or nipple? He wanted both. Kissing her deeply, he let his tongue play out the events that would soon unfold, working the kiss to a climax that he had to force his body not to follow. When he finished she was panting, trying to move her hips against him. Then he took the nipple he'd lusted after and started to move, tongue scrubbing over the tight bud, teeth holding her in place.

She whimpered, fingers gripping his hair, the sharp pull on his scalp just adding to his pleasure. He kept moving, setting a steady pace, even as everything in him was forging ahead, trying to find its own conclusion. Then her legs wrapped around his waist, using the leverage to up the ante, and changed the tempo and intensity to a crescendo.

Hollee was no longer asking. She was telling. She wanted more, and if he didn't give it, she was going to take it.

Well, honey, your wish is my...

He met her thrust for thrust, never stopping his contact with her breast. Every pump of his hips was hitting the right spot, if her moans and sinuous movements were anything to go by. His intent to reach between them and make sure she was getting as much pleasure as possible was stopped by the way her hands abandoned his hair and gripped his upper arms as if needing to anchor herself to him. It was a heady sensation and one he would never forget. Didn't want to forget.

He released her breast and glanced up at her. The sight of her head leaning against the upper cabinet, sliding upward with each thrust of his hips was the most decadent thing he'd ever witnessed. For a second he couldn't move his gaze. And then her eyes opened and caught him staring, her lips parting.

"Clance…"

Her breathing of his name was his undoing and suddenly he was thrusting into her at atomic speed, her cry warring with his groan as she contracted hard around his flesh. Over the edge he went, into the oblivion beyond, eyes jammed shut once again as pleasure poured over him, hot and wet and unbelievably long.

And then it was over, his movements slowing as things around him began to fall back into place. Her hands were again on the back of his head, but not frantic the way they had been, body softening as it accompanied his to the other side.

"That was…" Her eyes closed, and another tiny spasm gripped his flesh. "That was luscious."

Luscious. The word struck him, and he couldn't stop the chuckle that came out.

She frowned. "Is something funny?"

"Not funny. No. Not…not at all."

Her frown was still there. "Then what?"

"Luscious is not a word I've heard used before in reference to that."

She blinked. "And you've heard a lot of those words?"

He wasn't sure what to make of that. She didn't sound angry, but there was something there that had a little sting to it. Had she thought he'd been celibate all these years? "My share. As I'm sure you did as well."

With Jacob? Why the hell had he even said that?

He separated himself from her, unsure why they were even talking about this.

"I haven't been with anyone since my husband passed away."

And that did it. Hearing her call Jacob her husband made him turn and gather his clothes together. He knew exactly who she'd been married to. He didn't need anyone—especially her—to announce it to him. Especially after everything that had happened. After what Jacob had done.

If her aim had been to keep this simple and a one-time event, she'd just gotten her wish.

Only as he headed into the other room to get dressed, he wasn't sure exactly how he could use the word *simple* to describe what had happened between them. Because nothing in his life, including Hollee, had ever been more complicated than it was right now.

CHAPTER SEVEN

THE LAST TWO days had gone by with alarming speed.

Hollee was at the hospital with her bags, joining the others who were waiting on the bus that would take them to Bender. Rather than the tents she'd joked about staying in, FEMA had sent in small trailers to house emergency workers.

She hadn't actually talked to Clancy since that episode in her kitchen. By the time she'd dragged her clothes on and gathered her thoughts, plastering an empty smile on her face, he had gone, along with Gordy. Poor Tommie had stood at the door, whining after them.

"I know, girl," she'd said. "I think I just made a huge mess out of that.

Her emotions had already been starting to fray and to hear him talk about what he had and hadn't heard during sex had made her snap. All of a sudden she'd pictured that woman at the dog park and the dozens of women he'd probably been with, and it reminded her of how casually he'd turned his back on her ten years ago. How he'd found someone else almost immediately afterward.

His behavior had devastated her, and she wasn't sure why. Had he changed in the intervening years? She had no idea, because she'd blurted out the first thing that had popped into her head. It had been a mistake.

So was what had happened between her and Clancy? When he'd asked what she was doing, she should have made something up. Instead, she'd practically begged him to stay, saying they were both adults. It might have been true, but they weren't two objective bystanders brushing shoulders as they passed each other on the sidewalk. They had a past. Not much of one, granted, but still.

They'd shared an intense, heady kiss one day, and the next thing she knew he'd dropped her like a rock. That should have warned her that having sex with him— ever—was off limits. It was bound to make an awkward situation even worse.

And now she was going to spend two weeks with the man.

Thankfully she spotted Kristen getting out of a car with her bags and headed toward her, giving her friend a quick hug. "I'm so glad you got to come."

Kristen smiled back. "Me too!" Her friend flipped open a hospital newsletter. "And it looks like the hospital thinks you and the new doctor are getting along. *Really* getting along." She handed Hollee the paper, and she felt the blood rush from her head, her vision going white for a split second.

She and Clancy were on the cover. Well, not just them, there were a lot of other pictures as well. But the one of Clancy, her and Kristen was all she could see at the moment. And it was as damning as she'd thought it'd be. She and the plastic surgeon were gazing into each other's eyes, her mouth a round "O" of surprise, while Kristen smiled at them both. God. Just a couple of days ago, she'd joked about the communal showers and the rumors that could be set into motion.

It turned out it wasn't a shower that would set those wheels turning. It was a picture.

And the rumors would all be true.

Well, not exactly, because she had no intention of ever having sex with him again. She'd learned her lesson. At least she hoped she had.

"You were there. You know pictures don't always tell the whole truth."

"All I know is that I would have given anything to have one of those steamy glances aimed at me."

"You're crazy. There was nothing steamy about it."

Speaking of steamy, she sensed Clancy coming onto the scene even as she talked to her friend. Forcing her voice to sound more animated than she felt, she quickly changed the subject, aware that Kristen was still holding that newsletter. And it was still showing the damning cover. There was no way she could ask her to put it away without the other nurse reading more into it than there was, or without Clancy noticing and wondering why she was reacting so oddly. Maybe he'd already seen it and thought it was no big deal.

Kind of like their night together?

That thought hit her in the solar plexus and knocked the wind out of her for a second, because to her it *had* been a big deal. A very big deal. And that's what hurt the most.

She'd done all this talking as if their time together had been about two people having casual sex and then moving past it. Her problem was that she had trouble being objective when it came to Clancy de Oliveira. If she thought the sex would serve to close the book on that little crush she used to have on him, she was wrong. The book had crashed wide open instead, ripping a hole straight to the past. Then she'd had the gall to judge him for sleeping with other women. He had the right to live life the way he saw fit. How dared she act like he didn't?

Just as she'd run out of things to say to Kristen and had gotten the rundown on what their responsibilities were going to be, there was a call to load up the bus. Thank God. She didn't have to worry about facing him. In fact, she'd chosen the coward's way out and had left her mom to welcome Clancy and Gordy to her house. Hopefully that had gone well. She got on, sliding into the first empty seat she could find. Kristen sat next to her.

Clancy gave her a nod as he went by before he too sat down. In the seat directly behind hers. Great. Maybe she should have tried to find a time to meet with him and have it out, rather than just run every time she saw him.

Why did she need to, though?

They weren't involved as a couple, so she really didn't owe him anything. And he hadn't tried to contact her in the last two days either. So maybe that was how things were going to work. They'd just each stay in their own little corners of the world and not talk or have anything more to do with each other, except where Ava was concerned.

That made her incredibly sad.

No, sometime in the next two weeks she was going to make time to have a conversation with the man and see if they could get to a place where they were both okay, both on the same page.

About everything.

And at least she finally knew what it was like to have sex with him.

It had been fantastic. More wonderful than she ever could have imagined.

Ugh. And that just made it so much worse.

But she would find a way to make it better. Somehow. She just had to do it in the next two weeks.

After a six-hour bus ride, Clancy looked out at a scene of devastation. There were still huge puddles where the rivers had overflowed their banks and the smell of rot seeped through the closed windows of their vehicle, despite the cold temperatures.

Somewhere around ten trailers were lined up side by side, looking pristinely white compared to the neighboring mud-covered structures, many of them damaged by the tornado. Not a single sign of Christmas was in evidence.

Next to the trailers stood a huge wooden barn, which he assumed was being used for a staging area.

The bus stopped, and Hollee and her friend were two of the first people off. The other woman had left the hospital newsletter on their seat. He picked it up, so he could return it to her and caught sight of a picture of him and Hollee. He tensed.

It was a reminder of that day in the hospital—the place where he'd made his first big mistake. Right there in that room of Christmas cheer. Instead of letting the photographer handle the picture, he'd taken matters into his own hands in a very literal sense.

The memory had primed the pump and tickled the back of his skull every time he saw her, until it had finally gotten its way in her kitchen. The aftermath of that encounter hadn't been pretty.

He stepped off the bus and saw a small group of people shaking hands with the medical team. The weather was noticeably warmer than it had been in Arlington, but then they were further south. A little boy ran over to him, and turned his head, peering at the newsletter. "What's that?"

"Randy, leave the man alone." A grizzled figure came over and shook Clancy's hand. "Sorry about that. My son is excited that you're here, as you can tell."

"He's fine." He crouched in front of the boy. "Hi, Randy, I'm Clancy. This isn't anything that would interest you, but we have a few things that might. We'll tell you about them a little later."

The boy's father smiled. "We appreciate the help."

Clancy stood. "You live here in Bender?"

"I do. Rather, I did. Our house is gone. We're living with my sister and her family until we can decide what to do."

The man had a ring on his finger. "Your wife?"

"I lost her…" His throat moved and his voice stopped for a second. "I lost her and my daughter in the tornado."

"I'm sorry." Clancy had seen the physical evidence of the horror these people must have gone through, but hearing it spoken was a punch to the gut. He glanced at Randy, who probably didn't understand the full extent of what had happened, and a lump formed in his throat.

"Thank you. There are a lot of others in the same position. Whole families have been lost."

"I know nothing can bring your wife and daughter back, but we want to help however we can."

Someone motioned them toward the barn, and he grabbed his bag, smiling at Randy and his dad as he headed in that direction.

Once inside the building, he saw that a small room had been fashioned, using partitions. Someone he didn't recognize climbed up on a platform. "Hi, everyone, and thanks for coming. I'm Matt Gormley, and I'm overseeing the medical portion of the disaster relief efforts for FEMA. We've got room assignments for you in the trailers you saw as you pulled in. There will be four people per two-bedroom trailer, but meals will be cooked and served in another area of the barn by volunteers."

He glanced around at them. "I'm not going to lie to you. We have a lot of hard work ahead of us, since the only hospital within fifty miles was wiped out by the series of tornadoes that came through. We're flying urgent cases to Mount Retour, but there are a lot of skin infections, damaged limbs and sickness that flowed in with the flood waters. We've had long lines ever since we started operations. We want to get all of you signed in and set up with badges today. Current volunteers go home tomorrow, and you'll be briefed by them in the morning."

He went on to let them know where they could find their posted hours of service and lodgings. Evidently part of the barn had more walls erected as a makeshift surgical room and several exam rooms, but they were warned that waiting times were very long and they were still triaging patients as they came in.

Clancy could relate to that, since it was what he was used to. Then they were dismissed and asked to go to registration and sign in.

When he went outside, there was no sign of Randy or his dad, but he did see Hollee standing a few yards away.

What did she think of all of this?

He made his way over to her, her face revealing no sign of how the briefing had made her feel. But when he got to her, she gave him a stiff smile. "Did Gordy give you any trouble this morning?"

"No, if anything, he and Tommie seemed happy to see each other again."

"They hit it off." She bit her lip and glanced around before continuing. "Listen, Clance, I'm really sorry about…everything that happened. I think we were both tired, and the wine…"

He'd only had one glass of the stuff, so he'd been stone-cold sober. And if she tried to pass this off as a simple reaction to alcohol, he wasn't going to be happy. But she was right about them both being tired. He remembered saying he was too tired to worry about dinner. In fact, the whole cascade of events leading up to what had happened was a kind of a blur in his mind. Unlike the actual time spent in that kitchen. That had scorched a path through his skull that would be difficult to erase.

"Like you said, it was a one-time thing. We both made it to the other side, so why don't we put it behind us?"

She gave a sigh, like a weight had been lifted off her shoulders. And maybe it had been. Heaven knew, he was happy to finally get this out in the open, since the way they'd left things had been eating away at him.

"I would love that." She turned toward him and held out her hand. "Friends. Again?"

They would probably never make it back to the friendship they'd had as kids. But maybe they could somehow forge something new based on mutual respect and admiration. His fortune cookie's message came back to him: the past belongs to the past. Maybe this time he could leave it there.

He wrapped his fingers around hers with a smile. "Friends."

Hollee bumped her shoulder with his. "Are you ready for all of this?" She nodded at the room.

With her hair pulled back in a ponytail and almost no makeup on, she looked beautiful. There was no fear in her eyes, no hint of complaints about what they might find over the next couple of weeks. Instead, there was an eagerness in her demeanor that was contagious, even to someone as cynical as Clancy, who'd been in situations that had been shrouded in darkness and misery.

He tried to see things through her optimistic eyes. He felt old. Old and tired and not quite sure of his place in Arlington Regional, or in civilian life in general. He'd spent so much time in settings where everything had been so ultra-regimented that it was hard to adapt to some of his newfound freedoms. Maybe Bender, Virginia, would prove to be a bridge between those two worlds.

If so, he'd better make good use of his time, because he had a feeling these weeks would be over in the blink of an eye. Just like that night in Hollee's kitchen, when he'd felt the earth move beneath his feet. He still hadn't quite found his footing on it again.

Hollee had never been anywhere where people were treated in an actual barn, though the building hadn't housed animals in a very long time, instead holding the home owners' equipment, which had been sold when mining in the area had taken a downturn. And the hopelessness on the faces that lined the walls waiting their turns tugged at her heart. She worked as quickly as she could, but the crowd never seemed to thin.

By the third day she was more exhausted than she'd ever been in her life. To try to inject some tiny element of Christmas where there seemed to be none, she'd strung the Christmas lights in the small bedroom she shared with Kristen. But for the most part she was too tired to plug them in at night. Instead she fell into one of the twin beds feeling like she'd succeeded in moving a pebble up a very steep hill only to look behind her and see the landscape riddled with boulders, making her feeble efforts seem ludicrous. But they weren't. She had to believe that she—and the team before them—were making a difference.

Although many of the people they saw were poor, they cared for each other in a way that rivaled most families. And so everyone on their team owed it to them to do the best they could with what they had.

She'd barely seen Clancy, as she'd been dealing with pregnant women, and he'd been busy stitching up wounds and giving antibiotic and tetanus shots. Six o'clock found Hollee cleaning and sanitizing the exam room she'd been working in, since they were all taking turns with that chore. She was dead tired, but it was a good tired. She was wiping down the portable metal exam table when Clancy appeared in the doorway, dressed in jeans and a black shirt, holding some kind of tree in his hand. He looked like a lumberjack.

What in the world…?

She opened the door and ushered him in. Not seeing him should have been a blessing, but instead… She'd missed him.

"Have you decided to take up gardening instead of medicine?"

He chuckled. "Not exactly. But since we're in the first week of December, I thought we should at least have a tree."

"A tree?"

Holding up his prize, he said, "Yep. Not an actual Christmas tree, since I couldn't find anything that I wouldn't need an ax to cut down, so I found a shrub instead."

It did have the look of an evergreen, but on a smaller scale, dirt still clinging to the roots. "I don't think anyone is going to realize it's a Christmas tree if there's nothing to go on it."

"That's where the fun comes in. I thought we could have the children come up with creative, free ways to decorate it. We could hold a contest, and the participants get one of the presents we brought in for sick kids. We could vote on a winner and give that child a bigger prize."

It was a wonderful idea. She shouldn't be surprised Clancy had thought up something like that. Not after witnessing the way he'd played the role of Santa. "I brought a small set of twinkle lights, but I think I've only turned them on once. Why don't we use them for this instead?" She smiled. "Where are we going to put it?"

"How about outside the entrance to the clinic, since more kids will be able to see it there? I've already gotten permission from Matt, the organizer."

She nodded. "I'm sure it's something they didn't give much thought to. We've been more worried about caring for people who are hurting."

"There's only so much we can do in a situation like this. It will take them a while to rebuild."

"Some of the moms are planning on moving to where they have other relatives, if they can talk their husbands into it. I think a tree will make everyone feel better, at least for the short term."

"I thought the same thing. Once you're done here, can you help me get it up and get the word out about the contest? Or are you too tired?"

A few minutes ago she would have said yes, but seeing him left her energized in a way she didn't want to analyze. "I'd love to help."

She looked at him with eyes that saw past the gorgeous package to the man beneath. A man she had always known was there, but it was as if she was seeing him again for the first time without the emotions from their past. She didn't know why he had done what he had, and she might never know, but surely people could change.

"Looks like that Santa costume rubbed off on you."

He gave a half shrug. "I enjoyed being him more than I thought I would. I figured with this…" He haphazardly motioned to the left side of his face. "…I'd be the last person they'd want in that suit."

A sharp twist of pain made her take a slow careful breath, blinking hard to keep her emotions in check. Maybe she wasn't the only one who was insecure about who they were. Her fears were the result of two men she'd loved turning their backs on her. And maybe his insecurities were rooted in a fear that his scars changed who he was.

"Clance, you have to know that those make no difference. To anyone."

They might to him, though, and she suspected there was a matching set of emotional scars that he carried inside him. And she was learning just how bitter a poison regret could be.

A question teetered on her tongue, and she was debating whether or not to ask him when he suddenly squeezed her hand and gave her a smile that warmed her to the core. "Thank you for that," he said.

The awful clawing sensation she'd had a moment earlier subsided as he continued. "Now, let's get this set up, so we can take a picture and put a flyer up on the door of the clinic."

Her idea about going back to being friends suddenly didn't seem quite so farfetched.

Unable to resist, she went up on tiptoe to kiss his cheek, startled when his index finger hooked under her chin. The quick impersonal touch she'd meant to give turned into something that was suddenly very personal as her lips touched his. She swallowed, her heart flipping a time or two, before she got it under control. Then they both pulled away and he gave her a glance that made her tingle all the way down to her toes.

She struggled to find her emotional balance, grabbing the first subject she could find, and hoping it would break the spell he'd cast over her.

"I think I know where we can put it," she murmured.

"Excuse me?"

His voice had a strangled quality that made her laugh. And just like that, the moment was over.

"I was talking about the tree. There's a five-gallon bucket we've been using as extra seating."

All of a sudden the door slammed open and a man who was soaking wet stood there holding a child.

"I need help! Randy fell in the river. I don't think he's breathing."

Clancy threw the tree to the side and grabbed the child from the man's arms. "I've got him."

He laid the boy, who couldn't have been more than five, facedown on the table, pushing firmly on his back to drain any lake water. A gush came out, then another. He flipped him back over, feeling his neck as he did. "Slight pulse, no respiration. Come on, Randy, don't do this."

He acted like he knew this boy.

Hollee dragged the crash cart around and placed an Ambu bag over the child's mouth, squeezing the bag to pump life-saving oxygen into his starved lungs. God, this town had had enough tragedy. She glanced at the man, who was shivering, his lips a dark shade of blue, a despair in his eyes that she'd seen before. He expected his son to die.

"Clance, can you take over for me for a second?"

He turned his head toward her, and when she nodded at the panic-stricken man, he nodded and moved to the boy's head.

Going to a small metal closet, she grabbed a blanket and draped it over the father's shoulders. The barn was heated, but it wasn't airtight and there was always a draft coming in. He'd obviously gone into the lake after the boy and with the frigid temperatures outside, he was in danger of hypothermia.

The man started to shake his head and drop the cover

behind him, but she grabbed it and looked him in the face. "Take it. We don't need two patients."

That must have convinced him because he wrapped the blanket around himself.

"What's your name?" she asked.

"Samuel."

"Do you know how long Randy was in the water, Samuel?"

"I don't know. Maybe ten minutes. He was playing, gathering some twigs for my sister's fireplace, while I went back to get the fish we'd caught. When I glanced over, he was in the water, the current carrying him downriver. He looked so scared. So very scared." His voice caught, and he dragged a hand through his wet hair. "God, how could I have left him alone? I've already lost my wife and daughter. I can't lose Randy."

Her heart squeezed so hard it threatened to paralyze her. But she knew better than let it take control.

"You found him. Got him out of the water. That's what counts." She hesitated. "Let me go help him."

She went back over to Clancy, her lungs catching for a second when she saw he was no longer working the mechanical respirator. Instead, he had his stethoscope out, listening to his chest. "He's breathing on his own."

Never had she heard five more beautiful words. "His heart?"

"Believe it or not, it's strong. But I'm going to have him transported to Richland to be monitored for edema."

Sometimes, after a drowning victim had been revived, irritation and inflammation could cause the lungs to fill with fluid, a secondary complication that could be almost as deadly as the original event.

"I agree." She lowered her voice. "Do you know them?"

"I talked to them right after we got off the bus." He looked at her. "They've lost everything, Hollee."

"I know. He told me." She glanced back at the dad. "He said Randy was in the water for about ten minutes. In this case the frigid water probably helped slow tissue damage."

"My thoughts too."

The boy sputtered and opened his eyes, coughing for several seconds before trying to sit up. Hollee put a hand on his shoulder. "It's okay, Randy. Your dad is right here." She turned and motioned him over.

When the man reached the table, he practically fell onto it as he gathered his son in his arms, the blanket falling to the ground unheeded. As rough and tough as this man looked, his eyes told another story. "I don't know how to thank you."

Hollee draped the blanket back over him. "You just did." It was true. Not very long ago she'd wondered if she was making a difference. Here was proof that she was. That Clancy was. That everyone who came through this town, hoping to do some good, was doing exactly that.

"I'm going to arrange transport," Clancy said. They'd been flying critical patients out, but since Randy was stable for the moment, he'd probably be taken by car to the other hospital.

Within fifteen minutes, a woman brought Randy and

his dad some dry clothes and coats, then she hugged the pair for a long time. The sister he'd talked about?

Randy was well enough to wave at them as he was carried to a waiting car.

Matt, their liaison from FEMA, saw the pair off and then turned to her and Clancy. "Looks like you two have had some excitement this afternoon." He nodded at the tree lying in the corner. "And I'm taking it that that's going to be the Christmas tree we talked about?"

"It is."

Randy hadn't been the only excitement. It was a good thing the man hadn't walked in on their kiss or they might have been shipped home.

Why? Surely they'd had husband and wife teams here before. Except she and Clancy weren't husband and wife. And she certainly didn't want Kristen or anyone else from the hospital to get wind of what had happened in that exam room. It would give that picture of them in the newsletter a whole different connotation. And put paid to the idea that they didn't know each other well.

The fact was they knew each other all too well.

Matt headed back out, and an hour later, they'd planted their little tree in the bucket which they'd then wrapped with a canvas tarp. With a bit of artful folding and tucking, it made a passable tree stand, especially after winding a red strip of elastic bandaging around it and tying the ends in a bow.

They then watered it and set it just outside the door. "All we need now are your lights. Are you sure you're okay with us using them? You probably won't get them back."

"I'm sure. I knew there was a reason I wanted them so badly."

He put his hands on his hips, fingers loosely perched on the lean bones in a way that made her mouth water. "Matt said we can invite the town's kids and have a tree-lighting ceremony tomorrow night."

Right now she would have agreed with almost anything he suggested. Not that it wasn't a good idea. It was. And a little burst of excitement washed away the tiredness she'd felt just an hour earlier.

"The kids are going to love it." Maybe every volunteer group did something to help celebrate the holidays, and maybe this was as much about giving this town a shot of hope as it was anything else. But whatever it was, they were about to add a little bit of fun to their last week and a half in Bender, and maybe leave a little piece of themselves behind in the process.

CHAPTER EIGHT

AT DUSK THE next day, a crowd of around a hundred people stood around the barn's entrance. Hollee had agreed with Clancy that it was best to put the tree just outside the door. That way, all the children who made decorations could walk by and see it. It wasn't a huge tree, but at almost five feet tall, it was big enough to fit a fair number of decorations. And the tree would carry a piece of many of Bender's residents. It was another way to bring people together.

The rest of the staff loved the idea and were as excited as Hollee seemed to be. One of them had run to the nearest town and purchased a couple more strands of lights to add to Hollee's. But they'd agreed that all the other decorations would be handmade by the children and their families.

Matt addressed the group. "Are you ready for Bender's official Christmas tree lighting ceremony?"

"Ready!" The voices sounded in chorus, with some of the children clapping in excitement.

Clancy held the plug for the lights and waited for the other man to give the signal, very aware Hollee was standing off to the side. He didn't want her way over there. He wanted her next to him, and that bothered him more than he cared to admit.

Because of that shared moment yesterday?

Randy was there in the front row along with his father, having been released from the hospital after a night of observation. They'd gotten back to Bender just an hour ago, just in time for the tree lighting. He'd been horrified when Samuel had carried his limp form into the hospital. The outcome could have been very different. Seeing him well enough to join in the festivities made him glance at Hollee, who nodded as if to say she'd noticed the pair.

Matt looked at him with a smile. "Let's do it, then."

In addition to being a FEMA doctor, Matt would be here for most of the rebuilding and to help direct future volunteer teams as they worked toward that goal so Clancy could always write and ask for updates or maybe even come back at a later date and help again.

Clancy plugged in the lights and the tree sprang to life. Three strands might have been a little overkill, but they did the job, sending a message to everyone that the season was about more than just a man in a red suit.

An "Ooh" went up from those who were in attendance. The multitude of colorful bulbs stood out in stark contrast to the darkening skies.

Too many lights or not, all he wanted was for this to bring a tiny bit of magic to these kids. Especially after what they'd gone through. How many children, like Randy, had lost members of their families? He couldn't begin to imagine.

Matt had asked Clancy to explain what they wanted to do. So he asked the kids to get ready to use their imaginations.

"This tree needs decorations. Lots of them. But we don't want to buy them. We want you to make them." He paused to let that sink in. "So figure out something that you can draw or construct, using your own two hands. You can use materials you find around town. Recycled items would be even better. Don't worry about how to hang your decorations on the tree, just bring them in, and we'll figure that out."

When several voices started talking all at once, he knew they'd done what they'd hoped to do: put a tiny bit of excitement back in the season.

He raised his hand to quiet the crowd for a moment. "Bring your projects back on Wednesday—that's a week from today—and we'll put them on the tree. Everyone who participates will get a little gift, and the most imaginative creation will pick a prize donated from our hospital in Arlington."

Matt spoke up. "We're also going to have a Christmas party for everyone in the main part of the barn afterward. Those who can, bring a dish of finger foods to share. Those who can't, come anyway."

The level of excitement rose, and Clancy smiled, glancing over at Hollee to see that she too was smiling. She gave him a quick thumbs-up sign, which made him swallow.

She'd talked about being friends, and yet when she'd gone to kiss him on the cheek he hadn't been able to leave it at that. Damn. What was it about this woman that made him go sideways? Every time?

He'd toyed with telling her the truth about Jacob and seeing if that made it stop. But the time for that was long past. Why not let her go on thinking her husband had been a saint?

He hated it. Because it turned out that his old friend had been anything but. But this wasn't about him. Or about Jacob and his failings. It was about not hurting Hollee.

People filed through and shook their hands, thanking them for coming and for what they were doing, some of the kids already picking up twigs and tree limbs.

Hollee came over to him. "This was a great idea. Did you see Randy's face?"

"I did. It's good to see him back so soon."

She wrapped her jacket around herself. "Yes, it is."

"I like the idea of giving gifts out to the children who bring in ornaments."

"I don't think we have enough presents for every single child in town, even though the hospital added some useful items before we left, like fun cups and socks, et cetera. But it was the only way I could think of to make it fair."

A lot in life was unfair and right now he was suddenly peering through the fog of the last ten years and wondering if he'd done the right thing. If he'd not stepped aside for Jacob, would he and Hollee have wound up together?

Hell, what damn good did it do to rehash this again and again? He and Hollee were not together. And from what she'd said after that incident in her kitchen, she still loved Jacob. He was who she'd chosen to be with, so the jerk had evidently been right. Clancy hadn't deserved Hollee back then. But from what he'd seen at that hotel in Afghanistan, neither had Jacob.

Working with her here in Bender was proving to be an exercise in torture. He was dreaming about her at night and working with her during the day. A lethal combination.

Kristen came over to talk to Hollee, and he gratefully took that as his cue to leave. And that was fine with him, since he could use a nice cold beer. Or two or three. Bender had instituted a three-drink maximum at the local bar, partly to conserve their supplies and partly to keep the residents from trying to drown their troubles with booze.

Well, he wasn't trying to drown his troubles—plural—he was only trying to drown out one particular trouble. And that trouble had started the moment they'd begun working together.

Clancy had seemed off for the last several days, but she couldn't put her finger on exactly how. He'd been friendly enough, but there was an emotional detachment that hadn't been there earlier in the week. And certainly there'd been no more touching moments like they'd shared in that exam room, when his light kiss had lit her up as brightly as the Christmas tree standing outside the door.

She shifted her instrument tray, not used to playing surgical nurse, even though she'd done a rotation in it during her training. But the regular nurse was sick with a stomach bug and Matt had asked if she'd fill in, since there were no active labor cases right now. She'd seen Clancy's eyes when she'd stepped into the room. There had been a combination of dismay and resignation in them that had made her throat tighten.

He didn't like working with her, despite his assurances that they could be friends.

Maybe she'd been fooling herself. Two nights ago, he'd come up to her, and she could have sworn he'd had something on his mind, something he'd wanted to say, but in the end he'd just discussed the tree and ordinary things about the town and then left as quickly as he'd appeared.

It had been more surreal than the kiss they'd shared in the exam room.

"Suture."

She handed him the needle threaded with the suture material, bringing her mind back to the task at hand. Three-year-old Kaley was lying sedated on the table. The little girl had fallen while holding a glass of water and had cut her lip right through the vermillion border. They'd called in Clancy, since an error in lining up the edges would be noticeable as the girl got older. Strapping the child to a papoose board had quickly proved to be a no-go. The panicked child had screamed helplessly, causing her parents almost as much distress as it did Kaley.

Clancy had loosened the restraints himself, making soothing sounds as he carried the toddler over to her mom, and then asked the anesthesiologist to prepare a light sedation instead of physically restraining the child. It worked like a charm and soon Kaley was out like a light.

The sight of him holding that little girl had almost been her undoing. Just like seeing him with his niece, and later with Randy. He was so amazingly gentle with children. If he ever found the right woman, maybe he'd...

What? Settle down?

She didn't see that happening, and what Clancy did or didn't do was none of her business.

Four minutes later he'd finished the top lip and everything lined up perfectly.

Unfortunately the same couldn't be said of her dealings with Clancy, where nothing seemed to line up and where she was busy playing a psychological version of the mix-up-the-cups game. She was never sure which emotion was hidden under which cup at any given time. Pick up the wrong cup and—*oops!*—there it would be, on display for everyone to see. Like in that Santa picture.

She didn't need any more slipups like that one.

"Okay, moving to the lower lip." He glanced at her, his attention dipping to her mouth before tugging his loupes down and shielding his eyes from view. Maybe she wasn't the only one slipping up.

"Can you rinse the area again, please?

Okay, his brusque tone said she'd imagined that look. His mind, unlike hers, was completely focused on his job.

Using the bottle of saline, she washed the blood from

the area, granting Clancy a clear view of what he had to work with.

Should she do the same thing? Sluice some emotional saline and just come out and ask Clancy if something was bothering him? What if he gave her the standard "nothing's wrong" reply?

She couldn't force him to talk. And she wasn't really sure she wanted to know, especially if it went back to what had happened between them in her kitchen.

No, he'd seemed to put that behind him a lot easier than she had. Except he'd kissed her again in that exam room. And he had seemed to glance at her lips a few seconds ago.

Was Clancy really as indifferent as he seemed at this moment?

She didn't know. And she wasn't sure she wanted to know. She had time. There was still a little over a week before they had to leave Bender. Surely before then she could figure this thing out. And then she could go back to Arlington with an assurance that she knew exactly where he stood.

A week later, she was no closer to knowing where they stood than she'd been during Kaley's surgery, and time was up. It was decorating day. The crowds that had swamped their little clinic each day had again assembled outside the barn. But tonight it was for a different reason. And despite her uncertainties, the town's excitement was infectious. This was probably the first fun thing they'd done as a community since the disaster. Kids were chattering in animated voices, holding their offerings for the tree.

She allowed the turmoil and tension from working with Clancy to be washed to one side, at least for tonight.

Except he was the official MC for the event, since this had been his idea. She stood next to a large box that contained the gifts she would hand out to the kids who participated. There was also a pair of scissors and suture material that they would use to hang the ornaments. The tree was already lit, its glow like a beacon that made the crowd gather closer, their coats and gloves helping to keep the December chill at bay.

Clancy picked up the microphone, sending a long glance her way before turning back to the group in front of them.

Her heart tripped before righting itself.

Get a hold of yourself, Hollee.

That was hard to do when the man was heartbreakingly gorgeous. He always had been, that slight bad-boy air he'd carried with him as a teenager was still as potent as any pharmaceutical known to man. No wonder he'd had women swarming over him back then, her included. Even those scars did nothing to diminish his looks, as evidenced by the woman who'd slipped him that piece of paper at the dog park. Even here, he'd gotten sideways glances from some of the nurses, Kristen included, who'd asked if there was something between her and Clancy.

She'd flatly denied it. Did that mean Kristen was going to set her sights on him?

"I think we're ready to start," he said. "Who wants to be first?" He gestured at the lit but still empty tree.

Two kids moved forward—the resemblance between them unmistakable. They held matching stars made out of twigs that had been wired together.

Hollee peeled off her mittens and fashioned loops out of the suture material, before handing the ornaments back to the brothers and letting them choose where to put them. "Good job, you guys." She gave each of them a wrapped gift.

One by one they presented their treasures to Hollee for loops. The ornaments ranged from pictures scratched on bits of paper to a tiny wooden box that contained a nativity scene made from pebbles.

Very imaginative.

Another child had found a clear plastic soda bottle and cut what looked like icicles from it. There were twenty or so of them.

As things got more congested, Kristen came up to help her make hanging loops.

"Clancy came up with a great idea. I've never seen a more beautiful tree."

She hadn't either, and a sudden squeezing in her throat caught her by surprise.

"It's perfect." And it was. This dug-up-from-the-earth impromptu Christmas tree was somehow more special than all the trees at the hospital, or even the trees she and Jacob had shared over the years. The fear that its specialness had something to do with the man who'd spearheaded this event made her hands ball up at her sides.

She'd seen so many different sides of Clancy during this trip. Things that she'd never thought about or looked for when they had been younger. Like the way he'd taken Randy from his dad's arms—the intensity and determination behind his gaze making her believe that everything was going to be okay. Or the way he'd held his sister's baby with such tenderness. Or how he'd set up a tree for a struggling, heartbroken community and given them hope.

Dwelling on any of that right now was sure to turn her into a giant waterworks, so those thoughts would have to wait until she knew she wouldn't dissolve. Until then, she needed to hold it together.

It had to be the highs and lows of the last two weeks kicking in. It had nothing to do with Clancy, or what they'd been through. At least she hoped not. Because when they got back to Arlington things would return to normal. In every way.

So she sent her friend a smile. "Who is your pick for best decoration?"

"Those icicles are really cool." She glanced at where the maker was still hanging them on the tree. With each slight breeze, they twirled and sparkled, catching the light from the tree and magnifying it. "It's amazing what they came up with, and a good lesson for us all that keeping things simple is sometimes best."

"Yes, it is." She could apply that lesson to her current situation. She needed to keep things with Clancy simple and stop letting her feelings and emotions from the past bleed into the present.

Remember that fortune, Hollee. The past belongs to the past.

The icicles were up, and it looked like that might be all the ornaments. Then Randy's dad led him to the front of the crowd and gave him an encouraging nudge. He looked healthy but shy, hesitantly coming forward carrying something in a plastic bag.

Clancy looked inside, and his head cocked for a second as if puzzled. Then his throat moved with a quick jerk and he motioned for the child's dad to come up. Wearing worn jeans and a T-shirt sporting the name of the state football team, the bearded man moved toward them, draping his arm around his son.

"Hi, Randy." Clancy gave the child a smile. "Let's see what you brought for our tree."

Hollee's heart squeezed, that weepy sensation growing stronger. Maybe she'd fall apart after all.

Clancy pulled out a length of red yarn. Strung along it were bead-like items. Some were silver and shiny, and some were a dark dull color, almost like rust or—

"Oh, wow," Kristen said.

The words made her take a closer look, then she realized the part of the garland that was visible contained pieces of hardware. Odds and ends. Hinges and nuts and bolts and even a silver doorknob. Her chest tightened.

Clancy spoke into the microphone before holding it in front of the man's mouth. "I'd like you to tell us the story behind these items, if you don't mind."

The man took off his hat and nodded. "I didn't want the kids to step on nails after the tornado, so I borrowed a metal detector and started going through the streets and properties where…" He took a deep breath before continuing. "Where some of our houses used to be. I put them in a bucket, intending to throw them away. One bucket became two, and two became three. I realized these things were once part of this town and could be again." He rubbed a hand over his head. "They'd be a great way to remember what happened, to remember our loved ones. So I'm going to use them to rebuild my house. To rebuild my neighbors' houses. When the call came for items to put on the tree, Randy asked if he could use some of the stuff from the buckets."

He nodded at the bag. "These are what he chose."

The squeezing in her chest grew fiercer, and when she looked out over the townspeople she didn't see a dry eye out there. Some people were openly sobbing, including Randy's aunt and her family.

Clancy reached out and gripped the other man's hand, giving it a firm shake. "I can't think of a better thing to put on this tree. A tree that belongs to the people of Bender, Virginia. Will you both help me loop it around?"

Putting down his microphone, there was an almost reverent silence as Randy, his dad and Clancy wrapped the garland around the tree, carefully tucking it beneath the icicles and other ornaments, the gathered items a bittersweet reminder of what they'd lost, but also a picture of hope. These things would eventually be put back to use, showing that what had happened in the past could merge into the future, that it wasn't entirely lost.

Hadn't she just been thinking about that fortune and

her past with Clancy? And how it had nothing to do with the present? What if she was wrong?

The garland was on, and Randy and his dad rejoined the rest of the townsfolk. Several clapped the father on the back and gave his son a quick squeeze. Others took pictures of the tree with their phones. As Hollee gazed at it, she realized Kristen was right. She'd likely never see a tree like it again in her life.

"Is that everyone?" Clancy's voice startled her, and she couldn't stop the shudder that rolled through her at the words. At the thought of never seeing him breathe life into another child. Or having him hook a finger under her chin to tip her face up for his kiss. Once they were back home, it would be all over. They would go their own separate ways. Yes, they might see each other for Jen-Jen's christening or around the hospital. But…

Was that all?

It's only been a little over a month since he came back to Arlington, Hollee. You can't get attached that fast.

Maybe not, but what about over the space of ten years?

"If we have all the decorations, we're going to ask our panel of judges to pick a winner, but first let me say that this tree wouldn't be what it is without *all* of your contributions. I never expected such a variety of creative ideas. You've made something special out of what was once a scraggly old tree." He smiled and glanced around the group. "I hope you'll remember this as you grow up. It doesn't matter what you have as much as it matters what you *make* out of what you have. Randy's garland is a great reminder of that."

And sometimes you had something beautiful and didn't make anything out of it at all. Even her life with Jacob had turned out differently from what she had thought it would be. What it might have been.

One of the hospital staff members took several more photos of the tree from various angles, probably for Arlington Regional's newsletter.

Mixed in with the furor of other emotions was a hint of sadness over leaving this quaint mining town behind. The trip had been about caring and helping and...loving. She wished there was some way to stay in contact with Randy and some of the other folks she'd met over the past couple of weeks.

Maybe she could come back someday. Why not?

Clancy formed a huddle with the others on the voting panel, one of whom was Kristen, who'd excused herself to be with them.

Hollee was glad she wasn't on it. She could just enjoy the tree and not have to worry about that uneasy awareness that crept in whenever she stood too close to him.

Who was she kidding? All she had to do was lay eyes on the man and her traitorous pulse picked up its pace.

Five minutes later, Clancy stepped forward. "We've reached a decision. Randy, would you come up here, please?"

Hollee pulled in a quick breath, needing the shot of oxygen.

The little boy glanced up at his dad, who nodded. He hurried over to them, stopping beside Clancy, who put his hand on the child's shoulder. "I heard something else about you. Can you tell me if it's true? Someone told me that you're actually helping your dad collect some of the items that are on your garland, and that you spent most of the night stringing it." Randy nodded and Clancy looked up at everyone. "When you get a chance, you should come by and look at it."

Clancy knelt beside the boy while Kristen handed him a wrapped box. "We want to give you this to remember us by."

Randy took the present, fingering the stick-on bow. "Can I open it?"

"Yes, of course."

The little boy carefully peeled away the bow and paper and inside was a flat white gift box. Opening it, Randy's eyes got huge, and he looked up at Clancy. "This is mine?"

He nodded, picking up a white stethoscope. "Yep. Let me show you how to listen to your heart." He put the earpieces in the boy's ears and then held it to his chest. "Can you hear it?"

His head bobbed a couple of times and a huge smile appeared on his face.

"I used this same stethoscope to listen to your heart after your accident. You'll never know how glad I was to hear that strong beat thumping away in your chest."

Clancy removed the earbuds and draped the item around Randy's neck with a smile. Soon the boy was engulfed by his friends, the Christmas tree forgotten as everyone waited their turn to listen to each other's hearts.

Wait a minute. That was the 'scope he'd used on

Randy? She swallowed. Tomorrow was their last full day in Bender, and Clancy had just given away his personal stethoscope—which were normally closely guarded by their owners. He was leaving a tangible piece of himself with the boy he'd helped save. With the town he'd poured his life into over the last two weeks.

And that's when she realized Clancy had poured a part of himself into her heart as well, whether he'd meant to or not.

She loved him. Loved his selflessness and caring nature, even when he appeared to be at his most unapproachable. Loved everything she'd learned about him during their time in Bender.

Only there was nothing she could do about it. Not ten years ago, and certainly not now.

Not without risking her heart all over again.

Some of the partitions in the barn had been pushed back to allow room for a festive group of tables to be set up. People from both the Arlington volunteer team and the town had come together to make a wonderful spread of finger foods and drinks, careful to make sure that anything alcoholic was kept well out of reach of the kids. The three-drink maximum had been lifted for this one night, but Clancy doubted anyone would tiptoe over that line. Especially not tonight.

Clancy couldn't believe how fast time had flown. Soon they would be back in Arlington, far from the sights and sounds of what had happened in this town. And, truth be told, he'd miss it. He'd miss seeing the rebuilding process, especially seeing where the bits and pieces of recycled hardware from Randy's garland would wind up.

It was the first field hospital he'd worked in as a civilian, and the focus was so totally different from the military as to be like night and day. This was all about helping rather than defending, although he'd done his share of helping while in the army. But there was a freedom to come and go and decide things for oneself, within certain parameters. They still had to work as a team, but it wasn't as regimented as he was used to. Kind of like life at Arlington Regional.

He'd found Hollee standing by herself and went over to join her. There was laughter and music was playing, but it wasn't being blasted out of speakers.

Kristen came by before he'd said a word. "We kept the center clear for anyone who wants to do some… dancing." She said that last word in a sing-song voice, nudging Hollee's arm and grinning when her friend flashed her an acid glare.

Great. Dancing. He glanced around the room, wondering if Hollee would partner with any of the team.

It's none of your business, Clancy.

And it wasn't. But that didn't mean that he could just shut his brain off whenever it veered in the wrong direction. And this was definitely the wrong direction. Because he found himself wanting to be the one to dance with her. Despite trying to avoid her for the last week.

But it was the last night. Surely he could pass it off as something unimportant.

Like he had ten years ago? Not something he wanted to think about tonight.

The music went up a couple of notches, and some of the children and others headed onto the floor and started moving to the beat. At least this wasn't the stuff slow dances were made of.

He realized Hollee was still standing next to him. "Do you two want something to drink?"

Kristen shook her head. "Nothing for me, I'm headed out onto the floor in a minute."

"I'd love a glass of soda or even a beer if there's some up there," Hollee said. "Thank you."

He headed to the table just as Kristen tugged one of Hollee's hands. "Come on. It'll be fun. There aren't enough men to go around. Besides, most everyone in our group is married except a couple of the doctors, us and a few other nurses."

Hollee tried to resist for a second, but when her friend persisted, she gave a quick shrug, and then went out and started dancing. Clancy tensed, his instinct to stop and watch her whispering in his ear. He already knew he loved the way she moved but that was a temptation he should definitely resist. Even so, as he waited in line for his turn at the drinks table, he turned and glanced over. She was laughing at something Kristen had said, clapping her hand over her mouth for a moment, hiding that little dimple that he knew was there.

He'd already had a few moments of weakness when it came to her. To continue down that path might prove disastrous, especially with all the messiness that had happened with Jacob. She might not know about it, but if he tried to build a relationship with her, knowing he was keeping that a secret, he'd have a hard time living with himself. And he really didn't want to be the one to tell her.

Why couldn't you have done what you promised, Jacob?

Impulsive acts brought…complications. He'd found that out, and so had his former friend.

By the time he got back with their drinks, Hollee had changed partners. She was now dancing with…

One of the doctors. A man this time. He was assuming it was one of the single ones Kristen had mentioned.

And the man's gaze was as steady as a cobra's, poised to strike.

"Well, damn." The oath was enough to make someone at a nearby table glance at him.

You are crazy, Clancy. These are team members. No one is throwing cobra looks at anyone.

Holly wasn't dating. She'd said it herself, she hadn't slept with anyone since Jacob.

His teeth clenched at that thought. His friend had been dead for five years. Why *hadn't* Hollee gotten married again?

Because she was mourning him? Still? Or because she just hadn't found the right person?

Like this doctor?

He felt like a fool, standing there holding two glasses, so he went over to one of the tables and sat, putting one glass in front of the chair next to his. Then he took a long drink of his beer. At least tonight he didn't have to worry about driving. Not that he planned on getting drunk or anything.

The other man touched Holly from time to time.

Subtle gestures. Fingers to fingers, a palm on her arm. She appeared to take a step back at that, only to have the man slowly close the gap, making the move appear casual. He wasn't right on top of her by any stretch of the imagination but even so, a warning pressure began to build in Clancy's head.

He swallowed another drink of his beer. Kristen rejoined the pair, and a feeling of relief swept through him when Hollee seemed to glance at her friend gratefully, again laughing at something she said, while the other man didn't seem at all happy with the interruption.

What the hell was he doing sitting here, brooding in silence? He'd never been a man to sit back and ignore something he didn't like.

Like Jacob moving in on Hollee?

That had been different. Jacob had given him a pretty bitter pill to swallow, but it had also made him take a look at himself and decide to make a change.

Clancy was no longer the person he'd been back then. Did he deserve Hollee? Maybe not. But a single dance? That was a different story.

Taking one more bracing gulp, he climbed to his feet, leaving their glasses where they were. His initial goal was to tell her that her drink was ready. That goal shifted when the music changed, a much slower Christmas song thrumming through the speakers. Since most of these people were either colleagues or residents of Bender with a healthy sprinkling of children throughout, there probably wouldn't be a whole lot of slow dancing, and for that he was grateful. Because all he wanted to do was to draw Hollee into his arms, feel her skin against his, breathe her scent deep into his lungs. Even though it was a recipe for disaster.

Dancing with her. Standing across from her and letting the wistful tune carry them both away.

He made it across the floor, and as soon as he faced Hollee he saw her smile. Not just something polite that welcomed him to their little group but a genuine smile that warmed her eyes in a way that caused his lips to tilt upward.

"I knew I'd get you out here sooner or later," she said.

He blinked in surprise, until the other man excused himself. Then he realized why she'd said it. So he hadn't imagined her discomfort. Kristen leaned in and kissed Hollee's cheek, murmuring, "I had a feeling... Don't worry, I don't think you need saving from this one."

Then she, too, left.

"Sorry," Clancy murmured. "I wasn't sure if you were enjoying yourself, but I wanted to tell you that I have our drinks at one of the tables."

"I wasn't. Enjoying myself." Her eyes met his in a way that told him exactly what she meant. She hadn't liked dancing with that guy. And he was glad. Fiercely glad.

"It looks like you have a good friend in Kristen, then."

"Yes. She's been there for me, even when things got..."

"Got?"

"Complicated."

That made him frown, since it was the same word

that had flashed across his brain a few minutes ago. How long had she known Kristen?

"As in with Jacob?"

"Kind of." She shrugged. "I wanted to start a family, but that didn't…happen."

Because she couldn't? Or because Jacob had been against it? If he had been so consumed with other women, why hadn't he just divorced Hollee? An ugly thought came to him that he quickly discarded.

He and Jacob had always been competitive, but he'd never told his friend about the kiss he and Hollee had shared. And there was no way Jacob would have risked her happiness out of selfish ego. Would he?

But he'd always believed Hollee was deeply in love with her husband.

"I'm sorry that didn't work out for you. You would make a great mother." He paused trying to figure out how to word it. "You still could be one. There's always adoption. Or you might meet someone else."

"I don't know. I've given that some thought. But I'm so busy that I barely have time for Tommie, much less a baby. And I definitely wouldn't have had time to come on this trip if I had a young child."

"I'm glad you did."

"Excuse me?"

"I'm glad you came." Surprisingly enough, it was true.

Her pupils widened. "You are? Because you didn't seem all that thrilled that I was coming when you saw me in the conference room."

"I could say the same about you. Chalk it up to surprise, in my case." Which was also true.

And now here he was dancing with her. Smart move? Probably not. But better than letting that doc keep hitting on her, especially since she'd said she hadn't liked it.

A few minutes later the FEMA liaison tapped them on the shoulder. "How much have you had to drink?"

"Nothing," Hollee said.

Clancy blinked. What the hell? There was no way the man thought he was drunk. "Just part of a beer, why?"

"We've got a situation and several of us have already had more than our share."

Immediately on alert, he said, "What is it?"

"One of the residents in an outlying area is in labor. The roads are washed out and the midwife has run into trouble. She sent one of the kids to get help."

"God." Hollee's distress wasn't lost on him.

"Well, the kid made it here somehow. Have you got something that can get through?"

"Several of the residents have four-wheel-drive vehicles, but anything heavy is going to get bogged down in the mud. We already tried to get back into those areas last week."

"How did the kid get here?"

"He came on an ATV."

"If you can get me some directions and keep him safe, I'll get my gear together and borrow it."

"I'm going too," Holly said. "I've ridden on your bike with you. You know I can do it."

He did. He remembered a couple of times that he'd

had her behind him as they'd torn up some of the local fields. And then there was the night he'd kissed her.

"It's going to be cold going."

She frowned, her chin tilting up. "We don't have time to argue. This is what I'm trained for. Besides, you gave away your stethoscope. You'll need mine...and me."

Yes, he would. And he was beginning to think he needed her in more ways than one. "Okay, you grab a coat and I'll get my medical kit."

The ATV was one of the bigger ones, the wheels set wide apart and looking good and sturdy. It was also splattered with mud, attesting to the fact that it was going to be rough going.

"I'm going to need you to navigate," he said as they buckled on helmets borrowed from other Bender residents.

"Okay. My phone's GPS is working, so I'm going to try to use that as much as possible, but I have written instructions in my back pocket as well."

"Perfect." He climbed on, waiting for her to get on behind him. The slope of the seat tipped her tight against him, which was probably a good thing, even though it reminded him of the past and did a number on his head. "Hang on."

Soon they were off, the frigid wind whistling past them. A pothole threatened to rattle his teeth out of his head, but that would soon be the least of their worries once the pavement gave out. Which it did about five miles out of town.

He slowed down, the tracks from the kid's flight into

town plainly visible. "I see his path. Here we go." He eased the vehicle down into the mud.

Things got hairy for a while and maneuvering through the worst of the muck had them shimmying sideways a time or two. Hollee's arms squeezed his midsection in a death grip. He could remember a time when he might have chosen the worst spots for just that reason. Today was not one of them.

One of her arms left him. "Stop for just a second."

He immediately throttled down. "What is it?"

"Checking distance. We're about a mile out."

He again wondered about the wisdom of her coming, rather than leaving her to finish enjoying the party, but she was right. He would need her. Although he had delivered babies before, it wasn't his specialty, and Hollee had assisted with lots of them.

The last mile went quickly, and they pulled up outside a small bungalow-style log home. Clancy laid on the horn to let them know they were there before they both leaped off the vehicle. The front door opened in a rush and a man stood there.

"Thank God you're here! Please, hurry. The baby is…stuck."

His heart turned to ice, and when he looked at Hollee he saw that she'd gone pale.

"Not good," she whispered.

She wasn't kidding. He cast around for the training he'd had on shoulder dystocia, as he assumed that's what the man had meant by being "stuck." A wedged shoulder was a medical emergency, because once the baby's head was delivered, the rest of the body needed to follow quickly.

Clancy quickly introduced them to the man. "The midwife's with her?"

"Yes."

They were in the bedroom in a matter of seconds, asking her husband to wait outside. The midwife was calling out instructions, telling the young woman on the bed not to push, even as she attempted to reposition her legs and hips.

Clancy assessed the situation, communicating with the birthing assistant. "What's the status?"

"The baby's shoulder is wedged. I've tried everything short of attempting to push it back in and do a C-section—which I wouldn't, of course," she added quickly, "but I can't get anywhere."

Pushing the baby back in was a last-ditch measure and dangerous for both the mother and unborn child.

Hollee touched his arm. "We need to go through the maneuvers in order. We can help you with them." She glanced at the midwife and got a nod in response.

"I live just down the road. There's no way we could have gotten her to a hospital and there's nowhere to land a chopper back here."

"Yeah, I can see that. It's bad out there."

Clancy shed his coat and went into a nearby bathroom to sluice his hands with soap and water, Hollee appearing beside him to do the same.

With the midwife's help they positioned the woman so her knees were pressed to her chest. Then while Hollee put pressure on the patient's abdomen just above the pubic bone, Clancy attempted gentle rotation, hoping to free the shoulder. The woman's agonized cries tore at him, but there was no access to an epidural or other pain medication, and if they didn't get this resolved quickly, they were in danger of losing both mom and baby.

The baby rotated partially, but the shoulder didn't budge. "Dammit. I really don't want to perform a cleidotomy." The drastic measure involved a deliberate fracture of the baby's collarbone in the hope that the shoulder would then fit through the pelvis.

Hollee looked him in the eye. "We're going to do whatever it takes, Clancy. Whatever. It. Takes. But let's try the corkscrew first."

The midwife nodded her agreement. From the look of them, both the birthing professional and laboring mom were exhausted. If this failed, the next step was to get her up on all fours. But he doubted the young mother had the strength to hold herself up at this point.

"Ready?" he asked.

Hollee nodded, and when he directed a look at the midwife, she anticipated their every move.

This had better work. They were running out of options. Clancy slowly rotated the baby's head once again, being more aggressive about it this time, while Hollee located the baby's shoulder and pushed down hard, trying to dislodge it from beneath the bone. It stuck tight for a terrible few seconds, even as Clancy continued the rotation, then suddenly something popped and shifted. "I think we may be free."

"I think so too."

"Okay, let's push. But without a lot of force." He

added the warning, needing this to be a controlled slide otherwise the baby might end up wedged all over again.

The mom bore down, and the first shoulder appeared in the birth canal. Damn, it had worked.

"Keep pushing, you can do it!" he said. "One, two, three…" The midwife took up the count, guiding the process from her place at the woman's head. The look of relief on her face was unmistakable.

Two more pushes and, unbelievably, the baby slid onto the readied towel as if there had never been an issue. Carefully cradling the newborn, praying they'd won the race against time, he said, "It's a girl."

The baby's legs kicked, and then she squinched up her face as if registering her extreme displeasure with what had just transpired. He smiled, while rubbing her briskly with the towel to stimulate her, gratified to hear her sudden angry howl. "Sorry about all of that, sweetheart. You gave us quite a scare."

"Thank God. You did it, Maria." The midwife dropped a kiss on the woman's cheek. The new mom must have realized it was going to be okay, because she started weeping, her body going slack.

The midwife brought over surgical scissors, waiting until the cord had stopped pulsing. Then she clamped and cut it.

Hollee came over. "If you'll check her clavicle and make she wasn't injured in the maneuver, I'll make sure there's no postpartum hemorrhage as we deliver the placenta."

He'd just been about to do that. Once he was satisfied the newborn's respiratory system was working well, he laid her on the bed and ran careful fingers along the clavicle and humerus on the affected side. No breaks. He breathed a word of thanks.

She was perfect. Absolutely perfect. The baby had stopped crying, her big blue eyes struggling to focus on him.

"Hi, there, beautiful. You have no idea how happy I am to see you."

"So am I." Hollee was back beside him, her shoulder brushing his as she looked down at the baby. "She is beautiful. Rita—our midwife—has everything under control. I imagine she's dealt with things like this before, but sometimes it all happens so fast, and when you don't have an extra set of hands when you need them... well, it can get overwhelming."

"Yes, it can. Speaking of which, thanks for walking me through things. It's been a while."

"You did a wonderful job and delivered a healthy baby. That's all that counts in the end."

He smiled and touched a finger to the newborn's tiny nose, marveling at just how small she was. He'd had that same sense of wonder when holding Ava's new daughter. "It's amazing, isn't it?"

"Yes. I feel it every time I help with a delivery."

Clancy wasn't sure if that's all it was in this case. Maybe knowing how precarious the situation had been made him feel a little more exposed. A little more vulnerable. All he knew was that holding this little one felt right and good and—

"Is she okay?" Maria's anxious eyes were on them,

reminding him this wasn't his baby or Hollee's, but someone else's.

He gave a forced smile. "She's doing great."

Hollee took the baby, laying her on Maria's chest, skin to skin, letting them bond.

The woman murmured to her newborn, stroking her fingers through the dark tufts of baby fine hair.

"I guess we'd better let the baby's father know she's okay."

Hollee laughed. "Oh, no! I totally forgot about him."

So had he.

When Clancy went through the door, he found the new dad sitting on a couch, head bowed low, hands dangling between his knees. His slumped posture said he expected the worst but had stayed put as he'd been told.

"Everyone's fine. You have a healthy baby girl."

His head came up. "A girl? I have a girl?"

Clancy nodded.

The dad came over and grasped Clancy's hand in both of his, shaking it wildly. "A girl! I have a baby girl!"

How would it feel to hear those words? That he had a daughter? His heart squeezed so hard it hurt, a wave of remorse crashing over him. He could have had that. If only his friendship to Jacob hadn't meant so much— if he hadn't been quite so ready to believe the worst about himself. And Hollee had married Jacob, so that kiss hadn't meant all that much to her. Except Clancy had turned his back on her, pushing her away before it ever really got started.

But why was he still dwelling on things that he had no damn control over?

"Congratulations." He nodded at the door to let the man know he could go in and be with his family. Hollee passed him in the doorway.

"I came to see if everything was okay."

"It is. I'm pretty sure the news I handed him was not what he expected to hear."

"I'm sure it wasn't." She sighed and rested her head on his arm for a second. "I wondered for a little while if we were going to be able to deliver good news at all."

"Me too." He liked the feel of her next to him, just like he'd reveled in holding that newborn a few seconds ago. Hollee's closeness made him wonder if she could sense the turmoil inside him. "They probably should go to the hospital to make sure everything is okay, but with how hard it was for us to make it here, I'm pretty sure they won't be able to."

"I agree. My only real worry at this point is swelling. We've had patients who've needed catheters for a day or two after some of those maneuvers."

He nodded. "I want to come back and check on her tomorrow."

"Not a bad idea." She sighed. "Is it weird to think that this baby and Randy are the best things we've done since coming here?"

Since he'd had the same thought, he shook his head. "No, I felt it too. But I'm sure all the patients we've seen the last two weeks have been appreciative." He knew they had. He'd heard thank-yous from almost everyone they'd treated, despite the long waiting times.

"They have. It's just that it's almost Christmas. And after seeing all the hardship Bender has gone through, today felt like a miracle. A pre-Christmas miracle. Working at a hospital, I sometimes lose sight of those kinds of things. I think I'd like to come back to Bender to help as they get back on their feet."

As someone who'd been on the other side of the equation, working in the field where he'd railed against the lack of modern conveniences that could have saved lives, he wasn't sure he necessarily liked practicing under less than ideal circumstances. But he did understand where she was coming from. There was somehow a sense of accomplishment and gratitude when you saved lives, even when things were far from certain. When you worked your ass off and went the extra mile to make it happen.

"Field hospitals are not always what they're cracked up to be."

"You've already done all of this and more, haven't you?"

"The things I dealt with weren't pretty, neither did they produce something as beautiful as a healthy baby. But we did save lives."

Her eyes went to his scar. "You've seen horrific things."

It wasn't a question. "Yes, I have." He smiled. "But not today. Today was a good day."

"Yes, Clancy. It most definitely was."

The midwife came out, wiping her hands with a towel. "Good, I caught you. I hate to ask, but is there any way you could stick around until tomorrow?"

"We were already talking about coming back to check on things. I'm pretty sure there aren't any bed and breakfasts up here, though."

"Jerry—the father—actually has a little cabin out back that his mother lived in while she was alive. It's not much more than an efficiency apartment, but it does have a bedroom and a separate sleeper sofa in the living room. He asked if you'd be willing to stay there so someone is close. They only have two bedrooms and one has two other children in it." She smiled. "If there's not something crushing in town that needs to be taken care of, that is."

He glanced at Hollee, and she smiled. "I think that's a great idea."

The midwife blew out a long breath. "Thank you for everything. Gavin, their son, got through okay?"

"Yes, he did, and stayed in town so that Hollee could come with me. Let me call and make sure someone can keep him for the night. If so, yes, we'll stay."

"There are some canned goods in the pantry that should tide you over. I'm going to stay and sleep here on the couch. I can call if something happens."

"Please do." He gave her their cellphone numbers.

Now that it had been decided, Clancy's thoughts were straying back into areas they shouldn't be. Like the fact that he and Hollee would be alone in a cabin. Wasn't that the very thing he'd been thinking about earlier? About complications and possibilities?

Yes, but he'd better knock that last one right back out of his head. While he still could.

CHAPTER NINE

As THEY DROVE through the slushy backyard to get to the cabin, Clancy worked the controls on the handlebars of the ATV with the same dexterity he'd used to deliver that baby. He'd been sure and decisive, even as fear had tickled the back of her throat that they might not be able to pull it off. Despite her worries to the contrary, he really hadn't needed her help. He'd already been moving from one thing to the next in a logical order, climbing his way from simple to complicated.

Until he'd succeeded.

She had a feeling that succeeding was important to Clancy.

It was important to her as well, but there were things that mattered more. Like what they'd experienced today. That raw turbulence that made the human experience what it was. She wouldn't trade that for all the success in the world. Neither would she trade the rare vulnerability that she'd seen in Clancy after the baby had been born. He'd cooed to her and held her and had looked like he couldn't get enough of her.

Hollee had loved watching him with her. So much

so that she'd had to take a step back so she didn't get caught up in his emotion. More than that, she hadn't wanted to disturb that sweet connection he'd had with that little one.

She snuggled against him for the last couple of yards, needing that connection with him herself, though she wasn't sure why. Maybe it was the aftermath of the struggle for life that made up the human experience. Even though in this instance she was going to pretend that it was caused by the bumps in the path between the houses.

They pulled to a stop in front of a cabin very much like the main house, only on a smaller scale. She got off the ATV and turned to look at him. "This is really cute."

"Cute." One of his brows hiked up. "You took the word right out of my mouth."

His lips curved in that crooked smile that she'd loved so much when she'd been in the throes of that high school crush. People who crossed his path today no doubt wondered if the smile was the product of his scars, due to nerve damage. But Hollee could assure them that his sideways grin was one hundred percent Clancy. He'd probably come out of the womb with that adorably quirky feature. At the thought of a group of nurses swooning over a baby Clancy, she laughed.

"What?" He glanced over at her, climbing off the vehicle and pulling the keys from the ignition.

"Nothing. Just wondering something." There was no way she was going to tell him what that was. It was far too dangerous to her psyche.

"You looked good, holding that baby," he said.

The change in subject made her smile. "So did you."

When she realized there was more to his statement than a simple observation, her smile faded. She'd asked herself that same question repeatedly. But there'd never been a ready answer.

She tried to tack more onto the last explanation she'd given him. "It was just never the right time, I guess. Jacob just…" She swallowed back the rush of emotions that were still raw and yet, oh, so familiar. Why hadn't he wanted a baby with her?

"Sorry, it's none of my business."

She could understand his curiosity, though. Her mom had often pestered her about the same thing, but it was pretty crushing to have to admit that you wanted a child when your husband had no interest in that at all. And by the end he'd barely wanted to sleep with her. She'd done the asking, and he'd evaded her. The insecurities she'd felt back then had been crushing and horrifying. In her worst moments she'd wondered if Jacob was cheating on her, or if he somehow knew about that kiss that she'd shared with Clancy. But unless Clancy had told him…

Which she very much doubted. After all, Clancy had backed away from her as well.

She licked her lips and decided to bare one wound. "I wanted them. But in the end Jacob…didn't."

"Oh, hell, Hollee, I'm sorry. Did he give a reason?"

"Just that he wasn't ready. And after five years of marriage I stopped asking. For anything." It felt good to finally say that out loud, even though Clancy probably wouldn't catch what she meant by that last part. A weight lifted from her shoulders.

His hand moved under hers, palm to palm. He didn't close his fingers around her, but his thumb did stroke across her skin in a way that sent a shiver through her.

She decided if he could ask a question, so could she. "You never got married."

"Nope. I never did." As if a window slammed shut, so did the shared confidences, his hand moving out from under hers.

Stung, she withdrew, her fingers twining together. So much for baring her soul. That door evidently didn't swing both ways.

As if realizing what he'd done, he glanced over at her. "I didn't mean that to sound harsh. I just never really met anyone I wanted to settle down with."

Evidently not. Maybe that was why he'd dated woman after woman, never quite finding what he'd been looking for. He'd added her to that list of not-quite-right rejects.

She blinked. Except they'd slept together a few weeks ago.

Ha! No sleep had been had by either party.

But there must still be some kind of attraction on his part, unless it was just old-fashioned lust between a man and a woman. Even she'd tried to pass it off as that but had wondered several times if that was exactly true. Their time together had stirred up feelings she'd thought were long sent to the ash heap. But when she blew on them, a vague glow appeared. Just the barest hint of something left over.

He rotated one of his shoulders as if trying to rid

himself of something. "Let's go inside before it gets any colder."

Passing through the door ahead of him, she was surprised to see that someone had already started a fire in the woodstove in the main area. It must have been done while they'd been washing their hands and cleaning up. It was still chilly, but already warmer than it was outside. There was a stack of wood beside the stove that looked like it had been freshly dumped.

She walked over to the heat source, closing her eyes as she walked through a silky layer of warm air. In the background, she could hear Clancy talking on the phone to Matt, the FEMA liaison, telling him what their plans were and asking if there was someone who could take care of Gavin for the night. From the sound of it, that wouldn't be a problem.

That was good, because she was both keyed up and exhausted at the same time, each emotion warring for first place in her body.

So was something else, and it was making her feel slightly crazy. The waves of heat from the stove were starting to feel a little too good, were starting to remind her of other ways to stay warm. Like on the back of that ATV. Or twined together under the cozy weight of winter blankets.

Sex with him shouldn't have been as good as it was. But there she had it. A damn stove was reminding her how much she still wanted him.

"Are you okay?"

She blinked and mumbled that she was and started

to move away from the fire, only to have him stop her with a look. He came to stand in front of her.

"What's wrong, Hollee? You've been acting weird ever since we walked through that door. Before that, even." Oh, Lord, had he guessed her thoughts?

"*I've* been acting weird? I could say the same about you."

"It's been a stressful week." He stared at her. "Are you sure you're okay with staying here with me? I can try to get you back to town and return on my own."

"I don't want to go back."

She left it at that, her teeth digging into her bottom lip. When Clancy followed the movement, her breath stalled. In his eyes was a familiar heat. Something much more than the tiny ember from their past.

"You drive me crazy sometimes. Did you know that?" His fingers touched her arm, trailed up it until he reached her nape.

"You used to tell me that all the time when we were younger." She was treading on dangerous ground, and she knew it. But did she care? Not at the moment.

"I'm not talking about that kind of crazy."

She already knew that. But, then, of course, he didn't know that he drove her insane either. That she'd been sitting here thinking crazy thoughts herself.

His thumb stroked the sensitive area behind her ear. "Do you want coffee?"

Coffee? The last thing she wanted was a hot beverage. What she wanted instead was a hot...

Oh, God. Something was seriously wrong with her.

"No. I don't want coffee."

He gave her that slow, devastating smile. "That's good, because I don't either. Do you want the bed… or the couch?"

This time when his hand moved, his thumb toyed with her bottom lip in a way that caused her whole body to sit up and take notice. God, if he was seriously asking her where she wanted to sleep instead of where she wanted to be with him, she was going to be horribly disappointed.

He leaned his forehead against hers. "Damn, Hollee, tell me we shouldn't do this. That we could get a call any minute saying we're needed in the house."

"A minute is all it would take for us to get dressed." She licked her lips. "And I can't say we shouldn't do this. Because it would be a lie."

He leaned back to look at her, and she wondered if she'd just made a fool out of herself. If he was going to clear his throat and warn her not to get too invested in him, that he was only passing through…

"Lying is a sin."

The way he'd said that… Lord, it was getting hot in here. "W-we wouldn't want to sin, would we?"

Putting his lips close to her ear, he whispered, "I don't know. I think it depends on which of the seven deadly ones we're talking about. Because I can think of one I might like to explore. At length."

Her heart leaped at the seductive edge to those words, and suddenly she was floating in the clouds even as she tried to chain herself to the nearest solid surface. Because she'd just been thinking about this, and it looked like she was about to get her wish, sin or no sin. Right here. Right now.

Clancy walked her backward until her back was against the first flat surface he could find, shrugging out of his coat as he went, not caring that his cellphone was still in the pocket. And when he covered her mouth with his, he swore he felt something shift inside him. Something besides the obvious, which was doing some shifting of its own at the thought of having her again.

And that tiny nudge that said he might want more than one night? Well, he wasn't going to stop and examine that too closely. Better just to enjoy the here and now and not look too far into the future.

But the idea of actually waking up next to her tomorrow morning?

That was a heady thought. A new shot of adrenaline burst onto the scene, bringing with it the same urgency he'd felt the last time he had been with her.

Spinning with her in his arms, he pushed her heavy jacket off her shoulders, letting it fall next to his. Then he leaned down and picked her up, carrying her to the room just behind the living room, where a bed covered with a simple cotton spread was waiting. "Drop or place?"

She laughed. "Surprise me."

His inclination was to watch her fall in a delicious heap on that bed, but since he didn't know how thick the mattress was, he decided to lower her gently instead, setting her in the exact center, head on the pillows. He followed her down, covering her body with his, loving the feel of clothing against clothing, knowing soon enough that was all going to change. But if he only had one night, he was going to take pleasure in the small things. In every second he had with her.

He slid one leg between hers, enjoying the way her softness cradled his body. Those curves and swells that seemed to welcome him home.

Home.

She was. Even as his mouth trailed up her neck and slid across her jawline, something tickled at the back of his thoughts. A little yellow light that signaled, *Caution! Judge your distance and choose well.* Hell, right now he wasn't going to judge anything. He was not going to wait for that red light—he was barreling right through this intersection no matter what the cost.

Hollee murmured something against his mouth, and he leaned back slightly to look at her. God, she was gorgeous, even as her eyes fluttered open and looked up at him with a slight questioning frown. He trailed an index finger down her nose. "It's okay. I just needed to see you. Do you know what you do to me?"

"Pretty sure." She wiggled against him. "If this is what I'm hoping it is."

"Oh, it is." He laughed. "It definitely is."

With that all the questions were done as he rolled over, taking her with him until she was sprawled on top of him. And when he pushed up into her, she bit his lip hard enough to make a shudder roll over him.

He wanted this woman with everything that he was. "Sit up, honey."

Doing as he asked, she straddled him, her legs

pressed against the outsides of his thighs, giving a little wiggle. Hell.

"Like this?"

"Just like that." He reached up and slid his fingers through her hair, combing it back over her shoulders. "I want you to like this. Okay?"

"I promise I *will* like it." Her brows went up. "Okay?"

It was more than okay.

She leaned down and unbuttoned the long-sleeved black shirt he'd put on for the ceremony earlier—why did that suddenly seem like ages ago?—tilting back when her fingers reached the spot where the buttons disappeared between her legs. The implication of her long pause made his mouth water. Then she went up on her knees and tugged his shirt free, so she could get at the rest of the buttons. When she settled back in place, she was centered on him in a way that shot a burst of hormones through his system.

And lust. That sin he'd mentioned a few minutes ago.

"God, Hollee."

She made slow circles with her hips, a knowing smile on her face as she watched him. Then her teeth clutched her lip as the movements changed, rocking back and forth and adding a bit more pressure. If she kept that up, they were not going to need the entire night. He reached for her, shoving her turtleneck up her torso, glorying in the way she lifted her arms to let him pull it over her head. Next came her bra, exposing more silky skin to his touch.

"Come here. I want to kiss you."

Hollee leaned forward, her breasts mashing against

his chest in a way that made him take her mouth with a fierceness that surprised even him. She was heaven on earth. And she was all his. At least for tonight.

Her tongue licked across his lips, nipping at the corners, before she kissed him deeply once again. All the while her hips kept up that tormenting motion, making the fire that was already raging in his veins grow more intense by the minute. He did not want to ask her to get off him, but if he didn't he couldn't finish undressing her, and if he didn't finish undressing her…

He sat up, taking her with him, wrapping his arms around her back, his mouth still tight against hers. Finally he pulled back an inch or two. "Do you think you can stand up?"

"Possibly. My legs are a little questionable."

He chuckled. "Okay, then I'll do the standing."

Tipping her off to the side, she gave a squeal before laughing. "No fair."

"Nothing about this is fair." He stood, finding his own legs less than co-operative, but he somehow managed to shrug his shirt the rest of the way off, before divesting himself of his jeans and the remainder of his clothes. Then he undid Hollee's pants and tugged them down her legs, followed by her lacy undergarments. When he sat back down on the bed he was sheathed, his erection heavy and, oh, so ready.

Hollee must have sensed it as well, because in a flash she'd come around and straddled his hips again, her hands sliding up either side of his face. Her fingers feathered down his scars, her eyes following their track.

Before he could frown, she touched her lips to the one on his cheek. "So sexy. So very you."

Then she rose up just enough to position him before coming down hard, the sudden squeezing heat that enveloped him taking his breath away. He curved his arms up her naked back, palms cupping her shoulders as she continued to take him inside her. The intimacy of her whole body sliding against his was something he would never forget. Never wanted to forget.

Her lips were at his ear, her breath warm and sexy, hissing out with each downward pump. One of his hands slid deep into her hair, bringing her face around until her lips were barely against his. He brushed over them again and again, the light contact contrasting with the full-on impact of what was happening below.

His tongue tingled with the urge to thrust into her mouth, but he held off, knowing once he did that it was all over. With one hand still in her hair, the other trailed down her back, coming to rest just above her butt. He pulled her in tighter, trying to up the contact point between them. It worked, because she moaned his name, her movements growing slightly erratic as he kept her pressed against him.

He could feel the building pressure, praying he could hold it off long enough for her to get what she needed. He angled his hips higher. Pushed harder.

Suddenly her knees clamped against his thighs, using the leverage to propel herself up. Then she shoved herself down and held tight, her body going off all around him in way that brought ecstasy. And need. In a second he'd flipped her on her back and rode her even as he poured himself into her in a rush that consumed every thought in his head.

His movements slowed, her legs wrapping around him as if afraid he was leaving.

Not a chance. There was nowhere he wanted to be other than here. With her.

Nowhere.

That thought spun round and round in his head like it was a centrifuge, separating out the feelings that were packaged inside that single word and whipping them away until only one emotion remained. The most important one of all.

Hell.

He loved her. She'd just incinerated all those layers of denial he'd been building over these last few weeks, until there was no longer any hiding from the truth.

Somewhere in the middle of that revelation he'd come to a stop, his body resting against hers, not sure what he was supposed to do with what he'd just realized.

Why did he have to do anything? They only had tomorrow and then they were headed back to Arlington. There was plenty of time to think about whether he should act on this. Or whether he should just let it fade away. Again.

And until then he was going to do exactly what he'd said he was going to do. Hold her until morning dawned and hope by then he'd come up with a plan that actually made sense. So he rolled off her and pulled her back against his chest.

"Mmm… Clancy?"

"Yes?" He loved how rumbly her voice was. Loved that it was because of what they'd just done.

"Can I sleep in your bed?"

He chuckled. "I thought it was your bed. I was planning on taking the couch."

A deep sigh rolled up from inside her. "I could argue this point, but I won't. So I'll just change the question. Will you sleep in *my* bed?"

He tucked her tighter against his hips. "Yes. I will, Hollee. Gladly."

She couldn't remember the number of times he'd woken her in the night. But his need for her had been heady. He was still sound asleep, and as much as she loved watching him, she could already see light coming through the thin shades. The sun was up. Since her phone wasn't nearby, she had no idea what time it actually was. Or if their hosts were waiting for them up at the house.

Or worse, if someone came knocking on the door…

"Clancy." She breathed his name right against his ear.

His eyes fluttered open. He looked at her with a slight frown. "You're here."

Something about that made her blink. Where had he thought she'd be? She'd asked him to stay with her.

Unless she was putting emphasis on the wrong word. Maybe it was the "you're" she should be focusing on. Surely he remembered who he was sleeping with.

Her insecurities about all the women Clancy had slept with when they'd been younger melded with Jacob's later rejections and she stood in a rush, her legs not quite ready to hold her. She braced them beneath her.

Clancy didn't form attachments. She'd learned that the hard way. Had she expected that to change, just because it was her in his bed rather than someone else?

"Hey." He held out a hand to her. "What is it?"

"Nothing."

"Didn't we already talk about lying?"

She gritted her teeth for a second. "It's light outside. We probably need to check on mom and baby." She found her clothes, pulling them on as fast as she could.

He sat up. "Slow down for a minute."

"You were right last night. We shouldn't have done this."

Reaching out, he grabbed her hand, stopping her frenetic movements. "Why not, exactly?"

Blinking hard, she decided to just lance the poison all at once and let it out. "I'm not like you. I can't just sleep with someone and then move on to the next person."

There was silence for what seemed like forever. "Meaning?"

She shook her head, feeling foolish somehow. So what if she wasn't as experienced as he was?

God, she knew exactly who he was, so why was she suddenly attacking him for this particular character trait? It wasn't like he'd tricked her into sleeping with him. No, it had been her choice. Wise or not. She needed to own it. But before she could say anything, Clancy beat her to it.

"I remember Jacob once saying something very similar to me. Going on and on about how different he was from me." A pulse worked in his temple, and he got up and gathered his clothes together. His mouth thinned, and he seemed to be warring with something. "I know you think the man you married was a real paragon of virtue—someone worthy of sainthood—but you might be surprised."

There was an ugly bitterness in his voice that shocked her.

"What's that supposed to mean?" Was he actually going to talk badly about someone who'd once been his best friend?

"I mean Jacob wasn't who you thought he was."

She swallowed, waiting for him to say the words that she'd somehow known in her heart but had never really been able to face. "He cheated on me, didn't he?"

He didn't say a word, just stood there like the damn stone that he was.

The world around her turned white for a terrifying second before a wave of fury swept over her. "How could you keep something like that from me?"

He headed for the bathroom, but there was no way she was going to let him walk away from this.

She ran over and grabbed his arm, and he stopped but he didn't turn around. That's when she realized with startling clarity that he knew—*knew*—beyond a shadow of a doubt that what she'd suspected was true.

A question burned on her tongue like acid.

"Why do you think…?" She changed to different words. "*How* do you know?"

"I saw him. And he admitted it."

She let go of him, wrapping her arms around her midsection as wave after wave of hurt went through her. "And yet you said nothing. Just let him off without even a warning."

"You have no idea what I did or didn't do. But you're right about one thing. This was a mistake. One that won't happen again."

Before she could say anything else, he was through the bathroom door, shutting it behind him. Seconds later, she heard the sounds of the shower going.

She sank onto the bed, her thoughts swirling. Jacob had cheated on her.

And Clancy had known about it and had never seen fit to tell her. He'd just let her go on as if everything had been fine, when it hadn't been. He was supposed to have been her friend.

But evidently he had been Jacob's friend first.

So much for thinking her husband had simply not been ready for children. Had he and Clancy laughed about how gullible she was?

It all made so much sense now. Her horror grew until it was all-encompassing. She decided she wasn't going to wait for Clancy to get out of the bathroom. She was going to get her coat on and walk up to the house and see how mom and baby were doing.

And then, like it or not, she was going to have to ride back to town with him on that damned ATV. But that was the end.

She could either wallow in the past and rail against the present, or she could make a choice of her own: to finally move on with her life. Without Jacob or Clancy or the phantoms that would bang at her door whenever she saw him.

Maybe this had been about closure. She'd needed to know how the story turned out. And now she did.

Just like that, a long chapter in her life slammed shut.

As they headed back to town an hour later, Hollee only had one thought: she hoped like hell she was strong enough to leave it shut.

CHAPTER TEN

Two weeks and counting, and it still hurt.

It was Christmas Eve. The artificial trees in the hospital foyer still blazed with lights and fake snowflakes still twirled from the ceiling, but the holiday had lost its luster somehow.

And she knew exactly the reason.

Clancy had disappeared from the hospital a few days after they'd got back. The official word was that he'd taken a little personal time. But rumor had it that he was rejoining the military. And yet Clancy's shadow was still here. In the hospital newsletter about the trip to Bender, in the pictures of him as Santa that still circulated around the hospital from time to time.

Whoever had said it was better to have loved and lost hadn't known what the hell they were talking about. Because if she'd insisted on going straight back to the compound after delivering that baby, instead of agreeing to sleep over, she might not even know what she was losing. But standing here today...

She knew. And it hurt so much she could barely breathe.

She and Kristen had had a sit-down talk, and her

friend had vehemently disagreed with her for not going after Clancy. But how could she when he'd kept something so devastating from her?

When his life pattern was to walk away from anyone that might get too close?

He hadn't tried to contact her. She'd watched her phone for any signs that she'd missed a call. She hadn't.

She was just turning in the last of her paperwork for her shift when Ava appeared at the nurses' desk wearing an elf hat and long Christmas-tree earrings. Hollee smiled when she saw her, although her chest was tight.

Please, don't let her mention Clancy.

"You look festive."

"Thanks." Ava brushed one of the silver earrings and sent the bells on the tree jingling. "I have to wear this stuff while I can. Christmas is almost over."

Yes, it was. And right now she was glad.

"The baby?"

"She's fine. But Jen-Jen isn't who I came to talk about. Do you have a minute?"

Oh, Lord, this *was* about Clancy.

"I was just getting ready to leave, actually."

"It won't take long. And it's something you need to know."

A horrible thought hit her. "Is Clancy okay?"

"No. He's not."

Her lungs stalled. "Wh-what is it?"

Ava nodded toward the waiting room that was just down the hallway, setting those ridiculous earrings jingling. Once they got there, Hollee dropped into a chair, her heart clanging like a gong. "Ava, please, just tell me."

"I will, but I need to let you know about something else first. And I want you to know that I'm breaking a promise to Clancy in doing this."

"If he doesn't want you to tell me…"

"I have to. You'll see why in a minute. And I'm hoping it'll clear up a few things in the process."

This time Hollee didn't say anything, she just nodded for her to continue.

"It's about Jen-Jen's christening."

Maybe this didn't have anything to do with Clancy after all. "Please, don't feel pressured to invite me—"

Ava held up her hand. "Not only are you invited, but I want you to be her godmother."

Before she had a chance to digest that bit of information or respond to it, her friend continued.

"Jen-Jen's middle name is changing, though. I'm so sorry, Hollee. Clancy told me something that I didn't want to believe."

A chill washed through her, raising bumps along her arms. So he'd told Ava but not her? Wait, but Ava had been going to name the baby after Jacob, so she had to have found out recently.

"I think I know what you're going to say, and I already know. When did he tell you?"

"Just before Jen-Jen was discharged from the hospital."

"Before…" Which meant Ava had known before she and Clancy had made love that first time. Before they'd left for Bender. And he'd still kept it from her, even as they'd been intimate.

"Clancy told me you didn't know. He made me promise not to say anything."

"I wish he hadn't. I can't believe he didn't try to contact me. Not once. All this time, I thought that Jacob was…" She shut her eyes. "I deserved to know. I felt like such a fool when I finally found out."

"Which probably explains why Clancy is suddenly so set on getting back into the army. Did you guys have a fight?"

"You could say that." She wasn't about to tell her that she and her brother had slept together. On more than one occasion.

Ava leaned forward and laid a hand on her arm. "Listen, Hollee, we can talk about Jen-Jen and all the other stuff later. I don't want to pry, but Clancy cares about you. Probably more than you realize."

Did it matter? He'd joked about lying being a sin when he'd been maintaining the biggest lie of all, allowing her to think Jacob was someone he wasn't.

She couldn't think of anything to say, and maybe Ava took that as her cue to continue. "I am pretty sure he cared about you even before you and Jacob started dating. But I know my brother well enough to know that he wasn't going to step between you and his best friend. I think Jacob probably had a hand in that."

"You're wrong. Clancy dated pretty hot and heavy back then. He had a new girlfriend almost every week. He cared about me as a friend and that was it."

Ava stretched her legs out, crossing them at the

ankles. The leggings she wore were also Christmas themed. "I remember his dating life suddenly going on hiatus for a few weeks before it picked up again. I'm pretty sure it was just before you went out with Jacob that first time."

Clancy had told her that kissing her had been a mistake. She'd been so hurt and angry, that when Jacob had asked her out, she'd accepted his invitation. The more she'd seen how easy it was for Clancy to slide in and out of relationships, the more she realized she did not want a man like that. And so what had started out as a revenge date had morphed into an "I want a man like this, and not that" manifesto. She'd convinced herself that she loved Jacob, but maybe she'd been in love with the idea of what he represented. Someone who'd been happy to remain monogamous. Only he hadn't been, according to Clancy.

"Does it matter?"

"Not to me. But someday it might to you." She uncrossed her legs and climbed to her feet, a batch of reindeer bracelets clanking together at her wrist. "I'm his sister. I know him. And I'm telling you, that man is hurting right now. And that's all I'm going to say on that matter. I just thought you should know."

"Thank you." She hugged her friend and then headed for the door. There was no sense in being angry with Ava. None of this had anything to do with her. But it did give her a lot to think about.

Had she been rash in walking out of that cabin before they'd finished talking? Possibly. But she wasn't sure what to do about it now.

Clancy had told her that kissing her had been a mistake ten years ago, and he'd told her the very same thing two weeks ago. And she'd believed him. Both times.

But what if he'd been lying?

Maybe she should be focusing on that rather than on his choices from a long time ago. She'd hurled a lot of hurtful words at him. Had she expected him to just stand there and take it, and then start whimpering about how sorry he was? No. That was not how that proud, bull-headed man's brain worked.

And she'd been pretty bull-headed herself.

So what was she going to do about it?

First thing, she was going to call the army and see if he actually had re-enlisted. And if she found him and he refused to listen to her?

The thought sent a river of regret streaming through her.

If he wouldn't, then she was going to have to accept that whatever had happened between her and Clancy was over and done with. And there was absolutely nothing she could do about it.

Hollee arrived in front of her house feeling like her mind was full of sludge, much like what that ATV had traversed that day in Bender. Only she wasn't up to wading through it right now.

The last shift at the hospital had been stressful and busy, and Ava's words had sent a spear through her heart. Right now she just wanted to crawl into bed with her dog. Only Tommie missed Gordy. She hadn't whined or barked, but she did sit in front of the door listening for any sounds. And when she did hear something, she cocked her head and inched closer, tail thumping on the floor in the entryway. But it was never Clancy and Gordy.

Putting her key in the lock, she went in and closed the door behind her.

Tommie wasn't there to greet her, which was odd. "Hey, girl," she called out. "I'm home."

Still nothing. A chill settled over her. Tommie was still fairly young, but with the problem she'd had with her eye, anything could have happened. Dropping her purse onto the entry table, she hurried into the living room, only to stop short.

A huge Christmas tree rested in the spot where Tommie's pillow normally sat. Okay, unless she was in the wrong house or hallucinating, that shouldn't be there. She hadn't put up a tree this year because of the trip. And when she'd arrived home she hadn't really been in a good place emotionally. So...

And then she looked closer and her mouth dropped open. The decorations on the tree looked eerily similar to the ones from Bender. But only the people who had been there knew about those. Was Kristen having a joke at her expense? Or trying to cheer her up? If so, it wasn't working.

"Kristen? Are you here?"

"She's not." A form stepped from behind the tree. "But I am."

"Clancy?" The buzzing of a million thoughts roved her brain, looking for some kind of logical explanation before settling on one thing. "Where are the dogs? And how did you get in?"

"Your mom, on both counts. They're staying the night with her."

"For the night. My mom...?" Her mother was in on whatever this was? Didn't she know that Hollee's heart was about to split in two? "I normally spend Christmas at their house."

"I know. Let's talk about that later, though. Will you come and sit with me?"

In a daze, she went to the couch and eased onto it, only to have Clancy sit right beside her. A small remote appeared in his hand and the tree suddenly lit up, its multicolored lights seeming to shift and change as the seconds ticked by in silence. Clear plastic strips dangled from the tree, just like the soda-bottle icicles one of the kids had made. And there was a garland...made of odds and ends of hardware.

She stared at it. "How...? Where...? That garland..."

"I made another trip to Bender two days ago. Randy's dad let me raid his found-items bucket, which is now a fifty-five-gallon drum, since everyone is eager to help him with the building project."

"You went there?" She turned to look at him. "But why?"

"I'll tell you, but first I need to apologize. For keeping the truth about Jacob from you."

"Even Ava knew." A new wave of hurt washed over her.

"Not until she chose Jay for Jen-Jen's middle name."

"You still should have told me. A long time ago. When I could have done something about it."

"I would have, if Jacob didn't come clean to you."

She frowned. "But he didn't."

"I know. He told me he would, but he didn't get the chance. His chopper crashed before he came off deployment." He turned to look at the tree. "And once I knew for certain he was dead, when should I have told you? While we were standing over his grave at the cemetery?"

She saw his point. "If Jacob had lived and refused to tell me—"

"I would have outed him. I told him I would, and he had no doubt that I would follow through."

Glancing back at the tree, she was amazed at how closely he'd replicated the one from Bender. And he'd done it all while she'd been at work.

Ava had told her something else, and she could only move forward if she knew the truth. "You kissed me once. A long time ago."

"I know."

"But then…all those girls. You couldn't change them out fast enough."

"I think you can probably guess why. Jacob told me he loved you and the last thing you needed was someone like me messing up your life. Well, he didn't say it in so many words, but I knew myself well enough to know it was true. Jacob was on the fast track to success, while I was too busy having fun and cutting every corner I could find. So before I got the chance to fulfill his prophesy… I bowed out." He shrugged. "Was it the right decision? I don't know. What I can tell you is that I am not the same person I was back then."

"So what you said about it being a mistake?" Suddenly all the pieces slid into place, and she knew Ava's timeline statement was right on the mark. And maybe Jacob had even known what had gone on between them. It had always seemed like such a coincidence that he'd asked her outright as Clancy had seemingly cast her aside. But she would never really know her late husband's motivation.

"That kiss *was* a mistake. But not for me. For you."

Her heart clutched inside her and she chose her next words carefully. "And all those girls?"

"A smokescreen. And, no, I haven't been on a date… a real date…in a couple of years." He put his hands on her shoulders and turned her toward him. "If Jacob had never convinced me of how wrong I was for you, and if I'd asked you out, what would you have said?"

She sensed this was important. Very important. "I would have said yes, Clancy. I was ready to say yes. But you never gave me that chance."

"I know that now."

The time to be angry about the past was over. She could either sit here and fume and push him away, or she could try to understand the thought processes of a very young man who had just been reaching adulthood. Wasn't there a wise man who'd said that the greatest show of love was when someone laid down his life for his friends? Clancy hadn't laid down his life, but he had sacrificed himself. For her. And from the way Ava had talked, it had been a pretty big sacrifice.

"The past belongs to the past, time to make a new beginning."

"What?"

"Just something someone once found in a fortune cookie." And something she needed to take to heart.

He was here to tell her something important. The tree was the key to it, since he'd taken the time to replicate it.

She touched his face and gestured toward the tree. "Tell me why you did this."

"I messed up ten years ago. I wanted to make sure I didn't mess up again." He captured her hand. "Those kids in Bender made a huge impact on me, especially Randy and his dad. The way he said he was going to rebuild that town using the items he'd collected from the rubble of the past. So this is me, letting these things symbolize our past and hopefully using them to build a future. *Our* future. I love you, Hollee."

Had he really just said that?

"Ava said you cared. But I didn't think… I heard you were rejoining the military."

"I almost did, and then I realized it would be one more mistake to add to my list."

She laughed. "We could have a debate about who's made more of them, but now isn't the time."

"No, it's not."

"So you're not *in* the military?"

He squeezed her hand. "No. My commanding officer told me to go home and not to come back until I'd thought long and hard about it. So this is me, thinking long and hard."

Her eyes watered. "Then please don't go. Not this time."

Wrapping his arms around her, he pulled her against his chest. And the rightness of that was almost overwhelming. Hot tears splashed onto her cheeks, running into his shirt when she thought about all they'd lost. But more than that, about what they stood to gain by finally making things right.

"I was hoping you'd say that. I tried to show you with the tree, wanted it to be our starting point. As long as you love me back."

"I do. I realized I loved you when you gave your stethoscope to Randy. I may have even loved you ten years ago, but I was so young. Too young to really know my own heart."

He kissed her tears away and then slid his arm around her shoulders. "I want this garland to grow. To come to represent our lives. Good moments and bad, with us adding something to it every year until we're both old and gray and this string stretches for miles with the things that make us...us."

He pulled a tiny box from his pocket, and Hollee clapped a hand over her mouth.

Snapping open the top, he revealed a ring, one that was very different from the ornate band Jacob had given her. Instead it was a ruby, her birthstone, set in a plain band of white gold. "I know it's not a traditional diamond but—"

"It's perfect, Clancy. So very perfect."

His eyes met hers, the brown irises glowing in a way she'd never seen before. "Does that mean you'll marry me and help me add to our Christmas tree? And maybe even our family tree?"

Family...

"You want to have…"

"Children? Yes."

Her eyes closed, and the joy that had been slowly expanding in her chest was eclipsed by a huge burst of love for this man. They'd both made mistakes, but she wasn't going to make one now. There was only one possible answer to his question. "Yes, Clancy. Oh, yes."

He kissed her, his mouth seeking, asking in a way that needed no words. And she answered him in the same way.

And when he got up from the couch and swung her into his arms, walking with purposeful strides toward the back of her house, she laughed. "I see we're wasting no time in this family endeavor."

"We're not. Because the dogs are at your mom's house, but they'll be back tomorrow morning. And if we have that little addition I mentioned earlier, this may be the only time we're truly alone for many, many years."

She took one last look at the tree with its garland and wound her arms around his neck. Maybe that tree would never come down. Maybe she would teach their children what it meant, so that they too would grow up with a sense of wonder, knowing anything was possible.

If they just loved hard enough to make it happen.

EPILOGUE

HOLLEE HELD OUT her arms for her new baby girl. Somehow it was fitting that she had been born on Christmas Eve. She and Clancy had just sat down to enjoy the falling snow with glasses of eggnog—his with rum, hers without—when she'd felt a sharp twinge. And then another. Soon they'd been coming with enough frequency that there was no ignoring them.

And Clancy, who was normally as solid as a rock, had done the cute New Dad Shuffle as he'd fumbled to grab her overnight bag and call Hollee's mom to ask her to check on the dogs. In between laughing at his impatience when she'd tried to catch snowflakes on her tongue and the care he'd taken with making sure she hadn't slipped on the way into the hospital, she'd watched him with a sense of wonder and love that only grew deeper each day.

Her parents and Clancy's mom hadn't been nearly as shocked by the news that they were getting married as she'd expected them to be. Instead, they'd celebrated with them, even when Hollee had insisted on having an intimate ceremony with a justice of the peace and close family only. Her first wedding had been a lavish affair that had felt wrong in so many ways. She'd grieved about not confronting Clancy about that kiss being a mistake when it had counted the most. But Clancy had told her to let it go, that they'd both done what they'd thought was right at the time. Love had won in the end, and that was all that mattered.

And it was a good lesson to teach their baby. Or babies. Clancy wanted one more, and since she'd thought she'd never have even one, she was thrilled.

And they would all make a pilgrimage to Bender, Virginia, as soon as they were able to. She wanted to visit Randy and help where she could.

Her husband perched on the side of the bed as the nurses cleared away the labor equipment. He leaned over and kissed her forehead. "Well, first Jen-Jen and now our Elissa Marie. My mom is getting two grand-children in a little over a year."

"And my parents are getting their first. They're thrilled. Have you called them yet?"

"Right after I caught my breath, yes. But I asked everyone to wait about an hour before arriving en masse. I want you two all to myself for a little while. And you need to get some rest."

She reached up and touched his face, sliding her fingers over those beloved scars. She held off his frown by whispering, "They're sexy. And I love you."

"You're changing the subject."

"There'll be plenty of time to sleep. I'm so afraid I'll wake up and find out this is all a dream."

Just then Elissa let out a howl that threatened to take down the hospital.

Clancy laughed. "Definitely not a dream."

"Yes, it is. But as long as it's happening while I'm awake, it's okay."

Hollee had left the Christmas tree up all year and, true to what they'd said, they'd added their first piece to the garland, a hand-carved Santa to represent that day at the hospital when they'd both realized something special was happening between them. Clancy had actually insisted on having the picture of them from the newsletter framed, editing poor Kristen right out of the shot.

"Believe me, you are wide awake, sweetheart. And beautiful. I love you, Hollee."

"Love you too."

He leaned down, encompassing her and the baby in a hug that made her already mushy emotions even mushier.

She sighed, cradling her precious baby in her arms. "I'm so grateful, Clance. So very grateful."

"So am I."

Glancing out the hospital window, she saw the snow was still falling, the big fluffy flakes sticking to the glass and gathering on the sill. "It's almost Christmas."

"Yes, it is. Although I think Christmas arrived a few hours early. Elissa is the greatest gift I could possibly imagine."

She leaned her head against his arm. "Do you think Tommie and Gordy will accept her?"

"Are you kidding? They're going to love her. I'm sure of it." He paused, and she could sense he wanted to say something.

"What?" A curl of fear went through her before she forced it away. There was nothing to be afraid of. Not anymore.

"Would it be okay, if a friend of mine came over to see the baby?"

"Of course. Who is it?"

"My commanding officer. The one who talked me out of re-enlisting and told me to stay and fight for what I wanted."

She smiled. "I'm glad he did. Because if not…"

"I'd like to think I would have eventually gotten there. He just gave me a push when I needed it most."

Wiggling back to the far edge of the bed, she nodded at the space next to her. "Lie down with me, Clance. Because you're right. I'm sleepy. But I promised myself I was never sleeping without you ever again."

Clancy took the baby and laid her carefully in her bassinet and then slid onto the narrow mattress beside his wife, draping his arm over her. "Sleep. I'll watch over you both."

So, with the promise that he would be there when she woke up, she let herself relax against his lean frame. She was the luckiest girl on the planet.

As he tightened his arm around her she amended that thought. Make that two girls…they were the luckiest *two* girls on the planet. And she would make sure Clancy knew just how much he was loved.

This Christmas and every other.

* * * * *

SECOND CHANCE WITH THE SURGEON

ROBIN GIANNA

MILLS & BOON

Thank you to Dr. Ray Kobus
for putting my wrist back together again!

Also thanks to the wonderful occupational therapists
who helped me take it from useless, post-surgery, to
close to normal. Kathy, Janet, Paula and Heather—
you all are fun and fabulous! I would have expected
to be thrilled, walking out the door of the therapy
clinic for the last time after three months of visits,
but knowing I wouldn't be seeing you anymore
made it bittersweet. You all are the best! xoxo

CHAPTER ONE

"DOWN! DOWN, HUDSON. *DOWN!*"

Apparently the dog decided he didn't need to take her seriously because she was laughing, and he enthusiastically licked her face. She gave up for a moment and hugged his big body. How was it possible he'd grown so huge, when the shelter had guessed he'd be about average-sized? She was pretty sure that average-sized dogs couldn't slap their paws on your shoulders in greeting, but then again she'd known he was special the second she'd met him.

"You're such a good boy. I'm happy to see you, too." She grinned and shoved at his paws to take a quick step sideways—only nearly to trip when her other dog, a Yorkshire Terrier not much bigger than a city rat, bit down on her pant leg.

"No snagging my pants with your little dagger teeth, Yorkie. *Off.* Off, please!"

She yanked her leg loose and the slight unsteadiness of the movement didn't embarrass her anymore, the way it had when she'd been a child and even for a long time after she'd had surgery as a teen. Growing up with her legs different lengths hadn't exactly helped her fit in with the crowd, and had invited the kind of nasty teasing bullies were infamous for. Good thing those days were over. Now most people couldn't even tell she'd been a misfit for much of her life.

She crouched down to give Yorkie a hug, too, and the rambunctious greeting from her pups made her smile. Nothing like the unconditional love of dogs, was there? You didn't have to worry whether they really wanted to be with you, or were disappointed in you, or embarrassed by you. They just loved you, period.

"All right, I know you two are bored after being stuck in here all day. But working the early shift means I'm home early today! Plenty of time for a walk before it's dark."

The word *walk* incited yipping and excitement as Jillian walked the six steps it took her to get to the tiny bedroom in her New York City apartment, where she'd barely managed to squeeze in a double bed and a small dresser. It was an apartment that hadn't been designed to hold two dogs—especially one nearly the size of a motor scooter.

Familiar pain and regret stabbed at her heart when she thought about why she was living there instead of in the much more spacious apartment she and the pups had lived in before. The place they'd shared with her ex-husband until, after barely a year, their marriage had disintegrated. The place she'd heard through the grapevine he'd sold in order to move into an even bigger penthouse apartment in an even more exclusive area of the city. A place she'd fit into even less than she had before.

But there was no point in thinking about that anymore, was there? Her short marriage was over and done with.

From the first second her eyes had met her ex-husband's she'd felt as if the ground beneath her feet had shifted. It had been an earthquake like nothing she'd experienced before and she hadn't been able to escape.

It had taken only two dates for her attraction to morph from starry-eyed to head over heels in love with the man, and they had eloped into a dizzyingly fast and wonderful wedding even as her worried inner voice had told her all along it was too good to be true. She had always known, deep inside, that she wasn't the kind of woman who could measure up to being the wife of a man like super-surgeon, jet-setting, workaholic Dr. Conor McCarthy.

Unbidden, a vision of his dazzling smile, his messy thatch of blond hair and his heartbreakingly handsome face came into her mind. She squeezed her eyes shut, willing all that sexiness to go away. The fact that she just might have to see it for real every day made her stomach physically hurt.

How could she face having to work with him again?

Last week her boss at Occupational Therapy Consultants had told her she had to go back to the company where she'd met and worked with Conor, and the horror of it had made her feel so woozy she'd had to sit down. Apparently OTC was shifting its focus to work exclusively on lower body therapy, instead of hands and wrists, which meant she had to transfer back to HOAC, the hand and arm orthopedic center owned by Conor.

She knew that seeing him all the time would rip off the scab on her heart that was still healing, and she feared it might start bleeding all over again if that had to happen.

Escape was the only answer, and she prayed the job interview she had set up for next week in Connecticut would get her out of New York City and away from Conor. Housing there would be a lot cheaper, too, which would mean a bigger place for her and the dogs. And, while she'd miss the city and her friends, a move there would be a good thing.

At least she hoped it would be good. But, regardless, there was no way she could work again at the place where she'd have to see and sometimes share patients with Conor McCarthy.

She drew in a calming breath. No point in worrying about it this second.

Banishing all those scary thoughts from her head, she quickly changed from her work clothes into leggings and sneakers and a snug jacket. It was a surprisingly nice day for December in New York City, and she planned to take advantage of every moment of it before gray skies and cold and snow blanketed the city. To enjoy every minute of this crazy and wonderful place before she had to move away.

When the dogs saw the leashes in her hands their tails wagged so hard their entire rear ends wagged along with them, and Yorkie briefly danced around on his short back legs, helping her smile again. At least she still had these two. The two puppies she and Conor had chosen together at the shelter the very first week after their honeymoon.

Her heart pinched all over again at the memory of that day, and of their seemingly idyllic perfect days together until it all had fallen apart.

"Come on, you two!" she said, practically jogging them to the elevator in her hurry to breathe in some fresh air and banish the depressing thoughts that seemed stuck on repeat. "It's warmer today than yesterday, so this walk will be a nice long one. Happy about that?"

Tongues hung out in doggie smiles as they moved out to streets still lit by the low evening sun and all walked briskly toward the park, a few blocks away.

When they turned the corner they came face to face with two black dogs almost as big as Hudson, accompanied by a small elderly man. Normally Hudson and Yorkie were good around other dogs, but the second the other two saw her animals they growled and bared their teeth, which sent Yorkie onto his rear legs, barking furiously back.

"It's okay. Okay, guys," Jill said.

She turned to see if there was any way they could quickly cross the street. But traffic streamed through the green light, and just as she was tugging the dogs around the light pole to head in a different direction, the aggressive dogs lunged.

Hudson leaped away, pulling Jill with him into a stumble, and Yorkie rushed under his legs toward the other dogs.

Trying to firmly plant her feet, she felt a slight feeling of panic fill her chest as she worked to get her two dogs reined in. She could hear the man shouting, see him trying to control his dogs, but her two had got their leashes wrapped around the light pole, and as she tried to unwrap them she was yanked off her feet.

In one split second she went from standing to slamming onto the hard concrete, catching herself with her right hand, and the moment she hit the sidewalk she cried out at the intense pain radiating up her arm.

Damn it! Squeezing her eyes shut at the searing pain and the reality of the situation, she clutched the leashes with one hand and knew, just *knew*, without a single doubt, that her wrist was broken. How was she going to handle her dogs now?

"Sorry!" the man said breathlessly.

Jill blinked up at him and could see the light had changed. Thank the Lord he was now hurrying across the street, putting distance between her dogs and his. Gingerly, she rose to a sitting position and frowned down at her already swelling wrist.

A woman leaned over her, grabbed the dogs' leashes and finished untangling them from the pole and each other. "You okay?"

"Maybe not."

Shaking now, Jill struggled to get her bag unzipped to fish for her phone. Then she realized she had no one who could come and get the dogs while she went to an ER or to urgent care. Not her OT friends, who never answered their personal phones when they were working. Not her parents, who still lived in her home state of Pennsylvania, nor her sister, who lived in New Jersey and was out of town for work.

And not Conor. Not anymore.

"I need to get home."

"I'll help you with your dogs. You live very far?"

"No. Just a couple blocks. Thank you… I… Thanks so much. I've hurt my wrist and the dogs might be hard to handle on my own."

"Happy to help. Come!" The woman gave a quick tug on the dogs' leashes and they both dutifully came to stand quietly next to her.

"You're obviously an experienced dog-handler," Jill said, trying to smile. "And at this moment my guardian angel, I think."

"Ways to be a guardian angel don't come by too often, so you're making my day. Except that you're hurt, which I'm sure sorry has happened," she said. "I'm Barbara Smith. You need help getting up?"

"No, I…I'm okay."

Using her good hand to awkwardly push herself to her feet, Jill knew she was definitely not okay, and prayed it was a simple break. Nothing that would require surgery or weeks of the kind of therapy she helped her own patients with.

But, looking at the odd angle of her wrist, and the fact that it was already discoloring, she had a bad feeling she wouldn't be that lucky.

"Then show me where you live, dear, so you can get that wrist looked at."

"It's just a couple blocks north. I'm Jillian Keyser, by the way."

"I'd say it's nice to meet you—but the circumstances aren't very nice, are they?"

"Unfortunately, no."

Pain still radiating up her arm, she held it protectively against her stomach as they walked the few blocks to her apartment building. She didn't feel much like talking, which worked out fine because Barbara kept up a cheerful monologue about dogs and the city and the parks she often took her own animals to.

Beyond glad to finally get her pets inside the door, Jill turned to her guardian angel in the flesh. "I can't tell you how much I appreciate your help. Truly. I…I'm not sure what I'd have done if you hadn't been there when it happened."

"No thanks necessary. I was lucky to be in the right place at the right time."

"Thank you again."

The door clicked closed. Jill drew several steadying breaths before she struggled one-handedly to get the dogs fresh water, then debated what to do next.

The surgery center she'd worked at before her divorce had some of the best hand and wrist surgeons in New York City. One of them being her ex-husband. She'd been at her job at OTC for ten months, which had given her some idea about the other surgeons out there, but the truth was she felt more comfortable reaching out to someone she knew well. Someone she knew would fit her in right away for an X-ray, and who wouldn't blab about it to Conor McCarthy if Jill asked her not to.

She grabbed her cell phone, drew another deep breath, then dialed HOAC. The awkwardness of doing it made her think about how hard it was going to be to function with only one usable hand. Her years of working as an occupational therapist had told her a lot about how handicapping it was, but she had a feeling that having her own struggles would be eye-opening.

"Hi, this is Jillian Keyser. I used to be a OT there. Hey, Katy! Yeah, long time no see. Um…can I speak with Dr. Beth Crenshaw? Believe it or not, I'm pretty sure I've broken my wrist."

"Looks like a fairly light surgery schedule today," Conor McCarthy said to the two other orthopedic surgeons in the men's locker room as they changed into scrubs.

"Yeah. Glad the snow and ice season is coming. It's good for business," Bill Radcliff joked.

Conor couldn't help but chuckle, knowing Bill was kidding. "Don't let your patients hear that, or it'll be all over social media how you like to see people slip and fall so you can fix them up."

"It's an unfortunate reality that our jobs entail being there for people after they hurt themselves, and my patients love me for it." Bill grinned. "Always confounded, though, by the folks who decide to take up running in the winter, instead of getting into the groove while the weather's nice. Wouldn't you love to know what percentage end up falling and breaking something?"

"Yeah…"

The mention of runners made Conor think of Jillian, which sent all amusement from his chest, leaving it feeling hollow. A vision of her slender body in running tights or shorts that showed her shapely legs immediately came into his mind, along with her beautiful smile and the cute messy bun she always wore her hair in when she ran.

He'd loved seeing that bun bounce as she ran out the door almost every day, probably trying to make up for not being able to run for so many years. She'd told him that after the leg-length discrepancy she'd been born with had been surgically repaired in her teens, running had been the first thing she'd wanted to do. He'd always admired the hell out of her for her determination to overcome what some would have thought a handicap.

The ache in his chest almost physically hurt, and he dropped his hand when he realized he'd been unconsciously rubbing it over his sternum, as though he could somehow soothe his stupid broken heart. He'd have expected that after nearly a year apart he wouldn't be reminded of her by the least thing, but obviously he was nowhere near getting over Jillian Keyser.

"You close to finalizing that deal with Urgent Care Manhattan to partner with us? That would be huge, if they could move in next door now that the space is vacant," Bill said. "We're all counting on you making it happen."

"I have a meeting with them today, as a matter of fact. Hoping to close on it soon—before our competition woos them with an offer they think they can't refuse."

"I know you have a lot on your plate, but you're still planning to be chairman once the companies merge, right? With you there, making sure they're both managed the way they should be, I've got my check already written as an investor."

"Believe me, I'm going to make it happen and I'll

have them running as smooth as a Wall Street banker. So get your checkbook ready."

Conor took a last swig of coffee and headed toward the OR to find his surgery schedule. Studying the paper in his hand, he walked past several patients being prepped for surgery in cubicles only partly curtained off—and then the sound of a woman speaking caught his ears and he stopped dead.

He turned to see the owner of the melodic voice and felt his heart drop into his stomach. Her body was wrapped in a hospital gown, her usual sweet smile was on her face, and her hair tumbled across her cheek as she exchanged comments with the prep nurse and an anesthesiologist.

"Jillian? What the...?"

She looked up and his eyes met the gorgeous ones he'd missed so much. A mesmerizing mix of green and gray and gold—like clouds on the horizon with the sunlight shimmering through.

Damn it. The connection between them was still there. In spite of everything he could feel the electric zing of it, and his breath caught in his lungs.

Then she blinked, and her gaze shifted to the hallway behind him. Her smile flatlined and her lips twisted into a grimace before she looked at him again, cool now, all that feeling of connection gone.

"Oh. Hi, Conor. I...I broke my wrist. Distal radius fracture. Beth is putting in a plate and screws this morning to put it back together."

"How? What happened?"

"I took the dogs for a walk. A couple of big dogs

weren't very friendly, Yorkie freaked out, and we got all tangled up—next thing you know, I'm flat on the sidewalk."

"Ah, hell. Is it your right hand?" He stepped closer to reach for it carefully, and the feel of her soft hand in his felt so good his heart got all twisted up—which bothered him no end.

What was wrong with him? No matter how hard he'd fallen for her, he should never have married Jillian in the first place. He'd learned the hard way that he wasn't husband material any more than his father had been, obviously having inherited his bad DNA. He'd had a selfish, cold father and a mother who'd twisted herself into knots trying to somehow make his father happy—until the day he'd left. Which had made a bad home situation dramatically worse.

Their eyes met again, and he knew the pain and sadness he saw there had nothing to do with her wrist and everything to do with him. God knew he'd wanted his own marriage to be different. But she'd been right to leave. The last thing a special woman like Jillian needed was to be tied to a man who made her miserable.

Except he couldn't lie to himself. In the ten months since she'd been gone he'd thought of her every day and every night, missing her even as he'd forcibly reminded himself how much he'd hurt her. Disappointed her.

"Yeah. No fun, but I'll get through it."

"Titanium time!" Dr. Beth Crenshaw appeared in the curtained doorway with a grin that faltered a little when she saw Conor standing there. "Hey, Conor. Surprise, surprise, huh?"

"Definitely a surprise." It took some effort to release Jill's hand before he folded his arms across his chest. "Why is it no one has told me this happened? That Jill is having surgery here today?"

"Because I asked her not to tell you," Jill said in a stiff voice. "No reason for you to know."

The truth of that stabbed his chest all over again. "Maybe not, but I would have liked to know anyway. Who's taking you home post-op?"

As soon as he asked the question his heart jolted. If she had a new guy Conor hoped and prayed he wouldn't have to see him with her in Recovery.

"I asked Ellie next door. She's the only person I know who has a car."

"Wait. Isn't she the one who's about eighty and has a bum knee?"

Her lips twisted again, this time in a wry smile. "I know it's not ideal, taking advantage of her good nature when she has a tough time getting around. But they won't let me take a taxi by myself, as you well know."

"You should have told me you were having trouble finding someone," Beth said. "I can take you home. You'll just have to hang around in Recovery until the end of the day. You'll still be partially out of it for a bit, anyway. I assume you have a friend to take care of you tonight? You know you shouldn't be alone."

"I think Kandie from the other office is planning to stop by and check on me at some point. And my sister's coming sometime later this week. But she's got a big project at work and can't take off right now."

"I can't believe you haven't figured all this out already." Conor looked from Jill to Beth, then back. "She'll be coming back tomorrow to get the cast off, right? And what about the dogs? Plus, your sister's work schedule is almost as bad as mine, so how can you count on her to get here soon?"

"You know, I appreciate your concern, but frankly I don't see how this is any of your business," Jill said, her chin jutting out with that mulish look he was all too familiar with. At the same time he could see plain as day that she felt anxious about how she was going to manage everything post-op. "The dogs and I will be okay."

"Considering you've seen hundreds of patients, and know how they feel the day the cast comes off and you work with them to make a splint, I'm pretty sure you know how much pain you'll likely be in. How completely non-functional your arm and hand will be at first. Hudson's a big lug—not to mention there's no way you can take them outside for a walk. Not for quite a while—until your bones and the titanium plate and screws have fused. If you fall again before that happens it could be a disaster."

"I won't fall. And there are dog-walking services, you know," Jill said. "I...I didn't think to look one up before surgery, but I'm sure I can find one. And, like I said, Briana is coming as soon as she can."

"Let me check to see if there's a nurse or one of the office staff who wouldn't mind making some cash by helping you tonight and bringing you back tomorrow. Walking the dogs, too," Beth said, looking from him to Jill, then back. "Meanwhile, we have to get you into twilight sleep and to the OR—or the whole day's schedule will be messed up, which nobody wants."

Obviously Beth's calm tone was designed to keep Conor from getting upset about this, but it wasn't working. Jillian might not be his anymore, but that didn't mean he didn't still care about her. Wouldn't worry about her.

"I have a light surgery schedule this morning, so I can take you home," he said. "Though I do have a—"

Abruptly, he closed his mouth. He'd almost followed his comment about taking her home by telling her he had an appointment at one o'clock with some of the decision-makers from Urgent Care Manhattan, to go over the details of the potential collaboration with HOAC. Telling her that he'd take her home when the meeting was over. But his work and business schedules had been part of the reason why she'd left and how badly he'd failed her.

But this was an emergency, damn it. Much as he hated any delay in getting the deal closed, his competitor shut out and the urgent care department up and running, he'd just have to reschedule the meeting.

"I'll come to Recovery as soon as I'm done with my last surgery and I'll take you home. Get you settled."

"Conor, no." Despite her obvious need, her beautiful eyes widened in clear dismay. "I—"

"Perfect," Beth interrupted cheerfully. "I'll meet you in Recovery. And now, Jill, it's time for Dr. Fixit to fix you up."

Jillian opened her pretty lips to protest more, which

tightened his chest. Was it really that horrifying for her to have to spend a few hours with him?

Conor watched the anesthesiologist administer twilight anesthesia through Jill's IV. Her long lashes swept her cheeks as her lids slid closed, and he forced himself to turn away from her beautiful face in sweet repose. She looked very much as she had back when he'd held her in his arms every night as she fell asleep.

Damn. That ache pressed in on his chest again, but at the same time his heart strangely, bizarrely, lifted. He was going to get to be with her this evening for the first time in nearly a year. Drugged up and in pain, she wouldn't be like the smiling Jillian he'd loved. But knowing that she needed help, that he could be there for her at least for a few hours, made him feel better than he'd felt in a long time.

And never mind that the hollow loneliness he knew he'd experience when he went back to his regular life without her in it might feel every bit as bad as when she'd first left.

CHAPTER TWO

CONOR DOUBLE-PARKED IN the loading zone outside Jillian's apartment building and prayed he wouldn't get a ticket—or, worse, towed. Presumably it wouldn't take long to get her into her apartment and comfortable, and he could get the car to the parking garage down the street after that.

He jumped out of the car and ran around to open the passenger door. "Okay, I know you're still feeling weak and weird, so I'm going to hold you up in case your legs feel wobbly."

Her eyes blinked up at him and she nodded. He reached into the car to place his hands around her waist, pretty much lifting her out of the seat—which wasn't easy, considering she couldn't help much and he was worried about jostling her arm. Not that he needed to be concerned that he'd hurt her. It was covered in a cast and an elastic cover and would stay totally numb from the nerve-block for at least twelve hours.

"You're doing great," he said as she walked slowly beside him to the front doors of the building, keeping his arm wrapped around her waist to keep her steady.

Thank God he'd had the foresight to get her keys before they got out of the car. It would have been a serious juggling match trying to get them out of the pocket of the jacket he'd draped over her shoulders without her falling down right there on the concrete steps.

Once they were in the building, maneuvering her to her apartment wasn't difficult. He'd only been there once—the day he'd brought the dogs over to live with her after she'd moved out—but he remembered exactly where it was. Had often pictured her there when he was lying in bed at night. Wondering how she was doing. Wishing he was a different kind of man. Wishing things could have gone differently for them. Wishing she hadn't stubbornly refused any money from him so she could live in a bigger place. He had hoped she was happier now, even as the thought of her being happy with someone else tore him up inside.

The moment he unlocked her door he heard the dogs running across the hardwood floor. Worried that Hudson might accidentally knock her over in her current wobbly state, he turned her sideways and put his body in between them as a buffer, reaching to scratch the dog's head.

"Sit, Hudson. That's a good dog. Good boy."

It tugged at his heart that the dog obviously remembered him, whining and thrashing his tail back and forth so hard his hind end went along with it. Yorkie leaped up and down on his short legs, too, equally excited to see him.

Damn it. Letting down Jillian had been the worst, but the dogs' happy greeting reminded him he'd let them down, too. She'd wanted them to have dogs and he'd gone along with it. Had wanted her to be happy. Wanted to know what it would be like to live a completely different kind of life from the one he'd grown up in. To love someone who loved you back and have a family that was always there for one another.

Instead he'd turned out to be a bad husband and bad dog dad, incapable of giving any of them what they needed. Thank God they hadn't had children for him to hurt, too. He'd failed at being there for his mother the way he should have been, and he had failed at being there for Jillian.

That dismal reality had shown him that the focus of his life had to be only on what he was good at—and that was surgery and business and building his bank account and portfolio. Lonely, maybe, but at least he wouldn't hurt the people he loved. He believed providing for them financially, for their future, was the best way to show his love.

Jillian hadn't agreed.

"Sit. Sit, you two."

He held up his hand to signal that he meant it, the way the dog trainers had shown him and Jill when they'd first gotten the puppies. Jillian tripping over the excited animals on their way to the sofa would *not* be good, and he was both glad and surprised that they actually did as he told them to.

"Jill, we're going to walk to the sofa. I'll be holding on to you, so try not to trip over Yorkie if he jumps around again."

"Okay. I'm not as unsteady as you think I am."

"That's good. But I'll hold on to you anyway."

Because the feel of her body in his arms felt better than anything had in a long time, even as the ache of his failures burned in his chest.

He eased her down on to the sofa. "You feel like sitting for a while? Or do you want to lie down in bed?"

"I feel okay. Just groggy. But I want to wake up, not go to sleep. Once I'm feeling more alert you can head on home. Or back to work, probably."

"I don't have any surgeries or patients to see this afternoon. And I canceled a meeting I had scheduled, so I'm all yours."

Or he had been once.

But for today, at least, he had this chance to be there for Jillian in a way he hadn't during their marriage, although at the same time he somehow needed to keep a cool head and an emotional distance. Except looking at her now, with her arm in its huge cast, her hair all messy and her expression a little vulnerable, he wanted to scoop her into his arms, sit on that sofa and hold her close. Kiss her face and stroke her hair until she relaxed against him.

Bad idea for both of them.

He cleared his throat. "You hungry? How about a little soup and toast, or something like that?"

"Maybe in a little bit. I'll just sit here for now. Why don't you take the dogs out? Their leashes are in that basket by the front door."

"Okay. Come on, you goofs."

Wagging tails and little leaps from Yorkie had him smiling despite the weight he felt in his chest at being here. At the memories of him and Jill during happy times together. He'd never expected to be a dog person, but he had loved spending time with them. Loved seeing how much Jill enjoyed them. In some ways that seemed like a long time ago, and in other ways it seemed like yesterday that they'd lived together and loved one another until it had all imploded.

Heaving a sigh, he took the dogs outside. They were better behaved on their walk than he remembered them being as puppies, and he had time to ponder how it was going to work out, him helping Jill. He was pretty confident that she'd be okay on her own most of the time, so long as he saw her every morning and evening and took care of the dogs until her sister showed up.

Problem was her apartment was a long way from work, while his was just a couple blocks away from the surgery center. Somehow he'd have to find extra hours in the day, or look for someone to walk the dogs.

The animals were panting by the time they got back to Jill's door, and he pulled her key from his pocket and tried to open the door quietly, in case she was sleeping—then wondered why he'd bothered when both dogs leaped into the room, making all kinds of racket on the wood floor.

Her eyes were closed when he looked across the room at her, but her lids lifted and she sent him a surprisingly sweet smile. Probably because the drugs hadn't worn off enough for her to remember that she didn't like him much anymore.

"Seems like you just left. Were the dogs good?"

"Really good. You've done a nice job training them."

"Don't think I can take a lot of credit. They just needed to mature a little bit. But they still have their moments, believe me."

"Moments like when they get upset at other dogs and get tangled up and make you fall and break your wrist?"

"Yeah. Like that."

Her lips curved even more, into the kind of laughing smile he'd fallen for like a ton of bricks when they'd first met, and it felt good to smile back.

He stepped closer and crouched down in front of her. "How you feeling?"

"Arm feels like someone attached a log to me. Can't feel it at all yet. Sometimes I forget and lean down, then it swings out and I have to grab it back. I know you always tell patients that's what it'll feel like, but I've gotta tell you... Much as it makes me want to laugh when I lose control of it, it feels super-weird."

"It'll be numb like that for at least another eight or nine hours. Then it'll feel tingly, like you've laid on it funny and it's gone to sleep. Then it'll finally feel normal."

"I think you mean my *new normal*—for now. Painful and immobile."

"Yeah." He stood and shoved his hands into his pockets so he wouldn't reach out and tuck those wisps of hair behind her ears, as he would have before. "You feel like eating something now? I can get some soup from the deli? Or does something else sound good?"

"Something light, like soup and crackers, sounds perfect."

"You got it."

It would be good to have something to do besides talk with her and look at her. From the first moment he'd seen her in the occupational therapy room two years ago, he felt like he'd been smacked in the head by some unexplainable force. She'd stood up from the table, her athletic runner's body in a slim-fitting dress, and her laughter at something her patient had said slipped into his chest. When her beautiful gray-green eyes had lifted to meet his he could have sworn his heart completely stopped.

Looking down at her now, he felt waves of tenderness mingle with memories of that day. He wished that he could take away the pain he knew she'd be in as soon as the brachial plexus block wore off. Felt the desire to pull her close, to take care of her, to make all that pain go away.

"I'll be right back."

He made himself turn away before he reached for her, and then left for the deli. He chose two kinds of the soup he knew she liked, and a bagful of crackers. When he came back and opened the door to her apartment he stopped abruptly when he saw she wasn't on the sofa, and neither one of the dogs were in sight, either.

No way would she have decided to venture out while still half drugged up. Would she?

A panicked sensation rose in his chest and he strode to the galley kitchen, shoved the food onto the counter, then moved to her bedroom. "Jill? Jilly?"

One of the dogs whined before she answered. "In here. The bathroom. I... Go ahead and come in."

He pushed open the door. Was stunned to see both

dogs and Jillian sitting on the floor of the tiny room. Her sweatpants were twisted around her thighs and her good hand was held to her forehead.

He dropped to his knees. "What the hell happened? Did you hurt yourself?"

"Kind of. I'm so stupid. I had to go to the bathroom, and while I was sitting here I dropped the new roll of toilet paper. I leaned over to get it. Forgot all about my arm. It flung forward and dragged me off the toilet. I landed right on my cast and hit my head on the wall. Kind of funny, really."

She sent him an adorable crooked smile and his heart squeezed even tighter. He grasped her wrist to lift her palm from her forehead. "Let me see."

"Just a bump. Not a big deal."

"Maybe not compared to your broken wrist, but it still hurts, I bet." He wanted to lean down and kiss the offending red lump, and drew in a deep breath to quell the urge. "Let's get some ice on it."

He wrapped his arm around her back to help her up, and realized she was having trouble standing.

"You hurt your leg, too?"

"No. I just… I couldn't get my stupid pants pulled up using only one hand while sitting on the floor."

He lifted her to her feet. "Hang on to the sink while I finish pulling them up so you can walk."

"This is ridiculously embarrassing," she said, her face now stained pink and no longer smiling. "My ex-husband having to pull up my pants."

"Just think of me as your doctor. Not a big deal."

Logically, it shouldn't be. But the truth…? The sight

of the smooth skin of her thighs, of her round rear peeking out from beneath her panties and all the memories it conjured, made him want to tug those pants down, not up, and touch her and kiss her until neither of them could breathe.

He gritted his teeth and pulled up the sweatpants as fast as possible, before lifting her into his arms to move them toward the sofa. The scent of her wafted to his nose and he breathed her in. Who'd have thought the woman could smell so good after being in surgery and then Recovery half the day? But it wasn't perfume, it was simply her, and he remembered it so well it seemed they'd been holding one another just yesterday.

Damn it.

"I can walk," she protested.

"Yes, but this is easier and faster, and there's no risk of additional injury." He sat her on the sofa again. "I'll get some ice for your head, then you can have some soup."

"I don't need ice. It's just a little lump."

"Trust the doctor. You need to ice it."

"I see Dr. Bossy is alive and well."

Her pretty lips tipped into a smile as she rolled her eyes and the tightness in his chest loosened. He had to grin, remembering all the times she'd given him that look.

"I consider the nickname Dr. Bossy to be a compliment. Where are your plastic bags?"

"In the second drawer, next to the refrigerator."

Once a bag was filled with ice and wrapped in a towel he sat close beside her. Slipped strands of hair away from the bruise before he placed the bag on it. Their eyes met and he nearly forgot to place the bag on her injury, wanting so much to kiss her instead.

"That's cold!"

Thank God for that distraction.

"Ice generally is cold. It'll help with the swelling and make it feel better."

"Yeah, well, right now my forehead hurts way more from the ice than the bruise."

"Once your skin is numb it won't hurt anymore."

"Says the surgeon who lies to his patients about pain every day."

"Lies to my patients? I never lie. I may downplay what they're going to experience so they don't freak out, but I never lie."

"You forget I've heard you talk to patients when they're in occupational therapy." Her voice went into a bass tone. *"Well, sir, your bones are healing nicely and the ligaments are stretching out well. In no time your fingers are going to be playing the piano again. You don't play piano? Well, because of my magical surgical skills now you will."*

He had to laugh at her words and her cutely ridiculous expression. "I don't believe I've ever said that to a patient."

"No? I do sometimes. It's an occupational therapy joke that most people enjoy."

"And that's one of the many reasons why your patients think you're wonderful."

He knew they did. Her numerous thank-you notes and high patient satisfaction scores proved that. He'd always thought she was pretty wonderful, too, even though she hadn't believed it.

"Feeling any less painful?"

"Um…yes, actually."

He watched her lids slide closed and held himself very still so he wouldn't stroke her soft cheek or lean in to kiss her, which he suddenly wanted to do more than he wanted to breathe.

"Thank you. I'll take over holding it now." Her hand covered his on the ice before he slid his away.

"I'll warm your soup. Which do you want—chicken noodle or tomato basil?"

"I love both—as you know." She opened her eyes and turned to him, her expression serious. "I appreciate all this. I do. It's…awkward me being here with you, and I know it's awkward for you, too. I'm sorry about that. But I realize you were right. You bringing me home was lots better than trying to have my neighbor do it. She wouldn't have been able to steady me the way you did. Or pick me up off the floor and bring me food, and walk the dogs and all. So thank you."

"No thanks necessary. I…we might not be together anymore, but I'll always care about you."

And the truth of that made his throat close and sent him to the kitchen to busy himself and get her some food before he showed her exactly how much he still cared.

He helped her move to one of the two chairs at the tiny table placed at one end of the living room. "You comfortable enough to eat here? Or do you want to sit in your armchair and drink the soup from a mug?"

"This is okay. Smells wonderful."

"I'll take the dogs out again while you eat. Don't try to get up until I get back, promise? We won't be gone long."

She nodded, and he escaped with an urge to kiss the top of her head before he went, as he often had when he'd left for work or meetings in the past.

The dogs were excited to be outside again, and he wondered how often Jill had to walk them. Did she take them on her runs sometimes? Probably only Hudson would be up for that. Yorkie might have a big attitude, but there was no way his short little legs could handle the miles Jill logged.

Probably he should keep the dogs out longer, but he felt an uncomfortable niggle, worrying about Jill and how she was doing all alone, and hurried back after only about twenty minutes.

Seeing her still sitting at the table when he nudged open the door had him smiling in relief.

"I see you're being a good patient."

"Did you doubt me?"

The smile she sent back held a hint of the mischievous Jill he'd adored.

"I'm limiting myself to one event per day of finding myself on the floor."

"How about trying for zero events? The first one about gave me a heart attack."

"I'm still sitting here, aren't I? By the way, Kandie called and she said she can stop by after work tonight to check on me, see if I need anything. How would you feel about taking the dogs to your place until Briana gets here? I mean, I know you're super-busy, but you can hire a dog walker to take them out while you're at work. It…it wouldn't be for long."

How much he didn't want to leave her or the dogs shocked him, and his feet seemed rooted to the floor even as he'd been thinking about how difficult it was to be here with her.

"Is Kandie spending the night?"

"No, of course not. She has a young son, and there's no reason for her to do that."

"Post-op orders are for you not to be alone tonight."

"I feel okay. Barely woozy from the pain meds now. I'll be fine."

"Is the woman who just fell in the bathroom actually saying this?" He stared at her. "You'll need to take meds when you go to bed, to help with the pain when the block wears off. And what if you fall again with nobody here?"

"That's not going to happen."

"It did happen—and, since you're a smart woman, you know that's not something you can assume."

He folded his arms across his chest, ignoring her mulish expression. Two could play at the stubborn game, and he had no intention of losing because the thought of her lying hurt and alone chilled his blood.

He realized there was only one solution that would solve the problem, difficult though it might be.

"You and the dogs are coming home with me, and staying there until your sister comes."

CHAPTER THREE

JILL'S HEART BUMPED hard against her ribs, then seemed to stop for a moment before revving up again. Stay at Conor's place? Be close to him for hours on end, reminded of all the good and bad parts of their marriage and why it had fallen apart?

"No." A feeling of panic filled her chest. "I'm not doing that. Period."

"It's the only thing that makes sense. I live just a couple blocks from HOAC. Tomorrow morning you'll get your cast off and have a splint made, then you'll be able to easily go back to my apartment and get some rest."

"*No.* There's no way—"

"Listen to me."

He pulled the other chair close to her and leaned forward. His expression was earnest and determined, and she'd learned from the past that trying to fight him when he'd made up his mind would be like beating her head against a brick wall, bringing another bruise. But that kind of bruise wouldn't hurt nearly as badly as the one on her heart.

"I get that you want to limit how much time we

spend together—I do, too, to be honest. But remember my work hours that you hated so much? I'll hardly be around—just enough to make sure you're okay overnight. To walk with you to your appointment tomorrow morning. I'll find someone who wants to make some extra cash by checking on you when I'm not there and walking the dogs. It'll work out until your sister gets here. By then you'll be off the pain meds and able to stay alone."

She absorbed his words. The logic behind them. Her apartment was a good half-hour trek away from the center on the subway. When the numbness wore off and her cast was replaced by a splint she'd be in pain and still a little drugged up. Plus, she knew from talking with her patients that the challenge of trying to function with one hand wasn't going to be easy—especially with no one around to help.

Time for her to act like the mature and reasonable woman she was trying to be. The one who was fighting her insecurities and who didn't want or need a relationship until she'd dealt with all the baggage her marriage to Conor had proved she still carried around.

And maybe it wouldn't be too awful. He worked so much she'd probably hardly see him. Finding someone else to help her and take care of the dogs, with him basically an overnight watchdog for the next few days, was the logical solution.

Rock versus hard place. That described the situation to a T. She couldn't deny that trying to stay here alone, with her arm still in the nerve block, and then somehow making her way to the orthopedic center all by herself in the morning wouldn't be easy, even if she took a taxi.

"All right." She heaved out a resigned sigh, shoving down the dread that came along with it. "I know you're right. I shouldn't be alone right now. Just for a day or two, though. Then I'll come back here, and you can keep the dogs until Briana comes."

"Thank you." He stood and looked down at her, his expression hard to read. "I'll clean up the dishes while you rest."

Hating this whole scene, she reached for her spoon but managed to knock it off the table instead. Apparently clumsiness was part of this whole experience, and she sighed as she leaned over to pick it up off the floor. As she did so, her stupid dead arm swung out.

Yorkie had been standing there, waiting to see if some treat might be offered, and her arm in its heavy cast hit the poor pup right on his little nose, knocking him sideways to the floor as he yelped.

"Oh, dear! I'm so sorry! Aw, come here, Yorkie." She reached out her good hand and was glad he came over to let her pet him, clearly not holding a grudge.

"Damn. That thing is a lethal weapon," Conor said as he stepped away from the sink. He reached for her numb arm, currently held in a sling, and placed it back against her stomach. "Poor dog. And poor you."

He gathered up Yorkie, tucked him under his arm and scratched behind his ears, with an indulgent smile on his face which sent another stab to her chest.

This was the sweetness she'd fallen head over heels in love with. The thoughtful and considerate man who had treated her like a princess during that brief month they'd dated before they'd impulsively, excitingly, got married. The man who hadn't even particularly wanted the dogs, never having had a pet, but who'd wanted her to be happy. And then had seemed to so enjoy playing with them for the few hours a week he'd been free.

A thick lock of blond hair tumbled onto his forehead as he talked to Yorkie, and remembering how they'd felt about each other not too long ago made her heart pinch. How in the world were they going to handle spending time together again?

A deep fatigue crept through her bones and she found herself folding her good arm onto the table and leaning her head on it. Tonight and the next few days couldn't go by fast enough.

A large hand rested softly on her temple, its fingers caressing the top of her head. "You've had a big day. Let's get your overnight things packed up. The sooner you can get to bed, the better."

"All right. But you don't need to help. I can do it."

"Three hands are better than one." He sent her a lop-sided grin. "Show me where your suitcase is and we'll get it done."

It seemed to take longer than it should to pack a few clothes and toiletries, but of course there were the dogs' things to get, too. Their beds, with Hudson's being a big armful, their food and bowls, their leashes… Finally Conor had everything stowed in the car and had come back to help her to the curb.

"You want me to water your plants before we go?"

"Water my plants?" She stared, astonished he would

have thought of that. "You never even liked all the plants I brought to…to our apartment before."

"Just wasn't used to having living things around that needed attention." His smile disappeared. "And that was a poor choice of words, wasn't it?"

She knew he was referring to her. To her neediness and insecurities during their marriage. Something she wasn't proud of. "Accurate choice. And I'm working on all that."

"Nothing you ever needed to work on. I told you that. It was all me."

Not true, and she knew it, but it was ancient history. "Anyway… I just watered the plants a few days ago, so they'll be fine until I get back."

"Let's go, then."

He helped her down the narrow stairwell of her apartment, then eased her into the plush front seat of his car. "It's going to be a tight squeeze to get both dogs in the back seat, but they'll be okay, don't you think?"

"They haven't been in a car since…you know. When you brought them here." Lord, this was feeling more awkward by the moment. "But I think they'll be fine."

In minutes he'd returned with the dogs, who bounded into the back seat with excitement. Jillian had to laugh at how comical it was to see Hudson pretzeled in there, but his doggie grin showed he didn't mind a bit.

"This reminds me of a clown car," she said, glad to have the dogs to talk about. "How many Hudsons can you fit in a luxury sedan?"

"I believe the answer is one." Conor grinned as he slid into the driver's seat. The purr of the powerful engine competed with the sounds of the city as they drove through streets now brightly lit through the dark night sky.

Jillian wanted to ask where his new apartment was, but decided to stay silent, since she'd be finding out soon enough. Besides, he'd said it was close to HOAC, and that was only one block away from Central Park.

The car came to a stop in front of an old stone apartment building and Jillian's throat closed. Yes, the man had upgraded all right. As though his last apartment hadn't been prestigious enough…

"Your new apartment is off Fifth Avenue? Wow."

"It's a good location for work and a good investment."

He slid out of the car as a valet came from the building. She could see him talking to the man, who nodded and opened the back door to get the dogs as Conor helped her from her seat.

"Alfred will bring your suitcase and the dogs' stuff up, then get the car parked."

"You've really been slumming it, having to juggle with illegal parking in front of my place and walking up and down a bunch of crooked steps, haven't you?" she said, trying to bring some levity into this distinctly uncomfortable situation.

"I slummed it for plenty years of my life," he said quietly. "And *you're* the one who wouldn't accept any money from me after our divorce. Which still upsets me. I wanted you to live in a better and bigger place, but you hated me too much to take even a cent."

"I never hated you. I just felt there was no reason

for you to give me anything. Our marriage was a mistake for both of us and I just wanted to move on, like it didn't happen."

"But it *did* happen." He held her hand and looked down at her. "And I'm more sorry than you'll ever know that I made you so unhappy."

If felt as if her heart was shaking inside her chest. They'd both contributed to their mutual miseries, hadn't they? Definitely not all his fault. Something she'd come to see even more clearly over the past ten months.

"Conor, listen. I—"

The dogs leaped from the car, with Alfred holding their leashes, and Conor stepped over to take them. She wasn't sure exactly what she'd been going to say, but was glad the dogs had interrupted. Everything had been said that needed to be said—or at least most of it. Hashing over it again would make both of them sad or mad or critical or defensive—just like before. None of those emotions would accomplish a thing—especially considering she had to stay at his apartment for a night or two.

Cool and calm was the way to go. Starting now.

Conor led the way to the elevator, which opened on to a floor with only two doors in the hallway. Obviously his new place was way bigger than even his other apartment. He unlocked one of the doors and gestured for her to go inside.

"I'll keep the dogs out here for a second, so they don't knock you over on the way in."

"They're not that bad. Though it's true that they seem pretty excited to be checking out a new place."

It was like stepping into something from a magazine.

He'd clearly decided to start over completely, since not a single thing in the entire space looked familiar. Modern furniture in neutral tones sat near floor-to-ceiling windows that looked out over the twinkling lights of the city, and beyond the curve of the windows was a huge kitchen with an island and bar stools. It was surprisingly as comfortable-looking as it was breathtaking, and she wondered how his designer had accomplished that feat.

A familiar hollow feeling weighed down her stomach. The same weight she'd carried to every highbrow event they'd attended, knowing she'd never fit in to Conor McCarthy's life.

"It's…beautiful. Really gorgeous. Congratulations."

"Thanks. I like it." He unleashed the dogs, who instantly ran around, sniffing the room, then grasped her elbow. "How about sitting down until Alfred brings your things? Then you should take your pain meds and get to bed."

"Okay. I admit I feel pretty tired."

"I'd offer you a glass of the wine you like, but it's not a good idea to mix it with drugs," he said, a slight smile curving his mouth.

"Are you sure? Because a glass of wine sounds pretty good."

She was kidding, though at that moment she thought maybe mixing alcohol and painkillers would be a good way for her to completely pass out and not have to deal with how strange this felt.

He shook his head, probably knowing exactly how she was feeling since he doubtless felt the same way. Soon Alfred brought everything up, and Conor placed the dog beds at one end of the room, then filled their water bowls and placed them on the stone-tiled kitchen floor. Enthusiastic slurping by Hudson left puddles all around it.

"Being the neatnik you are, I guess you're glad to not to have to deal with doggie messes anymore."

"I got used to the messes. The dogs were always fun to be around."

But she hadn't been so fun to be around, which was why he'd been gone all the time.

The words came into her head but she fiercely banished them. This was the baggage she had to unload. These damned insecurities that flew into her head with the least provocation. Making a simple statement about the dogs, making small talk, didn't mean she should take it personally, the way she had before. That had to stop.

"I...um...guess I'll go to bed now."

"Good idea. I'll show you your room. Mine's at the end of the hall. If you need me for anything in the middle of the night, just yell."

"I'll be okay." And even if she wasn't she wouldn't call for him unless it was a dire emergency.

He carried her small suitcase as he led her down a hallway covered with lush carpeting, then went through the door of yet another beautiful room with a different view of the city. Two chairs and a table formed a small sitting area in one corner, with a large bed in the center, and another door that doubtless led to a bathroom.

He set her suitcase on a folding thing obviously designed for that purpose. "Okay if I get your things out?

I want you to take the pain pills right now, so they're working when the plexus block starts to wear off. Then I'll help you undress."

Her eyes lifted to his. They held only a cool detachment. No sign of what the words had made her feel, which was her belly jumping, her breath catching and her heart beating a little harder.

"I'm sure I can get ready by myself."

"Yeah? With that thing on your arm and it held in a sling? No way."

"Then I'll just sleep in what I'm wearing," she said. "I won't be the first patient to arrive at the clinic wearing the same clothes they wore for surgery."

"Suit yourself. But you're going to be overly warm and uncomfortable in that sweatshirt. And you'll need something with no sleeve to wear over the cast tomorrow when they take it off." He shrugged, seeming to not care one way or the other.

She knew he was right—damn it. "Fine. Can you pull the sleeve off over my cast?"

He did as she asked, carefully removing the sling, then pulling the sleeve off her arm before reaching for the bottom of her sweatshirt. He gently slipped it up and over her head, exposing the camisole she wore beneath. He seemed to be concentrating on the sweatshirt, but when his eyes met hers for a long, suspended moment his expression made it hard to breathe, and she was beyond glad when he turned to grab her toiletries bag from her suitcase.

"I'll get you some water for the pain meds."

The speed with which he strode from the room told

her she hadn't imagined it. This crazy situation was reminding both of them of things better left forgotten.

He returned with a glass of water and wordlessly handed it to her. "Take a drink, then I'll hold the glass and you can pop the pills."

Even taking pills with only one hand required either help or juggling, and she hoped and prayed her hand would be usable sooner than some of her patients experienced.

"Thanks."

"Think you'll need help to go to the bathroom?"

"I'm sure I'll be fine. Goodnight."

Her face burned all over again, and she could feel his eyes on her as she went into the chic bathroom and closed the door, leaning back against it. She stared at her toothbrush and toothpaste, sitting on the counter, and wondered how she was going to manage to put paste on the brush with only one hand, or wash her face.

Lord. How had her world gotten so messed up in one split second? No doubt about it—the next few days, and longer, were going to be misery in more ways than one.

And being close to Conor again was definitely at the very top of the misery list.

Thank heavens Conor had insisted she take the pain medicine. At about two a.m., when the nerve-block began to wear off, the intense tingling pins and needles sensation accompanied by pain surging through her whole arm was way worse than she'd expected—even though she'd had plenty of patients complain about it.

Another dose of medicine to get her through the night

left her feeling a little woozy in the morning and, as uncomfortable as she was being in his apartment, she had to acknowledge—again—that Conor had been right. If she'd tried to take the subway in to HAOC all by her lonesome to get the cast taken off, or even taken a cab, it would have been hard going, possibly even unsafe.

Except there was one significant problem she had to deal with right now. When Conor had simply and without expression stripped off her oversized sweatshirt so she could sleep comfortably in the camisole and sweats she'd worn yesterday it had been in a fairly low light, and quick enough that she hadn't had to endure feeling embarrassed, or whatever it was exactly that she'd been feeling, for very long.

This morning. Though… After struggling for a few minutes trying to get a loose short-sleeved shirt on over the giant cast, she huffed out a frustrated breath. Clearly not going to happen. What was it going to be like, trying to get dressed and undressed after the cast was off and a splint had been put on instead? Regardless, she was absolutely not going to ask Conor for help—even if it meant wearing the same clothes for days until her sister came.

Not going to cross that bridge until she came to it. But this bridge had to be crossed right now—because she couldn't exactly show up at her former workplace with only her thin camisole covering her torso.

"Um… Conor?"

She heard the rattle of cups and walked into the kitchen, ridiculously holding the shirt over her front even though he was facing the sink. As though the man hadn't seen her half naked last night and totally naked a hundred times in the past.

But they weren't together anymore, and she just couldn't feel comfortable walking around with her breasts visible through the thin fabric as if it was no big deal.

"Can you slip this over my head? Can't quite manage it."

He turned, his eyes meeting hers for a long moment, and she could tell he was thinking the same thing she was. That they were in a kitchen together, with him making coffee and her strolling in a few minutes later, just like old times. Except she wouldn't be wrapping her arms around him and kissing his back, and he wouldn't turn to pull her close, giving her a long kiss that would have the air shimmering with love and desire and sometimes would mean a quick trip back to the bedroom before they had to leave for work.

Wordlessly he stepped close, to take the shirt from her hands, and his gaze briefly slid to her breasts before he quickly tugged the shirt over her head. Gently, he took her big bandaged arm in his hand and carefully drew the short sleeve up and over it.

"How's it feeling? I assume the nerve-block has worn off?"

"Yes—and to say that did *not* feel good is an understatement. We have to be more sympathetic when patients come in to get their cast off."

"I'm always sympathetic. It's you occupational therapists who make them do stuff that hurts the very first day."

"That's our job. You get to play the good cop who does the miracle repair surgery, putting them back together, and we have to be the bad cop, making them do stuff to help them get it usable again. Which unfortunately means some pain."

"I'm sorry you're going to have to go through that pain yourself now."

For several seconds he skimmed his fingers across her cheek, before dropping his hand to his side, and the tension between them faded a little as he gave her a small smile.

"You being the bad cop when you were on the PT side of the table is maybe true, but you were always a very sweet bad cop. What do you want to eat before we go?"

"I'm really not hungry."

"Have to eat something." He rummaged in the refrigerator. "Have some yogurt and a banana."

"You're offering me a black banana to spur my appetite?" She held it up and chuckled. "Thanks."

"I've learned that if you stick them in the fridge they keep longer, even though the cold turns the skin dark. I'm too busy to go to the store much, so it's been good to know."

She often wondered how he'd survived before they'd married, when she'd taken over the grocery shopping and cooking. Later, she'd also wondered if that had made her an enabler of his workaholism, but probably he'd just have eaten out most of the time. Presumably he did that now.

She silently ate the food he offered as he got the dogs

fed and took them out for a short time. When he came back inside, so they could walk the couple of blocks to HOAC, it struck her all over again how tall and beautiful the man was, and she looked away to grab her purse, not wanting to feel the surprising skip of her heart and the ache in her chest that kept showing up uninvited.

Walking into HOAC was another strange moment of feeling as if the past was the present all over again. It felt like she'd worked there just weeks earlier, instead of leaving for the occupational therapy center ten months ago, after she and Conor had divorced.

It had been her decision to leave. Seeing Conor every day had been like a stab in her chest, and she was sure he'd breathed a sigh of relief, too, when she'd gone.

But she had friends here. People she still met with once in a while and missed working with. Several looked up in surprise when she came in, and her old pal Michelle Branson widened her eyes and then widened them even more when she saw Conor behind her.

"Jillian! What happened?" Michelle asked.

"Fell on the sidewalk. Distal radius fracture. Beth did the surgery yesterday."

"Oh, no! I'm so sorry to hear that." Michelle stood to give her a hug, and her side-eye toward Conor was obvious before she looked back at Jillian and gave her a sympathetic smile. "You always were one of the most dedicated PTs around here. Did you decide you had to know firsthand what it's like to deal with one of these injuries? I'm very impressed with your commitment to your work."

"Very funny. Not something I ever thought would

happen to me, I've got to admit. But hopefully it won't disrupt my life too much."

Except it already had, with her having to be with Conor for a few days of torture which she knew were going to be far worse than any physical pain and inconvenience she might experience.

"Jillian is living in a fantasy world," Conor said. "She thought she could go home and stay by herself last night, then get here alone this morning. I don't remember her being stubborn like that before—do you, Michelle?"

"I think I'll stay out of any conversations about that." She gave them both a half smile. "But maybe going through this *will* help you understand your patients better, hmm? You can give a talk about it to all the other therapists after your arm and hand are normal again."

"Maybe... I'm trying to remind myself that this will be a good experience in terms of sympathy and understanding for my patients. Already is, in fact."

"That's the way to see a silver lining. Here, have a seat at my table." Michelle gave her another hug. "I didn't realize that my patient this morning was *the* Jillian. Let's get that cast off, then Dr. Crenshaw will be here to talk to you."

"I'm going to take a look at my schedule," Conor said. "I told them I couldn't do any surgeries until later this morning, but I want to make sure I have plenty of time to take you home."

Home. His home. And yet he'd said it the same way he had when they'd been married...

Jill swallowed hard and couldn't help but watch him

as he left, until Michelle leaned close and spoke in a low voice.

"I couldn't believe it when I saw Conor with you. What's the scoop there?"

"No scoop. He saw me getting prepped in the OR, asked a bunch of questions, and decided he had to play hero by taking me to his place and looking after the dogs and stuff until my sister is able to come help for a few days."

"Because he's a *good* man."

"Just not good to be married to."

"Jill. I get that your man—*ex*-man—works too much and keeps ridiculous hours. But he's also—"

"I know. I do. I shouldn't have said that."

Immediately she regretted the bitter words. She'd thought those negative feelings weren't still festering in her, but being around him seemed to stir them up. Clearly she had a long way to go to get herself whole.

"It wasn't a party for him to be married to me, either. For a lot of reasons we just weren't right for one another."

"Well, maybe spending a little time together again means you can part as friends this time." Michelle gave her a hopeful smile. "I hear they're changing up at your office. Are you coming back here to work?"

"I have to—until I find something else. Working with Conor would be too uncomfortable long-term, you know? I need to start somewhere new. I have a job interview in Connecticut—though that might be delayed because of my stupid wrist."

"Well, we miss you, and would love to have you

back with us permanently, but I do understand. And we're going to do everything we can to get your hand working again."

Michelle gave her a warm, sympathetic smile, then got to work removing her cast. Beth came to take a look at the surgical site, check the stitches and talk with her, and all that was the perfect distraction to take her thoughts away from Conor.

"Looks good, Jillian. Pretty great stitching, if I do say so myself." Beth grinned. "As you know, the stitches will dissolve on their own. I'll want to see you again in two weeks for another X-ray, to see how it's doing. And of course you can call me anytime if you need to."

"Thank you, Beth. I hope I'll be the kind of patient who astonishes everyone with her amazing progress."

"So do I. I love to brag to the other docs that I'm the best surgeon here—especially Conor. Speaking of which…is he taking care of things? Do you still need me to look for a dog walker and helper?"

"Uh…maybe. I'll be working on that today, I think. I'll let you know—thanks for the offer."

Beth nodded, gently patted her swollen hand, and moved on to her next patient. It felt strange to be on the other side of the therapy table, watching as Michelle expertly began fitting the temporary splint to her wrist and hand.

"Swelling's not too bad," Michelle said. "Hopefully it'll become semi-usable more quickly than some."

"Here's hoping… I need to be functional as soon as possible."

"That's the goal." Apparently satisfied with her work,

Michelle sat back. "Still, I have a feeling this is going to be a whole lot harder than you think it will."

"Yeah…" And hardly being able to pull her own stupid pants up and down just might be the least of her worries.

"What are you going to do about work? Your hand isn't going to be usable for quite a while."

"I was thinking about that. I figure I'll take a couple days off, then come here and help as I can, since I was being transferred anyway. I know the bosses would give me time off with my current disability, but I can't just sit around at home twiddling my thumbs. Or thumb, as the case may be."

"You never were the type to just relax. And twiddling one thumb sounds very unsatisfying." Michelle chuckled. "But how can you do any work?"

"There are things I won't be able to do for my patients, but I can get them into heating pads or set up in the dry whirlpool. Help with evaluations. Bring everyone the therapy tools…keep them clean. And some things I can do with one hand, right? Like massage scar tissue, manipulate fingers and wrists, take measurements."

"Obviously you've thought a lot about this already. Sounds difficult, but if anyone can do it you can." Michelle squeezed her good hand. "My next patient just came in, but I'll see him at the other table. You can wait here until Conor comes back."

A good thirty minutes went by, which left Jill wanting to get up and help, proving that she wasn't cut out to take time off—especially since she couldn't carry on training for the marathon she'd signed up for now. No running while her wrist bones and the plate and screws weren't even close to fused. It was another depressing consequence of her injury, since running always helped clear her head of worries.

Fifteen more minutes had her thinking she should just head on back by herself. Conor was known for squeezing in patients who needed to be seen in the office right away, which could mean another hour or more. And why not? His apartment was close, and he'd given her a key. The pain meds had mostly worn off, which meant her arm hurt some, but she didn't feel woozy anymore. Not having the use of one arm didn't make her a cripple, right? And the break was protected by the new splint. She had to learn how to live this way for the foreseeable future, and there was no time like the present to start making that happen.

She walked to Michelle's second table, where she was working with her patient. "Looks like Conor got held up. Can you let him know I'm going back to his apartment?"

Michelle frowned. "I don't think that's a good idea just one day post-op. Grab a magazine and relax. He said he has all surgeries scheduled this afternoon and wants to get you home first, right? He'll be here soon, I'm sure."

"You know how his schedule can be. Could be forever till he's done. Plus, it's a nice day out. I'll be fine."

Maybe it was the thought of being close to Conor as they walked, enduring the awkward discomfort between them, that suddenly made her want to run out the door and get to his apartment. Not to interrupt his normal workday anymore. To take a nap and breathe at being alone again, not having to stare at Conor's handsome face and sexy body and think about what used to be between them.

She waved to her former co-workers and left. Outside, the December breeze against her skin helped soothe the chaos in her chest. Soothe all the bittersweet feelings that kept surging up every time he came close, or held her arm to steady her during those uncomfortable moments of him helping her get dressed and undressed.

How was she going to handle this? And would it be as hard on Conor as on her? Probably not, since his work had always been more interesting to him than she'd been.

She forced herself to walk slowly even though she wanted to get there and see the dogs and maybe lie down for a minute. She nearly took the stairs, as she would have at her own place, but remembered she should take it easy for a few days. Last thing she needed was to trip on the steps, landing on her newly put back together wrist and splinted hand.

The second she opened his apartment door the dogs greeted her excitedly, and much as she wanted to hug them she used a stern voice when she spoke to Hudson, making sure he didn't throw his paws onto her shoulders and knock her flat before she'd healed for even one day.

Her poor night's sleep once the nerve-block had worn off, combined with the events of the day, had left her feeling so tired she'd expected to conk out right away. But a half hour of trying to rest on the super-comfortable guest bed just sent her mind to places she didn't want it to go. Places like Conor's bedroom, which she hadn't let herself peek into, and wondering if he had women there with him sometimes. Of course he did. He might work a hundred hours a week but he was a hot-blooded man, wasn't he? And hot was an understatement.

Thinking about their fabulous sex life, and what other women he must be enjoying that with now, made her feel a little sick. She jumped out of bed and began pacing the gorgeous apartment. She stared out at the amazing view of the city and Central Park and decided she had to get out of there.

Surely she could walk just one of the dogs? Yorkie was the obvious choice, because he was small and couldn't pull her along the sidewalks and pathways like Hudson could if he chose to chase a squirrel, or something else grabbed his attention. She and Yorkie would both get a little exercise, and maybe that would clear her mind of all the unsettling thoughts that kept poking at her.

She grabbed the dog's leash and headed down the elevator and out through the door, managing to smile back at the doorman even as she wondered how many women the man saw coming and going from Conor's place.

Breathing in the crisp air and doing something as normal as taking a walk felt good, and it helped bring back her equilibrium. But once she and Yorkie had explored the park for only a short time a new fatigue began to settle in her bones, and she realized that maybe she was overdoing it for the first day after surgery.

After resting for a while, on a bench tucked beneath an old oak tree, she decided she should head back and take the kind of nap she'd felt too restless for before.

"Time to go, Yorkie. Okay with you?"

She'd barely taken ten steps, concentrating on not tripping over the uneven sidewalk, when Yorkie leaped forward with a yip and she looked up. She was stunned to see Conor McCarthy heading toward them, eating up the pavement with long strides, a thunderous expression on his face.

For some reason her heart started beating harder. She wasn't sure if it was the look on his face or the way he kept coming so fast, but she stopped dead and stared at him.

"What the *hell* is the matter with you?" His hands reached for her shoulders and he pulled her closer, anger practically radiating from him.

"Nothing. I just… I wanted a little fresh air, that's all."

"That's *all*? So you do whatever you want, not caring that it scared me to death? I was worried and mad when Michelle told me you left. How do you think I felt when I went in my apartment and you weren't there? I didn't know if you'd even gotten there until I saw Yorkie was gone, too, and Alfred told me you'd left. And then you didn't answer your phone! *Damn it*, Jill!"

His expression was fierce, but deep inside the fury in his eyes she could see how worried he'd been. Scared for her. Guilt stabbed, because she'd left without thinking it might worry him. And didn't that make her the kind of person she'd accused *him* of being when they'd been married? Telling him that he didn't care how it made her feel when he was hardly ever home?

"I didn't hear my phone… I forgot to turn the sound back up, I guess. And it didn't occur to me that you'd be worried, but it should have. I'm sorry."

He stared at her for a long second before his mouth came down on hers, hard and possessive. The shock of it had her swaying, leaning into him, loving the taste of him and the feel of his lips on hers that she'd missed more than she'd admitted to herself until now.

The tone of the kiss changed, softened, his mouth slowly moving on hers with more than a hint of the kind of tenderness they'd shared when they'd first fallen in love. His hands moved to cup her cheeks and her good hand lifted to his chest, curling into his jacket as her knees weakened and her heart began to thud in heavy strokes against her ribs.

"Jilly… Jill…" he whispered against her mouth, before he kissed her again, still soft, still slow, but deeper now.

Her focus narrowed to just him. The feel of his hands holding her face, his hot mouth on hers, his chest rising and falling as his breathing quickened. Only one thought was in her head. How had she lived without him in her life, kissing her like this? Making her feel like this?

The sound of Yorkie barking finally got through the mistiness of her senses, and she opened her eyes to see Conor opening his at the same time. His gaze was still fierce, his blue eyes dark, his face taut. In slow motion his hands slipped from her cheeks and he took a step back. Without a word he reached for the dog's leash with one hand and linked his fingers with hers before he turned to walk back down the path.

They didn't speak—and, really, what was there to say? Him scolding her some more? Another apology from her? A conversation about why kissing each other was the worst idea ever and how it was going to make staying in his apartment together even harder than it already was?

Now that his mouth wasn't on hers, short-circuiting every rational thought, she remembered that his kisses and the touches that had made her feel treasured and desired had happened less and less as he'd been gone more and more. His absence had tormented her, bringing every insecurity to the forefront of her brain, until living together was misery instead of joy. For both of them.

And now they were living together again, bringing all those wonderful feelings and those awful feelings, the guilt and the pain, to the surface. Even if it was only for a day or two, he couldn't want to revisit all that any more than she did.

They had to find a different solution.

When they stepped inside his apartment the large, lovely space felt excruciatingly oppressive. She squared her shoulders and turned to him.

"Listen. I don't think this is going to work. I'll figure out what I can and can't do and find solutions to problems. I'll be fine at my place and we'll find someone to walk the dogs. They can stay with you until Briana—"

"No. I get that this is strange and awkward. For both of us." He shoved his hands into his pockets and looked down at her, nearly expressionless now, compared to the anger and passion etched on his face ten minutes ago. "But you need at least a few days to get your bearings. Your hand is swollen and sore and in a splint, and you can barely move your fingers. Doing everything with one hand is going to take practice. I'm sorry about what just happened. I was freaked out and worried but it won't happen again. I promise."

"I think I'll be all right if—"

"No," he repeated, in a quiet voice that felt far more compelling than his angry tone of a moment ago. "I'm asking you to please stay. For me. So I'm not worried and anxious about how you're doing. You shouldn't be alone right now. We're adults and we can make this work—in spite of...everything."

"Conor—"

"Please."

She found her gaze clinging to the entreaty in his eyes.

"I know there's no reason for you to do anything for me. But please do it for yourself. For your safety. Please."

"I just... All right." How was she supposed to argue with him when he was looking at her that way? "Briana will be in New York soon, I'm sure. Just a couple more days and I'll be out of your way."

"You could never be in my way."

The soft sweep of his knuckle against her cheek seemed to shake her heart before he dropped his hand.

"Why don't you rest while I take Hudson out. I'll bring you something to eat before I go back to work."

"If you're working until ten I don't see how that's any different from me being alone at my place."

The sadness she heard in her voice wasn't supposed to be there. And the bitterness she was trying to banish for good.

She rushed to sound less pathetic and needy. "But, thanks. Some food would be good."

"I won't be working late. I've rescheduled my evening meetings until next week. So I'll be back as soon as surgery is over and I've finished the paperwork. Go lie down and I'll be back soon."

Maybe it was the big emotions of the past twenty minutes, but suddenly that deep fatigue seeped through her bones again. All she wanted to do was lie in that comfy bed, close her eyes and do nothing but start to heal.

She watched him get Hudson's leash and walk out the door, then sat for a long time staring out the huge windows. Admiring the amazing view of this city that was like nowhere else. Being together with him in this apartment, feeling her heart squeeze and tug every time she looked at him, already felt like torture. And there was no way that working with him again would be anything but painful, too.

Much as the thought of leaving New York made her feel more than a little sad, she knew a new job in a different state had to happen. Being far away from here would be the next necessary step in really addressing her insecurities once and for all and getting over Dr. Conor McCarthy.

CHAPTER FOUR

LEAVING JILL AT his apartment all alone had felt strange and uncomfortable, despite her assurances that she wouldn't try to go anywhere. Maybe he was being stupidly overprotective. Having only one hand was a handicap that would keep her from fixing her own lunch and give her other challenges, but she could still get around. So why couldn't he get the niggle of worry out of his head?

Was she in pain? Was she coping okay or was she miserable? When would her sister be able to come and stay with her, and for how long? The woman had a pretty demanding job in the advertising business, so he couldn't imagine she'd be able to stay with Jill for very long. How was she going to cope after that?

Not his problem, he reminded himself for the fiftieth time. She'd once been his everything, other than his work, but she'd seen soon enough that he wasn't the kind of man she wanted. And she'd believed she wasn't the kind of woman he needed in his life, that attending charity balls and galas and making small talk with work associates wasn't something she could do. That he didn't really desire her—which he still couldn't believe. No man touched a woman and kissed a woman and laughed with a woman the way he had if he wasn't crazy in love with her.

But she'd been right about the rest. He'd wanted a different kind of life from the way he'd grown up. Financial security, a special woman, children, stability... The first moment he'd set eyes on Jillian his heart had fallen at her feet. A month of delirious fun and lovemaking had had him rushing her into marriage, not wanting to wait one more day for them to be together forever.

Forever hadn't lasted even a year.

He'd made Jillian miserable. Not the same way his father had made his mother miserable, but still...

He hadn't realized until his monumental failure that the way he'd grown up had left him damaged, somehow. Anxiety about their financial security, so intense it had made him sweat and have trouble sleeping, had sent him working long hours, the way he had since he was a boy. He'd tried to ratchet it back, to make Jillian happier, but much as he'd loved her, loved being with her, the back of his mind had always been full of all the things he might be dropping the ball on. All the ways his businesses might fail and their future tank, leaving them destitute.

To him, providing for her future was the best way to show how much he loved her—but she hadn't seen it that way.

He'd begun to realize that intense worry and anxiety was some kind of mental health thing from his childhood, but in the end it had become clear that he had no clue how to be the kind of husband she wanted and deserved. When she'd walked out the door he'd accepted it, because the last thing he'd ever wanted to do was hurt Jilly any more than he already had.

He closed his eyes at the memories. It was over and done with. But seeing her in such pain from her broken wrist after surgery had about killed him. And being physically close to her, touching her through necessity as he'd helped her dress and eat, being near her soft skin and hair, later knowing that her warm, sweet body was asleep in the next bedroom over, had seriously messed with his equilibrium all over again.

Which was the best explanation for why he'd kissed her in the park. He'd been filled with an overwhelming fear when he'd seen she was gone with Yorkie, and he'd practically run from the apartment to find her. His relief had been joined by anger, and he'd kissed her before he'd even known he was going to.

Then the taste of her, which he'd missed more than he'd realized, the feel of her in his arms, the sweet scent of her, had robbed him of breath. Taken over his senses until he'd felt delirious with it. It was a good thing it hadn't come over him that way in his apartment, because he just might have picked her up and carried her to the bed, begged her to make love with him, broken wrist or not.

And what a terrible mistake that would have been. He absolutely refused to do anything that would hurt her any more than he already had.

He rubbed his hand down his face. Time to somehow get his mind off of her—and the best way to do that was to take care of the tasks in front of him. Paperwork on patients. Checks on his investments and stocks. Looking at the financials for some of his businesses. A few phone calls and emails to the Urgent Care Manhattan decision-makers to set up a new meeting—which had to happen soon.

Thinking about it not working out added another layer of stress to the turmoil already swirling in his head so he tried to refocus. Pulled up some X-rays for patients he'd be doing surgery on in the morning.

And then just as he'd thought he was nicely back in the work groove, he found himself texting Jill.

You doing okay?

She didn't answer, which probably meant she was sleeping. Or at least he hoped so.

The niggle of worry that he knew was ridiculous had him finishing up as quickly as possible. He strode through the teeming crowds on the sidewalk to get to his apartment, and when he saw a family waiting for the elevator he ran up the nine flights of stairs to get there faster.

When he shoved open the door, his relief at seeing her quietly sitting there reading, with the dogs on either side of the chair, weakened his knees.

"Hey. How are you feeling?"

She looked up and her eyes met his. It seemed impossible that just that simple connection made his heart beat harder, but he knew hurrying through the crowds and running up the stairs wasn't the reason he felt breathless.

"I'm okay. Feeling antsy to get out of here and take the dogs for a walk, but I figured you'd go ballistic if you came back and I was gone again."

"And you'd care about me getting upset?"

"I'm an occupational therapist—that means I care about people. So of course I don't want to worry you— though why you get worried about me, I don't know."

She *should* know. He tried hard not show it, but he worried about a lot of things. And, since he would always care about her, he worried about her, too. But he wasn't going to go there.

"Are you hungry?"

"I ate the last black banana and found some granola in a bag in your cupboard, so, no. Not yet. Though how you keep your healthy physique without any food in your place I have no clue."

"I eat out a lot. As you know." He watched her gaze slide down his aforementioned physique and tried not to get aroused by her unexpected perusal. "What do you think about walking the dogs together? So we can both get some fresh air?"

"I was thinking I'd walk Yorkie by myself. Then you can take Hudson out. Before you go back to work."

"I'm not going back to work."

"You're not?" She looked at him as though she found that incredible, but her being here was a special circumstance, wasn't it?

"Not tonight. I'll hold their leashes and you can stroll along at whatever pace feels good to you."

"Didn't we just talk earlier about how it's weird and

uncomfortable to be around each other again? I want to enjoy being outdoors, not feel nervous."

"I make you nervous?"

"You know you do. Or uncomfortable…or sad…or… I don't know, exactly, but I can't say I enjoy the sensation."

He wanted to lean toward her, touch her soft cheek and put a word to what she felt, what sensation might be happening to both of them, but forced himself to stay put. "I know I wasn't a good husband, Jillian. That I let you down. I do. But it would be nice if we could be friends. Or at least not enemies. Wouldn't it?"

"I…I suppose this time together could help us be a little more friendly than the last time we saw each other. And a walk sounds nice." Her troubled expression lifted a little. "You can't let dogs off-leash in Central Park until after nine, or before nine in the morning. But there's a small dog park not too far from here that a friend told me about. I take them to the one close to my apartment and they love running around there. Plus I read that there's a burger shack right around the corner from there, where we can grab some food and a milkshake."

"I remember how much you love a vanilla shake." Without thinking, he reached out to stroke the bump on her forehead. "You can hold the cold cup against your head before you drink it."

"Or not." She sent him an adorable crooked smile. "Okay, that's the plan. Give me five minutes to try to look presentable. Though I learned today that's pretty impossible, since my hair ended up looking a little like I'd stuck it in a blender after I washed it."

"I noticed it wasn't in its usual smooth, sleek fall down your shoulders, or in that messy bun you like to wear the rest of the time."

"Yeah… I also learned there's no way I can get it in a bun one-handed, and drying it without using a brush in my other hand does not turn out well."

"Are you taking notes? These are good things for a hand surgeon and occupational therapist to know."

"Don't laugh, but I actually am. I figure I'll give a presentation to the OTs after I've gone through all this. Maybe come up with some new ideas for patients as I go along."

"Not laughing at all. It's a good idea."

He'd been to a few of her professional talks in the past, both about her work and how she'd become a runner after her leg surgery. Her energy and warmth made her the kind of speaker who held everyone's attention, and he remembered feeling proud of her when others had told him how impressed they were.

"Make sure us surgeons hear it, too. Sometimes it's easy to focus on the bones and forget how surgery affects a person's everyday life. You're such a good speaker—I know everyone would get a lot out of it."

She sent him a smile so pleased it was as though in simply speaking the truth he'd given her a gift, and his chest expanded the way it had back when they were together. Back when she'd looked at him as if he was some kind of superhero.

That thought deflated the pleasure filling his chest,

because it hadn't taken too long for her to totally change her view about that.

"Thanks. That's a nice thing for you to say. I'll be back in just a few minutes."

He decided to stay in his scrubs for their visit to a dog park, and sat to scratch the pups' ears while he waited for her. When she stepped back into the room he smiled at her only slightly less messy hair, but decided it would be better not to comment on it. No reason to have her irritated with him before they'd even started their agreed-upon friendly outing.

"Ready?"

"As ready as is currently possible."

Once they were out on the sidewalk, he reached for her hand to keep her steady, but she tugged it away.

"I'll be fine. I'm learning to walk a little more slowly than usual, paying attention to make sure I don't some-how stumble and fall. You helping me isn't going to ac-complish that."

He nodded, but the truth was that steadying her hadn't been the foremost thought in his head. Mem-ories of all the times he'd held her hand had made it seem like the most natural thing in the world to reach for her that way.

He stuffed his free hand into his pocket as they walked the few blocks to the dog park. Both were mostly quiet, enjoying the crisp December air. He found himself enjoying being close to her, strolling along as though the ugly past between them hadn't happened. As if they were the two people they'd been for that wonderful short time, wildly in love. He tried to shove down how bad that made him feel now.

"It's good we're taking them to the park today," he commented when the silence had stretched on a little too long. "Supposed to get colder and rain later in the week."

"Well, that's a bummer. Rainy New York is not my favorite."

"It's nobody's favorite. Except for that time we were under an umbrella in Central Park, walking through that downpour. Laughing at how our shoes were soaking wet and yours were making loud squeaking sounds. Squeezing close together to try to stay dry as the wind blew rainwater all over us. Kissing and holding one another." Without thinking, he wrapped his arm around her shoulders and pressed her close to his side. "That was probably my favorite day ever in the city."

Her eyes shadowed and she pulled loose from his hold and looked in the other direction, which made him want to thrash himself. Why had that stupid memory come out of his mouth? Probably because the mention of rain as they'd walked close to one another had brought that day into vivid recollection, and his chest physically hurt, because he knew it would never happen again.

"There's the dog park," she said abruptly, pointing. "They can play first, then when they're tired we'll get some food and sit on a bench to eat."

"Whatever you want."

To take his attention from Jillian's sad expression, and the way his heart was squeezing in his chest, he looked around the area at all the people with their dogs.

"I've never been in this park before. It's nice. With Central Park so close to work and my apartment, that's where I usually go."

"You take time to relax in Central Park? Doesn't sound like you."

"You got me started on running to clear my head. I do that sometimes."

Talking about his focus on work and his other failings wasn't his favorite conversation to have with her, so he was glad the dogs had started pulling hard on their leashes and wagging their tails.

"They're pretty excited, aren't they? Do you put Yorkie in the little dog area, or keep him with Hudson?"

"Is that a real question?" She grinned up at him. "You know as well as I do that Yorkie has a big personality inside that little body. He does fine with Hudson."

He opened the iron gate to the park, unclipped their leashes, and both dogs took off across the gravel surface, excitedly running with the other animals there.

"Good thing you're wearing your scrubs instead of nice pants. Benches are usually none too clean in a dog park, which is why I wore these old sweats," she said as they sat.

"I figure old sweatpants will be your uniform for a while, until you can use your bad hand to zip and button again."

"Hey, I have new sweatpants, too, that don't make me look so ratty. I figure I'll mix up the tattered and un-tattered days."

"Old ones are looser—easier to slide up and down.

The newer ones I helped you pull up yesterday will take more work."

Memories of seeing her smooth skin, touching it as he helped her dress, and the entire conversation about dressing and undressing, made him feel short of breath.

Maybe she could tell where his mind had gone, because she turned away and pointed down the street. "You know, I've never been able to decide if I like the design of the Guggenheim or not so much. What do you think of it?"

"I like it. But my favorites are the Flatiron Building, Grand Central Terminal, the New York Public Library... And I can't leave out the Empire State Building, and the—"

"Are you going to name every iconic building in the city?" She laughed. "But I agree—and I've taken pictures of all of them. Along with Brooklyn Bridge and St. Patrick's Cathedral and a lot of others. After we... we broke up, I decided to take a photography class. I really enjoyed it. And now I just realized that's yet another thing I won't be able to do for a while. Can't hold a camera and take pics with only one hand."

"It won't be too long until you can manage that." Her frustrated frown had him reaching to cup her cheek in his hand, until he realized what he was about to do and dropped it. "I noticed a few photos on the wall of your apartment but I had no idea you took them. That's awesome. Could I talk you into letting me buy a few for my office wall?"

He'd love to have some photos she'd taken, to remember her by.

As if he needed anything to look at for that.

"I don't sell them—it's just for fun. But if you'd want a few I'll print them out."

"Thank you. Tell me about the class and where you took it."

The subject was a safe one, and she chatted about it as they watched the dogs run and play. Eventually both animals slowed down, tongues hanging out, and when Jillian stood up he went to retrieve them.

"There's a hose and a bowl for water over there," she said. "After you get them something to drink we can go to the burger shack."

"Dying for that vanilla shake?"

"Been thinking of nothing else for the past half hour."

He got busy getting the dogs some water. "Where's this burger place?" he asked.

"I think just around the corner. And they have...are you ready?...chicken ice cream for dogs. They love it."

"Chicken ice cream? You're kidding."

"Nope. Being next to the dog run, they sell a ton of it. Maybe you should give it a try, just so you know what they're eating."

"Think I'll stick with a burger, thanks all the same."

They shared a laugh, and Conor again had that urge to put his arm around her shoulders. They sat on a bench to enjoy their treats, and just as Conor was feeling as relaxed as possible around Jillian his phone rang. Digging it out of his pocket, he saw it was the lawyer who'd put together all the legal papers to present to Peter Stanford at Urgent Care Manhattan when they discussed becoming partners.

"Conor McCarthy."

"Hello, Conor, it's Sam Smith. I met with the new investors you told me about, and I've revised the paperwork accordingly. Thought you might want to read through it as soon as possible, since I know you're planning to reschedule your meeting with the Manhattan Urgent Care people soon. I faxed it to your office, and your secretary told me she'd put it on your desk."

"Appreciate that. Definitely want all the numbers to be up to date when we meet. I'll call you as soon as I have the date and time finalized."

He hung up and looked at Jillian, enjoying the soft, relaxed look on her face as she lounged near him, hoping it wouldn't get all disdainful when he told her he needed to stop into the office.

"Would you mind walking to HOAC with me? You don't have to if you're tired. I can take the dogs there and meet you back at my apartment. Or you can come with me and we'll grab a taxi to take you home while I walk back."

"I'm not tired. And I'm enjoying this dry weather while it lasts. Anyway, I need to get my strength back to start running again."

"Okay, but promise me no running for eight weeks to make sure the plate and bones are fused?"

"Yes, Doctor."

His heart got that funny feeling again, squeezing and expanding at the amusement on her beautiful face, at his memories of better times together.

He didn't trust himself to speak, and they walked mostly silently together the five blocks to HOAC. It was past seven, and long closed for the day, but as they approached he could see a boy of about ten pounding on the door.

"Need something, buddy?" Conor asked as they stopped next to him.

He turned with a grimace on his face and panic in his eyes. "I need a doctor who can fix my arm."

Conor's gaze moved to where he was pointing. The misshapen elbow joint and swelling were impossible to miss.

CHAPTER FIVE

JILLIAN WATCHED CONOR carefully reach for the boy's injured arm and lean closer to look at it. "How did this happen?"

"Part of the sidewalk was cracked and raised up and I didn't notice. My skateboard banged into it and I flew off into the corner of a building. Hurts real bad. I knew this place was here, so I came."

"Do you have a phone? Did you try to call your parents?"

"Don't have a phone."

"Here." Conor dug into his pocket. "I'll call them for you and you can talk to them. You need to go to an urgent care department to get this taken care of."

"I want to go inside this place and have them fix it. Why can't I do that?"

Jillian's and Conor's eyes met. His lips twisted. "It's not open right now. And you need your parents' consent before anyone can get X-rays and take care of you."

"I don't know if my mom'll answer. This time of day she's probably in a bar somewhere."

Jill's heart hurt for this boy whose mother apparently wasn't always there for him—something which she couldn't imagine, having been raised by wonderful, supportive parents. She looked up and saw that Conor's lips were pressed together.

"How about your dad? He wouldn't need to come here—we just need to talk to him and get permission to take you to get some care."

"I don't have a dad." Looking even more worried, the boy jerked his thumb at the door. "You sure this place is closed?"

"Yes. But I'm a surgeon here. Maybe there's something I can do." Conor's eyes met hers again. "Let's try to call your mom and we'll go from there. What's your name?"

"Noah Thomas."

Conor dialed in the number Noah gave him, then handed the boy the phone. After many rings Jill was about to give up hope when someone apparently answered.

"Mom, I hurt my arm. You need to say it's okay for me to get treated by an urgent care department, or something."

Her words in reply weren't decipherable, but the loud and angry tone was more than clear.

Conor reached for the phone. "Let me talk to her."

"Ma'am, this is Dr. Conor McCarthy. Your son Noah needs medical attention. I'd like permission to send him by taxi to an urgent care facility, and to call ahead to let them know to expect him."

Jill looked up at his grim face, not catching everything the woman said except the fact that she wasn't about to pay any urgent care fees and wanted Noah to just go home.

"All I need is your permission to treat him. I will take care of him here at my orthopedic center with no charge, but I need you to give your consent, which I will record."

There was more brief conversation, then Jill got the distinct impression the woman had hung up on Conor. "Did you get her permission?"

"Yes."

She could see him work to relax his expression into a smile before he looked at Noah.

"I'm an orthopedic surgeon, which means I specialize in bones. Since I can take care of you here, without charging your mom, I guess we'll go ahead and do that. Okay with you?"

"Yes! That would be awesome."

For the first time since they'd run into him the boy's expression lightened and he even almost smiled.

"All right." Conor punched a code into the keypad to unlock the door, and turned to look at Jill as the three of them and the dogs piled into the elevator. "I think Hudson and Yorkie will do okay in the storage room. You think they'll be tired enough to sleep a little after all that running?"

"Definitely. They'll rest while you and I find out what's going on with Noah's arm."

"What did you do to yours?" Noah asked, staring at her splint as he clutched his own arm to his belly.

"I fell and broke my wrist. Hopefully your arm isn't

broken, but we'll find out. Dr. McCarthy is a really good orthopedic surgeon, so you're in good hands."

"It hurts superbad and it looks awful. It has to be broken. Doesn't it?"

"Nope," Conor said. "Could be a dislocated elbow—that's a real possibility. Could be something else. We'll find out with an X-ray, then go from there."

They both quickly got the dogs settled, with more bowls of water, then moved to the X-ray room. "Sit down there, Noah, and put your arm on the pad just like that."

Jill stood behind the wall and watched Conor gently and expertly place Noah's arm in several different positions before stepping next to her and pushing the button to take the pictures.

"All done. Let's go take a look and see what they show, hmm?"

They moved to an office off the main hallway that held computer equipment and Conor pulled up the images.

"Take a look, Noah. See how the ball of your elbow has shifted out of the socket? That's called a posterior dislocation. And that's good news."

"It is?"

"Yep. It means it's not broken. I have to reduce it, which means put it back into place. It'll hurt, and we'll have to put it in a splint and a sling for a few days. Then check on it again. But it's much better news than if it was broken."

Conor sent him a warm smile that would have reassured even the most frightened patient.

Noah smiled back at him, and her heart pinched at how sweet Conor was with the boy. She'd seen him many times, meeting with a patient in the therapy room after surgery, but had rarely had the chance to see him talking with people prior to surgery—especially a child.

Conor patted the boy's back. "I'm going to give you something to make you feel sleepy when I reduce it, because it does hurt. But the medicine, which is called conscious sedation, will help you not really be aware of what I'm doing. Then, afterward, you'll wake up again in no time."

"Okay."

Noah looked up at Conor with a look of utter trust on his face and Jill drew a deep breath. Conor might have been incapable of being emotionally available the way she'd wanted and needed during their marriage, and unable to make her a priority ahead of his work, but in his own way he was still a good man.

She turned away. "I'll get the sedative."

When she returned Conor was carefully examining Noah's arm and hand, speaking calmly to him and telling him what to expect.

"Your circulation seems fine, which is more good news. No veins pinched in there, causing poor blood flow. Should be a simple procedure. Are you ready for me to give you the shot that will make you sleepy? It'll sting a little."

"Ready."

Cursing her one useless hand, Jill helped Noah get comfortable on the clinic bed before Conor injected the conscious sedation into the boy's thigh, and in moments his lids slid closed.

"All right," Conor said, looking at Jill. "I'm going to reduce the elbow. Are you able to hold on to his bicep with one hand while I manipulate it back into place? If not, I'll do it solo."

"I'll do my best."

Jill gripped the boy's arm as strongly as she could with her good hand, and watched in fascination as Conor grasped the wrist and forearm, slowly pulling and twisting. She'd never actually seen this procedure done in person, just in videos at therapy school. It obviously took skill to know exactly what to do, but in less than thirty seconds a loud popping sound came as the joint slipped back into place.

"Impressive, Dr. McCarthy," she said. "That was amazing to watch."

"Well, I *am* pretty amazing. Glad we were able to be here for him." He sent her a pleased grin and she smiled back.

"I think it was meant to be. I mean, we got to the door right as he was banging on it. I wonder what he would have done if we hadn't shown up?"

All amusement left Conor's face. "Struggled. Gone home to a mother who's only half there and barely able to take care of herself, probably, let alone a kid."

Something about his tone, which was not just grim but sad, too, had her wondering if there was something about his own childhood he hadn't shared with her. She knew his father had left when he'd been only five or six years old, and that his mother died when he was barely eighteen. He hadn't told her much more than that, other than saying she'd been ill for a long time.

Should she ask, or let it be, since they weren't a part of each other's lives anymore?

She opened her mouth, not exactly sure what she was going to say, but stopped as he turned to Noah and gently shook him.

"Hey, Noah. All done. You can wake up now."

The boy blinked up at him. "Huh?"

"Your elbow's back in place. Jillian here is an occupational therapist, and an expert at making splints for people. When you're feeling alert again we're going to make one for you. I want you to come back in two days. Let me know when you're feeling up to walking."

Noah nodded and Conor turned to Jill, his expression impassive. "Will you keep an eye on him as he wakes up? I'm going to find that fax I need. Be back soon."

By the time Conor returned Noah was feeling well enough to go to the therapy room with both of them.

"Sit right here, Noah. I'm going to fashion a splint for you out of this cool thermoplastic stuff," she said, holding up the sheet of hard material. "When I put it in hot water it softens, so I can form it to your arm. What color do you want?"

"I like that green."

"Green it is."

She dipped the sheet into the hot water bath, wondering how she'd manage with one hand. But with Conor holding one end as she placed it over Noah's arm she found she was able to form it to fit.

"Hey, I'm not as handicapped as I thought I was!" she said triumphantly. "My first success post-surgery!"

"I'm glad—but try not to be impatient and push it. You need time to heal just like Noah does," Conor said, smiling at both of them. "I'll cut the Velcro straps. I'm sure you can do it, but having two hands will make it a little easier."

"True. Not to mention that it's probably good for a high-and-mighty surgeon to do some therapy work once in a while."

"High-and-mighty? Is that how you think I come across?"

"No…"

And she didn't. He'd always treated everyone in the surgical center with respect, whether they were cleaning staff or a nurse or a worker in the office. Something not true of every surgeon—especially one who owned the whole place, like Conor did.

"Except when there's just one cup of coffee left in the clinic kitchen and you call dibs because you're heading into surgery."

"Well, I admit that's true. Wouldn't be good to fall asleep in the middle of cutting and drilling bones, right?"

His amused eyes met hers and they shared a long smile before he turned back to Noah and attached the Velcro straps.

"No skateboarding while you're wearing this," he said. "Your arm is going to feel sore and you don't want to be falling again while it's healing."

"I never fall."

Conor laughed. "You and Jillian. Both of you claim you don't fall, and yet both of you did. Stubborn and more stubborn."

"Not stubborn," she said, having to laugh a little, too. "Haven't I been good? Watching my step and walking slowly?"

"Yeah. You've been good."

His blue gaze met hers for another long, connected moment that made her heart race and her breath feel short until he broke the contact.

"You need to be good, too, Noah. I'm going to send you home in one of those ride-sharing vehicles. Then I want you to come back here after school in two days—and walk if you don't have somebody to drive you."

"I don't have any money for a ride-share," he muttered. "I'll walk and take the subway. I won't ride my skateboard."

"I have the ride-share app on my phone. So you don't have to worry about that." Conor reached to pat the boy's shoulder again, then gave it a squeeze before handing him a card. "Here's my cell phone number and the office number. If you're in a lot of pain or worried about your arm, call me."

As Jill finished adjusting the Velcro on the finished splint the boy stared down at the card in his hand before lifting serious eyes to Conor's. "Thanks. I… Thanks a lot for doing all this. Fixing me up and everything." He turned to Jill. "You, too."

She gave him a smile and small hug. "I'm glad we were here to help. You can take the splint off to have a shower, but otherwise I want you to leave it on until you come back to see Dr. McCarthy."

"All set?" Conor looked at her, his eyes still serious, and at her nod gave another quick pat to Noah's shoulder. "Okay, tell me your address and we'll call for a car. Jillian can wait outside with you while I get the dogs. And I'll see you here in two days after you get out of school. What time is that?"

"Three-thirty."

"I'll expect you here at four, then. Will that work?"

"Yes. Okay."

The boy shared his address and Conor typed it into his phone, then headed for the storage room.

Jillian and Noah took the elevator down and went outside, where the evening sky was now fully dark. He fidgeted a little awkwardly, and she made some small talk to relax him, talking to him a little more about the splint and how to be careful with his arm.

In mere minutes the car arrived and she opened the door for the child.

"Hang in there. I think you'll be fine until you see Dr. McCarthy again—but, like he said, if you have any worries, call."

"I will. Thanks again."

She waved, and as he waved back she could feel Conor's warmth behind her, the dogs on each side.

"That was your good deed for the day. Actually, maybe for the whole year," she said, smiling up at him.

To her surprise, he didn't smile back. "I hate that his home life is so bad. Did you hear what part of town he lives in? I wonder why he was so far from home to begin with? Probably doesn't want to be there with no-body else around."

"I didn't hear. But it *is* terrible that his mother didn't come for him. Didn't even want to send him to urgent care."

"Yeah… Maybe I'll talk with him a little about that when he comes back." His gaze seemed to focus on something in the distance for long seconds before he turned his attention back to her. "You've walked a lot, and it's dark now. I think we should take a ride-share of our own. Request a driver with a big enough car for the dogs."

"I admit I do feel a little tired now, but it's only a few blocks. I'll be fine." She pressed her hand to his arm and squeezed. "I want to say I think you're pretty wonderful, doing what you did for Noah."

He shook his head. "You of all people know work is the one thing I am wonderful at—which includes fix-ing up Noah. In another couple days you'll be rid of me for good."

She nearly protested, because there were so many things he was wonderful at, even if wanting to be with her during their marriage hadn't been one of them. In the end, though, she stayed silent, deciding there was no point in going there. As for being glad to be rid of him again…? The way her heart clutched and her stom-ach squeezed told her that a part of her didn't feel glad about that at all.

Early the next morning Jillian peeked out through her bedroom door, her heart bumping around in a ri-diculous pitter-patter. Expelling a relieved breath that

Conor wasn't visible, she shut the door and moved to the spacious bathroom.

Being in his apartment with him had sent all kinds of mixed feelings swirling around her chest as they'd watched mindless TV last night, sitting a respectable distance apart as he did his usual reading emails and texting, until she'd excused herself to go to bed, hyper-aware that he was just down the hall.

The discomfort of her wrist had made it hard to sleep, and the emotions swirling in her chest had added to her insomnia. Sorrow. Relief. A longing for the delicious past that she'd thought they'd have forever, until her insecurities and her inability to fit in with his wealthy cronies, combined with his workaholism, had proved that impossible.

His sweetness with Noah, the way he'd obviously been moved by and even upset about the boy's sadly less than optimal home life, had both tugged at her heartstrings and made her wonder about what Conor's own childhood had been like. Since he'd said so little she hadn't thought much about how had it might have affected him.

After last night she saw that she should have wondered. Should have asked. Their relationship was over, but maybe she should reach out anyway. Try to be his friend, as he'd suggested.

Was that possible?

And was it something she even wanted?

Confusion and uncertainty about all those questions gnawed at her, and she heaved a sigh as she undid the splint from her arm to step into the shower.

She held her wrist close to her body to protect it from getting bumped as she tried to make herself presentable for her therapy appointment this morning. Dumping shampoo directly on her head did not work well. Just like yesterday, even when she tried to distribute it at least a little evenly on her head, before rubbing it through her hair with the fingers of her good hand, there were serious globs in some places, and absolutely no shampoo in others.

She tipped her head back beneath the shower, trying to rinse out the soap. Apparently simple things like washing her hair weren't going to be simple for a while, and she just had to accept that.

Same with washing her body. Laying the washcloth open on the seat at one side of the shower, squirting body wash on it, then picking it up again, seemed incredibly inefficient, and all of it made her shower take about ten full minutes instead of the usual five.

Conor had asked if she wanted help getting ready. The thought of him walking in to see her naked in the shower made her feel both horrified and tingly and warm all over, which she knew had nothing to do with the water temperature. Proving that being close to him was making her crazy.

Flashbacks to them showering together popped into her head. Back when they'd been briefly happy, living in his old apartment. Where they'd laughed and made love and where they had seemed, for a very short and delusional time, to be perfect for one another.

Squeezing her eyes shut against the memories and the soap, she hurried to get the stupid shampoo fully out of her hair so she could dry off, get dressed, and stop thinking about how near Conor was and how much the part of her that kept forgetting their sad past wanted to drag him into the shower with her.

Yep. Crazy and crazier were good descriptions of her current headspace.

She twisted the knob so that colder water would rain on her head, which put a chill on that very wrong thought and motivated her to get out of the shower fast. One-handed toweling off was a different kind of challenge, and it took long minutes to blot her hair and get most of the moisture off her skin.

Finally giving up on being able to get it much drier than semi-sodden, she ran a hairbrush through the wet strands, put her splint back on and looked through her clothes options.

She'd already learned that getting a bra on and hooked was impossible, so it was a good thing her breasts were modest and she could get away without wearing one if the shirt fabric was thick enough. Pants were a different problem. She had tried to pull tight-fitting leggings on with only one hand yesterday… After wriggling and tugging and not even getting them past her thighs, she'd huffed out an aggravated breath and accepted that it was impossible. Zipping up and buttoning jeans? No way. Dress pants? Possible, but not easy.

She chose an oversized sweatshirt and managed to wriggle it on, which made her feel slightly better. Then she held up two pairs of sweatpants. Both had dog hair on them, with yesterday's nicely adorned with dirt from the dog park as well. Feeling bothered by the thought of not looking presentable around Conor, then annoyed that she should care about that, she flipped through the few other options, trying to find something that would work.

A knock on the door had her freezing in place and turning to stare.

"Can I come in?"

CHAPTER SIX

CONOR'S VOICE THROUGH the closed door sent panic through Jill's chest.

"I…I'm trying to figure out—"

Apparently he took her lack of an actual answer as permission, and came into the room. His gaze immediately slid to her rear, which was currently clad only in the bikini underwear she'd wrestled on, but at least her sweatshirt covered it a little bit.

"Uh…you need some help?"

"Well, actually…" Her voice trailed off but truthfully she did. And he was already in the room, staring at her half-dressed body, so what was the point in shooing him out now? "Yes. Can you help me put these pants on? Then blow-dry my hair? 'Cause I can't do that without looking like I've been in a wind tunnel, as you saw yesterday."

He came to stand next to her, seeming to study the contents of her dresser drawer very intently. "Which pants?"

"I guess these." She held out some black dress pants. "They're not tight, like my jeans or leggings, which are too hard to get on. But I can't get them zipped and stuff."

He reached for them, and when their eyes met his held a familiar expression that darkened his eyes and made her face feel warm.

Lord, this was embarrassing—and at the same time it was absurdly arousing. Apparently her libido hadn't caught up with the fact that they were completely wrong for each other, and divorced, and that she had zero interest in a relationship with anyone until she'dgot herself together first.

"Put your hand on my shoulder," he said as he leaned down. "Then lift your leg."

She'd almost forgotten the wide bones and muscular strength of his shoulders, and forced herself to hang on and focus on her balance instead of how his body felt beneath her hand. She slipped one leg, then the other, into the pants, but had to keep holding on to him to keep from toppling over.

He pulled them up to her hips, the backs of his fingers touching her skin. Their warmth slid around to her belly button and down to the zipper, then pressed into her flesh a little as he worked the button. Absurdly, she had to bite her lip to keep an unexpected sigh of pleasure from escaping. If the feel of just his fingertips on her stomach was enough to make her want to grab him and throw him to the bed, she was in serious trouble.

"Okay." He pulled her shirt down over the pants and their eyes met again, his dark with the same desire she felt pumping through her blood. "Not your usual combination. Dress pants with a big sweatshirt. Want me to help you with a blouse? I figure the sweatshirt was all you could handle on your own?"

"No," she managed. "I can't get a bra on, so I'm… I'm naked under it."

A soft groan left his lips and the hands that were still on her pants button moved to tighten on her waist. "Did you tell me that just to torture me?"

"No. Of course not."

Had she? Or had it been because being this close to him, with his hands on her clothes and her body, made her think about what it would feel like for him to strip off the stupid sweatshirt and lick her bare breasts?

"Okay," he said again, lifting his hands to run them through his hair before turning toward the bathroom. "I have no idea how to blow-dry your hair, but I'll try."

"Can't do any worse than I did with one hand."

She followed him, seriously pondering just letting it air-dry—except she didn't want to show up at her appointment looking like she was wearing a fright wig. Lord, this was awkward—especially because being so close to him made her feel stupidly quivery.

"Sit here," he said, pulling out the plush seat beneath the vanity. "Where's your dryer?"

"In the bottom drawer."

Trying to feel as if she was just sitting at a salon, she ran the brush through her hair again, then handed it to him. "Put it on the high setting, then brush while you point it at my hair."

He did as she asked and she watched in the mirror as he frowned down at her, his focus on the job so intense that the tight feeling loosened and she had to chuckle.

"You look like you're about to do surgery. Something like brain surgery that you've never done before."

"Because I *haven't* ever done this before. And I think it's clear I have no clue how, since I wash mine, comb and go. I mean, what exactly am I supposed to be *doing* with the brush?"

"Just sort of smoothing it as you dry. Didn't you ever watch me when we…? Never mind." Bringing up more memories of when they'd lived together was *not* a good idea. "So, brush the part you're aiming the dryer at. Just drying it, as I learned when I simply pointed it at my hair and left it flying around, makes it look like an eggbeater has been at it."

"Okay. No eggbeater look. I'll try—but, just so you know, I'm not promising how it'll turn out with me at the helm."

"Hey, I have an idea!" She turned to look at him, wondering why she hadn't thought of it before. "How about I use my good hand to brush, while you aim the dryer?"

Their eyes met and held, until he broke the connection by looking down again. "Good idea. Probably would work better than me brushing. Take this."

His voice sounded a little strained. Their fingers touched as she took the brush, and the buzz in the air between them practically crackled. She tried to focus on her reflection in the mirror, to see exactly where he was aiming the dryer and how her hair was turning out, but her attention kept being captured by him.

His shoulders were broad in the dress shirt and tie he always wore to see patients or for business meetings when he wasn't in his scrubs. His profile looked more as if it should belong to a male model than a surgeon. His strong jaw and sexy lips…

"I thought you were going to brush your hair while I dry—is your arm tired?"

'Um…no." She flushed. The distraction of his physical beauty had her completely forgetting to brush. "I just…you know…"

"Yeah. I know."

The blue eyes meeting hers were deeply serious, and at the same time the heat between them shimmered. Her breath caught as she felt his hand slide the brush from hers, then slowly sweep it through her hair. He turned off the dryer and placed it on the counter. His fingers dipped into the strands he'd just brushed before he leaned down to press his lips to the bump on her forehead.

Her eyes slid closed as he moved to press his cheek against her temple and over her cheekbone, in a warm slide that sent her breathing out of whack and her heart beating harder.

"I'm so sorry you're going through this. I wish there was something I could do to take away your pain. To make things better."

"I—"

"Woof!"

"Yip! Yap!"

Hudson careened into the bathroom, with Yorkie hot on his tail, sliding a few inches across the tile floor to bump into the vanity seat, jarring them apart.

"Hudson! Yorkie!" Conor said, his voice a little rough. "Sit."

Trying to focus her attention somewhere other than on him, she turned to pick up the forgotten hairbrush and gave her hair a few strokes. A glance in the mirror showed that her hair was surprisingly presentable. It also showed that Conor stood behind her now, his eyes somber as they met hers.

"No wonder you got knocked down on the street. I thought they'd be roughhousing less now that they're not puppies anymore."

"They're still fairly young," she managed to say.

"I'm going to grab a cup of coffee before I take them out for a walk. You want one?" He sounded for all the world as though the aching connection between them a moment ago had never happened. "I'll help you get your shoes on, and whatever else you need, then we'll go."

"Sounds good."

She watched him leave the room and turned back to look at herself in the mirror. Blinked to rid her expression of the melancholy she saw reflected there. Somehow, for the next couple of days, she needed to look and sound like Conor just had. Show him she could think of him as a friend and nothing more.

Whenever Conor showed post-op X-rays to patients, then talked with them about the results and their treatment plan as they met with the therapists, it usually took his full attention. Today, though, Jillian being in the same room was a constant distraction—and never mind that the occupational therapy space was massive, taking up nearly half the entire floor of the tall building where HOAC had its headquarters.

The building where, with any luck, a new urgent care facility would soon exist, with him as part-owner. It would be good for patients to be able to go directly from diagnosis to meeting with surgeons, then to the OR, then back here for post-op care. And it would be good for his financial future as well. A win-win all around.

Which reminded him—he hadn't heard back from Urgent Care Manhattan's CEO, Peter Stanford, and needed to call him to get their meeting set up again. The longer the delay in getting the deal closed, the better the chance that another surgical center would woo the group to partner with them instead.

But even as he was thinking about what he needed to do to expedite the process Jill caught his attention again. Jokingly complaining and grimacing as she used the therapy equipment to try to improve her hand mobility. Then chatting and laughing with the OTs during each brief break. The bright overhead lights brought out the golden highlights in her beautiful hair, and even when the smile he loved was directed at someone else it sneaked into his heart anyway.

Despite the uncomfortable feelings rolling around in his chest he had to chuckle, noting that her hair looked fairly smooth. They'd definitely somehow avoided the eggbeater look she didn't want, but how that was possible he had no clue. They hadn't even managed to fully dry her hair before he'd found himself kissing her bruise and loving the feel of his cheek against hers. If the dogs hadn't run in right then he wasn't at all sure he wouldn't have forgotten everything and moved on to kiss her mouth—which he'd promised her he wouldn't do again.

He drew in a deep breath and strode to the computer to look up some charts, needing to get his mind off the intense desire he still felt for her. They'd both regret being intimate if they gave in to the sexual heat that kept shimmering between them, which probably surprised her as much as it surprised him.

With all the anger and disappointment that had led to their divorce, he'd figured all those feelings would have been snuffed out. But being with her, close together in his place, had proved that wasn't the case at all. Somehow, though, he had to make sure he kept his hands and mouth to himself.

He went to his office and pulled out his cell. "Peter? Conor McCarthy. I'm sorry I couldn't make our meeting, but I had a family emergency to deal with." Not exactly family, but he sure didn't want to go into that with Peter Stanford. "When would be a good time for us to reschedule?"

"Unfortunately I have a busy week. I'll take a look at my calendar and get back to you."

"Thanks. I'd like to get the details worked out as soon as possible, so please let me know what would work for you."

Conor's gut tightened as he hung up. *Not* good that Peter had sounded so vague. With another surgery center wooing Urgent Care Manhattan to become partners, he had to make sure his proposal was laid out to them pronto. And if it ended up not being the first one they saw, he'd just have to make sure it was the best one.

He blew out a breath and was glad it was time to see patients. Some as follow-up, and others who were there to see him with new injuries, discussing their options for future surgery and what to expect.

After a couple hours he decided he should check on Jill and suggest she head back to his apartment to rest. He scanned the therapy room, frowning when he didn't see her anywhere. Michelle Branson was working at her computer, not with a patient at the moment, and he moved to ask her if she knew where Jill had gone. Then his gaze caught the shimmering waterfall of silky hair that covered half of Jill's face, turned in profile.

Instead of sitting and relaxing, or talking with the people she used to work with, or trying to do the exercises, she was in the laundry room, standing at a table to fold the towels they used under patient's arms and elbows during therapy. Then she gathered a heating pad to take it to a patient who had just arrived, smiling and talking with them as she folded it over his arm in preparation for therapy.

He shook his head. She'd said she wanted to get back to work as soon as she could, but wouldn't taking a few more days off to rest be a good idea? She'd had her own therapy session, and he knew she had to be in pain after it.

Nonchalantly pretending to look at his tablet, he watched her work with the patient. The stressed look on her face was obvious, even as she smiled. When she moved back to the laundry room he followed her there.

"Something wrong?" he asked.

"No. Why do you ask?"

"I thought you looked stressed."

"I am stressed. Worried that this—" she held up her arm "—is going to take forever to be normal again."

"It is going to take a while—which you know. So why are you working? You know you need to be resting, instead of messing around distributing towels and heating pads."

"I'm only using one hand and resting my other one."

"Why won't you take just a few days off?"

"Now, isn't that the pot calling the kettle black?" She rolled her eyes. "The surgeon who works fourteen-plus hours a day is annoyed that I'm bored and want to do something productive."

"I don't always work fourteen hours a day, and I'm not injured. You are."

Even though his chest felt tight with concern for her, he couldn't help but feel a tinge of pride that this amazing woman, the woman he'd thought he'd love forever, was such a tough dynamo, with zero interest in lying on a couch and watching movies for the next however many weeks as she healed.

"What's wrong with putting your feet up and letting people take care of you?"

"I'm hardly doing a thing. Mostly because I can't. Punching you in the nose isn't even an option." With a teasing smile, she waved her splinted hand toward his chin. "You can't imagine how frustrating it is only being able to manage a little of the work I usually do. To feel dependent on other people for things I'd never dreamed I'd need help with. As *you* are unfortunately aware."

Her voice held a joking tone, but he could see deep

inside her beautiful eyes that glum and forlorn were good words to describe how she felt. And, yeah, despite working with patients for a long time now, it was true that he didn't really know exactly what it was like to be temporarily or, in the case of some unfortunate patients, permanently crippled.

"Hey…" He reached to gently draw her into a corner, standing close enough that they could talk quietly. The frustration he'd felt with her just moments ago melted into sympathy and warmth, even as he tried to shore up the protective shell around his heart. "It's going to be okay. You'll get where you were before—I'm sure of it. It's just going to take time, patience and effort. Like you always tell your own patients."

"I know. But I'm not going to be able to run. I'm meant to be in training for a marathon, and I really thought I'd be able to beat my best time. I'm not going to be able to run at all for a couple months—which I hate."

"You're training for a *marathon*?"

"I started running marathons just after we broke up. It was cathartic. Now I'm addicted."

"Wow. Good for you."

He could just picture her training, driven despite the small handicap of her leg, working to achieve her best time. Her hair flying as she ran. He almost told her he'd like to watch her run, but stopped himself. After she was on her own again having any contact outside work wasn't a good idea.

"I'm sorry it's so frustrating that you can't run and train right now."

"I can't even tie my sneakers. Can't get dressed… I—"

The tones of a muffled "William Tell Overture" chimed in his ear and he knew it had to be her cell phone—because who else had that as their ring tone?

"That's you. Where's your phone?"

"In my purse."

She took a few steps to grab it off the counter and began fumbling to unzip it one-handed. Seconds stretched on, and he finally reached for her bag.

"I'll get it."

Digging inside her purse, touching her lipstick and her wallet and other things, felt strangely intimate, bringing memories he hadn't even realized were there. When he finally pulled her phone out from under a small notebook he was glad to be able to hand her purse back, so the smell of her perfume stopped wafting to his nose.

Despite telling himself not to, he glanced at the screen to see if it was some guy she might be dating, but it was just a number with no name. Of course if there was a guy, wouldn't he be around to help her? If she had a guy who wasn't here for her when she needed him he deserved to be dumped to the curb and never thought about again.

Though he'd been that guy, hadn't he? And she'd left.

"Here."

He passed the phone to her. Maybe it was a friend who was ready and available to help her out—he should be hoping that was the case. That would be good. Really good for both of them. Except his heart didn't seem to be wishing for that at all.

Carefully watching her expression as she glanced at the phone, he saw that it first held surprise, then concern.

"Hello?"

She moved to the other side of the small laundry room, her back to him. It was ridiculous that it bugged him that she obviously wanted to keep the call private. They weren't married anymore, and she had every right to keep whatever she wanted from him.

"I understand. Please let me know if there's another opening in the future. Thanks again."

Her shoulders visibly slumped and she ran her hand down her face before turning back to him with a grimace.

"What's wrong?"

"Nothing. Not important."

"Jill? What don't you want to tell me?"

He tipped up her chin to make her look at him, and all those conflicting feelings filled his chest again. More than anything he wanted to lean down and kiss her, to take away her worries. To taste her and fall into her and forget all the negativity between them. But he managed to stop himself.

"I had an interview for a job in Connecticut next week. I let them know about my wrist when it first happened, but it wasn't a problem because they didn't expect me to start work for six weeks. Now someone's left and they need a replacement immediately. So that means I'm out of the running—at least for now."

"A job in another state?" His heart jolted, then sank to the pit of his stomach—which made no sense.

She'd left to work at the occupational therapy clinic after their divorce ten months ago, and he hadn't seen her even once in all that time until now. So why did it feel as if her moving to another state would shove wide open the cracks in his heart that were barely beginning to heal?

"I'm sorry. But you know your job here is secure, regardless of how much time you need to heal?"

"Well…" Her lips twisted again. "For reasons I'm sure you can understand, I don't want to work here, have to see you all the time. It wouldn't be good for either of us."

Damn it. So he was the reason she wanted a new job in another state?

"We can figure it out. Maybe work on that friendship we talked about?"

"I've thought about that," she said softly. "And I think we both know we can't really be friends."

"Okay, I get it." He drew a deep breath. "But there are other jobs out there. Regardless, I don't want you to feel you can't work here because of me."

"Don't worry about it." She gave him a crooked smile. "I'll find something—and moving away from the city makes sense. You know I need more room for the dogs. I can find a bigger place a lot cheaper if I get a job in Connecticut, or somewhere else. Maybe even in Pittsburgh, since my parents are there."

"Will you please reconsider letting me buy you a place to live? You never believed it, but all I wanted was for us…for you…never to have to worry about money ever."

"Money isn't the answer to everything, Conor."

Her smile turned sad and wan, and he wished he understood why.

"Sometimes it just complicates things and makes them worse."

"I know money isn't the answer to everything. But it is—"

"Never mind." Her suddenly bright voice was at odds with her expression. "I've got to get back to work. I'll text you if I get tired and decide to go back to your apartment."

"Thanks."

Obviously the conversation was over, at least for now.

"Noah is supposed to be here in an hour. If you feel up to it maybe you could take a look at his splint with me, since he knows you."

"Noah? Oh, my gosh, I'd forgotten today is when he's supposed to come back to see you. Of course I want to help. I'll meet you right here."

CHAPTER SEVEN

JILLIAN PRETENDED TO focus on folding towels and tidying up the therapy space, but she was really watching Conor. An hour past the time Noah was supposed to show up, but hadn't, Conor was practically pacing the floor. He'd go into his office to do some paperwork, then come back to see if Noah had arrived, then pull up some charts on the computer, then check back again. Finally he came straight up to Jillian, a deep frown on his face.

"I'm going to Noah's house. If he comes, let me know and I'll get back here as fast as possible."

"You know where he lives?"

"His address is still on my ride-share app. It's pretty far, so I'm going to drive."

"What if he's not there?"

"He might not be. But I have no other way to find him, so I might as well start there."

The depth of concern on Conor's face surprised her. "I wish he'd come to see us, so we could look at him, but he's probably okay, don't you think? If he wasn't he would have come back."

"Can't count on that. Will you be okay getting back to the apartment by yourself?"

"Of course. But if you're worried about him I want to come with you."

"Not necessary. And his neighborhood is pretty rough. I work at a free clinic there every few months, and you have to watch your back."

"If it's safe enough for you, it's safe enough for me. And I'm the splint expert—not you. So let's go."

Their eyes met for a long moment before he finally nodded. "All right. I'll get the car from my apartment parking garage and meet you out front in fifteen minutes."

It was rush hour as they made their way through the city, though when it came to New York it felt like rush hour pretty much all the time. Horns blared and taxis swerved in and out of lanes.

As they got closer to where Noah lived the debris on the sides of the road increased and the buildings looked more dilapidated, some even boarded up. People looked up and then slipped away between buildings as Conor's powerful car nosed down the streets, finally stopping when the GPS told them they'd arrived.

Conor turned to look at her, his expression grim. "I have the address, but not his apartment number. Guess I'll have to knock on doors. Why don't you stay put in the car until I figure out which apartment it is and if he's even there?"

"It'll be a waste of time for you to knock on doors alone. We'll do it together, different doors on the same floor, and go from there."

"Why do I feel like that's a bad idea?" He sighed. "But all right."

The hallway of the first floor was pretty dark as they approached each door. A few knocks were answered, but nobody knew Noah. They went to the next floor, and by the third both of them felt discouraged.

"Can we find out what school a child living here would go to? Maybe we can do that, then contact the school tomorrow," Jillian said.

"Good idea. This isn't working out too well. Sorry."

"Don't be silly. I think it's wonderful that you care about him, and want to see how he's doing. I know a lot of people would be stunned to learn that you're taking a big chunk of your day to look for a little boy you took care of."

"Let's finish this floor, and if he's not here we'll head back."

The next door opened and a young man stood there, looking suspicious.

Conor held up his medical badge, which showed his photo and name. "I'm Dr. McCarthy and we're looking for a boy named Noah. He hurt his arm a couple days ago and I want to check on him."

The man studied both of them for what felt like a long time, until he apparently decided they weren't the police, or whatever it was he was concerned about.

"He's up one floor. 409, I think."

"Thank you."

They moved to go up the next set of stairs, and Conor paused. "You okay to climb another flight of steps? You can always go back to the car."

"I might not be able to use one arm, but the rest of me is in good shape, Dr. McCarthy."

"Don't I know it?" He flashed her a grin before heading up the steps.

After several knocks on the door there was still no answer, and Conor turned to her, his lips twisting.

"Looks like a wild goose chase. Let's—"

The door cracked open and Noah's face appeared. His eyes widened before he swung it open. "Dr. McCarthy! Why are you here?"

"You didn't come to your appointment today. So we came to you."

"I… Wow." After a quick glance behind him, he turned back. "I'm doing okay. It hurts, but you said it would. So I figured I'm fine."

"Still want to take a look. Can we come in?"

Obviously nervous, he glanced over his shoulder again. "I don't think that's a good idea. My—"

"Who are you talking to?" A woman's annoyed voice came from a back room.

"It's the doctor who…who fixed my arm."

"What?"

A woman, presumably Noah's mother, emerged from the back room, looking as if she'd just woken up.

"Who the hell are you?"

"I'm Dr. Conor McCarthy. I believe it was you I spoke with on the phone about Noah's arm."

Jillian was amazed at his calm tone in the face of obvious hostility.

"We want to check to make sure it's doing okay."

"He's fine. I've got no money to give you, so don't be coming around expecting any."

"We're not wanting any money. We just want to look at Noah's injury."

"I don't believe you. Everybody wants something." She crossed her arms and glared. "Noah's dad left us high and dry, without a penny, so you're wasting your time."

"Mom, Dr. McCarthy took good care of me and I want him to look at my arm again. He didn't charge me anything first time, right?"

"Then he shows up at the door? Ha! You've got a lot to learn, boy." She grabbed her purse from a worn chair. "I'm outta here. You want to pay your doctor friend, that's your problem—though I know you're as broke as me."

Jillian wondered if Conor would stop her, try to convince her he was offering his services for free and reassure her that he had Noah's best interests in mind, but he didn't look back as she left. Didn't even mention her as he placed his hand on Noah's back and led him to the sofa.

"How about you sit here while we take a look? How's it feeling?"

Jillian watched, amazed. For all the world you would have thought the two of them were sitting at HOAC having a normal doctor/patient visit. Was this something he did often? How had she never known he was used to working in communities like this and dealing with the various challenges involved?

"It hurts. Still really swelled up. But okay, I guess."

Conor took the boy's arm in his hand and carefully removed the splint, gently feeling all around his elbow, talking with him the whole time. He asked him questions and smiled, joking a bit, and the look of total trust and admiration on Noah's face made her heart fill with something warm and fuzzy.

Appreciation for this side of Conor she hadn't often seen. Pride in the man he was, even though he was no longer a part of her life.

In their brief time together she'd felt frustrated that Conor McCarthy had such an extreme need to make more and more money, through hard work, investment and business acquisitions. He'd made that the number one focus of his life. And yet this Conor McCarthy was a different person. This Conor cared about only one thing right now, and that was the health of this boy.

Together they adjusted the splint and refastened it, and then, to her surprise, Conor sat on the sofa next to Noah. "Tell me about your mom. Does she take care of you or is she not around much?"

"Sleeps most of the time when she's here. Otherwise she's not around much. She seems...sad a lot. I think I make her even sadder, so she goes places with friends."

"I doubt you make her sadder. Sometimes when people feel sad it's hard for them to see how the things they do affect others," Conor said quietly. "Was she sad before your dad left, too?"

Noah shrugged. "I don't really remember. That was a long time ago."

"Okay." He put his arm around the boy's shoulders. "My dad left us, too, and my mom was sad afterward.

Really sad. So I know about that, and how it feels. I'd like for us to be friends and get together to talk—about ways you can help your mom and about other things. Can we do that?"

"Sure. If you want."

The way Noah looked up at him said a lot more than those casual words. It said that having Conor be his friend and talk about the problems in his life was the most amazing thing that had ever happened to him.

"Good." Conor stood, and handed him another business card. "Call me next weekend. We'll get lunch or something. And don't forget this time."

"I won't." Noah stood and grinned. "I won't forget. Thanks for coming to see me."

"Good luck, Noah," Jillian said, fighting a lump in her throat. "And if you need help with that splint let Dr. McCarthy know and we'll get you into the office to adjust it."

"Okay."

Conor gave the boy another pat on the back before he opened the door and ushered Jillian out.

They didn't speak until they were in the car, heading back into traffic.

"I'm not sure what to say to you," she said quietly. "Except that you were wonderful with that child. Do you often mentor kids like him?"

"Sometimes. When the opportunity is there."

"How did I never know this? Why didn't you tell me?"

He didn't answer at first, then sighed. "Easy to move

from surgery to seeing a kid to a business meeting before I came home without making a big deal of it."

"I would have liked to hear about it. The children you mentor and why."

Again he was quiet for a long time. "Another one of my failings, Jill? I don't know how to talk about things like that, so I just don't. Didn't think you'd be particularly interested."

"I was your wife. Of course I'd have been interested in anything you were doing. Anything you were interested in. Anything that impacted your life from the past."

He turned to look at her, his eyes filled with regret. "Another thing I did wrong. Not explaining where I was after work sometimes. I know you wondered why I wasn't with you. Felt hurt by it. I wasn't smart enough to understand it. But we already know there's something big missing inside me, don't we? I proved that over and over again. I'm just sorry you were hurt by it. Sorry I didn't learn soon enough."

She opened her mouth to say that wasn't entirely true, that she wanted to talk more about what he'd just said. More about her own failings and issues, and what she'd learned about herself since their divorce. But he looked so grim. Melancholy. Was there any reason to go over it at all when their relationship was history?

"Conor, I—"

"What do you want to eat?"

He stared through the windshield and the interruption showed loud and clear that he didn't want to talk anymore. "I'll call and order something so it'll get to my apartment soon after we do."

"Um…pizza would be good. Something I can eat with one hand."

"Pizza it is. With mushrooms, as I recall?"

"And pepperoni. Got to have some greasy meat to help my bones heal."

A small smile curved his lips and she smiled, too, glad he wasn't feeling so bummed out anymore.

"Nothing better than mush and pep."

They didn't say much on the elevator ride to his floor, and then the dogs were a good distraction, jumping around excitedly when they came through the door. Conor laughed, and roughhoused a little with both the dogs, and Jillian's throat closed again. Why had she always focused on his absence and not paid enough attention to all the good things about the man?

She knew why. His glitzy life and wealthy friends and expensive apartment demanded a woman who'd fit in to all that, and she wasn't that woman. Focusing on his failings and inadequacies had been easier than focusing on her own.

"I'll feed the dogs, then take them for a walk while you wait for the pizza," Conor said. "That work for you?"

"Sounds good. I'll do that resting you keep nagging me to do."

"You've had a long day. And you know as well as I do that your body is putting a lot of energy into healing, which *has* to make you feel tired. It's not a weakness to let yourself rest—it's smart."

"I know, I know. And if you ever injure yourself, I'll have to remind you, the energetic Dr. McCarthy, of the same thing."

Their eyes met and she wanted to smack herself. Why had she said that? First, he'd hopefully never break any bones, and second, if he did, she sure wouldn't be around to remind him of anything.

"I'll be back soon."

Apparently, he'd decided not to react to her comment. The dogs gulped down their dinner, then excitedly left for their walk. The pizza came just as they returned, and Jill moved to the kitchen to get the dishes.

"Let someone else do the work while you can," he said, shaking his head. "You'll be faring for yourself soon enough. How about we sit on the balcony and look out over the park? You'll have to wear a jacket, but it's a really nice night. Pretty soon it'll be raining and snowing and freezing cold, so we should enjoy it while we can."

She figured there was no point in saying it would likely be the *only* night they'd enjoy his balcony together, regardless of the weather. "Sounds nice."

He carried plates and slid open the French doors to the balcony. Two chairs sat on either side of a small table, with chaise longues at the other end. Car headlights moved in both directions on Fifth Avenue, and the glittering lights of the city lit the panorama below. Beyond that, a half-moon hung above the dark silhouettes of the trees in Central Park.

"Wow," she breathed. "This is just beautiful. I see why you moved here."

"It is beautiful. But that's not the only reason I moved here."

"Because you're close to work? Because it's a good investment?"

"All of those reasons. And one more. Because I couldn't stand living in the place we shared together without you there with me."

His admission made her throat close, and she had no idea what to say in response. Their eyes met for a long moment until he moved back to the French doors.

"I'll get everything else."

He returned with the pizza, a bottle of wine and two glasses, pouring each of them a drink.

"Wine?"

"Your favorite—Chardonnay, as I recall. Since you're only taking your pain meds at night, now, I figured it would be nice to enjoy a glass."

"I'm not going to argue about a glass of wine with pizza. Sounds wonderful."

Without conversation they sat and ate and drank as they stared out over the park. For quite a while the silence was oddly comfortable, until it stretched out too long.

With the pizza finished and a second glass of wine in her hand, Jillian decided she was going to talk with him about Noah. About what he'd told the child about his own mother being sad, which he'd never mentioned to her. About why he'd never talked to her about what he did when he wasn't home during their marriage. Keeping it to himself. Feeding into her insecurities and fueling the belief that he didn't really want to spend time with her.

That was partly her fault, she knew. But she wanted to understand it better.

"Tell me about your mom," she said. "You said she was sad. Why?"

He kept on looking out over the park, his handsome profile seeming etched in stone. "Not worth going into, Jill."

"I think it is," she said softly. "How did you feel when your father left? How did it affect your mom, and your lives? Was that why she was sad?"

She'd begun to think he wasn't going to answer when he finally turned to look at her.

"I suppose I may as well tell you, so you know some of the reasons I was such a lousy husband." He sighed. "My father left when I was in kindergarten, but I still remember it well because my mother freaked. Which I didn't understand since he wasn't very present at home anyway. By that I mean he was gone a lot, and when he was home he didn't talk to me or my mom much anyway. So when he left it didn't really matter to me, because he obviously already didn't care about me one way or the other. But it mattered to my mother a lot. Changed our lives completely."

"In what way?"

"Well, number one was that we had no money after he disappeared, and he couldn't be tracked by the courts to pay child support. My mother stressed all the time about how to pay the bills, and once I was old enough to help I did what I could to get odd jobs. Mowed lawns, scrounged the neighborhood for cans to recycle, walked dogs—whatever a ten-year-old could do. Once I was a teenager I was able to get regular work, bagging at the local grocery store in addition to the other stuff, and help more. But paying the rent and everything was always a worry. When I heard her crying at night I always thought that was why."

"Oh, Conor." Jill reached for his hand. "I can't imagine how hard that must have been."

"I'd lie there and wonder what to do. Try to figure out other ways to earn a few bucks." He looked down at their twined fingers and she tightened her hold. "I vowed that once I was able to make real money we'd never be in that situation again."

"I see." She'd always wondered why the money he made had never seemed like enough to him, and tried to understand it better now. "Did your helping out that way eventually help your mother feel less stressed?"

"No—and I didn't get it. I hated that she was sad, but the horrible truth is I was focused on myself way more than her. My jobs. Friends. School. I resented when she'd go out at night, thinking, *What the hell? I'm working two jobs and going to school, and she's out having fun?* I didn't see what was happening. Didn't understand. Until it was too late."

"What didn't you understand?"

"That she had a mental illness. Was in a deep depression. Her escape from the pain of my dad leaving, of being alone except for me, who was hardly ever around, of the money worries—all that sent her to bars to drink.

To forget. To be with people who were just as sad and miserable as she was."

He lifted his gaze to hers, and the anguish she saw there made her throat close.

"I don't want to tell you the rest, but you deserve to know."

She dreaded to hear what was coming. "What happened?" she whispered.

"I didn't open my eyes to the depth of her pain. Her depression. Wasn't there for her emotionally. Then one night she drove home drunk, lost control of her car and hit a tree."

"Oh, Conor." Her fingers tightened on his, her heart in her throat. "And that's how she died?"

"That's how she died. And if I'd been paying attention to her, instead of just myself, maybe I could have gotten her help. Maybe I could have talked with her, been there for her. Maybe if I had she'd still be alive."

Jill stood and squeezed next to him in his chair, wrapped her arm around his neck and pressed her cheek to his. "I'm so, so sorry. But you know it wasn't your fault. Alcoholics rarely listen. Drinking buries what hurts and numbs the pain."

"I don't know it. After she died I made myself face all the signs I'd ignored. All the ways I'd let her down. All the things I could have done to be there for her. And when it turned out she had an insurance policy—a pretty good one that got me through college and medical school—it about broke my heart. Made me feel like the worst human in the world. Because I'd convinced myself she was self-centered, that she wasn't there for me just like my father. But all along she had been—as much as she could be. She'd been paying that policy when we barely had money to buy food, to make sure I was taken care of in case something happened to her. Truth is, it was me who wasn't there for her. Just like I wasn't there for you."

"Conor." She pressed her mouth to his cheek, her heart aching for the boy he'd been. "You were a teenager. Every kid that age is focused on themselves. You can't beat yourself up for being normal. Can't take responsibility for your mother's drinking problem. When you think of what you've accomplished with your life you have a lot to be proud of, and I know your mother would be proud of you, too."

He didn't respond for a long time, then finally shook his head. "Anyway. So now you know. All that made me think that I'd like to have what I never had. What my parents never had. A woman to love forever, to be a good father, to provide for my family." His hand lifted and cupped her face in his palm. "I fell crazy in love with you the minute I met you, Jilly. I didn't know then that I couldn't be the kind of man I wanted to be. That you wanted me to be. Bad genes, probably."

"Conor—"

His finger moved to her lips. "It's just the truth. I thought providing a solid future for us, making as much money as possible, was all I needed to do. The way to show how much I loved you. But once I saw how miserable I made you I knew I'd been wrong. That it wasn't enough, and that I'm missing something inside. That I can't be the kind of husband you want and deserve. I'm a one-dimensional guy, as sad as that is. And I'm more sorry than you'll ever know that I hurt you."

Her heart shook. She wanted to tell him he was wrong. But the truth was, everything she'd seen in the months they were married had shown he was right. No matter what she'd said or done, working and making money had been his priority. He hadn't been capable of, or even interested in, changing that. And she hadn't been who he needed, either. A wife who was comfortable mingling with people she didn't know, going places she would never fit in.

She wanted a normal life, doing normal things with normal friends. She wanted a husband who loved to be home, and Conor had proved he just couldn't be that man. Even if he'd thought he wanted to be.

She stared at him for a long moment, her heart hurting for both of them, until he wrapped his arms around her, pulled her onto his lap and kissed her.

Jillian slipped her fingers into his hair and let herself feel the emotion in his kiss. All he felt from his youth, from his belief that he'd let his mother down. His resentment over his father's abandonment. His grief. And tangled with all those big emotions was what they'd had together. The giddy passion, the deep love, the pain of failure—all of it hung between them as their mouths fused together.

He held her so close, her legs straddling his hips, that it almost felt as if they were one, and then the kiss began to change. It felt less about those big emotions and more about the connection they'd always had. The kiss softened, deepened, and the tenderness of it made

Jillian's heart flip inside out, reminding her of the brief time when it had been amazing between them and how much she'd loved him—how she'd believed, for a time, that there was nothing more perfect than the way they felt about one another.

"Jillian…" His mouth separated from hers just long enough for him to breathe her name. "Jilly…"

The kiss changed again. Hotter, wetter, sending her blood pounding and heat pumping through her pores. His arms tightened around her—until sharp pain had her crying out.

"God, Jillian!" He leaned back, looking horrified. "Did I hurt you?"

"My…my stupid arm."

"Damn it! I'm so sorry. I can't believe I forgot to be careful." He reached carefully to grasp her splinted wrist in his hand, staring down at it.

"Not your fault." She stroked his cheek with her other hand and kissed the top of his head, not wanting him to feel guilty all over again. "I'm the one who forgot about it and wrapped it around you. You'd think the splint would protect it from getting jostled, but I guess not. I suppose that's another thing for me to understand better and learn to talk to my patients about."

"How to make love while wearing a splint?" He looked up at her with a crooked smile, then lowered his mouth to her hand, gently pressing his lips to each swollen finger. "If you give that talk I'll make sure I'm not there. Wouldn't want to be in a public place while being reminded of how it feels to touch you and make love with you."

"We're not making love. Are we?"

"No. Because that would be a bad idea…wouldn't it?"

She nodded, but at the same time she could see the eyes meeting hers held something hot and alive, and before she could decide exactly what to do next he'd swung her into his arms and was carrying her back into the apartment and down the hall to his bedroom.

"Um… I thought we weren't sure if—"

His mouth dropped to hers again as he flicked the covers back and deposited her on the big bed. His talented surgeon's fingers had the buttons of her shirt undone in a blink, before he opened it, then slid it down and off her good arm. Getting it over her splint forced him to separate his lips from hers, and their eyes met as he slowly stroked his hands from her shoulders down her arms.

Jillian quivered, and she wondered if he could tell how he made her feel. Wondered if he felt as aroused and confused and uncertain about whether or not this was a bad idea as she did.

"It's up to you if we make love or not," he said, his gaze on her camisole before their eyes met again. "But I think you need some occupational therapy, regardless. To make your pain go away."

"You're a surgeon, not a therapist," she said, and couldn't help it that her voice was breathy.

"Sure about that? I seem to remember you liking my therapy treatments in the past."

"Please don't use the words 'therapy treatments' as a euphemism for sex. I'll never be able to work again with that on my mind." She started to laugh, then gasped as his fingers slowly traced along the lace of her camisole and lightly across her nipples. "But I admit that I'm curious to see what you have in mind to help me feel better."

"I *definitely* have some ideas about how to make you feel better."

Her heart kicked hard at his sexy, teasing smile. He leaned down to cover her breast with his mouth, his tongue teasing her through the fabric, and her good hand held the back of his head as she gasped. His hands moved to her waist and she could hardly bear the delicious sensation of his fingers trailing across her skin. He flicked open the button on her trousers and unzipped them, his mouth moving down to her stomach as his fingers stealthily dipped inside her underwear.

"You're so beautiful, Jilly."

God, it felt so good. So wonderful. The way it always had with him. The incredible pleasure of it tossed aside any worries that this might be a bad idea and she arched toward him, wanting him. Wanting this. Wanting him to forget the sadness and guilt of just a moment ago. Wanting to forget her physical pain and her heartache over him and enjoy the delirious bliss of being with him one more time.

"Conor?"

"Mmm…?"

"Make love to me."

"What, you think this really is some unorthodox medical treatment? Maybe being away from you for almost a year has made me lose my touch." Smiling, he tugged her pants all the way off, then brought his mouth back to hers as he caressed her again. "Just taking it slow. Slow and easy, right? I have to, or I might lose control and hurt your arm again."

"*Is* something wrong with my arm? I don't remember…"

"Ah, good. Glad to hear the therapy is working."

He laughed against her lips but kept up the heat, and she arched against the talented fingers that were making her quiver and burn. She could barely breathe at the goodness of it, and she pulled her mouth from his because she wanted to see his face. His eyes were smiling, but glazed, too, and he looked like he had so long ago. As if she meant the world to him.

It squeezed her chest and sent another layer of emotion into the incredible pleasure of making love with him again after all this time.

She'd just placed her hand behind his head to bring his mouth to hers for another kiss when she realized she was doing all the taking and none of the giving. And that she was nearly naked except for her camisole, but he was fully clothed.

"We have a problem here. I'm naked and you're not."

"I don't see that as a problem." He nuzzled her neck, licked her earlobe, moved his mouth to the hollow of her throat.

"It…it is a problem." She could barely get the words out, so she needed to talk fast before she couldn't talk at all. "Because I can't undress you. And I want to feel all your skin against all of mine. Will you take off your clothes, please?"

"In a minute…"

His mouth continued its leisurely trek across her collarbone, down to her nipples again, and the orgasm sneaked up on her before she knew it was going to happen. Waves of pleasure skated across her skin and through her body and she let out a soft cry.

"Ah, Jilly…" He kissed her softly as his hands moved to cup her waist.

Somehow she managed to open her eyes and look into his beautiful blue ones, filled with the same passion she felt. She waited to feel regret, the fear that this was a mistake. But there was no regret. Only want.

"Wow…" she breathed. "That was very…therapeutic. Thank you."

"There's more."

"That's what I was hoping," she said, reaching for his pants to wrestle with the button—until he stopped her.

"No. You're handicapped, remember? Tonight you're letting me do everything. Undress you…undress me. Kiss you and touch you and make love with you, while you just lie there and let me make you feel good."

"And here I was thinking that having a broken wrist was awful. Who knew it could lead to something so wonderful?"

"There's a silver lining for everything, I guess."

He smiled and kissed her again, softly and slowly, his mouth lingering so long she was torn between enjoying the bone-melting pleasure of it and telling him to get naked, already. Finally, he lifted his head and stood, stripping off his clothes until he was next to the bed gloriously naked.

She let herself admire his muscular body, his smooth skin, the jut of his erection. Thought about how she'd explored every inch of its beauty and how intimately she knew each small scar and imperfection.

Which reminded her of her own scars and imperfections. How she'd hated him to see them, and tried to hide them whenever they'd been naked together.

The thought briefly dimmed the excitement she was feeling—until he came onto the bed, kneeling above her. His gaze trapping hers, he slipped her camisole over her head, held her face in his hands, then began kissing her until everything was forgotten except how he made her feel.

"I think the safest place for your arms is over your head." He gently placed them there, and she shivered as he ran his fingertips down the soft skin of her inner arms, wriggled and laughed when he stroked down to her armpits, then gasped as he caressed her breasts. His fingers continued on, slowly tracing her entire body, then opening her legs and touching her *there* until she was making little mewling sounds she couldn't seem to control.

"I'm not sure if this is pleasure or torture," she said with a gasp.

"Pleasure. Only pleasure, I promise."

She was vaguely aware of him taking something from the nightstand and then he was inside her, moving, finding the perfect rhythm they'd always shared together. The pace grew faster, taking her higher, making her feel as if they were chasing the past. The best part of the past. Wanting to experience one more time what they'd had before they could never have it again.

His mouth crushed hers as they both moaned their release and her heart shook as hard as her body. Conor McCarthy was hers again, for this brief moment, and she would hold him close while she could.

CHAPTER EIGHT

JILLIAN SAT ON one of Conor's comfortable modern sofas and stared out over the city while she ate a banana that wasn't black this time.

The dogs were at her knees, nudging her and demanding attention, despite Conor having taken them for a walk early this morning, and she managed a crooked smile even as she inexplicably wanted to cry. She reached to scratch their ears, and when Hudson whined she rested her face on his big head.

"I know. I miss him, too. Which is *not* a good thing."

But, she reminded herself, she'd missed him even when they were married, hadn't she?

If only she'd known how things would turn out when she'd fallen so hard for him on their very first date. Except, if she was honest with herself, she had a feeling that nothing would have kept her from wanting to be with him, from marrying him, even if she'd known that her heart would be so deeply bruised when it was over.

After last night's conversation she understood him better. And that understanding made her heart hurt for him, made her appreciate why he hadn't seemed to want to change his ways even as their marriage had crumbled. It was good that she knew, and it would go a long way toward closure as she moved on to a new phase of her life.

The 'William Tell Overture' began so abruptly she jumped, then fished around for her phone. Finally finding it between the sofa cushions, she saw it was Briana.

"Hey, sis! What's the scoop?"

"I finally squeezed out some time to come stay with you," Briana said. "I'm really sorry I haven't been able to get there sooner. I'll be doing some work from there, but I figure that's not a problem, right?"

"Not at all. I have therapy sessions three times a week, and I even get a little work done for another hour or two. I'm not too functional yet, but you shouldn't have to stay very long. I'll be off the nighttime pain meds soon, and I am learning how to get along with only one hand until the other one starts to work again."

"Great to hear. I'll be there the day after tomorrow. I'll let you know what time. Can't wait to see you and the pups."

"Can't wait, either. Love you—and thanks."

Her fingers went limp with the phone still in her hand and she stared out the window again. This was it. Briana was coming. Time to say goodbye to Conor, except for the times they'd run into each other at HOAC. Besides getting her hand to work again, looking for another job would be her priority now, so they could say goodbye for good and never see one another again.

She should feel glad about that. Seeing him, and then making love with him, had seriously messed with her equilibrium and brought back some of the pain and heartache she'd been trying to move on from. It had also brought back wonderful memories of how much fun they'd had together when things had been good.

Which must be why her stomach felt hollow at the thought of never seeing him again. Of it truly being over with again.

But of course neither of them had any interest in going back in time. Conor was who he was, and she was who she was. Great sex was just that, and it had nothing to do with being right for one another in any real-life way.

She sighed and lay her head back against the cushions.

Apparently she'd dozed off, because the next thing she heard was the sound of the front door opening and Conor's voice saying her name. She felt his hand smoothing back her hair and opened her eyes to see him smiling at her as he crouched in front of her, wearing a suit and tie, crinkles at the corners of his eyes.

"Hey." He gave her nose a gentle flick. "How are you feeling?"

"Pretty good."

If she didn't count feeling confused. Wired from what had happened between them last night. A little sad that it wouldn't happen again. And relieved not to have to rehash all the bad things between them anymore.

"I'm glad. Because I don't have any surgeries scheduled today and I decided to get a bunch of business stuff done this morning and put the rest off until tomorrow so I could take the rest of the day off to spend with you."

"What?" She struggled to sit upright and his hands wrapped around her waist to help her.

"I know it's hard for you, being cooped up here when you're not at therapy or helping out there. Not able to run, or mess with your plants, or do all the stuff you usually do. Speaking of which…" He stood and walked to his doorway, then returned. "I figured the cool tones of the decorating around here needed a little warmth to make you feel at home. So I brought a couple of your plants to keep you company."

He set them on the coffee table and she stared. Reached out to finger one of the leaves as, inexplicably, a lump came to her throat. "That's…very sweet of you. Except there's no reason for me to try to feel at home anymore. Briana called and she's coming day after tomorrow. I'll be going back to my place."

His smile faded and their eyes met for a long moment before he put on a forced smile. "Well, that's good. I'm glad she'll be able to take care of you for a while."

"Yeah. It's good."

His chest lifted in a deep breath and neither of them spoke as their eyes met.

Finally, she made herself stand. "So, maybe you can help me pack?"

"You said she's not coming until day after tomorrow. And you know I never take an afternoon off. So let's enjoy it while we can."

She stared at his crooked smile and her heart bumped around in her chest. She couldn't believe he'd taken time off to be with her. Was that a good thing she'd be able to take with her when they parted ways? Or would it make her miss him even more than she would have?

"I…I don't know what to say."

"I hope you'll say yes," he said quietly. "I was thinking we could spend some time in the city, doing a few things we talked about but never got around to. Go to a couple of your favorite museums, since I never take time to do things like that. See the Rockefeller Center Christmas tree."

A bubble filled her chest, warring with the melancholy she'd felt earlier, balling up in there until she could hardly breathe. Incredibly, Conor had taken the afternoon off to spend it with her. Maybe it would be the best way in the world to put the chaotic feelings from their divorce into the past.

Her throat tight, she somehow managed to answer. "Well… Since I'll probably be moving sometime soon, that sounds like a nice way to say goodbye to both you *and* New York."

Conor let himself hold her hand, as he had from pretty much the moment they'd left his apartment. He'd convinced her he was making sure she didn't stumble and fall on the uneven sidewalk, but the truth was he wanted that physical connection with her for the short time he'd be able to enjoy it. What was the point of keeping his distance when they'd shared a kind of closeness last night that was bittersweet?

Sweet because they still obviously cared about one another, and immeasurably bitter because he couldn't be the man she deserved and he'd never put them in a position where he could ever hurt her again.

Jillian looked up at him as they left the last exhibit at the Guggenheim Museum and headed toward the coat check, where they'd stashed their lunch cooler. "This was fun. I feel silly that I've never come to this museum in the three years I've lived in New York."

"I haven't been here for a long time. And I'm still not sure about that weird exhibit that looked like giant cotton balls on pieces of wood and those big stones strewn around the floor—but, hey. What do I know about art?"

He loved the way she laughed, just like she had when they'd looked at the exhibit. Lighthearted, the way she had been long ago when they'd been happy together.

"Enough to know it looks like overgrown cotton balls. I thought we might get thrown out, joking about it. Good thing we moved to the Kandinsky exhibit or we might have."

He grinned. "Yeah. Good thing… I enjoyed most of the other stuff, though."

"Me, too."

The way she smiled at him had his chest feeling lighter than it had in a long, long time. She'd been right. He should take time to enjoy the city in a way he rarely did. He'd be going back to the grind once she was out of his life for good, but he'd take this day with her while he had it.

"Ready to go to Central Park for our winter picnic? It's already mid-afternoon, so you've got to be hungry." Conor took the backpack cooler from the coat-check clerk and adjusted it on his shoulders before they headed out the door.

"I am. Studying fine art takes a lot of energy."

He had to laugh at her cute grin. "How about we sit here in the sun? Unless it's too cold for you?"

"I wore my parka so we could be outside as much as we wanted. So we can see the Rockefeller Center tree after it's dark."

"My coat is warm, too, so that's the plan." He tucked her chilly hand into the crook of his arm and drew her close as they walked. "After we eat maybe we can go to the Metropolitan Museum before we go to the Rockefeller Center—unless you have another idea."

"I hear they've kept the boathouse at the Lake open late this year, because the weather has been so mild. I think it's closing tomorrow for the winter. Maybe we could rent a boat and row around for half an hour before we eat? I've walked by the boats on the Lake a few times and always wanted to do it, but never have. A couple times I had the dogs with me, and I was afraid Yorkie would jump into the water, like the goof he is. Plus Hudson's awful big for a rowboat."

Another knife-stab of regret jabbed him in the chest. He wondered if she'd wanted to do that while they were married. If so, it was another example of the ways he'd failed her, leaving her alone most of the time.

"I'm sure the dogs love the park, but for today I'm glad we came without them. Hitting the museums and riding in a boat couldn't be on our agenda if we had them with us."

"Not to mention that Yorkie would be trying to steal our lunch whenever we weren't looking."

He'd always been a sucker for that smile of hers, and he shook off the melancholy that had sneaked into his heart again. He wanted this day with her to be filled with good memories for both of them.

"All right. Boat ride it is, and then we'll eat."

They walked in companionable silence to the Lake and rented a rowboat. Conor set the backpack in the bow of the boat, then reached for Jill's hand. "Step in. I'll steady you until you've sat on the middle bench. I figure you want to row?"

He grinned at her surprised laugh.

"I *do* want to row. Except we'll go in circles using only one oar."

"Well, if you're going to make me do all the work," he said with an exaggerated sigh, "you might as well sit in the back."

"How about we both sit on the middle seat and each take one oar?"

This time he was the one who laughed. "I think that would be really difficult."

"Let's give it a try, anyway. I need to keep at least one arm strong."

He found himself falling into her twinkling gray-green eyes, felt his own smile forming deep inside his chest even as all those mixed emotions tangled in there as well. "All right. Who knows? Maybe we'll be trend-setters and everyone on the Lake will follow our lead."

"Not too many people out here on a chilly December

afternoon, with the boats about to shut down. Maybe they're smarter than we are."

"Or we're smarter than they are, having to sit close together to stay warm."

She laughed as he helped her onto the middle seat, then shoved the boat into the water and jumped in next to her. Their hips were smashed next to each other's and their shoulders bumped, too. Her beautiful face was so close her hair lifted to tickle his skin as he reached across to grab her oar for her, and suddenly he was incredibly glad she'd suggested this unorthodox and probably ridiculous way to row a boat.

"Ready?"

"Ready!"

They both dipped their oars, and for a few minutes they did fine. Then their rhythm got off-kilter and the boat began to move in a slow circle back to where they'd come from, making them both laugh and stop rowing.

"Seems to me we're doing what you said we'd do if you rowed alone," Conor teased. "Let's decide where we want to go, then we'll try again."

"How about over there by the rocks? Someone told me there are lots of turtles there. Maybe we'll see them."

"Okay. I'm going to row twice to turn us, then you're going to join me. Okay?"

She grinned up at him and nodded, and he got so fixated on her eyes and smile he forgot to start rowing. He leaned in to kiss her forehead, and let his lips linger there because he couldn't help himself.

"Your bump's almost gone."

"Probably that nasty ice helped it go away faster."

"Probably…" He let himself softly kiss her mouth and was glad she didn't pull away. "See? I do know what I'm doing sometimes."

"Sometimes. Especially when it comes to rowing."

She leaned up to press her lips to his again, and he closed his eyes to soak in how good it felt. Floating on the water with the sun on their faces and the cold breeze on their skin and the feel of her mouth on his. He wrapped his free arm around her back, wanting to keep kissing her. Wanting the moment never to end.

A loud splash nearby, along with some laughing, had them pulling apart, their eyes meeting. Hers seemed to be filled with the same longing and melancholy that kept threatening to ruin the day, and he resolutely shoved his own longing down. Appreciating and enjoying one another today would go a long way toward healing them both when they parted.

"All right, here we go. One, two, three, dip."

This time they managed to row in sync, slowly making their way across the Lake. Conor kept his arm around her waist, holding her close. Because it felt so good, because he wanted her to stay warm, and because he thought maybe it helped them move together in rhythm. Though that made him think about last night and…

He sucked in a deep breath. "Doing good now, aren't we?"

"Expert rowing, I must say." Her white teeth gleamed as she smiled up at him. "Though I haven't seen anyone else rowing like this. No trendsetting going on."

"Give it time. Next time you're here I'll bet half the people on the Lake will be doing it just like this."

"That might be a long time," she said, her voice tinged with regret. "If I move out of state I won't be coming to New York much."

He nearly told her that she didn't have to take the job if she'd miss the city so much. Then he remembered the reason she wanted to move and couldn't argue with it. He knew that it would be incredibly difficult for them to see one another regularly at work. When they'd been dating, and then first married, seeing one another there had been the highlight of his day. After their breakup it had been the worst torture in the world, and he knew she'd felt the same way.

Having no good response to her comment, he stayed quiet as they rowed across the water, glistening with late-afternoon sunlight on its gentle waves. They approached the rocky shoreline on one side and she pointed and exclaimed.

"Look! There they are—three of them, sunning on that rock. Wow, I didn't think we'd really get to see them."

"Pretty cool. Not too many places where you can see turtles on a lake with a skyline like that in the background."

"True. No place in the world like New York City."

There it was again. That tinge of sadness in her voice. He stopped rowing and reached to turned her face toward his. "Jill. If you don't want to move, you shouldn't. We can figure out a way to work near each other. Or you can stay at the OTC until you find another job in the city. I don't want to be the reason you feel you have to leave here."

"I know. But moving is a good solution in a lot of ways. The dogs will do better in a bigger place, and it'll be a lot cheaper for me to live. Those are pluses. And maybe up the road I'll want to move back. Or maybe I'll love it wherever I end up next." She stroked her fingers across his cheek and he could see the effort she made to smile. "Please don't worry. All things work out the way they're supposed to."

Did they? Maybe... Probably. Though he wasn't sure if that statement made him feel better or worse.

"Jill, I—"

"Let's go a little further—up to that pretty bridge," she said, interrupting.

Which was good, because he hadn't really known what he was going to say.

"Then we'll go have lunch?"

"All right."

He breathed in the lake-water-scented air, glad to move on from the subject even though he wasn't sure they'd fully talked it through.

After floating beneath the bridge, they turned around and headed back to the dock.

"You stay put," he said as he set the oars back in place and stepped out. Then he put out his hand. "Careful, now."

"I may be handicapped but I'm not an invalid, Mr. Mother-Hen."

The cute smile she sent him loosened the bands of

guilt and regret tightening his chest. "That's *Dr.* Mother-Hen, thank you. And I'm just trying to keep you safe."

He helped her step from the boat, then retrieved the backpack.

"If looking at fine art made us hungry, rowing should make us feel starved. I know a good place not too far off. Should have some sunshine to keep us warm."

They walked through the park until he found the spot he knew she'd enjoy. He tugged out the thin blanket he'd rolled up and stuck in the backpack and laid it down on the ground, with Jill helping spread it out as best she could. They sat in the center of it, her knee touching his as he twisted to dig into the cooler.

"Turkey sandwiches—mine with hot pepper cheese and yours with that yucky Swiss you like."

"Swiss is a classic cheese that many people around the world love."

"Yeah, well, they'd like pepper jack better if they tried it." He loved to tease her, if only to see her roll her eyes and the way her lips tipped up at the corners. "Potato chips, carrots—and, of course, dill pickles just for you."

"You like pickles, too."

"Not the way you do." He held one up to her lips and she took a smiling bite. Without planning to, his lips followed, pressing hers, and he gave them a tiny lick. "Mmm… On second thought, maybe I *do* like the taste of them as much as you do. In fact, I like it lot."

Their eyes met for a suspended moment, and he was about to go in for another kiss when she turned her face away and gently shoved her shoulder into his. "Then

I hope you brought plenty of pickles, because I expect my fair share."

"More than your fair share, I promise."

He pulled the rest of the food out of the pack as those mixed emotions kept on rolling around his chest. Sitting here with Jill so close to him it seemed every sensory sensation was heightened. The feel of the warm sun on his skin and the cold breeze on his face... The sight of her beautiful eyes smiling at him... It had him thinking about how wonderful she'd felt in his arms. About the taste of her mouth that he'd never get to enjoy again after today.

"I had them cut your sandwich in four pieces, so it would be easy to eat with one hand," he said.

"I have to tell you," she said, her suddenly serious gaze meeting his, "I would never have guessed you could be such a thoughtful caregiver. I mean, you're good with patients, and a great surgeon, but that's not the same as thinking ahead to someone's needs. You've really done that with me through all this."

"Can't claim to have spent much time thinking about other people's needs—which you know very well. But I've been glad to be here to help you as I could."

"Maybe it's time to rethink that about yourself," she said softly.

"Believe me, I—"

He saw her sit up straighter and stare over his shoulder, frowning, which had him turning, too.

"What?"

"Somebody just fell off their bike on that path over there. And they haven't gotten up yet."

CHAPTER NINE

CONOR COULD CLEARLY see the bike lying on its side, and someone flat on the ground next to it. After a full minute or so the person still hadn't got up, and Conor pushed to his feet. "I'm going over there to see if they're hurt."

"I'll come with you. But don't lag behind for me. I'll catch up."

He reached down to help her up, then strode to see what the situation was. When he got closer he could see it was a man lying there, clutching his wrist and staring at it as he struggled to sit up.

Conor covered the final distance at a jog until he stopped in front of the guy, instantly seeing that his index finger was turned sideways at the joint.

"I guess I don't need to ask if you're okay, because I can see you're not." He crouched down and helped him to a sitting position. "I'm Dr. McCarthy, an orthopedic surgeon. It's possible that it's broken, but my guess is that you dislocated your finger when you fell."

"Look at it!" The man looked up at him, his eyes

wide, obviously distressed. "It hurts like hell and it's freaking me out."

"Dislocated fingers do tend to freak people out, but hopefully it's not too serious." Conor gave him a smile he hoped would reassure him a little, because his skin had blanched to a pale gray and he was listing to one side so much it looked as if he might pass out. "Want me to take a look?"

"Oh, God." The guy stared down at his hand again and didn't respond to the question.

"What's…? Oh, I see," Jillian said, kneeling next to the two of them with the cooler bag in her good hand. She looked up at Conor, and as their eyes met it was clear that she, too, saw the guy was feeling seriously upset over the way his hand looked.

"Try not to worry. It's gonna be okay." Conor grasped the man's wrist and leaned in close to examine the finger as best he could, at the same time feeling for his pulse. "Jill? Can you get some ice out of the cooler? And maybe one of the paper lunch bags."

Their eyes met again, and hers telegraphed loud and clear that she knew exactly why he'd asked for the bag. The man's breathing was quick and heavy, and his pulse way too fast. Definitely beginning to hyperventilate. The sooner they could get it under control, the better.

"You'll have to help me get it unzipped."

"Sorry. You'd think I'd remember by now."

He shook his head and got it open for her, before he turned his attention back to the injured man, helping him sit more upright.

"Hang in there. I know it looks scary, but try to

breathe a little slower, down into your belly instead of your chest. You feel lightheaded?"

The man nodded, and seemed to have listened as he obviously attempted to alter his breathing. But the way he started to lean to one side again made Conor worry that he might completely faint.

"You're starting to hyperventilate—which is totally normal when something looks as weird as a dislocated finger. I'm going to have you breathe into a paper bag. In and out...real slowly."

"How about you hold it to his mouth while I ice the finger?" Jillian said as she emptied a paper bag and handed it him.

Conor realized there was no way she could hold it to his face with her current handicap, so he worked to get it open and around the man's lips in just a few seconds.

"Breathe in, then out. Slower. Like I said, breathe all the way into your belly. That's the way."

The man nodded and breathed, and after a minute or so Conor was relieved to see some of the color begin to come back to his face. He glanced down to see that Jill gently held a bag of ice on his hand, and as their eyes met again he saw hers filled with a warm smile.

"Are you going to try to reduce it?" she asked.

"No. I think it's probably just dislocated, but we should get an X-ray to make sure before it's moved back into place." He slowly lowered the bag from the man's face, glad that he seemed calmer. "Feeling a little better?"

He nodded, and Conor gave him a smile. "Good. You're going to need to see an orthopedic surgeon. You can go to an ER and have an X-ray done there, or you can go straight to the hand and arm orthopedic center where I work. Honestly, that would be the most efficient thing, with less wait time, and I can call ahead to tell them you're coming. They're open for another hour, but it's whatever you want to do."

"ERs can have an awful wait," the man said, with a grimace. "Your orthopedic center sounds a lot better. Where is it? Close enough that I can walk?"

"Not a good idea for you to try to walk there when you're hurting and a little light-headed. You might even have your finger jostled by pedestrians on the way, and you definitely don't want that. Do you feel up to taking a cab, or do you want me to call an ambulance?"

"Seems stupid to call an ambulance for a messed-up finger." The guy shook his head. "I feel better now. I'll take a cab. But…can you lock up my bike? The lock's around the handlebars. I'll send my son to come get it later."

"Will do. I'll call HOAC to tell them to expect you, then I'll walk you to Fifth Avenue and make sure you get in a cab safe, give them the address. Okay?"

"Okay. Thanks so much. Sorry I was such a baby about the way my finger looks—but, *wow*. Never seen anything like it." The man managed a weak smile. "I appreciate all you've done. And for taking care of my bike, too. Very nice of you."

"Glad to be here to help. And I can assure you most people are distressed by dislocated limbs and the way they look."

Conor pulled out his phone to call HOAC, then grasped the man's arm to help him stand.

"Hold that bag of ice on there, okay?"

The guy was definitely a little shaky, but he held the bag against his finger when Jill let go of it, and seemed okay to walk with Conor close to him.

Conor turned to Jill. "I'll be back shortly."

"Okay. I'll get the bike locked up over there." She pointed at a rack. "Will your son be able to find it, do you think?"

"Yeah. And if not I can come back myself, after whatever they're going to do to my finger—even if it's tomorrow."

Conor reached for Jill's hand and smiled at her as he gave it a quick squeeze. "See you in a sec."

After he'd got the man safely into a cab he came back into the park to see Jillian sitting on the blanket where they'd eaten their lunch. Her head was tipped back and she had her eyes closed, probably enjoying the warmth of the sun. The sunlight caught the golden highlights in her hair as it fluttered around her face, and his chest squeezed at how beautiful she was.

It seemed she must have felt his gaze on her as he stepped closer, because she opened her eyes and curved her pretty lips into a smile.

This would probably be the last time he'd see her looking exactly like this. Relaxed and appreciating the simple pleasure of being outdoors in Central Park. Enjoying being with him, almost like they'd used to be and yet not quite. They might have talked through their history and come to a new understanding, but some of the pain of those days still lingered. Probably always would.

Some of the love did, too. At least, it did for him.

As he approached and her smile widened the emotions pressing on his chest told him he would always love her. It was just too damn bad—crushingly pathetic, really—that he wasn't a different kind of man. There wasn't another woman in the world as special as Jillian Keyser, and a part of him wanted to grab her up and kiss her and beg her to come back to him.

But he wouldn't. He'd just hurt her again, and he couldn't bear to do that to her. What he *could* do was cherish these last hours with her and then keep the many perfect memories close to his heart, accepting the ache that would follow.

His throat closing, he glanced at his watch. "It's going to be getting dark soon. How about we head to the Rockefeller Center now?"

"I'd love that."

"It's about two miles from here. You feel up to walking that far, or do you want to grab a cab?"

"As I said before, I'm no invalid." This time she was the one who tucked her hand into his arm and stood close. "And walking in the city is one of my favorite things to do—especially since I can't run at the moment."

"Then let's go."

Their trek down the crowded sidewalk felt perfect in every way. They laughed together about the dogs' antics, about funny things that had happened where she'd been working, about all kinds of lighthearted subjects—which was exactly what Conor wanted for their last day or two together.

As they approached Rockefeller Center the lights of the tree glistened all the way down the street, and a cute squealing sound came from Jillian's lips.

"It's so beautiful! I never, ever get tired of looking at it. Do you?"

She lifted her face to his, her wide and happy smile making him feel beyond glad he'd been smart enough to take the afternoon off. That she'd wanted to come here tonight.

"Never. I've lived in the city for a long time now, but it wouldn't be Christmas without this tree, would it?"

"No. It wouldn't. And I just might have to change my mind and come back to the city every Christmas after I move away. Just to see it again."

He knew she wouldn't want to see *him* again, but refused to let that thought ruin the rest of the night.

They joined the crowds around the tree, watching the skaters on the ice rink next to it and listening to a band that had just begun to play. For a long time they stood together and soaked in the moment without speaking.

Gusts of wind whipped through the streets, more than earlier, and he moved to wrap his arms around her, pulling her back up against his chest.

"Are you cold?"

"No. I'm perfect."

"Yes, you are."

He rested his cheek against her temple and thought about how true that statement was. Jillian Keyser was as perfect as a woman could be.

"I'm not, you know." She turned in his arms and looked up at him, her eyes deeply serious. "We've talked about your past and how that affected you. But I haven't confessed about my own past and how that's affected me. And I think I should, so you know that all that was part of why our marriage failed, too."

"What are you talking about?"

"You know about my leg surgery... But I only shared the basics with you—like how old I was when I had the surgery, which as an orthopedic surgeon you would have known anyway. You assumed I'd left it all in my past. But I never really did."

He wasn't sure where she was going with this, and decided to stay mostly quiet and let her talk. "So it was traumatizing?"

"Yes. Growing up with one leg a lot shorter than the other, living with that kind of abnormality, was horrible."

"Why didn't you talk about that when I asked you? You told me it was so long ago you hardly remembered."

"That was a fib." She sent him a rueful smile. "I guess I just didn't want to talk about it. Which proves I've never fully dealt with how that felt, even though I thought I had."

"Did other kids make fun of you?"

She stared up at him. "How did you know?"

"Kids can be mean little things. Somebody stands out in some way...it makes them a moving target for bullies, unfortunately." The wind lifted her hair, and he gently ran his hand over its softness. "What did they do?"

"Called me lovely names—especially on the playground, where I had trouble doing some of the things the other kids did. You'd think that being called *freak* or *peg-leg* would be the worst. Believe it or not, though, the ones that hurt the most were *Jumpin' Jill* or *Jumpy Jillian*. Isn't that silly?" She shook her head. "I mean, it's such a stupid nickname I should have let it roll off my back. But I hated it."

"God, that's horrible. Makes me wish I could find them now and kick their butts—if they were guys."

"Both boys *and* girls called me those names. And, since I'm going into true confession about this whole thing, when I was about fourteen, the year before I had the surgery, was the worst. Not a single boy was interested in me other than those who wanted to torment me and make fun of me—and you know how self-conscious teenagers are anyway. It was awful."

"Damn. What idiotic fools." He tightened his hold on her, tucking her close. His chest tight for Jillian and what she'd gone through when she was young. "Why didn't you tell me this when I was giving my own true confession last night? We both had some rough times as kids."

"I know. Which brings me to what else I want to say to you."

He waited. Her beautiful eyes were so serious he wondered what could possibly be coming next.

"I blamed you for everything that went wrong in our marriage. Your working too much. Your extreme focus on making money. Your making me feel less important than all the other stuff in your life. It was all your fault—or so I convinced myself."

"We've already agreed I was a lousy husband," he said quietly.

"But now I'm admitting that I know that I was part of the problem, too. These past ten months I've thought a lot about what happened and how I reacted to it. I've come to see that all the insecurities of my physical abnormality have made me deeply insecure in a way I didn't understand. Didn't realize was still there. I was ashamed of the scars on my legs. That's why I always wore long dresses to the gala events we went to. Not just because some of the other women did, but because I didn't want those people—your wealthy, glamorous friends—to see them. To know how much I didn't belong there. That I didn't fit into handsome, wealthy Dr. Conor McCarthy's life the way your wife should."

"Jill…" He was so stunned at what she'd said he could barely speak. "I had no idea. You're always the most beautiful woman in any room. Your scars show nothing except that you're a warrior. That you dealt with something difficult and overcame it. Took up running. Trained for *marathons*, for God's sake! You—"

"Stop." She pressed her cold fingers against his lips as she leaned up to kiss his cheek. "I'm not telling you this to have you reassure me or compliment me. I'm telling you because I want you to understand that I know *my* issues were part of our problem, too. My insecurities had me wanting you to constantly prove that you loved me, that you found me desirable despite my scars. I'd lived with my wallflower status my whole life. I wanted to prove that I was the most important thing in your world, despite my inability to fit into it. I kept pushing you to let me do that, and when you didn't it dumped fuel all over those awful insecurities. Which made me push you harder about your work hours, which made you feel angry and frustrated. It was a vicious circle that couldn't possibly end well."

"I'm sorry." He pressed his forehead to hers, still reeling from all she'd said. "More than you'll ever know. I'm sorry I didn't give you what you needed. I'm sorry I can't be the man you deserve. And you deserve so much, Jillian. You deserve the world. You're the most special woman I've ever met. I don't know what else to say…"

"Don't be sorry." She pressed her palm to his cheek. "As much as our breakup and divorce hurt, it's helped me see how much I need to work on my inner self-confidence. Find it for real, in myself, and not expect to get it from anyone else. It has to come from me. That's the very important lesson I've learned from our relationship, so thank you for that."

He couldn't think of a thing to say that hadn't already been said, so he kissed her. He held her in his arms as the music swirled in the air around them, as people chattered and laughed, and he kept on kissing her.

Someone jostled them and he finally lifted his head. Their eyes met and he felt her shiver.

"You're cold." His voice was gruff. "Are you ready to go back to my apartment?"

She nodded, possibly finding it as difficult to speak as he did. Wordlessly, he took her hand and walked to Fifth Avenue to hail a cab. Sat silently next to her as the car whizzed past the lights and sounds and people of the city. Took the elevator to his apartment, where the dogs jumping around gave him a chance to fully gather his thoughts.

He got the dogs their food, and as they began to gobble it down he made up his mind. He'd failed Jillian in so many ways, but there was one thing he could do for her tonight—something that he wanted to do for both of them before they went to live their separate lives.

He strode to the sofa where she'd just sat down. "There's something you need to know."

He wondered what his expression looked like, because she looked slightly alarmed.

"What?"

He dropped to his knees in front of her. Reached for the leg of her loose-fitting pants and shoved his hand up to her thigh. Ran his fingertips down the long, white scars left from the surgeries she'd had, followed by his lips.

She tried to tug away. "Conor, don't. I—"

"You have to know that this is one beautiful leg. *Beautiful.* Soft and smooth and strong. It's a gorgeous shape and it does amazing things. Walks dogs. Runs marathons. Kickboxes." He lifted his face to see her staring. "I admire the hell out of you, and this leg, and what you've both done to overcome its start in life."

"That's…that's a very sweet thing to say. But I— *Oh!*"

She squirmed and gasped as he licked his way up her shin, tickled her knee, and began to move another couple inches up her inner thigh, until the sweatpants wouldn't roll any higher.

"What are you doing?"

"Showing you that you and your legs are sexy as hell. Showing you that I think you're wonderful in so many ways. Showing you that if anyone should have an abundance of self-confidence, it's you, Jillian. You are beautiful both inside and out."

"Thank you," she whispered. "And, though we weren't right for one another, you are special in so many ways, too, and I'll always care about you."

"I'll always care about you, too. And I'd be lying if I said I don't want to be with you now. Maybe it's a bad idea. But I don't care. I want one more time with you before we say our goodbyes."

Because that was true, he sat next to her, pulled her close and kissed her. Exerting a soft pressure, his mouth moved slowly on hers and she kissed him back.

"Just one more time," she breathed. "Once more…"

His heart thumped hard as the kiss deepened, and she gasped in protest when he broke the kiss and dropped to his knees again.

"Conor. What—?"

"Shh…" he murmured against her calf as he resumed kissing his way up her leg. "For once I can't be sad about your current handicap. Because I know these loose pants aren't going to be very hard to slide off."

His hands moved to her waistband, his thumbs slipping inside and tugging them down to her knees. This time his mouth followed the line of her scars on its way back down, and eventually he pulled the pants over her feet. Then he stood to tug her sweatshirt off and she gasped and laughed at the same time.

"No fair! You stripped me nearly naked in a nano-second when I can't begin to get your clothes off you."

"Handy, then, that I can do it myself." He got out of his clothes as quickly as possible and loved the way she was staring at his naked body.

"Well, okay, then," she said, leaning back to look him up and down with a sultry smile. "I guess being handicapped isn't so bad after all."

He laughed, then decided that moving to his bedroom was the best option. She squeaked when he picked her up and carried her toward the bedroom. The dogs had been lying on the floor, and got up to follow.

"Sorry, guys. You're not invited."

He kicked the bedroom door closed behind him and laid her gently on the bed, his body following. He managed to remember her injured arm and lifted it over her head again before lowering his mouth to hers.

"Got to protect this," he said. "Things might get a little rough."

She laughed against his lips and wrapped her good arm around his neck. Their kiss got hotter, wilder, as he touched her everywhere he could reach, and the sound of her small gasps and moans was so arousing he had to fight to not dive inside her right that second.

"Conor... Conor, I need you inside me."

Obviously she felt the same way he did, and he gritted his teeth against the insistent desire. "I'm not ready. This is not nearly long enough to make love with you."

"I know. But I want you *now*."

She stroked her hand down his belly, grasping him and wresting a deep groan from his chest, and he knew he couldn't hang on much longer.

"We'll go slower next time," she said.

"There won't be a next time." He hated the truth of the words that had come out of his mouth, but they were the one thing that managed to cool the heat. "Remember?"

"I remember. Except maybe we can renegotiate that deal the way you do in the boardroom? I'm not going back to my apartment until the day after tomorrow. Right?"

"Right..."

He loved the tiniest of smiles that curved her lips as he grabbed a condom from the drawer and kissed her again. Smashed her body to his. And as they joined and moved together his heart lifted and soared in a way that obliterated any and all thoughts of the past.

He broke their kiss to draw in a deep, ragged breath. Stared into her eyes as her name left his lips. "Jillian. Jilly..."

She cupped his cheek in her palm and emotion clogged his throat. As he nudged her over the peak she cried out and pressed her mouth to his, swallowing the moan that followed.

He pressed his face to the side of her neck and breathed her in as his heartbeat slowly settled. Her soft hand slowly stroked his back, and the physical and emotional sensations got all tangled up in his chest as he held her close.

God, how he loved this woman. But he would never put either of them in a position where he could hurt her again. And he knew with certainty that her leaving his life a second time was going to feel every bit as terrible as it had the first time.

CHAPTER TEN

JILLIAN WAS FEELING happy that morning. Her therapy had gone even better than expected, and her hand and fingers were becoming a little more mobile every day. It had nothing to do with the magical day she'd spent with Conor and their night together. Nothing at all.

She inwardly rolled her eyes at herself as she folded towels in the therapy center's laundry room. She shouldn't be feeling so lighthearted. She'd be moving back to her own apartment tomorrow. It must be because she and Conor had come to a better understanding than they'd had when they'd broken up. An understanding that had made moving on from that unpleasant experience much easier.

As though she could feel his presence, she looked up from the folding table to see the man in question moving toward her. The overhead fluorescent lights made his hair seem even lighter, his features even more handsome, and the smile he sent her made her feel warm all over.

"Hello, Jillian." He moved closer and tugged her into

a corner where curious eyes couldn't easily see them. "How did your therapy go?"

"Wonderful. I feel like I'm really making progress, and I can even use a few fingers to help fold these towels now."

"I'm glad." He shoved his hands in his pockets and looked down at her, his expression now inscrutable. "I have a question for you—and please don't be too quick to answer…just think about it."

"What question?"

"I know you don't love—okay, don't even *like* going to charity events. But there's one tonight I've been asked to attend to represent one of my businesses which is sponsoring an adoption event for an animal shelter. Since you're an animal lover, I was hoping you'd be willing to come with me."

A charity event. The thought sent a chill down her spine. She'd always felt so awkward attending them when they'd been married. Now that they were divorced would it be even worse? Or would it be easier, since she wouldn't have to prove anything as Conor McCarthy's wife?

"I don't know. I—"

"Before you answer—" he held up his hand "—there's another part to the question. How would you feel about one more night out together on our anniversary?"

"Anniversary?" She managed a faint laugh. "Maybe you're thinking of a different ex-wife, because we got married in January."

"It's the anniversary of your first day at the OTC. Of the first moment I saw you. Of our first date. And, yeah, that's unbelievably sappy, but I thought of it and thought it might be…fun."

"I can't believe you remember that." Her heart flip-flopped as she stared at him. "I'm…touched. But I think we both know that prolonging our goodbyes isn't going to make it any easier."

"I know. And I'm not trying to make it easier, because nothing will."

His somber expression shook her heart.

"When we said goodbye the day you left—or didn't say it—we were both angry and upset and hurt. I guess what I want this time is a different kind of closure. A positive kind. A nice evening that celebrates all the things we liked about one another. A bookend moment to mark when we met, and when we said goodbye again."

"Well, I… That does sound…nice. And the charity does sound worthwhile…"

She wasn't sure it would be "nice" at all, but wouldn't one more night with him, and the closure he spoke of, be a positive thing? Better than just shaking hands with him after she packed up her stuff from his place and left?

"Thank you. How about I take you back to your apartment so you can get a dress to wear? It doesn't have to be anything fancy—just the usual for an event like this."

"All right. That would be perfect. I'll be able to get some stuff done there, too, like water my plants, and then I'll head back to your place on my own. I'll take a cab instead of the subway."

"Good." He glanced around, then leaned in to press his mouth to hers in a short but unbearably sweet kiss, his eyes gleaming as he drew back. "I'll drop you off at lunch. Then see you back at my place before the event."

It felt a little odd to be back in her own little apartment. She'd called it home for less than a year, and couldn't say she had any particular attachment to the place. Fussing with her plants and doing some photography work on her computer felt nice, but part of her couldn't wait to get back to Conor's place. So she could see the dogs, of course.

She flicked through the formal dresses she'd bought during their marriage, glad she hadn't gotten rid of them as she'd considered doing. She reached for a floor-length gown she'd always liked the color of, then stopped and looked at a different one she'd never worn. A beautiful shade of sea-green, with a chiffon skirt that stopped an inch above her knee.

She thought about all she'd confessed to Conor. All the insecurities she had about herself and her scars and how she'd never quite fitted into his world. She fingered the silky fabric and then, in a quick decision, pulled the dress out, slipped it into a zippered garment bag, and looked for shoes to go with it.

This was her first step toward the new and improved Jillian. If Conor thought her legs were beautiful, that they didn't make her undesirable or a freak, shouldn't she finally believe it, too?

That bubble of happiness filled her chest again as she packed up her things and went out to hail a cab to Conor's place.

She took Yorkie out for a short walk, though the cold wind had her wishing she'd brought one of the dog's sweaters to Conor's, so he could have worn it. Then again, with Briana coming they'd all be going back to her place tomorrow anyway, so what was the point?

Refusing to let those thoughts put a damper on the evening, she got ready for the charity event. She swirled the skirt a little in front of the long mirror in the guest bedroom, pleased with what she saw. Proud of what she felt for the first time in her life. Yes, her scars were visible. But Conor was right. From now on she'd think of them as war wounds that she'd earned, overcoming her limp as well as she possibly could.

Her cell phone rang and she hurried to grab it, not recognizing the number. "Hello?"

"Hello, Jillian? This is Mary Rodgers, from Therapy Centers of New England. I apologize for calling so late, but we have another opening and we would like to have you take the job. The board has already looked through all your credentials, and we don't feel you need to interview. Are you still interested?"

Jill's heart jumped into her throat. Was she? Did she still want to move to Connecticut? Start a new life there away from New York City and far from Conor McCarthy?

Just a few days ago she'd been sure the answer was yes. But tonight, after their time together, and learning about Conor's past, and after her own questions and revelations about herself, it was possible the answer might be no.

She opened her mouth, then closed it again, not sure

how to answer, and worked to find her voice. "I appreciate the offer, Mary. I'm in a meeting right now, but can I call you back tomorrow?"

"Of course. I would appreciate hearing from you as soon as possible, because we need a replacement right away. Even with your injured hand we'd like to have you help train our newest therapists until you're able to fully work with patients."

"I understand. I'll definitely contact you tomorrow."

She hung up and slowly walked into the living room, looking out over the twinkling city lights and knowing she didn't want to move from here.

Would it really be impossible to work with him again?

Would it be impossible for them to be together again?

The thought made her head swim, because she'd never considered that. But now, thinking of everything they'd been through in the past, and the things they'd shared with one another now, could they have a second chance to be together again?

Her phone rang again, and she looked down to see it was Conor. Her hand shook a little as she answered. "Hi. Are you on your way here?"

"I'm really sorry but I got held up. I've been trying to pull this meeting together for a month now, and of course they wanted it to happen this evening. But we're almost done. How do you feel about taking a cab and I'll meet you there?"

"Um…okay. I guess I can do that." The idea of walking into a fancy gala event all by herself sounded daunting. But she was working on being the new Jillian, wasn't she? She could do it.

"Thank you. I'll text you the address. See you there."

The phone went dead—he'd obviously been in a hurry.

She sighed and got her coat and handbag. Said goodbye to the dogs, went downstairs. Alfred insisted on getting a cab for her, even though she could have done it herself, and in minutes she was on her way.

The lights of the city seemed in full twinkle tonight, and she absorbed the way living in this city made her feel. It seemed as though the entire place had a pulse to it, alive and vibrant, and she realized *she* felt alive and vibrant here, too.

She wanted to stay in this city. And she also realized, terrifying as the thought was, that she wanted to try again with Conor, too. He'd said it was the anniversary of the day they'd met—couldn't that mean it was the perfect night to tell him she wanted to make that happen?

Walking into the hotel ballroom on her own didn't feel as awkward as she'd expected it to. A few people she'd known back when she and Conor had been married approached her with friendly smiles. She'd always found it hard to make small talk, to feel comfortable in large groups like this, but it turned out to be good that this event was about finding homes for sheltered animals. It was something she cared about, and she'd adopted two dogs herself, so making conversation turned out to not be torturous at all.

She'd planned to wait to eat until Conor arrived, but

after an hour decided to try a few of the hors d'oeuvres. After another half hour she started to worry, and called Conor's cell phone. It went straight to voicemail.

She left a message. "I'm here, waiting. When do you think you'll get here?"

A text message pinged, and she hurried to look.

Sorry. Meeting ran late. Done soon, though. I'll be there shortly.

She blew out a breath. How late was he going to be? How long did she have to stand around and smile at people, feeling more and more foolish as time went on?

A man came and asked her to dance. She was about to refuse until her brain pointed out that it would serve Conor right to walk in and find her dancing with someone else. Then she regretted her decision, because talking to only one person on the dance floor was even harder than talking to a group. She found herself looking over the man's shoulder every time she could see the door, but unfortunately there was no tall, handsome surgeon walking in, looking for her.

Another hour or more passed. Much of the food was gone now, as were many of the people who'd been there earlier. Sitting alone at a table, she swallowed down the tears thickening her throat, and then told herself to stop it. She should be mad instead. After all they'd talked about, after all the times he'd said how much he hated it that he'd hurt her, after asking her to come here on some stupid made-up anniversary, he'd left her high and dry?

Oh, yes, she was an idiot.

The pain searing her heart was real, but Conor wasn't at fault for the damage to that vital organ. This time he'd stated loud and clear who he was, and said that he couldn't be anyone else. She'd known it but apparently had forgotten it. Or hadn't wanted to believe it after she'd had a glimpse of what they'd shared in the beginning. Of why she'd fallen in love with him.

She closed her eyes and sat very still, letting herself go back in time to when they'd first met. Those glorious early months of falling head over heels in love with each other. When every day together had seemed better than the last and the future had looked bright and brilliant.

But it hadn't been bright or brilliant. And now it was history. Over. Her wanting it to be different this time, believing it *could* be different, had been nothing but a foolish pipe dream.

She got up and headed out the door. Hailed a cab, slid inside and shut the door. As she struggled to put on her seat belt she saw a tall blond figure running to the front doors of the hotel—only to stop and stare at her. Their eyes met, and then he quickly strode toward the cab as her heart lurched, her stomach roiled, and the tears threatened all over again.

"Can we get going?" she said to the driver. "I need to get out of here. Now."

Conor leaped up the steps to Jill's apartment, his heart beating hard both because he'd been running, and because he feared how upset she might be. He'd blown everything sky-high, hadn't he? Hadn't shown up for the charity event. Just like so many times before.

He tried to tell himself she hadn't been miserable there alone. Probably hadn't cared if he was there or not, since it had been supporting a cause she believed in. And she didn't want to rekindle their relationship anyway, did she?

But he knew he was a damn liar. It *did* matter. It all mattered. They'd grown close again—so close that he'd begun to wonder if maybe they could try again. If maybe he could be a different man.

Making love with her, seeing her beautiful smile, being with her and sharing her joy in life, had had him feeling the best he'd felt since the day they'd married. And yet here he was again, being the jerk he'd known he couldn't help being. Letting her down like he'd let his mom down. Like he'd let her down so many times before. Just like he'd told her he would.

The meeting had dragged on with important business that couldn't be put off. He'd been so focused on the debate and conversation he hadn't even realized how late it had gotten until it was over. His heart had nearly stopped when he'd looked at his phone, and he had known he had no excuse to offer that was even close to good enough.

Hard as it would be, he owed her a face-to-face apology. And he owed her his assurance—again—that she was the most amazing, most beautiful woman in the world, and it was only his massive failings that had ruined everything between them. Both in the past and tonight.

He'd hoped for a closure between them that would be on a better note than the last, terrible one.

He'd sure demolished the chance for that, hadn't he?

If she screamed at him and told him what a loser he was he'd give her the chance to vent—because he deserved it.

He heaved a fortifying breath and knocked on her door. Knocked louder when she didn't answer. "Jillian?"

Still nothing. Would it be wrong of him to use the key he had? Would it scare her?

His heart was beating so hard he thought it might burst out of his chest, and anxiety churned in his gut. He had to see if she was there. See if she'd let him apologize one last time.

He slowly opened the door—then stopped cold when he saw her sitting on the sofa, wrapped in a robe, the arm with the splint resting in her lap. The eyes that met his didn't hold the anger or condemnation or disgust he'd expected. No, they simply looked tired and beyond sad, and his throat closed at the defeated expression on her beautiful face.

"Jilly…" He sat close in front of her, reaching for her good hand, and the soft feel of it in his made his chest hurt, knowing he'd never get to hold it again. "I'm sorry. I'm just so damn sorry."

"I know. I'm sorry, too. You should go now."

He had no idea what to say or do next, but getting up to leave before he'd let her know how he felt wasn't an option.

"I hope you know it's me, not you?"

"Yes, we've gone over this."

"And that you're the most beautiful, amazing woman in the world and I love you." It was true, and saying the words made his throat close again, but he forced out the rest of what he had to say. "I wish I could be different. But obviously I can't. I don't deserve you. I'm not good enough for you. You deserve so much more than a man like me."

"We've gone over this, too." Her lips curved in a smile that didn't touch her eyes. "Don't worry, Conor. I understand. It's simply time to say goodbye."

Her words were exactly what he'd been about to say, but they punched a hole in his chest and he couldn't speak for a long moment.

"If you stay in New York I promise I'll keep my distance from you at work. It…it won't be easy to be in the same building, but I want you to feel comfortable there. I don't want you to leave on my account."

"I've been offered a job in Connecticut. I'll be moving there soon."

He didn't know what the weight in his chest meant, because he should be *glad* she'd found a new job. But the finality of not seeing her again felt unbearable. Somehow it was almost worse than ten months ago, which he wouldn't have dreamed was even possible.

But it was.

"Do you…do you need help moving?"

"Conor."

Her lips twisted and she looked at him as if he was pathetic, which he clearly was.

"If I do, I don't think you'll be the person I call. We agreed earlier that this would be our last evening together, anyway. Let's stick to that. I…I don't want our goodbye to drag on any longer than it has to, you know?"

He looked down at her hand in his and nodded. He should feel the same way, but knowing he'd be leaving this apartment in a matter of minutes and never seeing her again shoved the knife blade currently sticking into his heart another inch deeper.

He lifted his gaze back to hers and stood, and was surprised when she stood with him.

"Remember, always, how special you are," he said.

"You, too," she said softly, shocking him by resting her hand against his cheek and giving him that sad smile again. "You're special, too, Conor, in so many ways. And I hope you find happiness someday that is more than just work. I truly do."

Emotion clogged his throat. She didn't hate him the way she had the last time they'd said goodbye, despite him deserving it. He wrapped his arms around her and held her close against him, just to feel her there one last time. When he made himself let her go he saw the sheen of tears in her beautiful eyes.

He knew there was nothing else to say that hadn't already been said. Somehow, he forced himself to turn and get ready to leave—until she reached out to touch his arm.

"I'll have Briana come get the dogs tomorrow."

"Okay. Have her give me a call." More words felt impossible, and he stepped to the door before he turned to look at her one last time. "Goodbye, Jilly. I hope your life brings you everything you want."

She nodded, and as she did so a few tears spilled from her eyes. "I hope yours does, too, Conor. Goodbye."

And with that he somehow made it out the door before a few tears of his own slipped down his cheeks.

CHAPTER ELEVEN

Packing up her apartment proved to be difficult. Jillian was thankful that Briana had gotten quite a bit done for her before she'd had to leave, and that now Michelle had been willing to stop by after work to help with the things she couldn't possibly do with one hand.

"I really appreciate this," Jill said, running the packing tape dispenser across a box as Michelle held the flaps closed. "Clothes and stuff weren't hard, and even putting things into the boxes just took me some extra time. But getting them secured and stacked? No way."

"Happy to help." Michelle lifted the box and put it on top of the others waiting for the moving company that would arrive at any minute. "But you know I'm still wondering if this is really what you want to do."

"It is. I'm sure."

Well, maybe she wasn't completely sure she wanted to leave New York. But did she want to have to see Conor's handsome face and infectious smile and think about how good it had felt to be together again for a few wonderful days? Think about how much she still loved him?

She briefly closed her eyes, picturing the face she missed so much, and swallowed down the stupid tears that threatened. Just as Conor himself had said, sometimes love wasn't enough. It just wasn't. He had demons that he didn't seem to want to battle, and she had her own. And even if she got a grip on hers, and felt she was making progress, she knew for certain now that if they tried once more it would end up in heartbreak for both of them all over again.

Not a place either of them wanted to go.

"I know from stuff you've said that you'll miss the city," said Michelle. "And I think it's wrong to let Conor McCarthy run you off if you don't want to go."

"He's not running me off. I'm choosing to go."

"Uh-huh? You're not kidding me. There was a new smile in your eyes when you two were seeing each other again—until he acted like an idiot, as usual."

"He's not an idiot. Just a guy with some issues. And I'm not sticking around to try to fix him, getting hurt all over again in the process. I'm going to concentrate on fixing myself. You should be glad about that."

"I don't know how much fixing you need, Jill. I think you're already there. As for Conor? He may have those issues you talk about, but he's more than worth fixing, in my opinion."

Yes, he was. But he didn't believe he could be fixed. And shoring up her own confidence had to be her priority—not trying to help a man who didn't believe he could be helped.

"It's too late for us," she said softly. "It just is."

Michelle sighed and moved another box. "What about leaving the city? You love it here."

"I do love New York. But the new place has lots of good things going for it."

She glanced out her front window and knew it was true that she'd miss this city. Yes, it was expensive, and crowded, and sometimes crazy, but there was no place like it and it felt like home to her. Even more after she'd moved into Conor's apartment for those first months they'd been deliriously, happily, married.

A sprinkle of raindrops began hitting the window and streaking down, and she held in a sigh. How appropriate that the unusually warm early December weather she'd enjoyed with Conor had given way to cold, gray drizzle this past week. It definitely reflected her mood. Hopefully the movers would have a way to keep her things dry as they packed them into their truck.

She turned back to Michelle and forced a smile. "Anyway, I can come back and visit New York any time, right? Expect me to bunk in with you about every three months or so."

"Uh…with the dogs?" Michelle shook her head and grinned. "Don't know that my roommate would be willing to share her bedroom with *them*—and there's only room for you and me in mine."

Jill laughed, glad to move the subject to safe ground that didn't make her heart hurt for something that couldn't be. "I'll find a kennel where they'll be happy before I visit, don't worry."

"Ready for us?"

She turned to see two guys in her doorway, wearing

matching shirts with the moving company's name on them. "Yes. We have a couple more boxes to close, but you can start to load up things while we do that, right?"

"Absolutely." He leaned down to scratch the heads of the greeting committee, known as Hudson and Yorkie, who were nosing the man's legs and wagging their tails. "Great dogs. The big one reminds me of mine."

"They *are* good dogs. Most of the time."

"So, the plan is to store your stuff in the truck overnight, then we leave in the morning. Right?"

"Right."

Tomorrow morning. The first day of her new life.

She managed to smile at the man before she and Michelle got busy packing the last few things in the kitchen as the men moved boxes and furniture.

Jill suddenly remembered the small bag of Conor's clothes he'd accidentally left that first day, when he'd brought her here after her surgery. She wanted to give it to Michelle, to take to work with her so she could return them. She didn't want to just give them to a charity shop, but also she definitely didn't want to call Conor to come get them. Their goodbye had been utterly final, and seeing one another again even for a moment would just dredge up those sad feelings all over again.

She moved into the bedroom and picked up the bag, then hesitated. The old T-shirt that he'd worn to exercise and walk the dogs poked up from the top of the bag and she tugged it out. Held it to her nose and closed her eyes to breathe in his scent. The smell she loved and that she'd never get to enjoy again.

Even as she told herself it was pathetic she opened

the suitcase she'd packed, so she'd have the basics handy at her new place, and folded the shirt inside. Zipped it closed even as she scolded herself that the last thing she needed was his shirt to wear. Something that would remind her of him at her new place and in her new life.

But she'd be thinking of him anyway, wouldn't she? Maybe in some strange way wearing his shirt would be a source of comfort instead of sadness.

With a sigh, Jill carried the bag holding his other things to the living room. "I just remembered I have some of Conor's stuff. Will you take this to work and give it to him?"

Michelle looked at her for a long moment, then nodded. "Sure. I've finished the last of the kitchen utensils. I think that's everything."

"Thanks."

She watched Michelle stack the box next to the door that was still propped wide open after the men had carried out the sofa. Then she realized that Hudson was lounging in his bed, but there was no sign of Yorkie.

"Where's Yorkie?"

She and Michelle looked all around the small apartment, and when it was clear he wasn't there a feeling of panic welled in her chest.

"Oh, my God, could he have gotten out?"

"I'll look in the stairwell," Michelle said.

"I'm coming, too." Jill shut the door behind them so there was no chance Hudson would follow.

When there was no sign of Yorkie on any of the staircases her hands began to shake and the feeling of panic grew.

"He must be out on the street! Who knows where he'll run? And he's so tiny…he could easily get hit by a car."

"Where do you usually walk him? Maybe he'll follow that route."

"I don't have a specific route, really," she said, trying to think through the cold fear clouding her mind. "I wonder if Conor did? He walked them a few times the day he was here."

"I'll call Conor and ask. Maybe he can give you some insight."

Jill's heart jolted. The last thing she wanted was to have to talk to Conor, but this was an emergency, and her feelings weren't nearly as important as finding Yorkie.

"Conor's not answering his cell. I'll call the answering service," Michelle said.

"Yorkie! Yorkie!" Jill hurried to the moving truck, calling to the men inside. "My little dog got out when the door was left open. Do you know where he is?"

"No. Damn—sorry about that. I didn't see him if he followed us."

Jill ran up the street, craning her neck and calling the dog's name with Michelle by her side, her phone still pressed to her ear.

"I need to speak with Dr. Conor McCarthy immediately," Michelle said. "It's an emergency."

"Here are the numbers I believe we can generate in the first year," Conor said as he handed everyone assembled in the boardroom the folders holding the calculations and projections he'd worked on for over six months. "The location next to HOAC is perfect for Urgent Care Manhattan to become well established as *the* place to go for non-life-threatening injuries and illnesses. No other urgent care clinic is situated within a twenty-block area, but there's a hospital only a few blocks away. If you needed to refer your patients there for things you can't take care of it would be easy to do."

"I agree the location is perfect," Peter Stanford said, addressing everyone in the room. "For all the reasons Dr. McCarthy just noted and because we can send patients directly to HOAC if they need to see an orthopedic surgeon. I believe that when we advertise that advantage a lot of patients with possible broken bones will want to come to Urgent Care Manhattan instead of our competitors."

Conor listened to the board members as they asked Peter various questions. Also asked their accountants about the numbers Conor had presented, and addressed some contract questions to their lawyer. For some reason he found he had to keep making himself refocus on the conversation. How that was possible he didn't know, because he'd worked on this project for so long he should be zeroing in on every word. Instead thoughts of Jill kept drifting into his mind, adding to the ache that still hung in his chest from the night they'd said goodbye.

He'd heard through the grapevine that she was leaving New York today. Taking the dogs and moving to another state. It was unlikely he'd ever see any of them again.

It was what he wanted. For her to find a new life

and a new beginning that made her happy. The kind of happiness he'd failed so miserably to provide. So why did his heart feel every bit as heavy as the night he'd walked out her door?

He didn't know. And it made him wonder how long it would take for him to feel even a little more normal. Which was the best he knew he could hope for, because he was absolutely certain he'd miss Jillian's lovely face and warm smile and beautiful heart forever.

He managed to focus his attention long enough to answer some of the board members' questions, but as two of them started to disagree over a few of the details his cell phone buzzed with its emergency call chime. He never answered his phone during meetings and he frowned, wondering what the problem could be, since he wasn't on call.

"Excuse me a moment," he murmured as he grabbed the phone and stood to step to the other side of the room.

"Conor McCarthy."

"Conor! It's Michelle."

Her voice sounded breathless and scared and his heart dropped straight into his stomach before it began racing. "What's wrong? Is Jill hurt?"

"No, it's Yorkie. He got out of the apartment when the moving guys were taking out the furniture. We're out here looking for him and Jill wondered if you'd taken him on any specific route when you walked him. We thought maybe he'd follow it if you did."

Damn! "Is she there? Let me talk to her."

"Okay—here…"

A muffled sound, then Jill was on the line.

"Conor? Oh, God, I'm so worried. Do you have any idea where he might go?"

His fingers tightened on his phone, because even sounding tense the voice he'd thought he'd never hear again slipped inside his wounded heart. "I don't. But let me think a minute."

"Call me if you come up with anything. I've got to go."

"Wait."

He stared out the window at the rain streaming down the glass, at the bright flash of lightning in the sky. Heard Jilly's voice sounding so panicked. Without another thought, he knew he had to help her through this scare. Help find little Yorkie, lost in this storm. The dog had been his once, too, and he had to be there for both Jillian and Yorkie when they needed him most.

"I'll be right there to help you look. I'll call after I park the car and find out where you are."

"Okay."

She hung up and he strode back to the meeting. "I'm afraid an emergency has come up and I have to leave. Please continue to go over the numbers and call me with any questions you might have."

"We'd hoped to finalize this tonight—it's important that you be here to answer those questions," Peter said, his eyebrows raised. "If it's a patient, surely there's another surgeon who can take over for you?"

"It's not a patient. It's my dog. He's lost and I have to go help find him."

Everyone in the room stared at him with varying degrees of surprise and disbelief on their faces.

Peter sent him a thunderous frown. "Your *dog*? Surely someone else can look for it?"

"They need my help."

"It seems to me perhaps you shouldn't plan to be president of this new company we'd be creating with the merger, then, if this meeting can't take priority over a pet."

"Maybe that's true. Sorry, Peter, but I've got to go."

Conor bolted to his car, waiting to be singed by gnawing regret. By worry that the deal that had been his priority for so long would fall through because of this. That all his hard work, all the money he and others would make as they improved and expanded patient care, was about to go straight out the window.

It didn't come. Even though his chest was tight with worry for Yorkie, it felt strangely light, too. As if he'd thrown a thousand-pound monster from his shoulders and was finally free of it. A monster that had been hanging there, controlling him, for way too long.

He wasn't sure exactly what that meant, but figuring it out had to take a back seat to the current emergency.

Right now Jillian and Yorkie were his priorities, and he drove as fast as he could through the traffic and rain, parked in the garage near her apartment and ran out to the streets.

"Yorkie! Yorkie!"

He strode toward the nearby park that the dogs liked, though he assumed Jill had probably gone there first.

He pulled out his phone to call and find out. "I'm near the park close to your apartment. Where are you?"

"Michelle and I were there maybe fifteen minutes

ago. Didn't see him. We're a few blocks over. I don't know how we're going to find him."

Her voice ended on a near-sob, and if he hadn't already wanted desperately to find the little pup her distress would have made him even more determined.

"I'll look here again, then call back, and we'll make a plan. Hang in there."

He strode through the small park, looking beneath the many shrubs and trees around its perimeter and in the thick groups near a few benches. "Yorkie! Yorkie!"

Bending over, he peered through a hedge that lined the brick wall, then did a double take, blinking the raindrops from his eyes. He looked again, and there, shining within the leaves, was a set of beady little eyes staring at him.

He crouched down and held out his hand. "Yorkie! It's me! Come on—you're okay. Come out now."

Conor held his breath as the dog just stared at him. He worried that Yorkie might be afraid and disoriented after he'd run off, and schooled his voice into a croon.

"Come on, now, big guy. Your mama is trying to find you. How about a treat? A nice treat?"

He drew the syllables out, the way Jill did when she talked to Yorkie, and sure enough the dog took a few halting steps closer. Close enough that Conor was able to quickly reach in, grab him, and pull him close to his chest.

A giant breath of relief whooshed from his lungs. The poor, wet dog was shivering, and he tucked him inside his coat. "There you go. You need to warm up."

Yorkie whimpered, and Conor knew there were two

priorities—one was to get the dog dried off and warm, and the other was to let Jillian know he had him safe.

Making sure he had a tight grip on the pup, he used his other hand to fish his phone from his pocket. "Jill? I have him. He was hiding under some shrubs in the park. Yes, he's okay. Just cold and wet. I'll meet you at your apartment."

"Oh, my gosh!" Her voice came on a new sob. "Thank you! We've doubled back toward my apartment building, thinking he might have tried to go home. So we're almost there now."

Conor talked to the dog as he walked and, now that he had him safe, spared a rueful thought for his clothes. A wet and muddy dog, not to mention pouring rain, just might ruin his suit—but he couldn't worry about that. He could buy a new suit, but finding the dog he loved and keeping the woman he loved from being scared and sad…

That was worth anything.

As he approached the front door of Jillian's apartment building he could see her running toward him through the gray rain and his heart jolted.

"Don't run! You could easily slip and fall on the wet pavement! I've got him and he's not getting away, I promise."

"Oh, Conor!"

She flung her arms around him and he wrapped his free arm around her and pulled her close. Both of them were soaked, but apparently she didn't care anymore than he did.

Water dripped from her sopping hair down her forehead and cheeks as she leaned up to press her wet mouth to his. "I can't believe you came. I can't believe you found him. I was so scared he'd be lost forever. I owe you so much."

"Don't be ridiculous. He was my dog once, too, and I care about him as much as you do."

It was true, and as he stood there holding her in the rain it was all he could do not to tell her how much he loved her, and that he'd learned something beyond important tonight. That work could never, ever replace the love her felt for her. His need to be there for her. With her.

His fear for Yorkie, and for her, had been so powerful it had taken precedence over anything else—including the meeting he'd so stupidly thought was everything. It might have taken him way too long to see that bright truth, but he'd never make that mistake again.

Except standing in the rain, with a wet dog tucked into his coat and a shivering woman held close in his arms, wasn't the best time to tell her all he'd learned and seen during the past hour.

"This reminds me of my all-time favorite moment in New York. Holding you in the rain in Central Park."

"Except that day we had an umbrella. And we didn't get soaking wet. And it wasn't freezing cold."

"True." Her smiling eyes met his, and it was all he could do not to lean down and kiss her. "Let's get inside out of this weather, hmm?"

She nodded, and when they got to the door a rained-on Michelle stood there. "Wow, you are *amazing*, Conor! I'm so happy you found him. I hope it's okay with you, but I'm going back to my apartment to get dry clothes." She grinned. "I admit I really want to just stay there and get warm in my jammies, but if you need me to come back and help finish packing in the morning, let me know."

"Thanks, but I think it's pretty much done," Jillian said. "I appreciate all your help so much, and you looking for Yorkie. I'll be in touch."

The two women hugged, then Conor and Jillian took the elevator to her apartment.

"There's a small problem," Jill said, shoving her wet hair from her eyes. "All my stuff is packed in boxes on the truck. Towels, clothes—you name it. I don't have any way for us to dry Yorkie, or you and me."

"Well, that *is* a problem."

He pulled Yorkie from his jacket and held him up. Both of them laughed at the way the poor pup looked as if he'd lost ten pounds, with his wet fur lying flattened against his little body, resembling an opossum more than a dog.

"You're a troublemaker, you know that?" Conor told him.

The dog licked his wet nose and yipped, and both Conor and Jillian laughed again—until Conor sobered, knowing the things he wanted and needed to say to her might be coming way too late. But knowing his future happiness, his life's happiness, depended on it.

"I…I have a lot of things I want to say to you."

Her eyes met his for a long moment before she gave him a slow nod. "All right. But first let me see if there's anything other than clothes in my suitcase to get York cleaned up."

"Let's use my shirt, first." He set the dog on his feet and pulled off his suit jacket, then began to unbutton the shirt that was mostly dry except for where York had been held against his chest, leaving a muddy stain. "It's probably ruined anyway."

He rubbed the dog all over, and being as small as he was, the shirt and Yorkie's repeated shaking, flinging droplets of rain around the room, seemed to do the trick.

"There. Bedraggled, but dry enough, I think."

"Oh, Conor. I'm so sorry about your clothes." She gave him a rueful smile. "Good news is I have a bag of things you left here."

She picked it up and handed it to him, then bit her lip. "Um…there's not a shirt in there, though. Let me… get it."

He dug in the bag and saw sweatpants and socks and a few other things, before she came back holding his T-shirt. Their eyes met as he reached for it, wondering why it wasn't in the bag with everything else.

"I kept it," she blurted, as though she'd read his mind. "I know it's stupid and silly, but I wanted to keep a little piece of you with me. Sorry I was going to steal it."

He dropped the clothes, wanting so much to reach for her and hold her close, wet or not, but he knew he had to tell her what he'd learned first and see if she'd possibly believe him.

"Stupid? That would be *me*, Jillian. A man who loves you more than anything in this world but still walked away."

"Conor…" she whispered. "It's okay. We—"

"Let me finish." He pressed his finger to her cold lips. "I let you go because I thought it was the best thing for you. Was sure it was because I'd proved over and over that I couldn't be there for you the way you deserve. That there was something wrong with me— something missing inside. And then tonight I finally got a hard hit to the head that made me open my eyes. Made me see that wasn't true at all."

Her eyes were wide on his now, but she didn't speak, and he reached for her shoulders and forged on.

"I was in the middle of a meeting with all the Urgent Care Manhattan board members, among others. About to close a deal I've been working on for a long time and that I thought was the most important thing to concentrate on. Critical to make it happen. But I was sitting there thinking of you, instead. Thinking of you moving today, and thinking how much I'd miss you, and how much I love you, and how much I wished I could be a different man."

"And then…?"

"Then I got Michelle's call about Yorkie. It scared me. And when I heard how scared you were I saw with an instant blinding clarity that I've been utterly wrong about so many things. That I'm not like my father at all. That *you* are the most important thing in the world. Way more than any work or money or investments could ever be. And that providing monetarily for you isn't the best way to show my love for you. It was like lightning struck me, and burned into my brain that if I let you go that would be the one thing that would truly make me a failure."

"You left the meeting?"

"I left the meeting," he confirmed. "And as I did all the things I believed about myself and my life fell away, and I knew with absolute certainty that all I need in life is you. Not more businesses, not a bigger portfolio, not a bigger apartment. Just you."

"Oh, Conor." Her lips trembled and she wrapped her arms around him. "I'd told myself our relationship being over was a good thing. A chance for me to believe in myself, be confident in a man's love for me someday, when I was ready to try a relationship again. But, listening to you now, I know for certain that you finally coming to believe in yourself was a process, the way mine was. And I believe we're both there now in a way we weren't before."

Her words made it hard for him to breathe, and he had to try twice before he could speak. "I know I am. I know that I love you, Jilly. I know that I'll always be here for you, and that I'll never be that guy who failed you ever again."

"And I'll never be that woman who wonders if you really love her. Because I can *see* it, Conor." Her voice wobbled as she smiled up at him. "I see the love I feel for you reflected right back. I see it so clearly I can hardly breathe from the happiness I feel right now. I love you. So much."

Unable to speak, he pulled her close and buried his face in her wet hair, not caring that her clothes were damp and cold against his bare chest. They stood there for long minutes before he pulled back and kissed her sweet lips, and the taste of them made his throat close all over again.

He lifted her wet sweatshirt away from her skin before reaching for her cold hands. "I know you need to get into dry clothes, but I can't wait even a few more minutes." He swallowed down the emotion in his chest so he could ask what he desperately needed to know. "Will you marry me, Jill? Again? This time I'll be the husband you deserve. I'll be the man you want. I'll be the man who is always there for you and who gives you everything you need—and I'm not talking about money. I'm talking about myself. I promise."

"Yes, I'll marry you. Again." Her fingers tightened on his. "I'll believe in you and I'll always be there for you. I promise."

Relief weakened his knees and he pulled her close, kissing her until the moist air around them seemed to steam and their wet clothes weren't even close to cold anymore.

When they finally separated he smiled down at the beautiful face smiling back. "How about we get these wet clothes off before you catch a cold? Then a warm shower."

"Sounds like very good medical advice, Dr. Mc-Carthy."

She gave him the impish grin he loved so much, and the fact that he'd get to see it every day of his life weakened his knees all over again.

"And here's something you'll be pleased about. I have

my hair dryer in my suitcase, since you're so good at using that."

He tugged her shirt off over her head, grasped her hand and headed toward her bathroom. "I *am* pleased about that. And I'd like to show you other things I'm good at, too. Prove that I'll always be good to you. What do you think about that?"

"I think being good to one another is the perfect way to begin our second chance together. Starting right now."

EPILOGUE

JILLIAN FINISHED THE measurement of her patient's hand strength and mobility, entered the numbers in the computer, then sat back with a smile. "Looks like you've hit all the required markers, Sandy. Congratulations! I'm graduating you from occupational therapy."

"I'm so glad! This sure hasn't been fun, except for working with you, Jillian. Thanks so much for everything. You've made a painful and frustrating process a whole lot better than I expected it to be. And my hand really works again! I almost can't believe it."

"I always knew you'd get there—and making therapy less miserable is one of our goals. If you keep up with your exercises at home you'll be almost as good as new in a few more months."

"I will. Thanks again."

Jillian stood and raised her voice. "Sandy's graduated, everyone! Time for her clap-out!"

All the therapists cheered and clapped their hands as Sandy laughed and waved on her way out the door.

Jill cupped her big belly and took a moment to stretch

her back before shutting down the computer and grabbing her purse.

She paused to look at her scarred wrist. The surgical line had faded to a pale pink, no longer obvious, and she smiled, thinking of how Conor sometimes still kissed and nibbled at it the way he did the scars on her legs, making her laugh until things morphed into another kind of kissing, then into making love, which brought so many emotions.

Feeling cherished. Feeling loved. Feeling blessed.

He was right. All her physical scars were simply life scars that everyone had, both inside and out. Things that showed she'd been through some tough battles and prevailed as the warrior Conor said she was.

He'd helped her see that, and had helped her work through the internal scars, too—the insecurities, that she no longer felt. And she, in turn, had helped him with his internal scars—and wasn't that what a close relationship was all about? She was grateful every day that they hadn't lost the chance to do that for one another forever. The chance to feel truly whole for the first time in their lives.

Jillian took the elevator to the fourth floor and walked through the glass passageway that connected the HOAC building to Urgent Care Manhattan, now Conor had successfully merged the two companies. Business for both had grown, even with Conor working only on the board and not as president, which had been his original plan.

She turned the corner and smiled to see all the children playing in the daycare center HOAC now offered their employees. Running and laughing, climbing the small plastic jungle gym, crawling on the floor, playing with toys. And sitting on the floor with them was a handsome man with familiar thick blond hair, playing and laughing, too.

Her smile widened and she shoved open the door to the play area. "Isn't Dr. McCarthy going to get his pants wrinkled, sitting on the floor like that?"

"I thought about leaving on my scrubs—but, since we're going out to eat before we see the Rockefeller Center Christmas tree being lit tonight, I figured I'd wear actual clothes and look presentable." He smiled down at their daughter and rubbed his hand down her small back. "You excited about that, Alyssa?"

"Yes!" Beautiful blue eyes looked up at Jillian, and she reached to slip the toddler's blonde hair out of her face. "Hi, Mama!"

"Hey, sweetie! What are you and Daddy doing?"

"We're pwaying cars and twucks and doctors. My twuck just smashed into his car and now the doctor has to come and fix the daddy's bwoken leg." Looking very serious, she held up a little plastic doctor figure.

"I see." Lowering herself to the floor wasn't easy at eight months pregnant, but she managed to get there. "I'll bet the doctor will do a very good job."

"Yes, a *vewy* good job."

Alyssa concentrated on the toy doctor and the car and the other small doll figures, and Jillian turned to Conor. "It's so wonderful that you insisted on having this daycare center built here. Thanks for convincing all the board members it would ratchet up employee satisfaction scores by making their lives easier and better."

"Well…" He leaned in to press his cheek to hers. "A certain person I'm crazy in love with showed me that having a work/life balance is important."

"Yes, it is." She wrapped her arm around his neck and tangled her fingers in his hair as she soaked in the warmth of his skin.

"Having daycare here benefits everyone—including me. I get to sneak over and visit my daughter for a minute if a patient doesn't show, and neither of us is struggling through the city to drop her off and pick her up from an offsite daycare. What's the point of owning a business if you can't make everyone's life better?"

"Making money would be one point…"

He moved his cheek until his lips slipped across hers. "That *is* an important one—making sure our family is financially secure. But my beautiful and wonderful wife has helped me see that it's not quite as important as a few other things."

They smiled at one another, their eyes meeting in a long connection, before he stood. "Let's get going. I'm hungry and I bet Alyssa is, too—aren't you, pumpkin? Then we're going to see the tree lit! Are you excited about that?"

"Yes!" Alyssa tossed aside the toys and stood, a happy smile on her face. "Weady to go?"

Conor grasped Jillian's hand to help her up off the floor and they both grinned. "Are you ready to go?"

"Yes. More than ready."

"Are we bwinging the dogs?" Alyssa asked.

"Not this time. But we'll take them some other day. Maybe they can watch you learn to ice skate with me helping you? What do you think about that?"

"Ice skate? Yes!"

Conor got Alyssa's coat and hat on, swung the child into his arms, and then the three of them headed into the city. After dinner at their favorite restaurant they walked the few blocks to Rockefeller Center. The place was jammed full of people, and Conor placed Alyssa on his shoulders so she could see everything.

A light snow began to fall and Jillian pulled Alyssa's hat down a little farther, to keep her ears warm. Excitement was in the air, and the countdown finally began.

"Five! Four! Three! Two! One!"

The rainbow of lights covering the giant Christmas tree blinked on, illuminating the night sky, and everyone cheered.

Little Alyssa clapped her hands and cheered along. "It's so pwetty! I love it!"

"I love it, too." Conor held on to the toddler's leg as he wrapped his arm around Jillian and looked at her. "And I love *you*."

"Love you, too. So much."

They kissed, then kissed some more, until the music began and people started to dance.

Alyssa wanted to dance, too.

Conor lifted their little one from his shoulders and she danced around for a few minutes, before reaching for Jillian's round belly and placing her hands on either side of it, her mouth pressed against it.

"You like the music, baby bwother? You like the lights? I *love* the lights!"

"He can't see the lights yet, Alyssa, but I bet he can hear the music," Conor said, looking down at their daughter with such adoration on his face it made Jill's heart fill to bursting. They had this amazing life together. The life they'd both wanted but thought would never happen.

"I'll bet he's dancing inside Mama's belly. What do you think?"

"Yes! He's dancing! Just like me!"

She began to bob up and down and back and forth so vigorously that both Conor and Jillian laughed.

Conor placed one hand on Jill's back and the other on her abdomen, leaning in for another kiss. "Does it feel like he's dancing? If he is, I hope he's not dancing quite as hard as she is."

She chuckled. "At the moment he's quiet but… Oh! Did you feel him kick?"

"Wow. I did." His eyes lit, then he sobered. "My third miracle. Alyssa was the second…"

"And the first?"

"*You*, Jillian. You're my forever miracle. You didn't give up on me even when you should have."

"And now you've given me everything I ever wanted." She placed her palm against his cheek as their mouths met again. "You, our beautiful babies, and New York City and the Rockefeller Center at Christmastime. What else could anyone need?"

He swept the snowflakes from her nose and smiled before he kissed her again. "I can't think of one single thing."

* * * * *

MILLS & BOON

Coming next month

THEIR ONE-NIGHT CHRISTMAS GIFT
Karin Baine

'We keep a few rooms made up just in case of emergencies.' Charles led her up the stairs to one of the bedrooms. She couldn't help but wonder which door led to his.

'Do you get many late-night, uninvited women calling in on you?' she teased, when he was such a stark contrast to the man who'd literally sent her packing in a previous lifetime.

'No, I don't, but sometimes we get patients arriving too late to be admitted to the clinic, so we put them up here for the night.' Her teasing fell flat with him, but she supposed his defence from her insinuations was understandable when she was accusing him of having loose morals. She knew nothing about him any more.

'I'm sure it's most appreciated. As it is by me.' She had to remember he was doing her a favour by letting her stay when she had no right to be here. Their risky behaviour in London had been her idea and as such she was fully prepared to take on the consequences single-handedly.

'Bed, bathroom, wardrobe. All the essentials.' He did a quick tour of the room before turning back to her. 'Do you need help bringing in your luggage?'

'I just have an overnight bag in the car, but I can

manage that myself. As I said, this was a spur-of-the-moment visit.'

'Ah, yes. The talk. Is this about what happened in London? I must admit it's been harder to put out of my mind than I'd imagined too.' He was moving towards her and Harriet's heart leapt into her throat at the thought of him kissing her again. She wanted it so much but that's not what had brought her here.

'I'm pregnant, Charles.'

His outstretched arms immediately fell limply to his sides. 'Pardon me?'

She sat down on the edge of the bed, wishing it would swallow her up. 'That night in London...I'm pregnant.'

Continue reading
THEIR ONE-NIGHT CHRISTMAS GIFT
Karin Baine

Available next month
www.millsandboon.co.uk

COMING SOON!

We really hope you enjoyed reading this book. If you're looking for more romance, be sure to head to the shops when new books are available on

Thursday 28th November

To see which titles are coming soon, please visit

millsandboon.co.uk/nextmonth